THE
WELSH FASTING GIRL

THE
WELSH FASTING GIRL

VARLEY O'CONNOR

Bellevue Literary Press
NEW YORK

First published in the United States in 2019 by Bellevue Literary Press, New York

For information, contact:
Bellevue Literary Press
90 Broad Street, Suite 2100
New York, NY 10004
www.blpress.org

Library of Congress Cataloging-in-Publication Data

Names: O'Connor, Varley, author.
Title: The Welsh fasting girl / Varley O'Connor.
Description: First edition. | New York : Bellevue Literary Press, 2019.
Identifiers: LCCN 2018047587 (print) | LCCN 2018049870 (ebook) |
    ISBN 9781942658634 (ebook) | ISBN 9781942658627 (pbk.)
Subjects: LCSH: Jacob, Sarah, 1857-1869--Fiction. | Anorexia nervosa--Fiction. |
    GSAFD: Biographical fiction.
Classification: LCC PS3565.C655 (ebook) | LCC PS3565.C655 W45 2019 (print)
    | DDC 813/.54--dc23
LC record available at https://lccn.loc.gov/ 2018047587

Bellevue Literary Press would like to thank all its generous donors—individuals
and foundations—for their support.

 This publication is made possible by the New York
State Council on the Arts with the support of Governor
Andrew M. Cuomo and the New York State Legislature.

 This project is supported in part by an award
from the National Endowment for the Arts.

Bellevue Literary Press is committed to ecological stewardship in our book
production practices, working to reduce our impact on the natural environment.

♾ This book is printed on acid-free paper.

Book design and composition by Mulberry Tree Press, Inc.

Manufactured in the United States of America

First Edition

1 3 5 7 9 8 6 4 2

paperback ISBN: 978-1-942658-62-7

ebook ISBN: 978-1-942658-63-4

DRAMATIS PERSONAE

THE AMERICANS

Christine Thomas, journalist
James Thomas, her husband
Douglas and Rupert Thomas, their sons
Gwen Thomas Blunt, their daughter

Philip Beckwith, publisher of *The Sun*

THE WELSH

Evan Jacob, a farmer, called "Tad" by his children
Hannah Jacob, his wife, called "Mam"
Sarah Jacob, their daughter (the Welsh Fasting Girl)
Margaret, Mary, and Esther Jacob, their daughters
Samuel and Saunders Jacob, their sons

Nell Daniel, Hannah's sister
John Daniel, her husband

Emyr, the Jacobs' hired boy
Evan Jones, vicar
Dr. Harries Davies
Reginald Pary, reporter

Alun Lloyd, reporter
Braith Lloyd, his wife
Lyn Lloyd, their eldest son

Mrs. Owen and Mrs. Morgan, innkeepers

Goyhebydd and Gwilym Marles, partisans

George Rees, coroner
John Cross and Neville Watkins, necroscopists

Thomas Davies, solicitor
Mr. Clifton, solicitor
Mr. Bishop, solicitor
Mr. Michael, solicitor

Mr. and Mrs. Brigstock, chemists

Dr. Lewis
Dr. Vaughan
Dr. Corsellis
Dr. Rowland
Dr. Pearson Hughes

Mr. Fitzwilliams, justice of the peace

THE ENGLISH

Vinnie Smyth, journalist
Dr. Robert Fowler
Elizabeth Clinch, the sister-nurse
Ann Jones, a nurse
Sarah Attrick, a nurse
Sarah Palmer, a nurse
Mr. Coleridge, barrister
Mr. Gifford, barrister
Sir James Hannen

THE
WELSH FASTING GIRL

PART ONE

Wales is a country interesting in many respects, and deserving of more attention than it has hitherto met with. Though not very extensive, it is one of the most picturesque countries in the world, a country in which Nature displays herself in her wildest, boldest, and occasionally loveliest forms. The inhabitants, who speak an ancient and peculiar language, do not call this region Wales, nor themselves Welsh. They call themselves Cymry or Cumry, and their country Cymru, or the land of the Cumry.

—George Borrow, *Wild Wales*, 1862

MARGARET

OFTEN THAT LAST YEAR, I would awake in the night's black heart to Sarah *fach* in the kitchen. Always the breaths of the bigger sisters were steady, and slow came the boys' whistles and sighs. In the byre on the other side of the wall where we slept, the hay crackled, stir of the cattle. In my nose, their beasty rump smell. When Sarah's feet went *pack-pack* going over the hardened clay floor, I burst up and followed.

In the kitchen, I stopped, and through the passageway always the sleeping curtains were quiet, Tad and Mam inside asleep.

At the front door, I saw Sarah running across the wet grass, feeding the hunger she felt for the wide, open sky. Though soon I could not see her, I knew she was past the pigsty and the chicken house. I scudded along.

She turned up the steep path to the stubby wild oaks by the lee, where she liked to pray. I waited for her in the open yard. She prayed in the language of the vicar, which I could not understand. "You will learn," Sarah said, but I did not want to learn English, nor pray. I knew she was asking to go to the angels, and I was saying "Do not let her go."

Once, my sister and I were lost in rain. On this day, the mist turned and came down and we were away from the yard, far out in the moors. Mam had said to walk straight back after Sarah fetched water, for tomorrow we would dig potatoes. But Sarah set down the full pail and said we must look for Fair Folk.

"No, Sarah," I said. The Folk came in the dark for white-headed children like me, stealing them off to the Fairy Land. They would leave in my place a gnarled troll.

Sarah laughed. "Don't be frightened." She pulled me along. Tad said there were no Fair Folk, that Sarah was fond of telling stories and conjuring what was not real.

"We won't go for the Fair Folk," she said, "if you are so frightened. We shall find the Round Pool." She knew how I wondered at the pool's depth, which no one had discovered. You could not even see the surface until you were practically there, for the trees and sedges and the nice muddy bogs.

We searched, but we could not find the pool, and I grew tired. The rain came. We had ventured far. I tried to follow, but I slipped in the mud. Sarah dashed ahead, as she would do, forgetting me, flying along to the voices only she could hear. I ran, calling for her, and slipped again, tumbled over a root and into the slosh of a gulley.

It was my leg. I could not stand. "Sarah. Sarah."

She knelt beside me. "Dear sister," she said. "Margaret *fach*." Her black hair lay flat on her cheeks and light leaked from the sky. She tried pulling me to my feet and I yowled.

"Forgive me." She tried to drag me, I yowled, and she tried to pick me up, but I was too big. She held my hand and said "Now then," and tried again.

She got her arms under me, staggered up, and carried me through the rain. We cried. We did not believe we would get back. My head at her shoulder and my face at her clenched jaw, she groaned and cried from the weight of me; still she did not put me down.

Far ahead a light wobbled, pushed at the rain. Two lights

bobbed in the water and then Tad and Emyr walked through the veils.

They carried us in their coats back to the house, where we were dried. Mam did not understand how Sarah saved me. My sister was strong. She got in beside me in the morning and held me.

"I love you."

"I love you."

We loved each other.

I can still smell the rain in her hair.

In the black nights I waited in the yard, Sarah would finish her prayers beneath the wild oaks by the lee. She would come back and squat in the grass and go to her bed. But I knew she prayed to go to the angels, and I said—I spoke to the stones and the stars and the pigs and the chickens and the earth, to the real gods—"Do not let her go."

CHRISTINE

Brooklyn, New York, U.S.A
10 May 1869

Dearest James,

Four years since the peace, as long as the war. Yet on many days I do not see how much progress we have made. Like babes we creep against the horizons, shadowed by pain. And while my countrymen and women struggle with rebuilding lives that are left, I dream of Wales.

Already I see the skies ever moving, shape-shifting—those clouds! We put up our hands and thought we could touch them. I remember the mist on your face, the obsidian rocks, the shale, the undulant patchwork valley fields, the rivers and lakes and the near sea, wafting far inland. The mountains' textures, etched and then softened in that brooding watery world.

Dear husband, I have found my story. Needless to say, without you, Philip Beckwith would never have agreed, no matter how good the story is, and it is good, he had to admit. Mild nepotism and a promise of personal cash for expenses (I finally have sound use for Father's money) convinced him. Now it is on to the children. It will be harder to ford that mercurial stream.

I am pasting in my copy of a letter that appeared in the Welsh press early this year to give you the outline of what I have settled upon. (Mr. Beckwith was most impressed and is after me to reveal my source.)

To the Editor of The Welshman
A Strange Case

*SIR,—Allow me to invite the attention of your read-
ers to a most extraordinary case. Sarah Jacob, a little girl
of twelve years of age and daughter of Mr. Evan Jacob,
Lletherneaudd in this parish, has not partaken of a single
grain of food whatever during the last sixteen months.
She did occasionally swallow a few drops of water during
the first few months of this period; but now she does not
even do that. She still looks pretty well in the face, and
though confined to bed she continues in the possession of
all her mental faculties. She is in this, and several other
respects, a wondrous little girl.*

*Medical men persist in saying that the thing is quite
impossible, but all the nearest neighbours, who are thoroughly acquainted with the circumstances of the case,
entertain no doubt whatever on the subject, and I am
myself of the same opinion. Would it not be worth their
while for medical men to make an investigation into the
nature of this strange case? Mr. Evan Jacob would readily
admit into his house any respectable person, who might
be anxious to watch it, and see for himself.*

*I might add that Lletherneaudd is a farmhouse,
about a mile from New Inn, in this parish.*

Yours Faithfully,
Rev. Evan Jones, BD
THE VICAR OF LLANFIHANGEL-AR-ARTH

James, you remember Carmarthen and its moorland farms,
upland from the beautiful southern coastal town of Laugharne.
That is the region. These days, Sarah's parish is accessible by

Without my connection to Wales through our precious bond, I might have sought out other extant fasting girls. There are girls in Brittany, Naples, and Lisbon, one even as close as Maine. I know there are common characteristics among individual cases and that something of what I may find in Wales may be found elsewhere.

But Sarah Jacob is attracting the most attention, and my research suggests that the case is approaching a climax. I must be there! I must slough off the garden parties and musical salon reports, James, and make my name. Oh, my dear, I want to write, to see, to search. I want to uncover developments in human life that will make it real to me again.

I will continue tomorrow. The confrontation with our children is about to commence.

Always,
Christine

～

CHRISTINE BLOTTED AND CLOSED the green notebook and stacked it on others of varying colors. The ten greens contained letters to James, begun two years ago. The single maroon was already fat with clippings pertinent to the case. Much had transpired since the vicar's published appeal. It was of utmost importance to depart by the end of the week. This morning, she had booked passage to London.

From the attic's filmy window, Christine peered out at the street, scanning for Gwen, who neglected appointments, arriving early or late, thrusting through passersby, dodging carriages, tearing her bonnet off at the front gate.

No Gwen. The faded black bunting sagged over the Remingtons' porch and for a moment lofted in the wind. It was spring, but for the Remingtons there were no seasons, only a single unending day. All three of their boys had been killed at the Battle of Fort Stedman, late in the war. At least they were found, Christine thought in habitual reflex. Then she fervently thanked the Lord for leaving her Rupert and Douglas, healthy and strong. And Gwen, too, dear Lord, she added with wryness. Just seventeen, Gwen had insisted on marriage to a much older man, so war-damaged in body and soul that at the engagement Christine stooped to bribery: "A trip abroad, a horse, whatever you want, darling, just wait a year!" But her girl would have none of it. The waste. Gwen inhaled Charles Dickens like air, devoured Melville like food, and her husband, Homer Blunt, liked "little ditties" as he said, "to steady himself" before going to bed. Moral songs and black-and-white tales—whatever did the two of them talk about? Marriage, in Christine's opinion, from her own positive experience, was a matter of compatibility—of true conversation and physical pleasure. Forgive me, Lord, she thought, if I blaspheme. But since the wedding, Gwen had spent more time at her mother's than she had at home. Well, now Gwen would have the whole house to herself. She could read novels all day in her old bedroom. Christine would not be there to remind her that divorce did exist.

Light of step, excited, Christine descended the two sets of narrow stairs to the kitchen, where she prepared tea and plated the scones she had baked this morning. Douglas, at any rate, might be pleased by the news of her first real assignment. She had already told him about Sarah Jacob, and he had heard of these fasting girls.

She checked her hair at the hall mirror, a still-thick gray-streaked brown, braided and hastily coiled. At fifty, she had a solid, dependable body—excepting recent minor symptoms she largely ignored. She glanced with regret at the dusty parlor but quickly forgot yesterday's resolve to tidy up, distracted by a book on the overburdened shelves. She put on spectacles hung from the chain on her bodice and tried to decide whether she needed to pack Dr. Johnson on North Wales for a trip to the south. She skimmed the spines of other volumes and followed those that trailed onto the floor and into the hall-way. Theirs was an intellectual family, but the book problem had worsened. Douglas had put up more shelves in the hall and the adjacent dining room, which caused the cracks in the wainscoting. Assessing the damage through the archway, she thought, go to hell. Let it all fall down.

"Mother!" Gwen called, and behind her voice came Doug-las's cough. That would be two of the progeny. The third, Rupert, had traveled west the previous autumn for the adven-ture of homesteading and ranching. He built a house with his one arm and by mail had fully endorsed her more extensive journalistic career. Oh, for three of them like Rupert.

"Hello, dears," she said, smiling at Gwen and Douglas as they came through the front door. "Don't bother to knock."

"You knew we were coming," Gwen said.

"Scones!" Douglas said, for their cinnamon scented the house.

"Go get them," Christine told him. "I meant to put the plate in the parlor. And there is tea!" she called after him.

"Is that all?" he replied. "Mother, it's lunchtime."

"I'm not very hungry," she said. "Are you?"

Gwen didn't look well. She stood, bonnet in hand, gravely observing Christine. Her hair, the same thickness and shade as her mother's, minus the gray, wasn't up, but spilled across her shoulders, as if she had five minutes ago risen from bed.

"Come to the parlor," Christine said, taking Gwen's arm.

"What is it you have to tell us?" Gwen asked. Her face had gone white.

"Oh—no, Gwen, it isn't—you know that—"

Gwen shook her off and collapsed onto the window seat.

"I told you," Christine said, "the news is about me. You didn't listen."

Douglas bustled in and out, serving tea and scones to his mother and sister. He was the eldest, also brown-haired and sturdily built, but with an assurance, a swagger reminiscent of his father's. Douglas was a doctor, and if Christine mentioned his cigarette cough, he would say, in excuse, that she could take care of his patients if she was so inclined, since they drained every particle of his strength. Unlike his brother, Douglas had not gone to war. He had remained at New York Medical College, and Christine suspected guilt plagued him. She regarded him tenderly, watching him eat with his usual rapacious hunger. Gwen did not take one bite, and Douglas said, "I'll help you with that."

"I know you must get back," Christine said to Douglas, "and so here it is. I have a big, big assignment." Gwen had her eyes on the street through the front window; Douglas grinned, nodded, and ate. "I'm going abroad," Christine continued. "I am foreign correspondent to Wales on the Sarah Jacob story. For Philip Beckwith at *The Sun*." Gwen turned to her; Douglas squinted and chewed.

"Beckwith?" he said. "*The Sun*? Why, it's absurd! Why would Beckwith send you all the way to Wales for a scruffy little faster?"

"*The Lancet*, for one," she replied, "has expressed a good deal of interest in the Welsh girl." The English medical journal would impress the importance of the case on him, and she couldn't resist adding, "You haven't been keeping up on your literature, Douglas."

"Americans won't give a flip about it," he said.

"Philip thinks they will."

"And you convinced him." Her son's expression had changed

to one of hurt. Ordinarily, up until this, whatever assignments she managed to wrangle had been for the less illustrious *Brooklyn Eagle*. Douglas—and Gwen—had easily gleaned that she had used the friendship between Philip Beckwith and their father—the *real* reporter—to jump ship, to declare that her hope for their father's return was spent.

She stood, in an attempt to quell the restlessness thrumming in her limbs, a sharp vibrating burn. "I leave in a week," she informed them. "May I have your blessing?" God, she would choke, gag, she would expire in life if they insisted on keeping her, yet breathing, buried in dirt. Gwen's mouth set, but it was Douglas who volunteered the most compelling reason for her staying home.

"Gwen's pregnant," he said. The worst had happened, sealing Gwen's fate. Christine took in her daughter's slumped figure, her son's stormy brow. She saw no exuberance in her children over the news, just the same grim constancy: the locked impossible wait.

Gwen wouldn't speak, allowing her brother the doctor to lecture Christine on her duty while Christine held fast. "I must go."

"Then go," he said.

"Douglas. We must live."

"And what better way than new life?" he asked.

It wasn't the only way—but she couldn't find words. Mother, wife, daughter, it was time to depart from her former selves and do for her future. She had no choice, quaked at who she might become if she stayed.

THE FOLLOWING WEEK, PHILIP BECKWITH himself transported Christine to the dock. As a frail apprentice in a corduroy cap loaded her trunks in the carriage, Christine walked out of the

modest brick Federal-style house she had lived in since arriving as a young bride. James existed in the house more than
anywhere else, and with him were their dead children, the two
infant souls she saw in ghostly trace against the black door.
Their lost remembered heat beckoned her back, ethereal hands
and eyes judging, as if in new league with the unborn! She
touched the door softly, tugged her cape close, and turned to
the gate. Across the street in the Remington house, the bent,
reclusive mother, framed by the morbid bunting, peeked out
her second-floor window. "Walk," Christine uttered quietly.

"Hail and salutations," said Philip, doffing his hat as he
helped her into the covered coach. "Good day to my star
reporter." With Philip in his puce suit and mink-collared coat,
stark bald and approaching seventy, she felt young and gay.

"What have you to say for yourself?" he asked as they
settled.

"There's been a watch on the girl."

"You don't say."

"And she has passed with flying colors."

"How so?"

She explained to Philip that the local vicar, incensed by
aspersions cast on his character by the English press, had
organized a group of local citizens to sit beside Sarah's bed
for twelve days—three men in the waking hours and three at
night—and see for themselves if she was given food or drink
by foul means.

"I should say, however," continued Christine, "that early on
the six men were winnowed to four. One, apparently, dozed
on his watch and another reported for the task drunk." Philip
barked out a laugh.

"But the remaining four were convinced," she said. "The
watch was a farce, really. No search was conducted before-
hand. And the girl's parents and younger sister, who is close to

Sarah, were not barred from her. A local surgeon, though, who was involved, has written in a letter published in *Seren Cymru* that he is genuinely perplexed, 'well knowing,' as he said, 'that nothing is impossible in the sight of the Creator and Preserver of all mankind.'"

"A case of religious mania," commented Philip.

"Religious feelings and divisions are serious there. The vicar has called the editor of *The Lancet* a 'Pope-editor.'"

Philip guffawed.

"Perhaps he deserves it. The press I've read is shrill. The medical men are behaving at least as poorly. A Dr. Pearson Hughes, in his thirst for scientific data, badgered and pawed at the girl without the parents' permission. The father pressed formal charges of assault."

"Oh, then," Philip said with satisfaction, "the law is involved." He meant, Christine deduced, that the doings at the Welsh homestead had become complicated, public, and remarkable enough for wide report. "Write it all up as your first dispatch," he said.

"I already have," and she brought from her handbag the folded pages. But she felt unsettled. One rightfully should, James had said, at the border of a story worth finding, worth telling. Still, her discomfort rankled. She turned her attention to the briny scent spiking the odor of horses and machinery oil. The openness of the nearing docks hollowed the rattling carriage tones and voices outside. A single consciousness could not encompass the frenetic activity everywhere in the streets, the building—scaffolding appearing each day like spring flowers—the transport of goods, of people, the announcements on walls, poles, and trees, the hawkers, and the smoky endlessly turning industrial wheels in contemporary New York.

Like a faint double vision cast by her anticipation, she pictured the Wales she recalled from thirty years ago. More than lovely, it was magnificent—unique and commanding in the grandeur of its land and the dignity of its people. She was upset with herself for reciting the case's developments in an entertaining manner to Philip, as he enjoyed and expected in conversation—and in print as well, to be perfectly honest. She was anxious to investigate her sources, to locate the serious import within the seemingly ridiculous goings-on, the nearly slapstick commotions. At the center was a child who was probably ill in body or mind, or both, although no one, at least from what she understood from a distance, showed much concern about that. A detail she'd recently fixed on was that every report from people who had visited Sarah remarked on the beauty of her visage, the perfection of her features. Christine wondered how much the girl's aura was achieved by her looks, and worried over what the world exacted from beauty.

They rounded a corner and the harbor rose up, crowned by the immense ocean liner. Everywhere were people, horses, carriages, and the apprentice hollered his team ahead.

Outside, the wind and sea smell inflaming her senses, clutching Philip's arm and holding her hat so it wouldn't lift off into the wheeling gulls, she surged ahead, within life, she thought, within herself, her body's breaths and her mind's actions. And then at the bottom of the plank angled up to the ship's mouth, from out of the crowd's indistinct hats, coats, and baggage emerged Douglas and Gwen. They had come to see her off.

"Hello!" she called, practically throwing herself at her son, knowing him well accustomed to his affectionate mother, for all her bookish predilections. "My dears," she said, grasping Gwen's hand.

After shouting back at the group conducting Christine's trunk toward the hold, Philip engaged Gwen in conversation. How fortunate she was, thought Christine, that her children were such essentially decent people. They had been tested for seven years by James's disappearance. Death itself, and the no longer unusual absence of death's bodily proof—for those buried in mass graves or eaten by animals in forests far from their homes or vanished in war camps or exploded to scum by canon fire in this republic of suffering—death was a calamity that in their time and society was so unfortunately common that Douglas, Gwen, and Christine felt it indulgent to reveal their pain, even to one another, while it remained lodged in their breasts.

Douglas said to Christine, "Perhaps you'll find him there." She knew he referred to his father's spirit and Cymru, where James had been born.

"Mother, don't let anyone tell you that medicine isn't young, or that it doesn't remain an art as much as a science. There are mighty clashes of will over Sarah. I have read more about the case. I find it appalling it's caused the ruckus it already has. For a thing in the air! The obsession with fasters is a stupidity epidemic. A girl doesn't eat her portion and the vultures fly low. Miracles and tricks are proclaimed. Do you know she had a serious illness that set off her fasting? She almost died and then recovered, but it seemed to have put her off food, and she may exist on very little."

"Yes," Christine said, "I need to learn more about how she was sick."

"They say that since then she has not left her bed," Douglas remarked.

Before leaving Christine to Gwen, he added, "If anything happens, I'll telegram." Christine was unsure whether he referred to his long-held hopes of his father's return or remains, or to Gwen's pregnancy. But she let it alone and went to her daughter. "I will be back for the birth," she said.

"You may be back sooner." Again, meaning blurred,

though Gwen's accusation came through. Truculence stiffened her. Douglas must have convinced her to come. Momentarily though, unable to sustain anger at Christine for long, Gwen drooped, still so young and unsure in the gray-blue velvet coat Christine had given her on her birthday.

They embraced, and suddenly shining, Gwen said, "I'm happy, Mother."

But her daughter's eyes, warm and bright in her childhood, clouded over again. "Happy," she insisted.

Christine kissed Gwen's soft cheek and said, "Then so am I." She promised herself to try to be kinder about the marriage. Gwen was nine when the war started, ten when her father was reported lost. She had witnessed Rupert's recuperation from his wounding—saw, inadvertently, when Christine changed Rupert's dressings, the pulpy stump that had been her brother's arm. She watched her mother burn the noxious blanket and coat from Rupert's long transport home. Once Rupert recovered, he had gone west. Now Christine was about to defect. How could she fault Gwen for clinging to old stalwart Blunt? She drank in her children and turned to the ship.

She had not been at sea since the journey to London and Wales with James in youth. They had always intended to return, but children came and then the war.

She mounted the plank, borne forward by the crowd. At the railing, she waved to Douglas and Gwen. Smoke plumed, whistles blared; the ship heaved. From the water, the New York skyline seemed to set sail. She watched it recede and felt years of care drop away, felt a bracing wash of relief.

ABROAD

I WAS YOUNG, BUT I REMEMBER. My leg needed to heal. I suffered, lying days in my shelf whilst sun cheered the ground and rain, which frightened me for a time, drove at the thatch. Sarah nursed me. She stayed behind when the others worked on the farm. Sarah knew hundreds of stories, of the Fair Folk and the Bible. I fancied the story creatures living in layers, the Fair Folk under the earth, the devils below them, the angels up in the sky—and the people trapped in between. She read to me hymns and poems. She was going to the purpose-built school and proud of her English. But because I am stubborn and occasionally must have my own way, I said, "Do not read in English. It is the sound of dry wood Tad brings in a drought for the fire."

"You are imaginative!" Sarah told me, "I like that!" I am not, she was, but for her to love me, I let her think I am.

Once I got well, I was different. My hurt leg is short, and I walk with a hop. "Never mind. You are fast," Sarah said, "and can run if children torment you."

My sister was my protector. She vowed to grind faces into the road, to kick and fight any mockers.

But I cared only for her. I trod with my sister through fields and paths and along the river. Together we worked, digging, picking, gathering, turning the molded butter as it set in the dairy. For the planting, men chopped the soil and we sprinkled the magical seeds. At harvest, I carried the jug of buttermilk, Sarah the oatmeal, to the workers for their tea. Sarah taught me that oats should be cut when the color of wood pigeon, and barley when the field bleaches to ripest white. A ready wheat field is brilliant gold. If the weather was fine and our work finished, we lay in the grass and crooned to the cows. We jumped up and chased the dumb, knobbly sheep. We teased the big sisters, milking and knitting with serious faces. We ignored the boys. At chapel, I liked the singing and jumping, but Sarah liked all of it, and I know how greatly she missed it when she became sick. At chapel, Sarah listened to every word. We lay in the wagon going home, and I saw her thinking and staring up at the revolving sky.

Then after that first harvest I was old enough to work, Mam went away. Tad needed the biggest children to finish the sheaves, and I swept and tended the kitchen. A change came in Sarah. She ignored me and silently crawled in at night, turned to the boards and pretended to sleep. "It is Margaret," I said, stroking her back, and she swatted me off, saying, "Don't." The next day I followed her, and she screamed at me to stop, "*or I will give you a knife to eat!*" I feared she was stolen. I watched for red in her eyes, like a fiery devil burrowed inside a body, as if he has found his home.

I saw her most often then from afar, with Tad, dragging a rake as they walked to the fields, her head down sadly, as she had not held her head before. One day coming back to the house after the others, Tad and Sarah stopped at the stile to the yard and he grabbed her roughly. They returned to the fields and didn't appear again until dark, and for the rest of the time Mam was gone, Tad kept devilish Sarah with him.

Missing her, nights I lay clamped in a panicky feeling, uprooted and scattered I knew not where.

Mam returned, her tall beaver hat marching closer until we

ran and shouted and snatched at her skirts. She brought a new swaddled boy who lay in a cradle and mewled. But with his coming and Mam home, Sarah was more her old self.

Then in dark February, Sarah was sick with dreadful sickness, pains in her stomach and frothy blood in her mouth. Mam said it was a cold, but on the third day she kept Sarah from school.

Sarah lay piteously. "Margaret *fach*," she said, "I am piteous." She held her belly and cried.

She was put in the cupboard bed, away from the other children, in the room where Mam and Tad slept.

She was rigid on her left side. She had fits, arching high up from the bed. She thrashed and vomited her food. The doctor said he did not understand her complaint or have any remedy that could relieve her, and the single being that could was the Great Doctor. But the Great Doctor did not come. Another, earthly one did and said she was dying from an inflammation of the brain. She seemed to sleep—they said in a trance. They said it was catalepsy, which I don't understand. But I stayed by her—and what better work is there than watching out for the person you love? I wet Sarah's mouth with water and table beer. Sometimes in her trance, she awakened, fretful. Mam said because I was hot and full-bodied and Sarah so thin and cold, I should get in the bed beside her. I did, and she calmed. "Stay with me," she whispered one night when I tried to get up. "With me," she said, "you are safe."

I was never afraid then of Sarah, not when she lost flesh, or her hair fell out in long clumps I collected and hid in the cupboard, thinking one day she might want them. I plundered the cupboard myself and smoothed the long black threads, pretending they were my clothes.

As she got better, our life was the bed, the counterpane

moss and heather and our hands animals galloping over my sister's legs.

She did not eat, but for milk and gruel that chocked her and brought the bloody vomit. Then she had fits if they offered it to her. She would take only boiled apple and dumplings, and finally only pieces of apple the size of a pill in a teaspoon. But everyone saw she was better if they left her alone. The fits were better, the rigid side loosened, and I combed the black fluffs filling in. Sarah read in bed, and when the haymaking came again, we were together alone in the house, even the baby with Mam in the fields. We did our work, watching each other and being together, and we were safe and well in Sarah's bed.

❧

Carmarthen, Wales
29 June 1869

Dearest James,

In London, I called at the necessary offices for what I needed and then stole a day to stalk our old haunts. So much has changed! London is a captivating city and a baleful one, where life is charming for a few and abysmal for many. Vinnie Smyth is the same except for her totally white hair, which she stabs into submission with a quill pen atop her smart head. She never did marry and has devoted herself to *The Times.* The paper exploits and ill-appreciates her, but she is content nonetheless. She has been enormously helpful, just as she was for you. I can't recall who connected the three of us all those years ago, but my closeness—and gratitude—to Vinnie persists. Beyond what she sent to me in New York about Sarah Jacob, she opened the way in London and determined whom in the press I should see when I arrived here, an event that transpired yesterday afternoon. Vinnie thinks I am mad for my interest in investigative reporting. Her current passion is finance. "Jolly bad business," she said, "to end up convinced that it all comes down to money, but so it is. Numbers are gorgeous. Stare at them long enough, Christine, and you will experience revelation."

So—Wales. The air was like champagne after the smog of London. The winding walls, the hedges, the turf, the castles rising in mist, lurking like medieval hawks on the sloping land riddled with stones—I am overwhelmed. I imagine I have reversed time, for it is the same, with minor modifications. Perhaps I have caught it on the cusp of change, before it is too late to know it as I did. I have taken up lodging in Carmarthen, twelve miles from Sarah's village. Twelve miles is a lot, but I need to be able to send my reports. The *Carmarthen Weekly*'s publisher has been most welcoming. Evan Jones, however, the notorious vicar, left a message that he had been called away to Swansea. And that we would have to postpone our trip to the Jacob farm until the following day.

I couldn't wait. Late yesterday, after my meeting at the newspaper office, I set out alone, crossing the river Towy by the stone footbridge and back to the railway station on the Cardigan-Carmarthen Line. It is three short stops to the town nearest the homestead. I thought, these iron chariots have set us free! I heard more English on the platform than I had in Wales before. I assume it is because of the workers who came from England and Ireland to cut the Welsh rock and lay the rails. English isn't just the language of the gentry and the professional, aspiring classes today. Yet the farmers speak only Welsh, and this was why the Reverend Jones had offered to escort me to the Jacobs, as translator. Foolishly, I decided it wouldn't be important the first time to speak, or to understand. I quickly discovered the ineptitude of my rusty Welsh, of how, for a language that sets so beautifully to music, it sits like barbs on a foreign tongue.

It was late in the day but summer, light flashed through the billowing clouds, casting the land radiant green. White sheep speckled the pastures and up the mountains. There were grazing Herefords and Welsh blacks, and the very Welsh wild oaks, stunted by wind. We were far from the sea, and yet on the train I detected its tang in the air. Then the sky turned dark blue and muzzy with mist. I had—and have—thus far little idea of the total geography of the parish, how one village bleeds into another, and the altered weather held the entirety in a further suspension.

Fearing the weather, I thought to take the train back, but the trusty guides waited nonchalantly on the platform at Pencader Station. Two bore placards reading, THIS WAY TO THE FASTING GIRL! and another had the same legend on a paper strip wrapping his hat. A family, parents and two teenaged children, enlisted the pair of guides, and I the guide who remained.

"Rain?" I asked, pointing out at the sky. I doubt he understood even this single Welsh word, but he gestured for me to follow.

We passed workmen and a refreshment stand doing brisk business. I am in Wales, I thought, where it *will* rain—the rain, I had heard, had been catastrophic this year—and I had better get used to it.

I'd expected to walk, but my burly young guide took such pride in the pony he asked me to mount, that I did.

We were led, I on the pony and the family in a hay cart, down a stony lane overgrown at each side by hazel bushes. Their branches reached like sticky arms through the mist, catching at my hat until I locked my hands above my head and went through by warding them off with my elbows.

My guide ducked and trod, content with the extra shillings I'd given him in confusion. I gulped mist, refreshed by its unearthly purity and my relief at the rain's holding off. But the pony's hooves made sucking sounds in the mucky road and the cart ahead of us lurched and bumped along.

James, it was outlandish! That a celebrity flourished in this remote place, that the guides I had read about really existed and I had traversed an ocean to be met by them! I knew that rivers encircled Sarah's village, the Teifi, Tyweli, and Talog, and the mineral festering scent of river water wove through the phantasmagoria.

My guide helped me off my beast in a clearing. At the hillside, past a rich turf broken by thick slabs of rock, I had my first sight of Lletherneuadd, the plain whitewashed longhouse afloat in a parting of gray. It was then again obscured and just its smoke twisting into the sky led us nearer.

I was wet from the mist. My dress dragged heavily as we proceeded. They could have lived a thousand years ago, I thought. There were no neighbors within sight. We were invaders, come to chivy them out.

The darkness inside the house increased the sense of timelessness and displacement. The smell pulled my throat closed: rennet, mold, cattle, burning peat, urine, spoiled milk, and, underneath, the smell of bodies asleep. White objects loomed in the dark center room, sheets on a line, perhaps washing brought in from the mist to dry. The darkness was interrupted by a glowing fire in the open hearth; a cauldron hung from a chain rising up to the rafters. The guides led us to the fire and directed us to wait. Out of the darkness, shadowy densities took on the shapes of a table, a dresser, and a settle, and two women on stools mended cloths by the firelight. Two young boys of the house, whom I took to be Sarah's brothers, chattered in low, excited Welsh to the guides. A baby cried from another room and one of the women got up to see to it. Though summer, and though it was hours until nightfall, I felt cold emanate from the very walls. I decided the women were young and likely Sarah's elder sisters. A group of six emerged from a deeper darkness and another guide ushered them out to the yard. A shrill voice in what increasingly sounded threatening to me—Welsh—because, somehow, I could not penetrate it in the least—a voice half-chanted, half-sang three chords of rolling, semiguttural words. I shivered. The voice laughed. It was a young girl's laugh, Sarah's, I felt sure.

My fellow curiosity seekers and I were led through a passage to a bedroom. I hung at the rear, adjusting to candle glow. I looked down at a child crouched on the floor at the foot of a curtained bed to my side. She got up and danced—that was how it seemed—swiftly and silently out of the room and then back, to crouch again on her original spot. Her white-blond hair was short, sawed jaggedly off at her forehead, and her features were both very sharp and elfin—the cheekbones extremely pronounced and the eyes huge in their hollows and seeming to eat light. They watched with such energy and focus.

In front of me, and central to the room, was a cupboard bed holding a girl, flanked by her mother and father. I was certain of their identity because they were so obviously her attendants. The mother cast short bows as we arranged ourselves in the small space. She was dressed in traditional Welsh country style, full patterned skirt, her hair capped and a shawl over her heavy jacket. Her face seemed to me older than it should have for a young mother, but maybe from shadow. Her bearing was deferential to us and to her husband. Though she hovered about the girl, he oversaw the proceedings with nods and motions. He stood exceedingly straight, proud-postured, stern, a long-faced, dark-haired man who made me feel, as I observed him, startled by his humanity, that he was, like me, flesh and bone, and yet, together, we were enacting this drama. His serious mien in the wavering light, in the cold, bespoke orchestration.

But the girl—Sarah, surrounded by books, her hair wreathed by flowers and ribbons, a fur tippet gracing her shoulders—taper-lit as a corpse set out in the parlor would have been, the girl didn't give me the same impression.

She was indisputably beautiful, fine-featured, with slightly winged black eyebrows set off by large scintillating eyes. I thought of the cult of Ophelia, of princesses ravaged by warring lords, of legend, that is, rather than sham. An open book was propped on a stack of other books in her lap. Her father helped raise her higher in the bed, and when she was settled, he signaled her to read. She began—Bible verses they may have been, in Welsh, in that language sounding so harsh and ineffable and even dangerous to my ears—and it was then that rain spilled from the sky and splattered the thatched roof with gushing violence and her voice lifted and fought and droned on with the rain, and I thought her insane, driven to sickness by her own beauty and this place, this weather, this house, this darkness.

The others about me were rapt, becalmed, awed as if in a high ceremony in church. They stood in a dark clump as one creature, sung over, baptized by rain.

The pouring diminished, but Sarah continued to read in a loud voice, pausing now and then to glance up at us and gauge our attention. She wasn't coy, but she seemed highly aware of her effect.

She stopped, as if spent. She lay back and, for a moment, the father laid his long hand on her shoulder.

Each visitor filed by Sarah before they departed. The two adults placed coins on her chest—which balanced there oddly and glittered like Sarah's eyes. I was again hanging back and at my turn could find in my purse no coin smaller than a florin. I put it on her and she grasped my hand—a startling leathery touch, but no, her hand was gloved. Our eyes met, she said, "*Duw bendithia ti.*"

I followed the others into the rain. We set out, the pony and cart sinking fast in the mud. The steady rain soon put the pony in mud to his hocks, and the cart toppled, was righted, and the mud effigy family climbed back in. The branches were whips, but they were the least of our problems. I prayed I would survive to sit on the train.

This was granted to me and I was delivered to Carmarthen, where I crossed the bridge in the dark, and the rain that hadn't stopped pooled around me and beat at the water beneath me and I was beyond cold, even beyond feeling.

I got to my room and stripped off my sodden clothing and put on two flannel nightdresses and shivered to sleep under the blankets.

Asleep, I rode the ship again, except its immensity filled the world, entirety only the ship and the dark. I heard Sarah's voice, or Gwen's, but I couldn't identify words, determine location. At length, the voice faded to silence. I was alone, darkness behind me and darkness ahead. But then you were with me, James, and the ship regained proper size. I knew there still existed a place to which I could arrive.

I awakened at first light. Disoriented again, I threw open the shutters to the soaring stones of Carmarthen Castle, so near to my room. Its size seemed to strike to obliterate me. But I was warm and dry. I took up my notebook and pen and wrote to you.

Always,
Christine

WHEN SHE WAS WRITING TO HIM, he seemed to listen. After she put down the pen, her conviction of his presence lingered. He seemed to wait, making notes in the small tablet he carried in his coat pocket. You could sit him anywhere, as you chose a hat, or checked a schedule he hadn't consulted, trusting his memory, which was quite fine but not as fine as he trusted it was. They had been twenty together in Wales, twenty! He was a patient, unflaggingly interested twenty, and he didn't lose those qualities during the next twenty-three years.

Their youthful trip to Wales had yielded his first published articles back in the States. As Vinnie had said when she encouraged Christine to investigate Sarah Jacob, there would be rightness in Christine's return, and maybe a settling. No one knew about Christine's notebook letters to James. At first, she wrote with the intention of giving them to him if he returned, after she tired of posting into a void. Now the letters served another purpose.

She liked to rehearse her analysis and impressions to him before she fully believed them herself, and now she was here, before she wrote for the public. Not that any of what she had written today would survive to see print. Maybe a few facts, but in the light of the clearing day—it dripped outside, a soft, steady drizzle—she distrusted most of what she had surmised through weather's veils and newness's shock. What she wished to avoid was casting the Jacobs as wild Welsh, as supernatural, archaic, devious, and rightfully demeaned. She had been as astonished at herself as she had been by them, at her plunge into the situation with scant supplementary context—which the vicar, in his letter, had just begun to provide—and at her loss of composure: Without language, she quivered and shrank into her lesser self.

She had to get her reporter's legs back, and starting that night, for three hours after dinner, she would study Welsh.

She finished dressing and arranging the room in an orderly state; looked again at the castle filling her window and closed the shutters. She had left her soaked clothing in a pile on the slate floor, to save the wood furniture. Now she wrung each garment into the ceramic basin. The water turned muddy brown and released the mineral river scent and a whiff of the hovel's peaty, sooty damp.

CARMARTHEN, THE COUNTY TOWN of Carmarthenshire, was the oldest town in Wales. Until recently, it had been the most populous. That is, until the population seeped down to the mining communities and burgeoning Swansea and Cardiff. Christine would familiarize herself with Carmarthen's business district, its stone and colorful washed town houses. Markers were the castle and the pastoral vista beyond the city center—beyond, but always in sight.

The river was rushing today from the rain. The stone bridge led one away from the town and the castle's ramparts banking the river, to the grassy slopes and the station.

The Reverend Jones was of the professional English-speaking class of Welshmen. He had taken his post at St. Michael's Church in 1860. The village—and civil parish—of Llanfihangel-ar-Arth derived its name from the church, translating to Holy St. Michael's on the Hill. By 1864, Evan Jones had established a school, which Sarah attended. She was a fine pupil, the vicar had written Christine, at a time when many girls and indeed many Welsh received no education. He had grown fond of Sarah and her family. He admired Sarah's ambitious father, who had expanded his thirty-five-acre smallholding to a hundred and was respected by the community. Like most farming Welsh, the Jacob family was Nonconformist, worshippers at a Congregationalist chapel, one of numerous denominations and chapels in Wales that opposed the dominant Anglican Church. Jones, as the Welsh vicar of the Anglican St. Michael's, aimed to reconcile the opposing forces. He delivered his sermons in Welsh. And though he did not—in his favor—deem English a superior medium of instruction, at his school Sarah learned the language of the courts and the professional classes. Even tradesmen today, Christine understood, needed English and, she had gleaned, an Anglican baptism.

When Sarah became ill two years before, Jones had visited her, and in November that year, when she had recovered but was said to remain in bed without eating—October 1867 was the date claimed that she entirely stopped—the parents sent for him. Perhaps the Church would be interested in Sarah's health, which had bloomed without food—was it not a miracle? Everyone in the village knew the girl had been close to death. The exhausted parents, after months of caring for the sick child, had at last taken an oath together on the family Bible that they would no longer offer Sarah food, for she had fits and further sickened whenever they did and grew healthier when they did not.

The vicar, wary of folk belief, of fasters and miracles from times gone by, impressed continually on the parents that it could not be. Despite his affection for the family, he warned them against deception's grave danger.

That November 1867, Sarah confided in the vicar fear for her immortal soul. The vicar baptized and admitted her into the Church and over the next fifteen months he visited her weekly to discuss religion and listen to the Bible verses she memorized.

Gradually, he began to change. The girl had about her the light of the uncanny. Her ability to grasp theological questions and subtle human predicaments surpassed what a bright child, even one in bed reading continually, could be expected to absorb. Her astonishing comprehension derived from an intellectual flowering coincident with her fast. There was no evidence that she ate, no motive for any imposture. "Money!" the vicar had scoffed in the letter he wrote to Christine in London, a lengthy response to her inquiries from New York. Although the Jacobs weren't well-off by any means, they had no need of the change visitors left for the girl. He said it amounted to nothing.

And were the English, so ready to dismiss the claims of his letter to the *Welshman* early this year, infallible arbiters of the invisible? He thought not, and he wasn't alone in further distrusting their stewardship here in the visible world, given last December's election, in which the more prosperous Welsh tenant farmers were, ostensibly, granted a vote. The landlord Tories pressured the farmers to vote against the Liberal candidates they favored. Those who refused to capitulate were evicted from their land and left homeless.

Eighteen sixty-eight had been, he wrote, a divisive year. Agitation against the Anglican Church had increased, scaling back the advances he had made with the people in the parish. Now the endless rain tested the farmers.

Yet in Sarah he saw hope, a Welsh child bringing the Welsh together against the new god of materialism, against science and earthly power as the summits of our mortal journey.

No, he would side with the meek, with those who came to the lamb as little children, and the Welsh would yet rise up if they were held in contempt. The age of miracles was perhaps not yet ended in Wales.

He sounded rather more charismatic than Anglican, Christine had thought. Like many Welsh, the vicar straddled two worlds, and the strain seemed to have set him spinning. He and Evan Jacob, Sarah's father, were in their middle thirties, and they would have lived through the Rebecca Riots over the toll gates and taxes and the harsh judgment cast on the common Welsh in the famous Blue Books of 1847. Nothing about this conquered land was simple. Nothing was entirely new, disconnected from age-old struggle.

But young America was a friend to Wales, Reverend Jones reminded Christine. Many Welsh had emigrated—among them, James and his father—and thrived. Jones would be honored to meet an American journalist and to help bring their miraculous story to the American public. He had followed with great admiration America's Civil War, its holy quest for emancipation.

At Pencader Station, a carriage sent by the vicar awaited Christine. The driver, an old man holding a horse whip, stalked the platform amid the famous guides and the pilgrims and dairymen bringing their milk cans, and Christine had to ask him if he had come for her, he seemed so distraught and disoriented by the throng. Of course, he spoke no English.

She was able to say, in Welsh, that she was American, and the old man's eyes exploded with light.

The vicar, in turn, made a dramatic first appearance, standing before his church underneath an umbrella, on guard to convey Christine to shelter. Together, they entered the shadowy nave.

St. Michael's present structure had been built by the Normans in around A.D. 700, but its history went back to Celtic times, marked by the church's long stone, standing rough and ancient and beautiful—an oblong gray object about three feet in height, engraved with faded exotic letters—alongside the more recent Christian artifacts, the crosses and prayer books. These stones were everywhere in Wales, Christine remembered. She had noticed on her first visit to the country traces of past beliefs incorporated into the present. Now, the vicar said that most old Welsh Christian churches had their Celtic stone, signs that the past could not be expunged.

He touched the old stone and then held it, grasped it as if it were his. "It anchors me," he said. "I include it in my prayers."

His hand, milky white, looked to her unhealthy, and as he showed her around the old stone church his demeanor was different from what she had imagined from his writing—weaker, exhausted. He had a broad face and reddish hair; his black eyebrows slashed a substantial nose, and his short beard was glossy. But his thin body as he moved about suggested convalescence.

When they emerged, the rain had stopped, and they walked the short distance down into the valley. "The Jacobs' nearest neighbors would be at the mill," Jones said, "half a mile away. The nearest farm, a mile or more's walk across fields. There are twelve farms in the village, and cottages along the rivers. We have a butcher and a village shop, and the smithies and carpenters and our good cooper service all the villages of the parish. The mainstay of the Jacob family income is milk yield. They have fine, handsome cows, perhaps a dozen." He gained vigor as they walked, taking such giant strides that she had to trot to keep pace.

"I am most grateful you have come," he said. "Many newspapers reprint the story from other presses, without sending their own correspondents. You will see for yourself and make up your own mind."

"My opinion," she said, "is irrelevant. My job is to get the story to my American readers and they will decide for themselves." She preferred not to mislead him into thinking that conceivably she, or many of her readers, would believe in his miracle. Her prime intention was to understand the belief, and why it incensed the unbelievers.

"I saw Sarah yesterday," she confessed. Best to get it out in the open if she was about to be recognized.

"You went alone?"

"Oh, I paid for my haste. I got stuck in the mud and sopped through in the dark going back."

"You shouldn't have." Curt. For precious sake, she was old enough to be his mother. His censure was out of order.

He walked even faster, until she was well-nigh running at his side.

"Stop," she finally said, staking a spot and alerting him forcefully of her absence. "Are you trying to hobble me?"

"Good madam . . ." He retraced his steps, conveying a note of chagrin but also impatience. "Forgive me," he said. "I am most often alone. On my own, you see."

Not any time lately, she thought, with the village show you have drumbeat into existence. Besides, by the ring on his finger, she saw that he was a married man.

It was an issue, she knew, of control. People thought reporters came to take dictation. Analytical inquiries made them unpopular. Jones didn't question the gall of an American reporting this Welsh story, but he did desire that she report it as he revealed it to her.

They walked silently for several minutes, she listening to their boots squash in the rain-softened ground and the distant lambs' call, the deeper-registered returning call of the sheep.

"Are you a Christian?" he asked, humbly, she thought.

"I am," she replied. "I couldn't live without belief."

"You wrote that you are a widow."

"My husband was lost in the war." He didn't answer, and she kept her gaze on the lushness around her, as James would want it—she did feel him here, in the purple-and-blue parting clouds, the rain-dappled bushes and trees, the washed turf soft as a rug.

"We'll approach from the side," the vicar said. "The acres surrounding the house are richly fertile, whilst other portions of the farm are poor and hilly. Humid land lies to the west. Do you know—the natural adversities had a share in keeping the Welsh purely Welsh? We are cut off by the geography of the mountains, we are tested by our small percentage of arable land, and our language, for having been spoken by few for a thousand years, is unsullied by mixing and sounds much the same, they say, as it was spoken by the Celts. Our sorrows are also our genius. Our rural folk possess particular wisdom, as they have been forced to cleave fast to the land, to what was originally theirs."

She said nothing, appreciated his truths up to a point and suspected his aggrandizing of hardship.

"Look," he said, sparking with pleasure, "I see Mary and Esther are out in the field!" Once they had traversed a short rise, grazing cattle came into view and, beyond them, the smoke and hump of the homestead. "They are the older girls," he explained, "Sarah's sisters. A different breed altogether. But dear girls, hardworking girls." When they drew close, Christine could see the young women milking two of the cows in the pasture. The sisters were dark-haired, in plain apron-topped dresses. Goats grazed among the cows.

Jones greeted Mary, the elder girl, who greeted him back without looking up from her task. The younger, Esther, smiled widely at the vicar and twitched, oddly, when he said her name, but then, taking the lead from Mary, she hunched into her cow and renewed milking. Nearer to the house, chickens strutted the yard. A dog raced to the reverend for a petting, its harsh barks muting the lamb calls Christine could still hear. After the dog came the flash of a child, the dancing child from the day before, the light-haired girl.

"Well, Margaret," the vicar said, "how is Sarah today?"

He spoke Welsh, but Christine understood enough to get his meaning. The little girl didn't dance; she limped. One of her legs was short, but her small stature and the fleetness with which she moved gave the impression of dancing—an extra hop and skip in her every step.

Margaret shook her head at the vicar's question, as if all were the same. She was stone serious and as unusual in her appearance as she had seemed to Christine yesterday—her facial hollows, from the deeply set eyes and prominent cheekbones, in juxtaposition to the red puckish mouth. Though her height indicated a child of six or seven, judging by her demeanor Christine put her closer to nine. Margaret scolded the dog, and the grizzled red-and-white energy ball stopped barking and sat at her feet obediently.

"His barking disturbs Sarah," the vicar said to Christine. "Margaret is devoted to Sarah. Look at her hair," he said with distaste.

"The fringe?" Christine asked, feeling uncomfortable speaking English in front of the child.

"She cuts it herself as she likes," he said, and Christine figured he was referring to the sawed-off effect.

"I have a daughter," he said, "and, believe me, she doesn't cut her own hair." Propriety, Christine thought, is a relative virtue in this arena, is it not? He continued: "I fear Margaret is developing eccentricities in imitation of Sarah. I wrote you about the costumes Sarah wears. They do not help our cause. But the mother claims Sarah has few remaining joys, and I suppose she is right. People bring Sarah bonnets and such.

"We're coming," he said to Margaret. "Run along and tell Mother."

Christine caught the meaning. They crossed around to the front entrance, where four women sat by the house, eating a picnic.

A picnic! Nonetheless, the break from the rain, the animal life in the field, and the introduction to the children produced a sense of normalcy, in contrast to Christine's first visit. The sense continued as Hannah Jacob greeted them at the front door.

The vicar had told the Jacobs about the American reporter, and this morning he had sent a message saying that today she would come. Evan Jacob—called "Tad" by the children—was away from the house, but Hannah had arranged for Christine to speak with Sarah alone.

Christine studied Hannah, her long pointed nose and thickly lashed eyes in a careworn face under a snowy white cap. Each time the two women met, the clash between Hannah's fastidious dress and her rough hands, hanging like leather grappling hooks from her sleeves, caused Christine to ponder whether it was possible for adult hands to grow over the years of a farmwife's work. Eventually, she would consider that Hannah's hands were swollen and fear they would not last the life of their necessity.

Jones translated between the women in the doorway. Hannah told Christine that her husband had a bit of English and Sarah spoke it well.

They entered the main kitchen room with the hearth fire, a room about twelve feet by nine, Christine calculated.

"Over there," and Jones nodded to the left, "is where the children sleep. At the far end is the byre, with a loft above for storage and a bed for the hired boy, Emyr."

"Emyr," Christine repeated. "What are his duties?"

"Whatever is needed," Hannah said through the vicar. "He is very capable, and we feel for him as if he were ours."

At the main room's far end, they ducked into two closet-size icy spaces, impeccably clean, where cheeses lined shelves and dairy equipment crowded the floor space—churns, cans of buttermilk, whey, and copper vats. Jones wanted Christine to describe the homestead accurately to her readers.

Back in the dark main room—even on a lighter day, given the small single window—Christine perceived the darkness as less oppressive, and the smells today combined into a pleasant farmhouse smell. She recognized the scents of oat-cakes and cawl, the Welsh vegetable-oat stew that simmered in the cauldron over the fire.

Through a passageway to the right was the parlor-bedroom where the parents slept in the curtained bed and where Sarah lay. Christine wrapped herself against the cold, unsure why the second, smaller hearth in the room was left unlit.

Those tall tapers burned around Sarah, and Margaret sat up on the bedstead with her. Hannah spoke briskly to the younger girl and she scampered away.

"Hannah feels Margaret is too much with Sarah, and I agree," said the vicar. "She should be busy learning her sewing and cooking."

Sarah wore an elaborate embroidered jacket and a large red bow with yellow streamers in her hair. Books in English and Welsh scattered the bed. A shelf at the bed's head held more books, and trinkets: carved religious statues in wood and stone, a miniature rocking horse, dried flowers in bunches, bells, ivory and tortoiseshell combs, folded colorful shawls, bonnets, an India ball, and a child's spinning top.

The room was small, about the same size as the kitchen, with one small window. A chair had been placed by Sarah's bed, and the reverend suggested Christine sit in it. Hannah bowed and left.

Christine sat, knowing full well that Jones wouldn't leave, despite Sarah's reputed stellar English.

Although Hannah hadn't recognized her, Christine could see Sarah did. Her finger still caught in her book—the gloved right hand, the left hidden under the covers—she regarded Christine quizzically, almost with amusement.

"I am happy to see you again," Christine said.

"And I you. You are from America?" The words were strongly accented but clear. Christine hadn't any idea what to say, and then she remembered the list of questions she had forgotten to bring. They rested atop her note-taking pad, which she had left at the inn.

"What is it like, America?" Sarah asked.

"Big," Christine said. Sarah looked puzzled and turned to the vicar, who shrugged.

"It is hard to describe?" Sarah asked.

"Yes," Christine said. "My children are half Welsh," she added impulsively. "My husband's people are from Gwynned."

"The north," Sarah said. "I would like to go there."

"Then you shall someday," Christine said. Sarah sobered and shook her head no. Her face was so exquisitely rendered, it was hard to observe, while still unfamiliar, and her gaze seemed to realize and rue this.

"No north?" Christine said. "Why?"

"I—may not live long enough." Said, after the brief pause, matter-of-factly.

"I'd hate to think that," Christine offered.

"You would?" Sarah said sweetly, hopefully. And Christine believed the entire situation had to be based on a misapprehension. Sarah looked perfectly healthy. Why should she lie in bed? When Gwen was ten, she insisted that her father came to her at night and this was why she couldn't sleep, because she must wait for him. She sat up watching the window, developed violet stains beneath her young eyes, and dragged through the days. Her behavior originated in the trauma of her father's disappearance and described a sort of wishful solution. She was therefore insomniac for a reason. Perhaps the trauma of Sarah's illness was to blame for her dissimulating behavior.

"Sarah, why do you not eat?" Christine said.

"It sickens me, madam."

"Do you have pains?"

"No. I used to."

"You look very well," Christine said.

"It is a mystery," Sarah said.

"Do you have miraculous powers?" Sarah looked at the vicar, who nodded. "The miracle," she said, "is our Father and His abiding love for sinning creatures."

"Do you sin?"

She lowered her eyes. "Very much."

"Oh, I'm sure you don't."

"Why?" she asked, looking back at Christine.

"You're young. You haven't lived long enough yet to learn any of the really big sins."

Sarah laughed, and then frowned. "But I am—mature?"

"Precocious?"

"I think so."

Christine laughed. The last quality she would have expected in Sarah was a sense of humor. "Do you love life?" Christine asked.

"Too much." Her eyes filled with tears.

"I don't think one can love it too much."

"Oh, yes. We are but clouds."

"Life's brevity shouldn't concern you just yet." Interest in what Christine said shone in Sarah's eyes.

"What do you love, Sarah?"

"Reading. Religion. My family. Wales."

"Don't you miss going outside?"

Again, Sarah looked at the vicar. "Why, answer!" he said.

"The earth is the Lord's, and the fullness thereof, and they that dwell therein." Her gaze shifted to her gloved hand, fingers still tucked in the book she had been reading. "Yet I miss it," she admitted.

"What is your book?"

"Poems, madam. Would you like me to recite? These are Welsh, but I am learning to translate."

"Please, yes, recite."

"I will say in English what I have so far." She closed her eyes. "Mountain stream, clear as—"

"Crystal," the vicar said.

"Mountain stream, clear as crystal, tumbling down the valley, telling its heart to the reeds—oh, that I was like the stream!"

Truly, her English was excellent.

"It reminds me of haiku," Christine said.

"What is that?" Sarah asked.

"Japanese—the people of Japan. A form of their poetry."

"I have seen Japan on a map. Have you been there?"

"Reading their poetry, I feel that I have. I'll bring you some."

"Haiku? Thank you, madam!"

"Are you tired, Sarah?" asked Jones.

"No, I was thinking—may I ask you, madam? You write for newspapers and you are a woman?"

"I am definitely a woman." They laughed. "Women do this now, yes. Not many of us, but—would you like to?"

"No. I would like to write books."

"Ah, a noble aspiration."

"Perhaps a religious recitation is in order, Sarah," said the vicar.

"Oh, yes!" and she closed her eyes once more. When she opened them, she was transformed, transfixed, and she chanted in rhythmical, powerful Welsh, as she had in the rain, and Christine remembered now when she had heard

Welsh sound like this. It was in a Welsh Methodist chapel thirty years ago with James—the incantation of the revival. During the service, worshipping scores in wooden clogs jumped to the chanting and singing. If nothing else, Sarah was an exceptional mimic.

Sarah stopped, and tears wet her beautiful young face. "I am sorry," she said. "I am so glad, so glad in the Lord."

"And you will bring many to Him, Sarah," the vicar said.

"Thank you," said Sarah.

"Thank you," Christine said to Sarah.

"You will come again?"

"Yes, to hear the rest of the mountain stream poem."

"It will be ready for you!" She is so anxious to please, to be loved, Christine thought.

Outside, Christine spoke with the group who had finished their picnic, while the vicar translated, and then the group went in for the next show. The old man in the trap waited to drive Christine to the train and Jones back to the vicarage.

"What did you think?" asked Jones on the ride up the stone-addled lane.

"She is a sweet girl." Christine opened the object in cloth that the little one, Margaret, had thrust into her hand as she departed the house.

"What is it?" he asked.

"Oatcake. From Margaret."

"Ah, she is strange. She needs religious training and school."

"She's kept from school?"

When he nodded, she allowed disapproval into her tone. "I suppose she will be schooled when her sister is recovered?"

"I must tell you, Mrs. Thomas, that Sarah's special condition is a trial to us all, particularly the parents. Farm people have no time for invalids, certainly none for a prodigy."

Prodigy? So far, Sarah struck Christine as bright and carefully tutored.

"The fits, the screaming," he said, "you cannot know. Mrs. Jacob insists on fresh bedding twice a week and fresh gowns for Sarah daily, at the cost of backbreaking work. And changing the bedding! Well, stay for a while and you will see for yourself. As you see, Sarah likes finery. We endure it because she is valued. I don't believe in finery! Now Mr. and Mrs. Jacob, these hardworking, responsible parents are accused of using the child for their own gain. Gain! I ask you. What do they gain?" A vein worked in his crimped brow. "What do they gain?" he asked again.

"Why, I haven't accused them of anything," Christine said.

With his umbrella, he hit at the hazel branches that tore at their heads. "What have *I* to gain? Do you know what the Welsh are calling Anglican priests? Ministers of the National Whore! Not the Jacobs, not the fine people of my parish, I mean—" He threw down the umbrella and subsided against his seat. "We are at an impasse," he said.

"I see that," she replied.

Was he ill? Feverous? No, only caught in an awful muddle. He said he would translate again at the station if Christine wanted to interview anyone there. Outside the homestead, the four women who had eaten the picnic told her that they were visiting Sarah because one of them had a sick baby at home in her village the next county over. The baby wasn't well enough to travel, and the other three had agreed to help grant the mother's wish for Sarah's blessing. The mother was more than painfully thin, Christine realized now, recalling the woman's shortness when she stood up from the ground. She was stunted, deformed from meager food in her poverty's history—a stark, grotesque contrast to the apparently blooming health of the fasting girl she hoped would heal her child.

On the platform, Christine felt all at once as exhausted as the vicar looked. "I won't interview anyone else today after all, Reverend Jones." She wanted to catch the train pulling in. "Thank you," she said, putting out her hand. They shook.

"If I may be of further service," he said.

"We'll meet again soon," she replied.

Probably he had expected an entirely different type, she thought on the train—an American woman! He must have anticipated a believer in spiritualism, or a thrust-from-the-heart lady of means who had read about Wales in Romantic poetry and would prove easily swayed by any fight for the noble cause. His cause, to heal the rift between the English and the Welsh, to educate, to respect the peasantry—and his resistance to bowing utterly to scientific paternalism that righteously held itself high above other possible authorities—it was all good without any question.

But why had he latched onto the girl? Christine had taken his measure in London, after she read his letter. He was using Sarah, could be in cahoots with the father. Christine recalled the father's hand on the girl's shoulder. She recalled the vicar's hand clutching the Celtic stone. A Welsh girl to bring Welsh people together, he had said. Jones wrote that Evan Jacob was a deacon in his chapel and an overseer of the poor. Compounding the rigors of his own life, what might Jacob have seen in his dealings with the poorest in his parish? What might he have heard at the anti-English revivalist gatherings? Would a father sacrifice a daughter to further justice?

Sacrifice, not exactly. Clearly, she ate. Was the whole family in on the ruse? How could the two men coordinate the scheme? And what, as the vicar had said, did it gain them?

Disdain. Only the least educated Welsh, and some that sympathized with them, gave any credence to the fast. Old miracles shot through by inevitable advances could not redress wrongs.

If Jones thought he could use Sarah to rally righteous forces, then he was a fool, and he wasn't that. What he was, she felt certain, was acutely distressed because he could see that somehow in the slippery course of events he had made a mistake, to his regret, but for reasons she couldn't discern he believed there was no right way out.

The dark blue sky predicted rain. A storm was coming again, to close down the little bright day. In memory, she heard the calling lambs, and Sarah chanting; she smelled the melting tallow—and saw James's eyes.

Looking out at the land running by, she smelled the oat-cake, the greasy package she had tucked in her handbag, the gift Margaret had given her—or had it been Hannah sending a belated token of hospitality to her American guest? Or had Sarah herself sent the food, a symbolic, unreadable message? And where in Carmarthen would she find English translations of Japanese haiku?

No, the vicar wasn't a hard man to read. Opinions of him she had already formed would in essence hold. But Sarah was and would continue to be harder, a turning prism in light, taking on colors, first this and then that, scattering shards in magical patterns a person could almost catch in her hand.

DOUBT

I WAS RELIEVED TO BE EXCUSED from school. One reason was the Welsh Not. Sarah said it was never used in the vicar's school, but I heard of schools in the neighboring towns where it was. They hung the Welsh Not sign around your neck if you forgot to speak English, and stood you in front of the class. They took it off when another child lapsed, and the child who wore the Welsh Not at the end of the day was beaten. The Welsh Not made illiteracy, it was said at chapel, a condition of honor. Mam said it was all we could do to let the boys go to school, once Sarah got sick. Sarah disagreed, and Mam said, "I will thank you, Miss High and Mighty, to leave Margaret to herself." Sarah decided to teach me reading and writing in Welsh. "I like to *hear* stories," I said. "If I have to make out black marks for a story, I will soon give them up."

And so she went back to telling me stories, and teaching me with them about life. One was the story of poor Dai Sion, the son of a clog maker. I had seen the towers of clog blocks cut from the alder trees, drying in the open air. The stacked wood pieces fit like a puzzle and miraculously did not fall. The towers were round and wide at the bottom, narrowing toward the tip. Whenever I came upon them I lingered and admired them. But Dai Sion had no feeling for craft. He was hapless and dreamy. He liked to roam, and one day in his roaming he was startled to come upon a fairy ring, the mushroom rings where the fairies have been. He knew not to step in the ring, but he dipped in a foot and jiggled his leg. "Ah! That felt fine! Now I had better go home."

But near where his father's wattle-and-mud cottage should have been stood a handsome stone house. The sight told Dai Sion to mistrust his eyes: It was a fairy trick! Why, his foot touched the ring for seconds, and no one could build a stone house in that time. The house was imaginary and insubstantial.

He hurried along a familiar path to his father's dwelling and came to the thorny bushes he recognized. He tested their reality by pricking himself with a thorn. "These are no fairy hedges," he said, sucking blood from his finger. Even so, there were no clog blocks in what should have been his father's yard. A dog barked at Dai Sion viciously. "Rhapsody!" he cried. "Do you not know me?" Still the dog barked, and her color was changed. Dai Sion thought he must have gotten turned around and was nowhere near home. Only then he saw the long stone, *Y Garreg Hir,* and there was no other like it.

Alerted by the dog's barking, a farmer came out of the house. "Young man!" he said. "What is the commotion?" The beggar he faced stood in rags. "Who are you?"

"I know who I was," Dai Sion said sadly. "I lived here this morning."

"Why, that couldn't be," the farmer said. "This house was built by my great-grandfather. None but my family ever lived here."

"I would doubt my own mind," Dai Sion admitted, "except for Garreg Hir, which ever stood before my father's cottage." And he told about the fairy ring and how it may have worked fairy tricks.

"Come," said the farmer, sorry for the lad. "We will call on Cati Shon, an old woman wise in the magic of *y tylwyth teg.*"

But no sooner had they set off than the farmer, leading

the way, stopped hearing footsteps behind him. He turned
around, to find Dai Sion crumbled into a pile of black dust,
no higher than an anthill. The farmer continued on to Cati
Shon's ancient hovel, and when he questioned the woman, she
vaguely recalled a clog maker, Sion, *y crdydd of* Glanrhyd. Her
grandfather had told her about Sion's son, who didn't come
home one day and wasn't heard of again. People said fairies
took him, and Cati Shon remembered that Sion's house had
been close to where the farmer now lived.

ALWAYS AFTER I HEARD THE STORY, if I saw the clog block towers, I would squint my eyes hard so that the blocks shimmered
and the towers lost their shape. But my eyes watered and I had
to let them relax. Then the towers were firm, and it was impossible to believe they were anything else.

"It isn't that they are something else," Sarah said. "It is that
there may be other realities behind what we see with our eyes."

"You mean God?"

"The towers could be shoes," Sarah said. "You understand
that. The blocks are there temporarily until they are turned
into shoes. And so, everything changes from one thing into
another."

"Not fast."

"Not usually. Sometimes it can be fast."

"He was a silly, dumb man," I said.

"Oh, no," Sarah said. "He just liked to roam, and he was
curious."

"He paid a price."

"That he did."

The Bible speaks of time and generation, as well. But I
thought there was something else behind the story. A thing
Sarah couldn't put into words, or I couldn't understand.

≋

British Medical Journal of 24 April 1869 (p. 374)

State on 7 April 1869—She was lying in a low bed, on her back, the shoulders and head slightly raised, and her right arm outside the clothes, which she moved at will. Her face was not emaciated, but moderately full, with slight flush on her cheeks, and the nose and colour of lips natural; her features were perfect, and good-looking; the skin of her face was healthy; her front teeth were normal, and it was said that the remainder were so, though I did not see them. She was not able to open her mouth: she never put out the tongue. The temperature of the forehead was natural; the eyes were bright; the irises of hazel brown colour. The general aspect of her face was that of being delicate, not cachectic. As her examination required to be proceeded with cautiously, her body was not uncovered, but my hand was applied immediately to the front of the chest and the abdomen. The skin covering these parts was warm; there was no excessive emaciation felt; the abdomen was not depressed, but was of the usual position of a slender child. Occasional flatulent rumbling noises were heard in the abdomen. The whole of the right arm was seen, and the legs; the colour and texture of the skin of these parts were healthy; the hand looked delicate, and the nails well formed. The pulse was feeble, but distinct, and variable, from 100 to 108 per minute. The temperature in the axilla, after three minutes' rest, was 95 degrees; the temperature of the feet rather low. During my visit she had three attacks of unconsciousness; one caused by a barking dog; she partially closed the eyelids, and remained perfectly still; the colour of the face was not altered. After two or three minutes, she heaved a sigh, made a slight sound, and seemed like one suddenly awakening from sleep.

She is once a day removed from one bed to another, for the purpose of shaking her bed; during this time she remains in a state of unconsciousness, or what they call 'a fit,' and does not recover until replaced in her own bed.

The foregoing account is drawn up, after a visit to the girl, for two objects: to satisfy the curiosity of persons at a distance who are desirous of knowing the history and present state of the Welsh Fasting-Girl, and also to awaken the attention of those who have the leisure and the scientific ardour to visit the case, and investigate and judge for themselves.

—*Dr. T. Lewis of Carmarthen*

Carmarthen, Wales
23 July 1869

Dearest James,

I have gotten quite used to the town and try to accept the continual rain. I sometimes feel lonely. Though there is real warmth in the people, they are understandably cautious with me. Perhaps it is best I discern what I can inconspicuously for the present. Welsh sounds more natural now to my ear. The pronunciation is fairly straightforward. It is the rules of mutation I wrestle with nightly, those words changed by gender or the last letter of the word before—the slur, the elision in a language you once said was so precise! The mutation device is a safe, whose code I am too dense to crack.

One interview I absolutely must conduct is with Dr. Harries Davies, the physician who treated Sarah during her original illness. I have waited three weeks, and at last he agreed to a visit day after tomorrow. Perhaps, as he says, he has been busy. Perhaps he distrusts me. Harries Davies is the man who, at the behest of Evan Jacob and Evan Jones, oversaw the watch on Sarah.

To my knowledge, just two doctors have examined Sarah other than Davies. One, Dr. Lewis, is a local man, like Davies, of whom I hadn't heard until a reporter at the *Carmarthen Weekly* showed me his write-up in the *British Medical Journal*. I should have known better, since nothing is self-evident in any aspect of the case, but when I read about the "rumbling noises" in Sarah's stomach, I asked why this didn't put it all to rest. Weren't rumbling noises proof that she eats?

"Proof," the reporter scoffed. "For people who until recently trusted in conjurers, a physician's word wouldn't convince. And if I asked my old auntie for her 'diagnosis,' I believe she would say that poor Sarah's stomach grumbles from hunger pains. That the Lord must sustain her, but as she is clothed in mortal flesh, she likely suffers."

Perpetual circles! Personally, I suspect the locals are cannier than the reporter surmises. I sense they are very concerned about the scandal that has developed around the case, and this makes them wary. The two Evans, Jacob and Jones, are Welsh and their neighbors, and if the Evans are committed to Sarah's claim, people feel there has to be something to it. They feel sympathetic to the mire Jacob and Jones are caught in and, possibly, just accept trouble there—complicated trouble, whose outcome they will have to await. I learned that the Magistrate's Court threw out the assault charge against Dr. Pearson Hughes—the other physician who examined Sarah, with too much zeal—after hardly a listen. In contrast, Carmarthen's Dr. Lewis clearly described his examination of Sarah but also refused to shut the door to differing opinions, concluding his report with a call for further investigation. Anything I have seen written by English doctors is haughty, dismissive, ridiculing the vicar and the parents and the entire uproar as an embarrassment to any with heads on their shoulders.

Yet ink from the English doctors continues to pour. Douglas has written to me that their engagement with the case in the papers lends credence to what they proclaim is beneath consideration. It is a feature, he says, of their campaign to legitimate medicine as the ultimate arbiter. The conquering English are intent on extending their rule to the last realm of bodies, and they will not rest until their authority is accepted, much as they are so anxious for their English to subsume the Welsh language in Wales.

Thus far, English doctors are keeping a physical distance. It is said that, here, people were swayed by the watch a few months ago. Two watchers were highly skeptical of Sarah's powers, but they left convinced. Rather than putting the controversy to rest, the watching fueled the flames. Dr. Davies, as I reported in my first dispatch, stressed the omnipotence of the Creator alongside his medical opinion that physiologically speaking Sarah's fast is impossible. Now I feel that he *may* have so published in deference to the continued interest and reinforced conviction in favor of the miracle.

Meanwhile, Philip Beckwith threatens to withdraw from the fray, writing that while my reports have been read with interest in the States, if something sensational does not happen soon, it all will have been, in the end, a minor story. Well and good; I'll pack my bags and return to my family.

Also in Douglas's letter, I received the news that Gwen is no longer pregnant. Douglas assured me that she is healthy and there was no miscarriage. Gwen never was pregnant. Douglas assumes she misread the signs, and I will, too. But I worry. I hope it wasn't a ploy to keep me in Brooklyn. You would tell me she *could* have been wrong . . . and what can I do from here? How much was I able to do anymore for Gwen at home? And when didn't I worry about her? Born a girl. But her brightness convinced me that she could be happy, as I was for so many years.

Well. My children are grown, and it is fitting that I strike out into my singular future. Vinnie put it like that. I will carry on here and try to keep Philip satisfied. I suppose I should attempt to speak with Dr. Pearson Hughes, only I've heard he is an abrasive, unpleasant person and wholly sides with the English.

It is not that I am *against* the English; I am as distressed by the Welsh, at least by Evan Jones and Evan Jacob. Jones informed me that Jacob considered my exclusive interview with Sarah inappropriate. Since then, I have seen Sarah thrice more with a group, and her father present. The last time, he greeted me heartily in English, but the Welsh in him throttled the words: He choked out the vowels.

I stood paralyzed, sweaty, straining for comprehension, when, at last, like vapor had cleared from a mirror, I understood.

How you like Wales?

I jabbered back something inane, and he observed me with utter composure. He has a force. I can't put my finger on it. As a tenant farmer in rain-driven Wales, he toils like an ox, or the family wouldn't survive, and yet he waits on Sarah and propagates this bizarre campaign. His wife and children look up to him; I think excessively so. None of them ever sits in the special chair by the fire where he reads the papers. He is literate in Welsh, unlike Hannah. I don't feel violence in him; that doesn't seem it. I would say he has magnetism and a quiet contempt he employs to his personal benefit.

At my last visit, yesterday, I filed by Sarah in a group. Then Jacob allowed me to speak to her in his presence. I had brought poems Vinnie kindly sent from London, a pair of haiku I'd promised. Sarah liked the poems, but after I read her *the first cold shower / even the monkey seems to want / a little coat of straw*, Sarah said she hadn't heard of monkeys and asked what they were. I described monkeys, explained where they lived—when I felt Jacob's withering stare. His eyes bore through me, found me ridiculous, chattering about monkeys while he battled torrential rains, or some such—played his part in the land's drama and now, because of Sarah, on the large social stage. What I felt was a quiet assertion of his importance and my inconsequence. I don't know how much of it had to do with my being a woman. Most Welsh have accepted the woman reporter more readily than Americans do. I don't know what Evan Jones may have told Jacob.

Evan Jones continues to disturb me. I keep thinking of the weekly meetings he had with Sarah for fifteen months, a long time. I imagine what was said in their religious discussions, how he may have influenced her. Two hale middle-aged widows run the inn where I stay, Mrs. Owen and Mrs. Morgan. They are tall and rangy, of the bodily type more common up north—they remind me of you dear, and our tall Rupert. Mrs. Morgan knows no English, but Mrs. Owen does. She spoke to me about Sarah. As I said, I don't want to seem prying or aggressive. But Mrs. Owen herself brought up Sarah one morning when I was about to leave for the newspaper office. I hadn't told her why I was here, but she knew. "Have you met Sarah?" she asked. "She is a good little girl. Too pretty for comfort, but otherwise a polite, studious child. She kept to herself. Wasn't overly attentive to the boys. We have a long tradition here of holy girls, you know. There was handsome Mari Jones, who walked through the Black Mountains in winter, barefoot, for a copy of the Welsh Bible. Gaunor Hughes was a great Protestant mystic and beauty. She lived a life of constant

ecstasy and visionary experience. She lay in bed without eating for many months, only slaking her thirst with water from
what is now a holy well." I nodded politely and started out.
"It is bittersweet, thinking those days are over," Mrs. Owen
added. Sarah has likely heard the legends, and clearly, they
cling to the collective imagination.

Why is it the holy sufferers are always women, and beautiful? It occurs to me that since Moses fasted for forty days
before receiving the Ten Commandments, and Jesus before His
enlightenment, and the hermits of the Gnostic era subsisted
on bread and water in their huts and caves, we have heard of
few men living on nothing but spiritual sustenance. Catherine
of Sienna supped on bitter herbs and perished of malnutrition
at thirty-three. Fasting was fundamental to female holiness
until 1500. A shift occurred during the Reformation, when
fasters were cast as demoniacal, heretical, and insane. They
were whipped in the street, executed, and believed fed by the
devil. But the uncertainty about whether bodies could persist
without food—and hope of the soul's independence—kept
interest in fasting alive.

In 1669, sixteen-year-old Martha Taylor, the "Derbyshire
Damsel," took no food "except now and then a few drops of
the syrup of stewed prunes, water and sugar, or the juice of a
roasted raisin," and was proclaimed "a wonder of the world."
Scientists cited food abstinence in hibernating animals. They
looked to how women nourish fetuses with their own blood.
Fasters might live on bodily ferments, might absorb nutritive
particles in the air or on the skin, for, it was written, "putting
one's limbs in brandy one gets drunk." Picture the experiment!
Willing volunteers plunged into barrels of brandy. How they
kept the volunteers from sample sipping, it is hard to say.

What I have learned is that there are vast accounts in newspaper morgues, documents detailing the energy expended

across many years on food refusal. I surmise the momentum doesn't easily halt. Bother the fact that oxygen was discovered in the late eighteenth century and proved digestion to be a combustion process with absolute laws.

And what of Sarah? Who are these women and girls said not to eat? Those who sicken, who are estranged from their own flesh? They are rewarded by sainthood, denigrated and watched, and what is the cure? One harsh cure that was really no cure at all came about with the watching of the Englishwoman Ann Moore, the "Fasting Woman of Tutbury." Moore's fame was transatlantic. Her figure in wax was exhibited at a Boston museum. I find the case doleful. Moore's repugnance for food began after daily changing the bandages of a man who suffered from seeping ulcers. He was her employer and probably fathered her illegitimate children. Somewhere along the line, she began claiming to eat nothing and spouting religious text, though she could not read—I would suppose she deduced that this was expected of her. Witnesses reported that she was emaciated. She passed a watch; she benefited financially from gifts people brought over five years—it is important to note that she had always been poor. At last, a "stricter watch" was conducted, and Ann's method of staying alive was exposed: as her daughter washed the bedridden Ann's face, she fed her with cloths dipped in gravy, or vinegar or starch. The daughter passed morsels to her mother in kisses.

Ann was exposed in 1814, but she is mentioned in medical textbooks and held up as a cautionary example in discussions of Sarah. She stands as a symbol of "female cunning and deceit." Ann wrote and signed a humiliating public confession, admitting how she had mocked Christian piety and scientific learning. The scientists and the clergy, it seems, came together in the instance of Ann.

Was she not ill? Had not her distaste for food arisen from desperate circumstance? She may have sickened from the attentions of her scrofulous employer. Was she not seeking refuge from trials she endured? The last trace I found of her in later life was that she went to jail for robbing her lodgings.

A thief, a con artist, I suppose. She was a grown woman, as Sarah is not. I fear I am overly sympathetic.

What say you, husband? Shall I write a "History of Fasting" for *The Sun*? I doubt it is what Philip has in mind.

Talk at the *Carmarthen Weekly* is that Evan Jacob and Evan Jones are angling for a stricter watch involving the English. They may be, if they are intent on humiliating Sarah. But it is 1869, not 1814. And to be fair to the father, I doubt he will surrender Sarah to the English. After Dr. Pearson Hughes, it is said Jacob's distrust of doctors congealed into positive loathing.

Silence. Rain at the glass. When the children were young, I prayed for ten minutes of silence. My prayers have piled up like snow.

Do you listen? James? I am feeling unwell. The thrumming, burning sensation in my legs has returned. I feel tightness in my throat, a shortness of breath.

I am alone, my children across the ocean, my husband gone when I'm growing old.

Good night, love,
Christine

❧

DR. HARRIES DAVIES LIVED over a blacksmith shop in the nearby village of Llandysul. A hand-painted sign in garish reds and greens proclaimed H. H. DAVIES, SURGEON, atop stairs slickened by rain.

Christine found him hardly more than a boy in his warren of rooms, well-heated and packed with books everywhere—even the surgery, smeared by a frightening splash of blood on the floor. "Oh, dear me, Mrs. Thomas, I—the char was supposed to clean up. I had a tyke in, sliced his chin badly this morning." Davies threw down a rag and, with his foot, wiped the evidence away. He cut the tour short and settled his guest in the parlor: books, a cozy fire, cake, tea, and a giant birdcage that flickered with pale orange lovebirds he called Henrietta and Haley.

"What a relief to sit down," he confided. "If the bell rings, don't breathe, don't talk; we'll just sit until whoever it is goes away." He helped himself to cake and encouraged Christine to do likewise. The lovebirds whistled and chirped, prompting frequent shushing: "Girls! Henrietta and Haley! We will hear no more about it!"

She thought him adorable, warm and fussy, round, with a full moon face and moist, expressive gray eyes. "How are you surviving our rain?" he asked. "It is beastly this year. I would like to move out to your Utah. I have relatives there."

"My son has settled in Missouri," she said.

"Send him a telegram," said the doctor, "and say I'll be there in a fortnight. A fortnight?" he asked himself. "Oh, well, I'll fly. Where is your notebook?"

"I remember each and every word I hear," she said.

"Seriously? How convenient for your profession!"

"Oh, yes," Christine replied, nodding sagely. Let the rumor get around. Truthfully, she had forgotten her notebook yet again. "Thank you for having me."

"I am sure," and he sighed, "you want to ask about the watch. I did hope it would lead to the end of our little drama."

Drama? She waited.

"Sarah is well," he said. "The parents are coping as best

they can. Obviously, her condition's biological cause eludes our comprehension. That should be that."

"She isn't well," Christine countered. "She's a well-looking child who lies all day in bed, one who told me she thinks she will die."

He wiped his mouth daintily and asked, "She said 'die'?"

"Yes."

He put down his plate. "How may I help your reporting?" He seemed sincere, as if anxious to get to the bottom of the case and truly have it over.

"I'd like to know about Sarah's original illness. Do you agree there is a connection to her present condition?"

"Oh, well, obviously. Historically, prodigious abstinence often began with a shock to the system. Sarah was gravely ill, though I and another physician called at the time were unable to agree on a diagnosis. Eventually, she rallied without help from us. Praise the higher forces, *y Doctor Mawr.* Do you know any Welsh?"

Christine pointed at the ceiling to indicate God, "the Great Doctor."

"Eat cake," said Davies. "It is special Welsh cake."

"I'll wait," she said. "Must concentrate on my memory."

"Of course. Dr. Hopkins gave her up for dead from swelling of the brain. I gave her up myself, after finding her skeletal and comatose. This was a month or so after she was first stricken with stomach pains and chest congestion. She developed paralysis of the left side, acute sensitivity, and spasms. Nothing I did produced improvement. I didn't want to take any more money from the Jacobs. I left them with directions on her management."

"You mentioned 'prodigious abstinence,'" Christine said. "Do you mean in the absence of organic causes, of disease?"

"Yes, but, well, the insane don't eat. Many don't."

"What about the slightly insane?"

"Slightly? Girls! Henrietta and Haley!" He considered for a moment. "I didn't diagnose Sarah as hysteric."

There, thought Christine, was the word she had waited to hear. Hysteria was the catchall woman's disease for illnesses supposedly related to female conditions: the onset of puberty, pregnancy, and the cessation of monthly courses. Medicine claimed these natural functions, without which the human race would cease to exist, drove girls and women crazy.

"Catalepsy was my diagnosis," he said. "A nerve disease. She may be suffering from hysteria now, but it is unlikely. Sarah is a good girl. There may have been damage to nerves at the time of active disease. . . ."

"And?"

"We don't know. I am not afraid to say we don't know."

"You referred to prodigious abstinence in a historical context. Do you mean the saints?" she asked.

"Some of them, yes," he said.

"Do you believe Sarah eats nothing?"

"I don't know. Girls! Henrietta and Haley! We will hear no more about it!"

"Do you?" she repeated.

"Mrs. Thomas, I do not wish to have my words quoted and believed, when I don't know what I believe myself."

"You wrote that physiologically it is impossible."

"I also wrote that from my experience with similar ailments, what an incredibly small amount of nourishment may support life."

"Then she may take small amounts of food."

"She took small amounts when she was ill before."

"And now nothing?"

"It is what the Jacobs claim, and they are admirable, truthtelling people."

"Good parents."

"They didn't give up on Sarah and they haven't yet."

"It isn't a designing scheme?"

"I don't see the motive."

The bell jangled at his door. He started, put his finger to his lips, and, on a grunt, stood and said, "I can't. Excuse me."

Interesting. If Sarah was a "good girl," she could not be a hysteric, like Ann Moore, presumably, that paragon of female cunning and deceit.

"Only my lemon drops," the doctor announced, returning with his bag of candy. "Do try one. Surely they won't interfere with your recall."

"Thank you." She held a drop. "I did want to talk about the watch. A committee was formed. After the watch, the watchers reported to the committee what they had seen. Were the reports recorded?"

"Most likely," he said. "The press was there."

"Really? I found nothing published."

"You might try the *Weekly*."

"I will. What about Pearson Hughes?"

"He was rough with her. She is a sheltered, modest, religious child. She had not in her life been examined by a doctor before I attended her during her illness, and Hughes was insensitive to the decorum we endeavor to employ with our young patients."

"What happened?"

"I don't know exactly. He isn't from around here, and no one is anxious to hear from him again. Don't you like candy?"

She put the damn lemon drop in her mouth.

"Bad for the teeth," he said, "but I can't resist."

She sucked; he said, "Tasty?" She nodded. The birds chirped quietly. "I don't know what else I can tell you. You've spoken with Reverend Jones?"

She nodded; clever way to get her to stop asking questions; the drop was too sweet.

"Poor Jones," he said. "The pressure he's under from the case, and the political pressures, I'm sure you heard about the evictions? Yes, and then his wife . . . Oh, she died! Yes, last year in June. Typhoid. He has a small child of four. Not very much comfort at that age—they don't understand." Christine knew typhoid fever from its ravages in the Civil War. More soldiers died of it than of wounds. At the hospital where she volunteered, she had seen typhoid, patients writhing with fever while their bodily fluids flooded the beds, leaving husks, like shucked corn.

So, the vicar grieved. It explained his fragility. He had described last year as divisive. Politically, yes, but he had also suffered this absolute human division. Surely his faith was tested, prompting a desperate belief in Sarah's powers?

Davies awaited further questions, but this latest information felt revelatory. She needed to think—and to check the *Weekly*.

She felt overly warm, anxious to leave. The lovebirds screamed, and Davies said, "Girls! Henrietta and Haley!" She thanked Dr. Davies and quickly departed.

At the *Carmarthen Weekly*, she stopped by the office of Alun Lloyd and Reginald Pary, reporters, and asked Lloyd whether he had been present at the committee meeting after the watching. Lloyd didn't look up from his heaped desk, where he sat with his thin legs entwined, sipping his herbal mixture, evidence that his stomach problems were acute this afternoon. "Wasn't there," he said. "Pary was."

"Where is he?"

"Marching, I should imagine."

Reginald Pary, a wiry sprocket of a man with kinky black hair, liked to pace. Whenever he was stuck on his writing, he took to the hallways.

"Thank you!" She didn't find Pary on the ground floor and, raising her damp, muddy skirts, she rushed upstairs to the second. "Mr. Pary," she called. "May I talk to you?" Hands clasped behind his back, feet beating a steady tattoo, he said, "Join me." They paced the second floor and back downstairs to begin again.

"You ought to have your skirts shortened," he suggested. "Get a pair of clogs."

"I ought to," she replied. "Were you at the committee meeting after the Jacob watching?"

"For how bloody long will we have to think about it," he muttered. "I was," he conceded. "What do you want to know?"

"Have you notes?"

"Yes, and you can see them if you like. They're mildly amusing. Two of the watchers were Harries Davies's nephews, did you hear? No? Well, nobody volunteered and he had to get someone. I couldn't determine the point of the watch. Safeguard the Jacob family honor, Jones said. I guess that was it. But, honor? Hard to keep a straight face, even, when the watchers kept bringing up the sheets. Wet and unpleasant, had to be taken to the kitchen for washing." He made a sharp turn and, once more, they climbed. "How these men are convinced, two medical students and a farmer among them, that the girl doesn't eat and only gets—what, her lips moistened every fortnight, and somehow, forgive me, urinates like a horse?" A door slammed shut as they passed. "The mother said it was the shock of the watching brought it on. Smelly sheets. For, as we know, up to the watching, the girl neither ate nor drank for seventeen months."

"What else?"

"Read the rest. You can analyze her fits and her tics and her spasms."

"What do you know about Dr. Pearson Hughes?"

"I was there when the case was heard at the Magistrate's Court. The acquittal didn't go down too well here. Hughes shoved his hand down her back, feeling for bedsores. There were none. Read about it yourself. I am monumentally restless, so I'll be out here. Go to my office, third file to the left. Bloody Welsh."

After she'd read the file, Christine returned to her room. The file detailed what Pary summarized. Just one further comment caught her attention.

One watcher said, "I told the father to leave it alone then, to let Sarah to her own ways. But make no mistake: I came to the watching a disbeliever and I left in doubt." Mass delusion, she thought, the force of suggestion, the accumulated months and years of Sarah's legend.

She sat down at her desk and opened a green notebook for letters, then shut it. Opened another, wrote, "Proofs: Urine. No bedsores."

Evidence that Sarah ate was abundant, for anyone who wanted to look.

What was Hannah's part in it? she wondered.

She shuddered. Gwen, she thought, and pictured the girl in her velvet coat at the harbor—her cool, clouded eyes.

THE TIDE TURNS

I N AUGUST, TAD TOLD US NEST WAS DYING. Sarah cried bitterly, and Tad said there was nothing he could do. Nest could stay a day more in the barn with the others, and then she must go. My sister and I agreed that Nest was the most beautiful of the cows. Nest's was the first animal face Sarah saw in this life. When she lay in the field with Mam as a baby, Nest's face hung so near that Sarah reached out her baby fingers and touched the cow's moist nose and lips. Nest opened her mouth and showed her big square teeth and let out a breath and sprayed Sarah all over, and how Sarah laughed!

As the rooms darkened on Nest's last night in the barn, and Mam cleaned the kitchen and Tad read his papers by the fire, I crawled in with Sarah. Mam would soon shout me out, but my sister and I had this time together.

When, later, I went to the kitchen, Sarah was just putting on her secret soft shoes. I gathered oatcakes from the crock for quieting the dog, Dilly, and hid a match in my stocking for the oil lamp Sarah took from the table. Quietly, we left the house, went around to the barn door; Dilly whimpered, gobbled a cake, and we got inside. Scurry of rats and afraid they'd scrabble my feet in the dark, I lit the lamp, pouf! The cows awoke, lifting their heads: Belle, Clovis, Bronwen, Nansi, Eilund, Rhian, Malt, Gronwy, Megan, Ruth, Salomé, and Nest, lying farthest away. She did not lift her head as the others had and already she could have died. Sarah gazed at the dirty board walls; the scythes hung on the wall, seed baskets, rope, reaping hooks, flails, spades, rakes, awners, milk cans, and the new plow Tad bought this year. It was Nest's life and Sarah's and my life, and Sarah missed it. She approached Nest, happy yet scared, and suddenly, swift as a hawk to the ground, she grabbed a reaping hook and slashed at the air and said, "*Nest! Arise.*"

"You are well," Sarah said. "Stand up and walk to me, Nest. Do you hear me, Nest? Walk." I watched the glinting curved hook in her hand, and the quiet cow.

We heard steps above us. Remembering Emyr, the hired boy who slept in the loft, we looked up at the opening and thought we saw him, a bump in the black.

"Emyr?" Sarah said. "Don't answer me, then. Listen: If you say a word about us in the barn, I will tell such truths of you that they will turn you out onto the road!"

He was silent. But he was there in the dark triangle.

"Watch us, then," she said.

She turned to me and smiled. I recalled the healer who had come to my sister's bed the day before, a crooked man with fuzzy whiskers, who said to Sarah, "Arise. You are well. Get up and eat."

We smiled at each other. Sarah replaced the reaping hook on the wall gently, followed its blade with her eyes as it settled back into place.

She greeted Belle and Malt, rubbing their bristly backs. She said, "Boo, Clovis!" And the parti-colored cow shifted, for always Clovis was apprehensive. Sarah touched Bronwen's long eyelashes, Rhian's high head ridge, and said "Your Highness" to Salomé of the tall, queenly neck. She kissed Nansi, Gronwy, Eilund, Ruth, and Megan. We had black, brown, and parti-colored cows. But Nest was most beautiful, with her curly white topknot and white face above her black body. She looked very human. She loved music more than the others and would stop grazing and come to us if we sang to her. We sang to her now. I edged closer, with Dilly beside me, and Sarah sat on a stool by Nest's head.

> A happy place I was in today,
> Under cloaks of lovely green hazels . . .
> And the eloquent slim nightingale,
> From the corner of the grove near by,
> Wandering poetess of the valley, rang to the multitude
> The Sanctus bell, clear to its trill,
> And raised the Host
> As far as the sky . . .

We grieved. The music opened Nest's eyes, but she did not lift her head. Her side was a huge bellows riding her great arcing ribs. I studied the nicks in her coat, the missing ear tips from frostbite, and her gnarled, tender feet.

Sarah looked at Nest for a long time. She put her face close to Nest and said, "I smell the grass and turnips she has eaten in her life. Barley. Oats. Straw. I am smelling her life."

The next morning, Tad and Emyr put Nest in the wagon and drove her away.

❧

Carmarthen, Wales
17 September 1869

My dear Gwen,

Are you well? It has been weeks since I've heard from you. Please write, darling, or Mother will worry. I hope the summer heat is finished and that Mr. Blunt is in good health. The Lord continues to spray South Wales most days. If it is warm, steam rises to meet the low-hanging clouds and we move half-blind through this strange, not always annoying but sometimes piquant manifestation of the ephemeral nature of existence. That is Wales, one waxes poetic, it cannot be helped—the poetic is locked in the molecular air.

I've had a letter from Rupert, have you? He mentioned a woman! Would that not be lovely? A helpmate and consolation, for as much as he craves solitude and fancies himself the Thoreau of the West, I hate thinking of him completely alone.

On fine days, when the rain tires and the sun peeks from its hiding, I hurry with my friends Mrs. Owen and Mrs. Morgan to sit outside and knit. We knit in rain, too, but our plein air knitting meetings are especially jolly. I don't exactly chatter in Welsh, but I understand more and converse in a correct if stiff fashion. You and Douglas will have enough hats, scarves, mittens, and sweaters to last you forever.

The main reason I write, dear, is to say that just at the moment I felt sure I was about to come home, Philip Beckwith told me not to. He was emphatic. A distinguished doctor visited Sarah last month and published a lengthy report in *The Times*. The letter was reprinted and responded to throughout England and Wales, in leaders and correspondence columns. You may have seen my summation in *The Sun*? I know you dislike newspapers, but you cannot get all of life from novels, and it is a terribly interesting case. [Christine thought to cross out the previous line and rewrite the page.]

The interest derives, and *interesting* may be the wrong word, from difficulties in what has been a colonized nation since 1235. Essentially, Dr. Fowler, who is English, has politicized the Sarah Jacob case by calling on the landowning gentry and the Anglican ministers to save the girl from "the credible Welsh." Nothing like this had been said overtly in print before, and emotions are pitched higher than ever. I cannot say I am happy about it. I don't think most people care about "saving" Sarah, and I don't see how this debate will help the

Welsh who have suffered. The Nonconformist religious movement, however, has given the peasantry a renewed pride, an
awakening from mute acceptance of injustice. One can hope
that this argument over the "truth" about a sick girl will open
further discussions about the real matters at hand.

I will certainly be home by Christmas.

Your loving,
Mother

❧

DR. ROBERT FOWLER, DISTRICT MEDICAL OFFICER for the London Union, was on holiday in Cardigan when his friend, Mr.
Thomas Davies, solicitor, asked if he should like to see the
far-famed Fasting Girl.

On the rare sunny morning of 30 August, the pair jour-
neyed along the Teifi Valley, leaving their horse and carriage
at the Wilkes Head Inn, Llandysul, and proceeding by train
to Pencader. They continued on foot down the winding lane
and soon arrived across the moor to where "the marvel," as
Fowler called Sarah, was living.

At the house, it was washing day, and since dawn Hannah had hauled and boiled water, scrubbed laundry in abrasive
soda crystals, rinsed and wrung out the bulky wet linen, with
only Margaret to help. Evan needed the others in the fields.

Sarah and Margaret were whiny and distracted since Nest
had gone to the slaughterer. Sarah constantly called for her
sister, and Margaret, who was often enlisted to mind the
baby—now a strapping toddler of nearly two—would leave
him to wander off and, for all anyone knew, drown in the
river while she attended Sarah.

On many mornings, and this was one, Hannah didn't
know how she could go on as the situation existed. She

opened her eyes out of a sleep deep enough that she might have emerged from the earth's pitch, the earth's bog, one of those primeval bodies hauled to the surface after its centuries' sleep. She prayed, "Make her well or have her proclaimed, but Lord, have it done." Of her prayer, she was ashamed. One day, she would say these things to Christine, but never until then and never again.

Dilly pricked her ears and barreled outside. Margaret caught and yanked the dog back from the fine gentlemen—she saw they were fine from their waistcoats and top hats and shiny black boots high as Dilly's head, and so she had waited a heartbeat before she grabbed Dilly and let the visitors to their ease.

Having returned to the house, she said, "Mam, fine men are coming."

"I'll see to Sarah," Hannah said. "Keep them outside until I tell you."

Sarah lay staring at the ceiling. "We have fine gentlemen come to see you, my girl."

Unmoving, Sarah said in a listless voice, "Must I today?"

"Why ever not? That is unlike you." She helped Sarah sit, and tended her hair. The child was warm, cheeks red and eyes unnaturally bright. "Have you pains?" Hannah asked.

"My stomach," Sarah said. "But I will see the men. It is my duty to one who suffers most—God."

"A crown for my princess." To the wreath Hannah affixed to Sarah's head, she attached dangling ribbons joined beneath Sarah's chin by more flowers. She helped Sarah into a jacket and added an emerald shawl and the crucifix on a string of gilt beads. But her daughter sagged, bedraggled under her finery. Hannah moved to take Sarah into her arms, saying, "My Sal, what is it, darling?"

"Off me!" Sarah said, all at once filled with the strength

of rage. "I'm not a baby, and there is nothing"—she exaggerated her syllables, producing venom in each sound—"you can do for me."

"It is mean to take it out on your mother, who only wants what is best for you."

"You," Sarah said as Hannah left. "Turn around." Hannah did. "Can you not see?" Sarah asked.

Hannah was at a loss, as she had most often been for the life of this passionate, quick, unmanageable, sickly, mysterious creature Evan said was their blessing, trial, and test. "See?"

"See," Sarah said. "See. See. Look."

"If Tad were here—"

"But he isn't, then, is he?"

Already Hannah's back and arms ached, her hands burned, and it wasn't but nine in the morning. Was she supposed to think also? See? What was there to see?

"Don't talk in riddles, Sarah," she said.

"Oh, go," Sarah said, "I'm ready."

Hannah went to the kitchen and through the open door saw Margaret and Dilly sprawled in the grass by the washing they'd put out to dry in the sun. The gentlemen stood by the fence. There had to be linen out when they came. She hadn't the skill for being watched, almost every hour, and Sarah, too, watching her, and Margaret lolling on the ground in the posture of an exhausted laborer! "Margaret! Come in!"

Spotting Hannah, the men started toward her, stepping carefully around the linen. Hannah's breath caught—the catch of fear with her for as long as she could remember near any of their class, the catch full of danger that fogged the air in their proximity. Sarah would laugh at her for feeling this. Evan laughed. To his peril, he laughed.

The younger man with the waxed mustache greeted her in

Welsh. The elder made her so nervous, she called him "Your Honor" throughout the visit.

Fowler. If she'd known any English, she might have thought *foul*, for his lordly big head and pendulous features, for how he pursed his lips when he ducked to get through the door and entered her house, as if he had entered a privy. He fingered the gold watch chain crossing his belly and made his request, through his translator, to examine Sarah.

Evan forbade physical examinations after Dr. Pearson Hughes, and Sarah was in a mood today, but what was Hannah to do? Thomas Davies represented the landlord, and her husband and the vicar talked about the value of English doctors coming through—Mr. Davies said this one was from London. She sent Margaret to fetch Evan and ushered the men in to see Sarah.

Fowler frowned. As he would articulate in his letter to *The Times*, his first impression of Sarah was distinctly unfavorable. What a show they made of her! Dressed like a bride! Very pretty, undoubtedly, plump in the face and her cheeks and lips a fresh rosy color.

"It is pleasant to see you again, Sarah," Thomas Davies said. "I was here in spring, and you are looking much better." He said to the doctor, "Remarkably better."

"You said she speaks English?" Fowler asked.

"How is your English?" the solicitor asked her.

"Very poor," Sarah said.

Hannah stood clasping her hands. When Sarah denied her English, she was poorly indeed. She had proudly greeted the men, but as they drew closer, fear glinted her eyes.

Mr. Davies said Dr. Fowler had requested him to stay and translate, and Hannah's knees weakened—two men. She wanted to wait for Evan, but like her daughter she was afraid.

"Now, now, Mother," Fowler said, "all will be well."

"You must be careful," Hannah said anxiously. "Else she will go into fits. Tell her what you are about to do?"

"Little miss," said the doctor, "this is my stethoscope. With it, I can hear your little heart, lungs, and tummy." As his words were conveyed back in Welsh, he attempted to disarrange the child's dress, and Sarah whimpered and pulled back, eliciting sympathetic clucks from her mother, "Now Sal, the kind man won't hurt you." If this man would make her well, make it all *stop*—but none of them had. Sarah cried at the touch of the doctor's fat hands, his frightening deep voice, which he failed to disguise with his simpering inflections.

"She'll faint! She'll faint!" Hannah warned.

"She isn't fainting, Mother," the doctor said, chastising her. "Nothing for tears, miss." He pressed Sarah's stomach and she swooned.

"There!" Hannah said. "She's gone now, you see! Being touched hurts her. Sal? Sal?" Sarah's eyes were closed, and her head thrown back on the pillows.

Pursing his lips, Fowler opened one of her eyelids and detected motion of the eyeball. Her coloring hadn't changed, and her pulse held steady. He pulled the covers back farther while Mother said, "Careful, be careful!" He saw no marks on her ankles and feet, despite the thin flock mattress she lay on. For someone so long in bed, her muscular development was normal, her fat layer not inconsiderable.

"I need to look at her back," Fowler said.

"No, no, you cannot!" the mother cried, and Sarah half sat, putting her right hand to her head in a studied manner.

"Pull up the covers," he told the mother with distaste. The only unusual findings were the girl's perspiration despite the cool room, her flexed feet, and the clear indication that her left side was weaker—and cooler—than the right, perhaps a vestige of the earlier paralysis written about by a local doctor. The stomach region was tense and drumlike, as he had expected. "Put out your tongue," he said to Sarah.

"She cannot open her mouth," Hannah said. She had opened her mouth very well to cry, Fowler thought. "Take my hand," he said to Sarah, whose eyes grew enormous. "I need to feel your strength," he said.

"She has no strength," Hannah told him.

"Why can I not see her back?" Fowler asked. Hannah explained that this could only be permitted when Sarah was moved for changing the bed. And yet the changing, Hannah babbled on in contradiction, caused fits and was therefore done as quickly as possible—so that she had not seen or washed the child's back for two years.

Evan and Margaret came in. "Tad!" Sarah screamed. "Tad!"

"Dress her," Evan said to Hannah. But Sarah recoiled from her mother's touch, crying, saying pitifully, "Tad. Tad."

"Leave us," Evan said, and the distinguished doctor, the solicitor, Hannah, Margaret, and Dilly went out of the room.

Hannah seated the gentlemen at the table and sent Margaret and Dilly away. "I am sorry, Your Honors. She is a sick girl, sick."

Sarah's crying stopped, and Evan emerged from the bedroom. Thomas Davies explained, and Evan put out his hand to Fowler; they shook.

"If need be," Evan said, "you may go in again to Sarah. We are glad you are here." Hannah looked at him.

"No, no," the doctor assured him. They sat at the table for the history. When it was finished, the doctor turned to the solicitor. "My good fellow," Dr. Fowler said to Thomas Davies, who conveyed the sense to Evan, "at this young age, Sarah's case is in all probability curable."

Evan said, "None but the Great Doctor could cure her."

"Come, come," said Fowler, "admitted to a London Hospital,

or into the Carmarthenshire Infirmary, the child would, doubtless, be quickly relieved. Leave her as she is, and her condition may become chronic, and develop into some physical or more severe form of mental disease."

Here Evan inquired, "Mental, you say?"

"My good fellow—" the doctor began, but Evan's expression stopped him.

Evan said through his teeth, "How can you London doctors make my child eat, without making a hole in her?"

Fowler absorbed the words and stood. Quoting Evan exactly in his letter, the doctor would dub him "the silly father."

Fowler scanned the kitchen. "Have you a privy?" he asked.

"Nay," Evan said, on his feet now.

"You've a chamber pot where Sarah sleeps?"

"Where we sleep, as well," Evan said, "and she does not use it."

Fowler deduced that it could be so. The girl's physical condition rendered her fully capable of relieving herself outside. As for food, Fowler identified hiding places in the "old Welsh cupboard bed," and he would write that no sensible doctor, unless guaranteed perfect control, would undertake treatment in the girl's home.

"We shall be going, Mother," Fowler said to Hannah, and with a glance of undisguised pity at Evan, he ducked into the yard, followed closely by Thomas Davies.

The dark hues that weather had wrought in Evan's face collected into livid necrotic regions. "Evan—" A shift of his shoulder and Hannah bit off her words, watching him, riveted by the lit doorway, the tunnel to wherever the fine men had gone. The doctor had said Sarah could be cured! But when Hannah brought it up later, her husband scoffed, saying that hospitals were dreadful places for the insane and the desperate.

But were they not desperate? Nay, Sarah could die in a hospital, apart from those she loved. Better to trust in the Lord.

Margaret slinked into the doorway. "Tad, people are coming."

"No more today," Evan said. "Send them away and go to your sister." He turned to Hannah. "See they are settled, and then we will need you for the corn." He left.

Hannah scooped broth from the simmering cawl into a bowl, crumbled in oatcake, and ate her porridge greedily; she had missed breakfast.

After Margaret went to Sarah, Hannah shooed Dilly out of the house, rinsed her bowl, tamped down the fire, and checked on the girls.

They were asleep—the scruffy blond head, the sleek black, in each other's arms. Hannah moved closer, but not close enough to disturb them. She left the emerald shawl and Sarah's headdress on the floor, still alert to the air ushered in by the doctor, and it stifled her energy, impetus, and hope. She realized that, in his innermost self, Evan left her long ago. The house had felt scoured of the husband she knew since baby David came home.

Thinking it sinful, she stopped herself from praying for Evan to return. For we must bear what He sends, Hannah thought, and she went out to the fields.

By September, Christine sat nights in the public room at the inn—or outside with the innkeepers, as she wrote to Gwen. After dinner, she and Mrs. Owen settled down to knit. Later in the evening, Mrs. Morgan dragged in and collapsed, put up her feet, and hum-sighed at the click of her knitting needles brought from her bag. The dinner smells from the dining room lingered; the clopping of horses on the cobbles outside now and then subsumed the quiet hiss of wool. Sometimes only a few words were said; other times, many.

Christine had planned to lease a house, in the event of an extended stay. But one evening when she felt lonely enough to break out of her skin, she recalled that guests were welcome in the public room at night, although no one took up the offer—the Welsh widows just knit. And the American widow joined them. At first, she brought paperwork, but the night she brought knitting was the momentous occasion on which they seemed to accept her.

The weary Mrs. Morgan did the cooking and physical labor, while Mrs. Owen dealt with guests and kept the books. Like a schoolmistress, Mrs. Owen corrected Christine's mistakes in Welsh; Mrs. Morgan giggled at them. Mrs. Owen's was the long-nosed Welsh face; Mrs. Morgan's the broader type, with widely spaced eyes. The height of both women turned out not to indicate northerly origins; they had lived all their lives in South Wales, right here in Carmarthen.

"I always did say," Mrs. Owen announced after reading Dr. Fowler's lengthy letter, "that the vicar's campaign would come to no good."

"Inviting the public into a sickroom!" Mrs. Morgan agreed.

Locals would call on the sick, leave money if needed, and even the romantic idea of a miraculous Sarah that had earlier appealed to Mrs. Owen, as a reminder of bygone days, was acceptable if it didn't go too far—did not invite inquiries the Welsh didn't need. But Evan Jacob, the widows said, influenced by Evan Jones, refused to leave well enough alone. By extending the situation—by allowing any ragtag or Tory in to see Sarah—they had provided an opportunity for the English press and establishment to, yet again, mock and deride the nation.

"The Welsh have sound reason to keep to themselves," Mrs. Owen said.

"Hard enough these days," Mrs. Morgan said, "without requesting trouble."

Although the Welsh widows didn't agree, Christine felt Dr. Fowler had offered convincing medical propositions in his published letter. Where he had erred was to draw a line between the peasantry and the gentry. He appealed to the gentry to "save" a child from her own parents. Then *The Lancet*, which all along showed a distinctly anti-Welsh bias, in response to Fowler's incitement, outright attributed the claims made for Sarah to "the credulity of Welsh persons." The journal articulated what, until then, it had implied.

The enlightened English versus the ignorant Welsh: That was what it came down to. Now no one would hear anything else. Even blasé Reginald Pary and other Welsh journalists who had tired of the case were newly energized. Soon, any blame the Welsh widows cast on Evan Jones and Evan Jacob receded beneath their anger at the English, and Christine thought the modest widows themselves could have been radicals, full of fervor and flash.

They were thrilled when into the tinderbox, riding the still-fresh outrage over the evictions, shot the spark of a shining Welsh star: *Gohebydd*, "the correspondent," in Welsh. A writer for the nationalistic Welsh press and a leading Nonconformist, Gohebydd's hope for Wales in the modern age had infected thousands—and when he called on Evan Jacob in September, Sarah's case had stepped solidly into the broad public sphere.

"Today in the papers," Mrs. Owen said one night, "I read that Goheybdd has enlisted Gwilym Marles in the cause."

"Why, I heard him speak!" cried Mrs. Morgan. "He orates in the magnificent Welsh style," she told Christine, "and no better man lives."

"Goheybdd and Marles will set it right," Mrs. Owen said.

Set *what* right? Christine thought. The medical watch Gohebydd stridently called for in the press would bring exposure, not vindication.

She got up her courage to ask the question.

"You misunderstand," Mrs. Owen said. The tall woman stood and added a log to the fire. She paused, seemed to listen to voices outside—or to inaudible voices of another time—then sat again and explained. "The call for a watch must come from the Welsh. Any outcome—the truth, you see, must be shown to be what we seek. We cannot be cast as savages any longer."

Of course, and Christine colored for her foolishness. But where was Sarah in all this? What was actually going on in the private cauldron of the family? "Then politics is the point," she said boldly.

"For Gohebydd, yes," said Mrs. Owen.

"And Marles," Mrs. Morgan added.

"And as important as the medical aspect may be," Mrs. Owen said, "it isn't the issue for average folk."

Putting aside miraculous intervention, what was left besides the political was the medical strand, Christine inferred, one too intangible and esoteric to consider. How like invisible God were the mysteries of human bodies! And minds. But if Evan Jacob flatly resisted help for Sarah from the medical priests—which everyone knew he had done, from Fowler's letter—would he give over his child to a watch on their terms? He and Jones had gotten themselves into a quandary indeed. Fowler emphatically labeled Sarah hysteric, and suspected that as a part of her illness and an explanation for holy claims, Sarah deceived her own parents.

He had written, "The cunning stratagems and deceptions practised by young girls afflicted with hysteria are well known to medical men, though not so generally credited by nonprofessionals. I can, therefore, quite understand these poor simple parents being easily deceived by their own child, the more especially as in their ignorance they seem to implicitly believe that there is a miracle. . . ."

Evan Jacob, it was said, felt persecuted. Since June, the toadying *Western Mail* insulted him daily—now Fowler's attack and *The Lancet*. At this point, couldn't someone as shrewd and grand as Gohebydd persuade him of anything?

The widows dismissed Fowler's diagnosis.

"Hysteria, yes, I know all about it," said Mrs. Owen. "A malady of fine English women with nothing better to do. Sarah's a farm girl."

"She is a very intelligent girl," Mrs. Morgan said. "One for the books."

"And since when, Mrs. Morgan," said Mrs. Owen, "are books a crime? It would benefit you to read a book now and then! You are Welsh, after all."

"Well! Some of us cooking and cleaning from morning until night may not have the leisure for books."

"My argument exactly. Hysteria is a disease of ladies with leisure."

"And mine is that books give little girls notions."

Mrs. Owen smirked. "Soon you'll be saying it is best that girls are kept illiterate!"

"Never!"

"Notions, Mrs. Morgan, come from everywhere. Books didn't invent them. Do you follow along, Mrs. Thomas?" she asked Christine.

"Carry on!" Christine said, inwardly panting with her efforts to comprehend.

The paragraph in Fowler's letter she had thought most about was this: "Being made an object of curiosity, sympathy, and profit is not only totally antagonistic to this girl's recovery but also renders it extremely difficult for a medical man to determine how much of the symptoms is the result of a morbid perversion of will, and how much is the product of intentional deceit."

It made scant sense to locate the ruse in the cunning of a twelve-year-old. "Why should she deceive her parents?" Mrs. Morgan asked, a valid question. And if Sarah deceived, how had she gone undetected for so long? Could be the parents had reasons not to detect. Possibly Hannah was blameless, but Evan? Instinctively, Christine couldn't believe it. Making Sarah an object of curiosity, as Fowler said, wasn't "simple."

But what *was* "intentional" on Sarah's part, and a "morbid perversion of will"? What scenarios spooled in Sarah's mind, what misapprehensions? Even so-called hysterical women had reasons, let alone a child who had experienced what Sarah had in the last twenty-three months. Perhaps private dramas elude us always, Christine thought, but what is the truth without them?

WALKING TO THE TRAIN ONE COLD October day, Christine considered winter in Wales, blackest nights James described, driving wind and rain, squalls casting snowdrifts higher than rooftops, mountaintops shrouded for months, all of life clamped under the substance of vast, unknowable heavens. It occurred to her that neither her husband nor any of the Welsh she had met ever spoke of their mountains as hills. They were not very high compared to the mountains of the western United States or southern Europe.

Hyperbole and dread: Were they not part of the national character, of the weather of minds? She had never grown used to the castle outside her window. She kept the shutters closed always, and quickly passed by its ramparts, where Irish vagrants, the poorest of the poor, worse off than the Welsh tenant farmers, congregated by fires, around which they huddled and drank, sang and cursed. Prostitutes walked there at night. She had glimpsed them in the flickering, coming home late. The northern section of the castle farthest from the inn housed the jail. How apt, locking them up in the very stones of historical empire. Prison reform was in the papers these days. In England, they had begun to house prisoners in single cells, which, apparently, for people unaccustomed to sleeping alone, was a cruelty worse than fearsome strangers, worse than the exposure of the multiply housed: They were going mad in their modern isolation. Prisoners howled for release. They scratched themselves to death with shards, managed to fashion their shirts into nooses; suicides threatened to alleviate a good portion of the prison population. More guards were required, and they were keeping the lesser offenders out of their cells and at work for more hours. But the lucky Welsh, behind the times, were still incarcerated in groups of eight and ten. She pictured them in there, squirrels curled in a nest, rats in a hole.

She had seen Sarah twice in September, supervised by her father. Everyone looked shifty-eyed, worried, and Sarah looked tired. She was thinner. Despite Fowler's reference to her "not inconsiderable fat layer," she was a very slender girl, and Fowler himself conceded that, even if she had the "propensity to deceive very strongly developed," she probably also had "the power or habit of prolonged fasting." One could surmise prolonged fasting hurt. How hard it had been, Christine recalled, for Gwen to stay up those nights waiting for her father. When, after weeks, Gwen quit her mission and slept again through the nights, Christine had asked, "What was it like, Gwen?" Gwen answered that staying awake had been exceedingly hard, achieved by brute willpower only.

She missed Gwen. She missed Douglas and Rupert and her house, her long-used mahogany desk, where she wrote in her notebooks mornings, looking forward to puttering about afternoons in her kitchen. She missed America—Brooklyn, where there was always someone to talk to.

On the train, she felt weak and feverish, then icy cold, and finding the guides gone, she braced for the walk because she couldn't face a return to her room this early in the day.

On the lane, leaves crackled and swirled, and on the moor, wind whistled in emptiness. Smoke spiraled over the homestead.

No one was about, no pilgrims. Inside, the elder girls knit by the fire, the boys played a hitting and running game in the kitchen, the baby wobbling about, trying to keep up with his brothers, as Hannah watched, smiling. A young man whittled wood near the older girls, and Christine learned he was Emyr, the hired boy.

She had greeted Hannah in Welsh, and for the first time she spoke to her in the language, saying, "Everyone seems well today!"

Hannah grinned widely and laughed, showing a missing bicuspid, but her lightness, her unusual carelessness made her look younger anyway.

"Yes, we are well!" Hannah said. "You speak Welsh!"

"But a little," Christine replied slowly. "Is Sarah receiving visitors?"

"Mr. Jacob isn't here," Hannah responded uncertainly. "But never mind! Sarah!" Hannah vanished, returned; shrieks and hard clumping and clattering followed her out of the room. "Silly girls," Hannah said happily. "She'll see you."

"It is all right?" Christine asked.

"Yes," Hannah said, the one word breathy, full of relief.

It seemed to mean more: It is all right now. Everything will be all right.

The clatter was Margaret jumping up and down in heavy clogs, her scraggy white hair leaping like flames and her face patchy red from exertion. "Jump!" she shouted. "Jump for the Lord!"

Reposed beneath quilts, capped in red wool, Sarah appeared delighted by Margaret's antics, though seeing Christine, she waved her good hand at her sister to quiet her.

"No chapel!" shouted Margaret, paused from motion. "Brought the chapel in here!"

"Yes!" Christine said, pleased at getting the meaning of the little girl's Welsh.

"Jump for the Lord!" Margaret cried, starting again.

"No!" Sarah abjured, and Hannah bustled in, saying, "When we have a visitor! Margaret, be still." But Hannah was obviously feeling too sanguine to deliver a firm rebuke. She chuckled when Margaret, too elated to quiet immediately, jumped a figure eight around Sarah's bed before stumping out, her mother behind.

"Where have you been, Mrs. Thomas?" asked Sarah. "Why haven't you come to see me?"

"It hasn't been two weeks!" Christine reminded her, settling in with Sarah's English—in the *mood* for English. Needing rest and relief—her face felt flushed as Margaret's, her heart would not stop its drum.

The house quieted. But to Christine, the paper's speech as Sarah rustled a batch couldn't cover her thundering heart. It calmed, so maybe it was her imagination. Bodies! Traitorous bodies. Hysteria was a specious diagnosis. Where were the people on earth, outfitted in flesh, who rested secure in such fickle houses? Where was the division between body and mind? How could these confident doctors accuse a girl of deception and imposture while saying, too, that she suffered from a disease? It is under her control, they implied, and out of her control.

Sarah studied one of her papers. "I thought to translate haiku," she said. "The poem about the frog. I hoped to discuss it with you first."

Christine pulled up the one chair. "'Old pond,'" she recited. "'A frog leaps in / water's sound.'"

"You say it beautifully," Sarah remarked. "I learn from your English."

"American English."

"A dialect I quite like. These days more than ever, yes?" she joked. "To me, the poem turns on two meanings. In one, water is sound. Water and its sound are one. When the frog leaps into the water then, he also leaps into sound.

"And the other?"

"The sound causes him to leap into the water. It excites him."

"But a pond is a still body of water."

"Not *afon*? A pond isn't a river?"

"A pond is a small lake. It doesn't move as rivers usually do."

"Then it has no sound, until the frog jumps?"

Nodding, Christine said, "And what about the observer?"

Sarah thought hard and then said, "The ears of the observer and the jump of the frog sound the old pond."

Impressed, Christine said, "I like how you phrase it."

Sarah wrote on her paper. "Now in Welsh I can find the proper equivalents." She looked up, searched Christine's eyes. "I have a stanza from Welsh I put into English for you." Holding her gaze on Christine, she said, "'On hill, in valley, in islands of the sea / Every way one goes / From Holy Christ there is no escape.'"

"It is—austere."

Sarah still stared directly at Christine's eyes. She touched and then gripped Christine's arm. "I am afraid," she whispered.

"Why, dear? Sarah, tell me. What is it?"

But she shook her head, released her grip, and said, "Not good enough."

"You are not good enough?"

Sarah's eyes closed; she folded into herself, submerged in her own pool of self, subjectivity, secrets. It looked less like a fit than that she had recoiled. In the cold room, moisture beaded her brow, and her sweat wafted to Christine in waves—vegetal, strawlike, acidic. *How could this be borne, to see it and to have nothing to do?*

Sarah's eyes opened and fixed on the ceiling. "I am tired," she said.

"I'll go." Christine waited.

Sarah turned her head and reached to take Christine's hand. "I did a very bad thing," Sarah said, "but I didn't mean to."

"I'm sure you didn't. Have you told—did you talk it over with the vicar?"

"No." Sarah's face spoke regret, saying she would never talk about whatever it was with the vicar and that Christine had entirely missed her meaning.

"Would you like to talk it over with me?" Christine asked.

"No," Sarah said uncertainly. "Do you believe me?"

"I think you are saying you unintentionally committed a sin, and, yes, I believe you." She waited. "Maybe we'll talk about it more when I next visit?"

"I don't know."

"We can if you like."

"Kiss me?" Christine kissed Sarah's cheek, and the girl kissed Christine's hand.

"We're friends, Sarah, aren't we?" Sarah nodded. "Shall I stay?"

Sarah shook her head, acting tired again.

"Well then, I will be back before long."

"Thank you." Sarah's eyes closed. Sputter of candles; the cold, cold room; it was no more than two hours after noon and how late it felt: *to lie day in and day out in this room.* Christine looked down at Sarah once more and went out to the kitchen.

"Sarah is sleeping," she told Hannah.

Hannah indicated she sit at the table. She brought her strong, sweet tea. They drank together. "Your children?" Hannah asked.

"They are grown."

"Your husband?"

"Is dead," Christine told her.

"Oh, madam, madam!" Hannah's face wrinkled with sympathy.

"Thank you," Christine said.

"Thank *you*," Hannah said. "You are kind to my Sarah." All but the elder girls at the fire had gone away. Dour Mary was large and comely; Esther darted her head, and her eyes snapped when Christine observed her. Mrs. Owen said Esther "wasn't right" and had always been like that. Mary supervised Esther; they were as much a pair as Sarah and Margaret.

The women finished their tea and Christine took her leave. The moor stretched before her, the olive green grass, the rocks jutting like interruptive corrections, the bristly reddish brush and short trees—sloping land cupped by the hills. The sky showed blue, the sheep were mute, the wind calmed, but the air refused to relinquish its bite. Christine thought of the Welsh words James had first taught her. *Hwyl* described a stirring emotional energy. Margaret jumped today from *hwyl*.

Literally, it translated as "sail" and also referred to that Welsh method of chanting in poetry and rhetoric when a person filled with inspiration as wind swelled and drove a ship's sails. The other word was *hiareth*, so different, or the other side of the same coin. It described longing, nostalgia, wistfulness, or that very Welsh internal reach for a Wales long ago.

James was eight when he emigrated to America with his father. The century's hard early years had dealt harsh blows to James's family. One by one, his four sisters languished and died, and his mother was taken in her attempt to give life to a fifth. In old age, James's father told Christine about the corpse candle he saw rolling cobalt blue, big as a wagon wheel, at a ferocious speed down the road to their house. He had been coming from work in the quarry, unaware of any threat to his wife's health. But theirs was the only house on the road, and the blazing force told him his wife and the child would die. When a week later James's mother and the baby lay dead in the parlor, James's father instructed him to smash a front window, so the souls could escape. The bodies were buried in the churchyard that afternoon, and the following morning the father and son set out for New York. All his life, James cherished the smashed window's comfort, the freedom it symbolized—the certainty from the smashed glass that the souls were no longer contained in the bodies and his mother wouldn't be left in the ground. "I believed she flew with us," he said, "and brought us fortune on the water and in the new land."

At the station, Christine met Alun Lloyd, the lean, dyspeptic reporter who shared the office with Reginald Pary. Lloyd's dress was a rumpled version of a London toff, wool coat missing all but a button, still-shiny top hat scored at the brim.

"Well, well, Mrs. Thomas. We've just missed the train." It would be over an hour before another. "Care to trundle down to the public house for a rejuvenating beverage?"

A fire would be welcome; Lloyd might have news or a rumor. He hadn't been especially friendly before, but then, he was often sick. "Sick?" Reginald Pary had recently confided. "Sick from the drink or drunk because sick?" The herbal mixture Lloyd often sipped from to treat his roiling gut was spiked with a hearty dose of gin.

The Eagle Inn, just across the road from the vicar's St. Michael's, wasn't far. They walked, discussing the case.

"And have you been out to see Sarah this afternoon, Mrs. Thomas?"

"I have. She isn't well."

"Well? The lot's off their heads! But she'll get hers soon enough."

"That isn't a generous view, Mr. Lloyd."

"Oh, we need to get on with it. Bring in the doctors from England and expose her. With the money they've taken, she might even be charged."

"Do you think so?"

"Why not? She is legally old enough to be charged with a crime." Yes, it was so, although Christine hadn't considered legal danger for Sarah.

"You are no longer of the opinion that the parents put her up to it?" she asked.

"As I said, the whole lot's off their heads! Pack the lot up in Carmarthen Prison and teach them their lesson."

They proceeded silently on.

"Oh, Mrs. Thomas, I know, I know. Tenants. Not much education. Fault of the vicar, if you know the whole story—I grasp how you feel; I saw the girl once myself, though I didn't go back. She had an excessive tenderness, as girls that age often do, and a sort of power. But Wales can't afford her, no ma'am. We've had enough of her shenanigans."

"A watch might unhinge her," she said. "A real one."

"She could go mad?"

Christine didn't respond immediately. Sarah's kiss—and her fear—had very much moved her. "I don't know. I've gotten too emotionally involved; that, I know. I have children myself and—"

"I have children, too."

She looked up at the narrow yellowish face he turned to her.

"Don't judge," he said.

"I don't. If you have seen my reports, they are overridingly sympathetic to the Welsh. I've bent over backward to—"

"Don't get upset! We're a prickly lot, aren't we?" And he laughed. "Oh, why might that be? I have read your reports. I perused each one with care."

He certainly hadn't, she thought; he may have skimmed a few pages in the telegraph office.

"I did my best, as an outsider," she said, refusing to be rattled. It was just too outrageous of him to take affront. Was he drunk already? Had nips throughout the afternoon from his gin and herbs?

"I have often wondered," he said, "if after the emancipation of the American slaves, your country will look to its Indians?"

She would not take his bait. "We are an evil lot, Mr. Lloyd—the human race. I am glad Mr. Darwin removed God from the equation, since He isn't to blame. Let's bring in the scientists, I say. See if the scientists can do a better job than the rest of us have."

"Ha! Rich, Mrs. Thomas. You've a wit on you."

"And what brought you to Pencader today, Mr. Lloyd?" In answer, he removed a small object from his coat pocket and handed it to her. She recognized the inch-high silver rectangle as a double portraiture case; one side bore his photographic portrait and the other a lock under glass of his dull brown hair.

"What d'you say?" he asked, leaning down for a peek, pleased by his image, the thin homely face—the eyes forever shocked in the frame. "Handsome chap, that," he said. "Picked it up for the wife; it's her birthday today."

She handed it back. They had stopped as they rounded the bend to the Eagle Inn, a solid lime-washed structure cater-corner to the quaint stone St. Michael's and its yard of graves. Christine had sought out the grave of the vicar's wife one day, read the inscription after her name and dates: *Beloved wife, eternal companion.* Should it not have been "beloved wife and mother"? Lloyd's miniature had given her a start. She no longer carried the one of James. She had opened it once and gasped at his frozen eyes, his stiff expression, and put away the portrait she had insisted upon before he went off. "You would think I was going to soldier," he had complained when they both sat for the photographer. She wondered if her face moldered in his grave—stayed with him in the place she had decided he was found, in Virginia. She had once been to Virginia with her father as a girl and was soothed by its mountains, gentle and blue. She imagined compassionate strangers saying prayers for her James and laying his Welsh body to rest.

Inside, Lloyd asked for beer. It was brought to their end of a long table—she could see the graves through the window to her side. The inn cheered her, the mutters in Welsh, the stove and the soft planks beneath her feet. She tasted the pewter mug's iron against the dark, foamy brew. She and James liked beer, got drunk in the North once and fell out of bed making raucous drunk love. They simply continued on the slate floor, and from the chill to their flesh the next morning they suffered pains, like the old, and stayed the day in bed, kissing and stroking and tending to each other: "Oh, poor girl, it's a sad arm I see there, a poor hurting thigh, and I must tend it immediately!"

"Do you know much about the vicar?" she asked Alun Lloyd.

"Goodness no," he said. "Why would I?"

"He has a child, doesn't he?" That, Lloyd allowed.

She recognized dairymen from the train station, and even strangers had about them a familiarity now. Would Brooklyn in future feel strange? The beer's heat rose into her face, lingered there, as if she had no pores to breathe it out. She set down the mug. She otherwise felt fine—heart calm in her chest, throat as it should be, the thrumming sensations she'd suffered lately inconsequential, the anxiety tamped down.

A motion outside drew her eye. "It's him," she said.

"Jones?" Lloyd squinted at the window. "Out to care for the wife's grave."

"What?"

"Does it every day by himself."

"Oh. Good of him, I suppose."

"More like obsessed. He sent the child away after the wake and didn't come out of the house for six weeks. People left food outside in baskets. Those he took. Otherwise, he bolted the door and the shutters."

"And you told me you didn't know much about him," Christine said. "Excuse me. I need to talk to him. I'll meet you outside."

The cold air stung her flaming cheeks. She took her mittens from her bag and, drawing them on, crossed the road. Past the gate he worked among the graves—Lewis, Thomas, Hughes, Griffith, Morris, Owen, Davies, Jones, people within many families represented by those perennial Welsh names.

He'd thrown on an overcoat, leaving it open. No hat, his hair reddish black against the chalky sky. His wife's grave stood at the far end of the yard, marked by an obelisk and flanked by a wooden toolshed, its door ajar.

She opened the gate and called, "Reverend Jones."

He turned as she approached—black slash eyebrows ironic above the clerical collar.

"Still here, Mrs. Thomas? I thought you'd departed." She suspected he very well knew she'd remained.

"I couldn't leave now," she said.

"Your paper acknowledges the import of our cause?" He picked with a rake at wet leaves clotting the elaborate carved vines that wound around the stone's base.

"Your wife," she said.

He didn't ask how she knew. "She gets the worst of it on the slope. Mucky stuff blows and the rain sticks it on like paste."

He remained thin—but strengthened, rejuvenated; it was in his carriage, in his blithe responses. Not blithe, just easily confident. He squatted and picked with his bare hands in the crevices.

"Have you any news?" she asked.

"Why, yes. Evan Jacob has agreed to a watch."

"On Gohebydd's terms?"

"They're of a mind," said the vicar.

"Which is—"

"We await details." He rose and brushed at the words *eternal companion*.

She shivered, pulled her cape closer against stirring wind. Her face seethed. "Tell Evan Jacob to renege."

He tilted his head, as if he hadn't quite heard. "Why ever would I do that?"

"For Sarah."

"You exaggerate my influence."

"I think not." He faced her, black slashes joined above the bright eyes. The few sips had gone to her head—maybe the reason for his enlargement, looking taller, of fuller stature.

"Do you truly believe Sarah eats nothing?" she asked.

"We have discussed it," and he turned to rake the monument's ground. "Go back to your inn, Mrs. Thomas. You're not looking well."

How dare he? Deflect his disease, have the gall to cast her as weak while he bloodied the name of Almighty God.

I see you, she thought. I can see into your mind and your past, the instant you grasped at an airy nothing and fashioned it to your desire. I know the hallucinations of grief, black ash covering all you believed, held dear. Your very mind, heart, life, cut loose, extinguished, no more than a guttering candle—vanished with your love until you walk with the dead, the living unreal. Rake at the ground as if she were there. Howl in the night. No one can hear you.

You sat by the bed of fresh life, minister. You heard an echo of what you lost and mistook it for rebirth, for proof of what you could no longer grasp. You took it, took her as testament.

"I thought you were fond of her," she said.

"Sarah?" He put the rake in the shed, closed and locked it, brushed off his hands on his coat. "Good day."

She watched him walk through the yard, open the gate, and cross to the front of his church.

Alun Lloyd stood in the road, waving for her. She waved back and started out. Little boats, she thought, moored in the dark.

GOHEBYDD

*Update on the Progress of a Scientific Watch
on the Welsh Fasting Girl*

Special Dispatch to The Sun, *24 November 1869*

By Christine Thomas

*In Wales, clouds wreathe the tops of the mountains
and winter grips more deeply into the valleys. Harvest-
ing in South Wales was a difficult process, with the
wind and rain that flattened the corn crop. It has been
confirmed that Evan Jacob, the father of Sarah Jacob,
"should be glad to have nurses to clear their character, that they had always been a quiet and honest family and never charged with falsehood." Now Mr. John
Griffiths, better known as Gohebydd, the correspondent
and famous Welsh champion, has brought Mr. Jacob's
wish to the brink of realization. Since September, in
response to the letter by Dr. Robert Fowler summarized
in this paper, Gohebydd widely appealed for a second
watching, without taint of local bias. "Not only must
justice be done, it must be seen to be done," Gohebydd
wrote. In his quest for "fully professional watchers,"
Gohebydd contacted his eminent countryman, Dr. J. J.
Williams, assistant physician accoucheur of Guy's Hospital, London, to request the case be scrupulously tested,*

105

*using the expertise and care of trained nurses. Enthusi-
asm spread from the parents to the community at large
when, as announced on 6 November, Dr. Williams
obtained permission from the Superintendent and
Treasurer of Guy's Hospital to proceed. On 23 November, Gohebydd called on the Jacobs to discuss details. A
public meeting has been announced for 30 November
and a commencement of the watch shortly later. Sarah
Jacob looks well. She is calm and in good spirits. Bad
weather and continued dissent has not diminished the
arrival of pilgrims from as far away as France.*

❧

AN EXTRAORDINARY CHANGE HAD COME ABOUT in Christine's
relations with the vicar and, in turn, with Evan Jacob. To gain
closer access to Sarah, Christine sent copies of her dispatches
to Jones. She enclosed a note, stressing that her Welsh husband
rendered her more than a neutral party; Jones could consider
her a friend. Reporting objective events was well and good, as
far as it went—and every day it went further from the heart
of the matter. Sarah's welfare counted for less than it ever had,
and reporter or no, it counted for her.

Jones liked what she had written and, as Christine had predicted, he shared with Jacob her "friendliness" to their cause.

At the homestead, Christine became a special visitor, ushered in to Sarah immediately. Hannah brought her tea, and
the girls happily accepted the picture books Christine selected
for them—jungle animals for Sarah, with many exotic monkeys, and *The World of Dogs* for Margaret. She brought Hannah and the other children gifts of food, and tobacco for Evan
Jacob—that oddly doting father, that carnival hawker, and
why? Why to the lengths a watching would go?

She was feeling her way into the autumn, into this place,

this language—these people. She had been certain of her role as a reporter in the beginning; now she wasn't anymore. She wanted no one hurt, she wanted it over, and she wanted to go home. She wanted to stay forever and never go home. In the black afternoons, the shrinking days, she felt the strength of Wales. It was not what she had expected to feel. She had thought to feel new strength in herself, rising confidence, a renewal of self. Instead, coming back to Carmarthen from the train in the brittle dusky afternoons, to sheep voice, the teeming water beneath the bridge, the darting fires of the itinerants banked by the castle, she felt Wales's power across its hardships, endurance, long struggle, long hope, and it buoyed her and brought her ballast she felt in her body, in her legs and feet, the strength of ghosts who walked before, not God, but men and women who breathed the air. Primal. Real. Evan Jacob said foxes had taken many of the sheep this year, and crossing the bridge she would think of this, hearing the fox calls she had learned to identify: barks of alarm, a stuttering throaty chatter she thought of as play, howls, whistles, yodels, and the vixen's scream scratching over her skin like nails, human, daunting, leaving her lonelier in the silence that followed, in the space the scream tore. A city person, she had never considered foxes. She felt herself expanding, growing sharper ears, knowing, understanding what was out there in the dark.

In deepest night, she woke in sweats. She couldn't write to her husband. She'd lie awake, unable to see him, feel him. Her fingers had held for seven years tactile memories of his body—his lips, the soft thickness of skin at the back of his neck—and they were fading.

Again, she accused him, as she had when he left. No cause to go. There were stories here, in Brooklyn, and throughout the North. He wasn't as young as he had been. Leave it to the young. There was Gwen to consider, their one girl. She hung on her father, needed him. The effects of the war were already too hard, what it did to the heart, the mind, even for those nowhere near the battles—why go?

"To see," he said.

"See? What is this 'see'?"

"You wanted it once."

"It was before I had children. You have children, too."

He argued that he would be far from the fighting, protected. "But not from disease," she said, "sniper's bullets, your own fearlessness."

He seldom showed fear, only after the babies died—after the three-day-old boy and the girl who had lingered a week, he refused to touch her. He said he feared making death, and when at last he succumbed to his own desire and her exhortations for love, new life, his body to quiet her grief, he had wept, saying he thought it was wrong. They had Douglas and Rupert and Gwen, but it had taken much longer than she would have chosen for them to arrive. It had been as if his seed held fear, resisted her still.

Age would have taken them from each other soon enough. Such love they had. And him flung like a dirty sack into the black universe, Rupert off by himself or with a stranger woman far, far away, Douglas ceaselessly laboring over the sick—and Gwen writing to her about nothing but life in novels, so that her mother would not know how lost, how sad she remained. And herself, alone in Wales, stubbornly trying to *see*.

She would drift off and awake again, damp, confused. "It is modern life," Vinnie Smyth said, "casting us hither and yon. We don't know ourselves anymore."

It was war, pride, and empire. Christine had not understood when James cried to make Douglas and Rupert and Gwen that his grief, too, was for himself as a boy—a Welsh boy watching death, smashing a window against all the death before crossing the ocean to meet her.

On 30 November, the day of the public meeting, Christine traveled to the Eagle Inn with Alun Lloyd and Reginald Pary. The men discussed the money the Jacobs had made since Sarah took to bed.

"*The Lancet* put it at fifty pounds back in May," said Lloyd.

"You can't trust *The Lancet*," Pary insisted. "But the money's important insofar as it bolsters suspicions of the parents' collusion."

"Righto, they're bilking the public!" Lloyd said. "What do they do with it? Hide it? Stack it up and take it to market? Oh, yes, they have people put coins on the little girl's chest, so the parents don't touch it. It's Sarah's, they claim. Fat lie. Look here, in spring I reckoned she collected five shillings a day. This fall, there've been reports of people leaving two shillings or half a crown. If pilgrims go in six or seven at a time and even a few leave two shillings, and the rest one, it adds up to significant money."

"If we count six days of visitors a week," Pary calculated. "With a group or two a day, at minimum."

"Two Englishwomen in the spring left a sovereign," said Lloyd.

"I'd lie in bed for those ladies myself," said Pary.

"They could be saving the money for Sarah when she is grown," Christine offered, knowing how feeble that sounded.

"They'd better be," said Lloyd. "Because at her exposure, they'll have to pay it back."

"Will they?" Pary asked.

"So I'd think," Lloyd replied.

"What does the law say?" Christine asked.

Pary made a note to check. "And how is the girl? Now that she's your niece." Both men admired how Christine had ingratiated herself with the family, though she assured them that sending her dispatches was to demonstrate her lack of hostility; she hadn't implied that she favored a watch. The Jacobs read into her reports what they wanted to see. Evan Jacob was probably flattered by ink flowing in distant America, as by the attentions of Gohebydd and Marles. She didn't put it beneath Evan Jones, either.

"Lloyd," Pary said, "don't you think women will be the reporters of the future? She gets closer than we do."

"Depends where," Christine said. "I doubt I'd get very close on a battlefield. But in answer to your question, Sarah is calm. They're all calm."

"Makes no sense," said Lloyd.

"Except if they have nothing to fear," Pary said. "Only how could that be?"

The three turned to the window, where snow flew. Early snow, harbinger of inevitable winter, halted speech, left in its wake silent awe—in concert with the awe the three felt, as the train chugged along, that the case remained alive and had gathered momentum. It would be over soon, though. This was the general consensus.

Sarah had said nothing else about fear and refused to acknowledge that her secret had ever come up between Christine and herself. Nothing personal whatsoever had passed from Sarah since that day. Christine imagined Sarah thought better of confiding in her, given recent developments. Christine was sure "the bad thing," Sarah's sin, referred to not being what everyone wanted—a real saint. And as she neared exposure, her calmness suggested more mental imbalance than Christine had assumed—or misguided faith. Did she suppose God would see her through? Or did she fear something more than exposure? Did she, like many in the community, see an end in sight, and in place of humiliation, relief?

Already the public house was thronged when they arrived. Men stood in the passageway and filled the main room, where tables were pushed against walls to accommodate rows of benches—and farmers, tradesmen Christine recognized, and several women took any space to be had. Sprightly Reginald Pary shouldered a path inside as the vicar waved them ahead to the area by the stairs to the loft where he stood with the Jacobs. Hannah wore her tall beaver hat, a woolly shawl, thick gloves on her swollen hands; Evan Jacob was hatless, his straight dark hair, his ruff of a beard setting off his determined, frowning face. Nods passed, murmured greetings in Welsh mixed with the stir of the room—of stamped feet, low conversations, scraping benches as space was made. Jones directed them to the stair steps, where other reporters, from the rival local paper *The Welshman* and further afield, perched, crows on a fence, voracious eyes shining.

Gohebydd and Marles entered to cheers, followed by scattered applause. Christine had never seen either of them, but the greeting could have been for no one else.

"Gohebydd," Pary said to her, indicating the rugged man shaking hands, removing his cap to reveal a pointed pate— a bald top pushing through whorls of ginger hair, as if his brain forcefully sought to escape the confines of a skull and its typical hairy covering.

Gwilym Marles was small and neat, more ordinarily bald; thinning spirals of dark hair clung wistfully to his head, and his drooping eyes matched his drooping mustache. Long battles marked him. Marles had campaigned on behalf of the Liberal Party in the parliamentary elections, led the farmers in the tithe wars against the compulsory tax, and would one day be evicted from his chapel for similar activities. The hot stove and the bodies blunted the chill. The clutching damp loosened its grasp and the swirling snow at the windows subsided as the meeting was called to order—as if, she thought, the people had at last gained purchase on the intractable land. The scent of wet wool, dripping stone, sodden wood lay against a gun-metal smell, animal heat, and dried sweat. Those on the steps pushed aside to allow late arrivers to climb to the loft, from where they observed the proceedings.

The currier Twym Hughes—she had met him in summer, remembered his blackened forearms from rubbing leather—called the meeting to order. Gruffly, in Welsh, he announced the chairman, Evan Jones.

The vicar stepped onto an overturned trunk to cries of "Hear! Hear!" He addressed the people in Welsh, and it was exclusively spoken from then on. Christine occasionally leaned toward Pary or Lloyd for translation.

"There's Harries Davies," Lloyd said to her. His moon face glowed from a seat by the stove. "And the solicitor Thomas Davies, who brought Dr. Fowler to Sarah." Waxed mustache. Dressed for London, blue topcoat, white scarf, and unnatural glistening hair.

Jones was better in Welsh, she observed. Welsh lent further stature to the sense of size she had recently felt in his presence.

"I greatly rejoice," he said, standing tall beneath his slashing brows, "that the matter of the Welsh Fasting Girl is being thoroughly investigated. It has long been my earnest desire. I beg leave to remind you that this long fasting went on for sixteen months before it was published to the world. During this time, no strangers visited the Jacob farm, and no money went into the pockets of the girl's parents."

"Hear! Hear!"

"As you are all aware, I sent a letter to the local papers,

expressing my opinion that there was strong evidence of the truthfulness of the parents' statement."

But Christine was sure he wrote in his letter that *he had no doubt whatsoever.*

He'd lied.

"I invited members of the medical profession to make an investigation into the case. Few accepted my invitation, and I was ridiculed by medical journals. The situation continued until a committee was formed to institute a watch over the fasting girl. Yet all sorts of imaginary faults were found with the conduct of those watchers."

"Hear! Hear!"

Imaginary? Christine thought.

The vicar's expression hardened. "But those who formed the committee felt convinced that it was fairly and honestly carried out. In a matter apparently contrary to the laws of nature, the committee did not, perhaps, consider the evidence sufficient to convince scientific men; but they did believe that it supplied strong prima facie evidence in favor of the claim. It proved that the case required further investigation."

Pary said in the pause, "Puts a different spin on it, doesn't he?"

"Don't you just love logic after the fact?" Lloyd rejoined.

"I rejoice," the vicar concluded, "that the claim will be thoroughly tested. What we all want is the truth."

"Hear! Hear!"

"Gohebydd," said the vicar, "a gentleman well known throughout Wales, has been kind enough to take the case in hand, and we are grateful." People strained forward; repositioning rustled the room. In stentorian tones, Jones pronounced, "I call upon Gohebydd to explain the proposed arrangement!"

"Ever met him?" Christine asked Pary and Lloyd.

"Many times," Pary said.

"Gives the crowd their money's worth," Lloyd said. "His style is unusual, modern, you'll see." Gohebydd was speaking with the parents, but after the vicar stepped down, he mounted the trunk. The crowd cheered.

"I beg you," he began, and quiet returned. He wore a dusty old coat; he could have been one of the common folk, the *gwerin*. Thinking, he rubbed his fingers together at his sides, as if he were alone and not in front of fifty-odd people.

His voice was intimate and disarming. "I'd like to say why I am here. I am not a Carmarthenshire man, nor am I a Cardi." They laughed. He meant he was not from Cardigan. He acknowledged the laughter shyly. "I am a Welshman, jealous for the honor of my country, for the good name of my countrymen and countrywomen." He looked gently at Hannah.

"Hear! Hear!"

He evinced, Christine thought, an immense sincerity and seriousness directed utterly at Wales; his speech revealed for his country profoundest passion.

"I visited Lletherneuadd last April and again in September. I read the letters and leaders written about Sarah Jacob. . . . And I am sick and tired of constantly seeing paragraphs headed 'the so-called fasting girl'; this week a letter from a London doctor, next from a self-proclaimed Welsh bard from *somewhere—*" The rubbing fingers lifted and, with a flick, brushed off that *somewhere*. People nodded, sighed, laughed. "From somewhere," he continued, "giving their 'opinion' on the case of the girl. Now, the matter seems to me not a question of opinion, but a simple matter of fact."

"Hear! Hear!"

"Is the girl fed? Or is she not? This is all we have to find out. To be or not to be fed, that is the question."

There came surges of laughter.

"How long a human being can live without food, we may

divorce from our considerations. It is a question for scientists, not for the public to discuss." He sounded adamant there, and Christine scratched a note in the pad she had, fortunately, remembered to bring. "We do have it on authority from so exalted a writer as William Hamilton that 'there is no ground for inferring a certain fact to be impossible merely from our inability to conceive its possibility.'"

"Hear! Hear!" Cheers. They believe, she thought. Many of them genuinely believe. Faces lifted to the Welsh patriot lustered in attention, hands fisted in laps—and Christine thought of the words she had overheard in a shop: "We are more than gristle and fat, more than the animals in the fields; we are made in His image and saved by Christ our Lord."

Gohebydd said, "Individual opinions on the matter, mine, yours, do not amount to much." And on this note of anticlimax, he read the letter from his connection at Guy's Hospital, London, putting forth rules for the watching.

Four nurses from London—one of Welsh background, as the father had requested—would watch to see if Sarah partook of food. As it was asserted that the action of the bowels and bladder was suspended, special attention must be directed to those organs. The family would stay at a distance from the girl. Sarah's body and room would be thoroughly searched, and Jacob would sign a legal agreement, giving his daughter entirely over to the nurses for two weeks. The nurses would report their findings to a local committee and local medical men would stand ready to act against serious symptoms.

Gwilym Marles rose in his weary dignity and proposed that the sensible, cautious rules be accepted, and a vote was unanimous.

Christine thought, it really will happen. She watched the vicar, thinking, you lie.

Darkness fell, and the wind huffed outside, sifting powdery

snow across the roads. After committees were voted on, people left quietly, hunching into the cold.

❧

Carmarthen, Wales
7 December 1869

Dearest James,

I beseech you to help me. I cajole, I entice you to stay with me in spirit if spirit you are. If you walk—and God Himself help me, for as you recede, I begin to believe again in your persistence in tangible shape. It is as if you sleep like the Welsh warriors still in their armor, not dead, but resting under the land, until Wales is ready and the call comes to arise. From deep in the mountains, the knights will shout, "Is it time?" The stories the children brought to me over and over, the first year, the second, the fourth, and the fifth of men staggering back from the war destroyed me. In my heart, I buried you, dear; I dug a grave for my husband, who had no other I could see, stand over, pray to, water with tears. I washed your wounds and wove your shroud. I formed the words we would have said to each other had you died in bed. I found my strength for the children. I held Rupert's pain, bore his slow healing, and then you were torn again from my heart's grave and tossed into wandering twilight, deathlessness, lifelessness, and again I stood over upturned empty ground and—again, I buried you, darling. When Douglas went south to seek you, I didn't believe anymore. There was no grave, no life, and so I decided to write to you. I need this, James. I need to feel that you hear and help me. I need to feel that what I do is not futile, that life is not futile. I need to forgive you. I need this, as the change of life is upon me and all I see is a world again and again and again full of fire.

It is sad, your Wales, in a froth of confusion, hunting

itself, drawing regret and urgent anticipation into this watch, another attempt to see, I suppose, but not for themselves, for others to see them for what they so earnestly believe they are. What is acceptable and what is not? What are the limits of sacrifice? Across the veil where you dwell looking down on me, I pray, do you know? Is it finally clear to you and, over there, have you discovered the gold of every quest? Peace? Justice? Truth?

She is but a child. Her father has instructed her on what will happen tomorrow. He has explained to the family procedure, preparation, and some of these have already commenced. Mary, the eldest, is more to the fore than she has been, checking on Sarah, appearing concerned, but also going about her usual tasks. Of course, they are all in the house more in winter. I have visited every day since the public meeting, a witness to the rhythm of their winter life, the cows going only as far as the yard for milking, the attention to darning, repairing, the grain put away in the loft, the tending to pigs and chickens in the outer shelters, the tasks in the dairy that go on the same, except the resulting cheeses are winter pale—and the readying of the house for the nurses.

The second girl, Esther, has taken to sucking her fingers. I think she bites her nails to the quick and they bleed and hurt. She sucks them, sitting off in a corner of the kitchen floor, her snapping eyes gazing after the goings-on.

The boys are quieter, studying lessons at the table by the fire. The hired boy, Emyr, watches the book learning curiously as he whittles wood—love spoons he sells at market. It is artful work, each spoon one of a kind.

Hannah told me Evan saved Emyr. The boy's father died, and the mother and children were evicted, put off their land and out of the county to wander in search of a village that might take them in. Hannah does not know their fate. Emyr ran from the others and hid in the rocky promontory edging the Jacob land. Evan found him near death and decided he could take in this one. The boy was nine then and would be sixteen or so now. His blue eyes aren't the fishy pale of Evan Jacob's, but a startling cornflower blue. A birthmark, a pale red stain, seeps from his hairline.

Baby David keeps up Hannah's spirits. The ruddy little boy laughs continually, charms pilgrims, and chases poor Margaret, who hates him. Margaret has loudly signaled her hatred of everyone. The parents relaxed their strictures on her closeness with Sarah; this helped. They sleep nights together in Sarah's bed, though Margaret knows come tomorrow she is back in the children's room, for Sarah must sleep alone.

I heard Evan speak to Margaret severely, thus: "If you disobey me, I will send you from the house for the watching. Is this what you want?"

She hates silently now, without obstreperous outbursts. I was encouraged to think she liked me, after the book bribe. But Margaret sneers, scowls, and looks ready to spit when I talk to Sarah. She watches us, her light-sucking eyes following my every move.

"Is Margaret your guard?" I asked Sarah playfully one day.

"She is," Sarah replied—as if it were self-evident and entirely reasonable. "We are each other's port in the storm."

Sometimes, though, I think Margaret is angry with Sarah, too. I have long suspected that Margaret harbors the truth if anyone does. How much she knows, what her role is, the impossibility of gaining her trust to discern any of it—these repeatedly tap on my brain like a drip from the pump. But what would I do with the truth if I knew it? What *could* I do? And why has it come to mean so terribly much to me?

People accept now that the case is larger than any simple truth, though they say all they seek is the truth. My head aches with my effort to articulate these recalcitrant snarls. I told Sarah I was thinking of writing a book about the case when it is over—that a book would be fairer, presenting the total story. She liked that. I thought it might get her to talk to me more. It didn't.

Her father has finally called off the pilgrims, but even today, the last day before the nurses arrive, while expressing her usual affection for me, Sarah said nothing new. She was feeling quite well, she said. She read her Bible and prayed, asking God to help her love His will, learning how to bow before His authority.

The fire in her room remains unlit because of the dairy, adjoining the parlor-bedroom, on the other side of the wall by the parents' bed; Hannah requires the dairy ice-cold. But atop the cold hearth, new gifts to Sarah have collected and she likes to lie looking at them; her father has lit extra candles for their illumination.

"Did you see my portrait?" she asked me. I did, a line drawing of an every-girl, a pious-faced maid someone did for a broadsheet and brought to the homestead.

"Well, it looks nothing like you," I said.

"What do I look like, then?" she asked.

"Your face is finely etched, Sarah, and vivid. It is very—alive." This thirst for confirmation, what did it mean? I found it more difficult daily to separate the whims of an adolescent from messages, symptoms, and signs. My daily presence was my own signal to her that I waited to help, if help she wanted.

"If I had a photograph," she said, "I could see myself." She had brought up the photograph before, after a London man offered to bring his camera and Evan Jacob turned him down, without a steep fee—that man, Jacob, adding another to the list of his endless inscrutable actions.

"Did you see the map?" Sarah asked. Margaret lay against her like a lover, her face buried in Sarah's hair.

I picked it up. "It's the valley, isn't it?" I said.

"Take it," Sarah said. "You can copy it out and publish it in Brooklyn. And here," she said. "I've translated one of my poems for you." She removed a tightly folded paper from a book and handed it to me.

She seemed, today, to believe her own myth, to be flattered, as I had suspected others of being flattered. But she is twelve, and what does that say? Only a day ago she had protested to her father, after she was required by a pilgrim to lay her hand on a boy's withered leg, "I didn't want to touch it! I can't do anything about his leg, Tad!"

"Be silent," he said to her quietly. "If it balms their pain to believe, what is the harm?"

"If I could be lame for him, I would," Sarah said, a great tear rolling from her eye. "I could be lame here in bed, couldn't I? It wouldn't make any difference."

Jacob didn't act worried by my witness of the scene, and it was the one lapse in Sarah's composure, the single expression of pain.

"Well, I will see you very soon, Sarah," I said, putting the poem in my bag. The family had asked for my presence when the nurses arrived. The vicar required a member of the press to witness the search.

"Kiss me?" Sarah said.

"Are you all right?" I asked.

"Yes," she said.

"Good-bye, Margaret," I said to the lump beside her, the girl burrowed completely now under the covers. Not even a grunt back.

"She isn't in favor of the watch," Sarah said.

"That much is clear," I replied.

I made my farewell to the others and Hannah insisted I drink tea before setting off. I opened my bag and glanced at the poem: "On the Death of a Little Girl." Shaken, I put it back. To show it to Hannah, I thought, would be futile. I inquired after the whereabouts of the vicar and learned that, as it was late day, he was likely at his church.

One of the boy guides, bearing a lantern, conveyed me by pony to the train station, where I was able to hire a trap for my conveyance to St. Michael's.

Dry, cold—at last we arrived, and I went inside.

Already the church was sunk in darkness, and inside the gloom pierced by starry candles the vicar sat in the first row of pews, head bent in prayer. I sat in the last pew and waited. Next to me, on the wall, the names of vicars going back two hundred years were chiseled in stone for the ages.

I looked away, picturing Sarah as she would be if it were up to my divination—a girl on the cusp of womanhood in a white dress wading through grass, all of her future before her. I pictured her invalid's books stacked on a desk in a school-room, her head bent above them, the writing ignited by her new mind into a clean conflagration. Then I read the poem,

On the Death of a Little Girl

A little girl went home today
She rests where she belongs,
And now she plays upon her harp
The sweet and heavenly song.
And though she was so precious
To her parents dear
Christ He sent to fetch that girl
A pearl whom he'd have near.

She leaves behind a world of grief
And all its tempting gain
She leaves behind her troubles
And all this world of sin.

And now she stands beside the throne
With Jesus and the holy throng
And in her hands she holds a harp
And plays the Heavenly song.

The vicar finished his prayer, raising his head to the glowing altar. I walked up the aisle to him. "Is anything wrong?" I asked.

"I've just come from Dr. Harries Davies," he said. "Mr. Morris, the tinsmith, was killed. We had the black ice after the thaw, and his horse slipped on wet leaves that covered the ice. Davies tried to save him, but it was no use. The horse fell upon him and his chest was crushed." I didn't know what to say.

"May I help you?" he asked wanly.

"It's Sarah." We sat together, and I handed him the page. "She gave this to me today. I'm concerned."

"I know it," he told me. "I saw it before."

"Oh, when?"

"At the time of the first illness, when she was badly sick. Shortly thereafter."

"When she'd almost died."

"Yes."

"Then it isn't expressive of her fears for tomorrow."

"There is nothing for her to fear," he said. "Oh, it will involve unpleasantness, we can venture to say."

"Why are we putting her through it?"

"'We'?" he said.

"I feel complicit."

He smiled. "You are not a very good reporter, Mrs. Thomas. It is why I like you."

He wouldn't lie about the poem, I thought, definitely not. A crushed chest—deaths, one after another, these were the lives of the minister and the doctor and here I was. . . . Champion of—what did Douglas call her? "A scruffy little faster," he said, "and for that they are sending you all the way to Wales?" I hadn't succeeded in protecting Gwen from the abandonment of her father, hadn't been able to stop her from throwing herself away on a sick old man. I judged myself inept, and so here I was, aging and widowed and carrying on. I took back the poem and refolded it.

"I must go tell my servant to mind my daughter for tonight," he said. "And then I must go sit with Morris's family."

"Yes," I said dully, stunned by my inability to effect any change.

"All will be well, Mrs. Thomas. Trust in the Lord."

Outside, the trap waited. I petted the muzzle of the sputtering horse to comfort myself. I rode the train through the darkness, recalling my father—how he wouldn't get on a train, did not deem it safe, an attitude common in the earlier generation.

Nothing was safe. I thought that if the train rode into the dark sky and crashed in the mountains, it was all one.

This is bitterness, James. It is a leveling out. It is a place we cannot afford.

After dinner and a sit in the parlor with the widows, I felt no less troubled. Reginald Pary marched because of his restlessness, but it didn't allay his insomnia, and, a bachelor, he often worked at the *Weekly* late into the night.

I found him in his office, a windowless closet tacked, floor to ceiling, with maps, drawings, graphs, articles, lists. He elbowed the sides of a thick book, head in his hands, clutching the weave of his kinky black hair in concentration.

"Is the wind down?" he asked without looking up.

"It's calmed."

"Colder?"

"Rather warmer, I think."

"There's nothing but weather, is there?" He came to a stopping place and turned up the lamp. "You're out late."

"What are you reading?"

"Background for a story on one of the mining communities."

"Where?"

"Are you familiar with Swansea?"

"Thirty years ago," I said.

"You'd find it changed," he said drily.

"Doubtless."

"Care for a spot of gin?" he asked. "I teetotal in summer, but winter calls for extraordinary coping mechanisms, wouldn't you say?" He got up and took a bottle from Lloyd's desk. "Sit." He removed files from Lloyd's chair and, placing them on the floor, said, "I've cups somewhere—aha!" At my nod, he poured. "Before the religious revivals, everyone drank," he said. "Babies had it in their pudding." He silently laughed, saying, "I joke," and I cringed at myself for being unsure. Trapped, I thought, caught again, unfair to the Welsh.

"Well now, bad day?"

I sipped. "What is this? Just gin? It's marvelous."

"Fairy milk," he said.

"Delicious." I drank about half of it down, felt my heart kick, the flush rise to my skin; closed my eyes; opened them. "Sarah won't die, will she?"

"Of course not! Good grief, what are the doctors for, then?"

"Why fourteen days?" I asked. "How long does it take to starve a person to death?"

"Mrs. Thomas—"

"Christine," I enjoined. Were we not friends?

"The value of a scientific watch is its safety," he said.

I laughed. "Forgive me. I'm sure you're right. But really, how long can we live without food?"

"I don't believe it's been established precisely. Depends, I'd imagine."

I put a hand against my flushed cheek to soothe it. "I came a while ago from the vicar." I thought of giving the news about the tinsmith, but I didn't care to bring it up. I said, "He called me a bad reporter and meant it as a compliment. He's right. I'm unsuited for this work. My father—is it all right if I chat a bit?"

"Needed a break," he said.

"Thank you. My father would have liked what I've done, late in life, true, but he wanted a life of the mind for me, ever since I was small. It was just the two of us, and without a son, he dreamed through me. He was a banker, but he loved books—philosophy, history, literature—and he read four newspapers front to back every day. My late husband's father also loved books, and he set down my James, as my father did me—plucked him out of the cradle and set him down at a desk. We were meant for each other, little gnomic creatures blinking in daylight, keen to go back inside to our learning. More?" I asked, indicating the gin. He complied. "It's unloosed my tongue," I said.

"Good. I'd begun to think you were just hatched, day before you embarked for we lot here in Wales."

"Meant for each other," I repeated, musing. "Marked from the age of fifteen. But I was a girl, and that made the difference. I fell in love, children came, and I fell in love with them, too." I remembered—felt—their tiny hands wrapping my finger, smelled the milky, soft, baking scent of their heads. "I didn't stop reading. I'd dandle a baby on a hip and hold a book in my other hand. When there were three, I stuck them most days in a wagon with my books and we set out to play and read. My father was disappointed I didn't continue formal education. I think he envisioned me at Harvard. So—autodidact, I guess. Anyway, Harvard could not have competed with children even had I a brain that fine—and was a man. Now my husband, James, didn't go on with education, either. First time he walked into a newspaper office, it was what he wanted." I looked at Pary's wallpaper, his messy scraps. "I like your curiosity," I said. "I think I am more easily satisfied." Hogwash. This wasn't what I wanted to say, what I meant. I wanted to say that I didn't know anymore why I was here or why I had wanted to be a reporter. "Perhaps I should go home and open a nursery or a school," I said, without having that ambition at all.

"You wouldn't feel—confined?" he asked.

"I might. Hard to say."

I liked this office, tick of the clock, night.

I said, "Trouble is—one can't go back. To a previous life or even to the person one was before. I'm changed. I'm fallen under the spell of Wales."

"It does that."

"What is it?"

"I tried to leave once," he said. "Struck out for London, thinking I would go farther, that London was the initial step. But I was called back. Trouble in my family, in Wales—convulsions, deaths. Thing about trouble, it bonds you. It calls forth—love. The family house—burned to the ground, and I never wanted to leave again."

"I came here on money my father left me," I said. "Seems fitting, but now I'm paid. I accomplished what I set out to do here, made a name for myself in Brooklyn—a little one anyway. It is strange."

"Answered prayers," he said.

"One for the road?" I asked. "I'm giddy."

"Not drunk?"

"A little."

"I'll walk you."

"No need."

"Be careful."

"I'm fine," I said. He wasn't courtly, a bachelor par excellence. They would find him asleep with his head on the book in the morning.

With utmost care, I embarked, stepping determinedly out of the room. But the complex scent of the foyer, the thick empty-building air, its pause and its secrets, arrested my progress and I stood in its silence, in the grip of its suggestions, until my vexing, unceasing warmth urged me outside.

In the cold air meeting my heat, steam could have poured up out the top of my head. I was equalized, comfortable. I walked a few blocks by the haloed gaslights. You could hardly smell the dung in the cold. It must have frozen, and they'd scrape it up in the dawn. Boneless, I felt, thought I ought to get drunk more often. Feel sad and have a good melt. Why they did it, drunkards. Or you got God. I didn't have God. Sometimes I believed, but I didn't really. God was a trope, an automatic response, a hopeful yearning. Gin in the pudding. Horse fell on his chest. A woman passed me, and looked back: painted face, shabby bonnet. I followed her, picked up my pace so she couldn't escape. Didn't think why; passed the corner where I should have turned and started down the incline behind her to where the fires burned by the castle. I stopped and watched her walk into the darkness, the flickers, where I could see other figures, and tents. Mesmerized. Reminded of the displaced after the war at home, and slaves coming north, the ones I had seen in shanties. These people,

I surmised, were escapees from famine, itinerant members of the convulsions of their land. Flotsam. I belonged with them, but they wouldn't have me. The woman turned and started up. I waited, certain that facing possible danger was the price I must pay for what I thought she could tell me, what I needed to know. I was ready to hand her my bag.

"Madam?" she said. She knew me, had seen me in the streets? She spoke in Irish-accented English. "Why are you here?" A young painted face, chapped, kindly. "Are you lost?"

"Yes," I said.

"What are you looking for?" she asked.

What everyone looks for—a way ahead.

"I remember now," I said. "It's up the next road."

"Go home," she said.

"Yes," I promised.

As ever,
Christine

THE WATCHING

E VEN THE SISTER-NURSE, ELIZABETH CLINCH, twenty years older than the others and in charge, hoped to the last minute for a reprieve from their task. She hoped at Paddington Station, where no reprieve came and a group of reporters blocking their path blathered questions. "Forward!" she ordered her charges. "Say nothing." She hoped in Wales, where thicker crowds shouted for them to show themselves on the platforms. At her directive, the four nurses stayed put straight through to Carmarthen, where the gentlemen they had been told to look out for got on as escorts to Pencader Station. Trains, she thought derisively, they could have arrived by coach and no one the wiser. The noisy commotion, the steam blasts, their ungodly weight slicing the land—trains inflamed people, made the simplest folk believe they confronted IMPORTANCE. Boys leaped at the windows, bearing welcoming signs in English and Welsh. At Pencader, they were forced to emerge, she ushered ahead by Gwilym Marles, with Gohebydd trailing behind with the Welsh girl, Ann Jones, and Sarah Attrick, and Sarah Palmer. Young Jones, Attrick, and Palmer lacked seniority and were therefore obliged to this folly. She, Elizabeth Clinch, was strong-armed, and she thought that if she retained shreds of her former enthusiasm for nursing, this job could well prove the straw to break that camel's back. Still she hoped, en route to their lodgings at

Blaen-blodau farm, where they bade the Welshmen good-bye. She and Ann Jones lay speechlessly after supper in the wee corner loft smelling of wood smoke. "We could still be called home," she said to Ann the next day as they traveled with the committee members to Lletherneuadd.

Animal den, she thought in the Jacob dwelling, earthen creatural silence and heaviness, December dark, cows on one side of the house, the anxiety of the parents palpable, but they were cooperative, and the brothers and sisters drifted like wraiths on the edge of it, over the next days, cropping up unannounced in the doorway—faces glimpsed at the parlor window, looking in at the fasting girl. Once the search was complete and the nurses sat two at a time in eight-hour watches, wrapped in flannels against the damp cold, hot bricks at their feet, they had little to do if the girl slept but watch the clouds of their breath, and Elizabeth Clinch attempted to write the details of the day in her diary, helpless to keep the ink from running and blurring in the dampness—damp books, damp stains on the walls, the heavy brown furniture ominous and sad. They couldn't eat, for the girl would faint at the sight or mention of food. Stiff and hungry, trading places at the end of the first shift, the sister-nurse and Nurse Jones cast glances, as if to say, Well, here we are, it has happened, no calling off. At least we'll be out of here before Christmas.

At the front door, Elizabeth felt a tug at her skirt and a little girl she would learn was Margaret handed her food, oatcakes, Nurse Jones said. For the journey, she told Elizabeth, translating the girl's words. Jones thanked her in Welsh. Elizabeth stared for a moment at the girl's eyes—grim eyes, like the eyes of the London urchins, the children who saw more than they should. The mother apologized, found a cloth for the bare food.

Outside, getting into the trap, traveling back to her narrow bed in the loft, lying awake in the echoes of the day, Elizabeth thought of, still felt the child's atmosphere, and Margaret, once the nurse was gone, thought of her, without any real focus of wonderment, only a following of her out into the night world, out to those places that already felt gone from her. She knew the gravity of the watch, knew it a standoff, the still point they had all along moved toward. Already she felt the house under her unloosed, pulling up from its roots, and the mountains outside drifting away from their bearings, the ground in a shift, as if a giant had dug his hand under it all and held it, had softly closed his fingers around it and they were inside, breathing the steamy vapors of his skin.

CHRISTINE HAD WAITED WITH ALUN LLOYD at Carmarthen Station for the nurses' arrival. She counted the crowd at about forty, a snappy, predominantly young crowd of shopkeepers, mill workers, and the service element—barkeeps, bakers, grooms, washerwomen, some with their families. Dry day, the sky iron gray, bone-cold, kids racing in circles, and then the temperature change of the tracks, or so she imagined, premonition of the train. People straightened, grabbed back the children, and the inexorable force screeched in billowing steam, the majestic land and sky peeling away, the landscape seeming to slink itself down and put up its belly like a dog to the traveling tonnage man had made.

Gohebydd and Marles emerged from a shaded coach and stepped up to the train. When the nurses didn't come out, they went in.

"That's it?" Lloyd said. The train stoked its engines once more and left, flinging grit and scorched fumes.

"Do you believe in Sarah?" Lloyd asked in Welsh of a pretty shivering woman.

"You're from the paper," she said.

"That I am, ma'am."

"None of your business."

Christine laughed. "Want to ask anyone else?"

"Too damn cold," he said. "You?"

"I've a splitting headache; I'm going back to bed."

"Aren't you called forth by His Royal Highness the vicar for the search?"

"It's tomorrow; they want to let the nurses settle in."

Communications were in place, contacts at various points to telegraph news, errand boys hired for conveyances, reliable rumormongers identified. The inns burst with national and foreign correspondents, trains added extra runs, and what, Pary had remarked this morning, would everyone do when the fasting girl no longer fasted?

Yesterday, Christine had learned that Gohebydd was paying the four nurses' fares and wages. The local committee, scheduled to meet periodically at the Eagle Inn over the coming weeks, had arranged their lodging. Neighbors and relatives of the Jacobs had volunteered to help with the farm, with laundering and other tasks in the days ahead.

Early today, coming down groggily for the breakfast she couldn't eat, Christine found an envelope at her place at the table. Inside was a note from the vicar, who had enclosed a lock of Sarah's hair. The vicar explained that when the parents emptied Sarah's cupboard bed, they had found swatches of Sarah's hair from her original illness, hidden by Margaret, they learned. Margaret battled them, claimed the hair hers, and was swatted and put to bed. Before throwing it out, Hannah clipped locks and tied them with pink ribbons, requesting the vicar to distribute them as he saw fit but to be sure not to forget kind Mrs. Thomas.

Back from the train, in her room, Christine held the lock

up to the lamplight, which cast a false lavender sheen on Sarah's black hair. Why did people fetishize, clip parts, create their eerie representations, trot out talismans, charms, double and distance us from breathing flesh, mock the original, cast up wizards and genies—because it was unbearable sometimes, being alive.

She tucked the lock in a bottom drawer, leaving Hannah's motives for later. She drifted off, any mirrored future unreadable, draped in her mind's eye by verdigris and smoke.

THE NEXT DAY BROUGHT FREEZING RAIN. But it diminished by afternoon, with the congregation of the local committee and the available members of the medical committee, and Christine, struck by the scene smack up between her eyes.

The four nurses, the parents, Christine, and nine men crowded into Sarah's back room, the men with their heavy beards, coats, boots, and bodies, and the girl sitting up brightly in bed, costumed by Hannah with a headband garland of paper violets and yellow ribbons, topped by a pink-and-white check silk bonnet. On Sarah's slight frame, a black velvet jacket and white shawl pinned by a gold broach completed her outer attire.

The nine included: Evan Jones, Gohebydd, Gwilym Marles, Dr. Harries Davies, Thomas Davies, and others new to Christine—one, she heard, was Sarah's uncle, a draper.

"Now, Sarah," the vicar said, "Only the nurses will watch. Is this acceptable to you?" The committee had objected to the father's request for neighborhood girls to sit with Sarah.

The girl nodded sweetly, and the search commenced, under the eyes of the observers. Sarah was lifted by her father from her cupboard bed and set down on her parents' bed. While she lay in one of her fits or withdrawals, her bed was pulled apart, a chest opened, overturned, a cabinet scraped from the wall and thoroughly investigated. Sarah's trinkets and books were tipped up and shaken; a bell dropped with a weak tinkle and stuck in the claggy floor, wetted by boots. The linen presses Hannah kept in a corner were removed from the room at the sister-nurse's request. Finally, Sarah's bed itself was stripped. Sister Clinch looked askance at the thin stained mattress on sacking tied by a rope to the bed frame and said, "May we have a clean mattress?"

Consultation between the vicar and the father led to a decision to make the bed up as it was, and Evan Jacob instructed the nurses on how his daughter liked best the bed made. When it was done, they brought Sarah back to it. She came to and smiled.

"How are you, Sarah?"

"I'm fine, Da-da." Never had Christine heard her call him that.

"We'll search her now," Sister Clinch said, and in the cold dimness, Hannah, lips tight, eyes brimming, removed Sarah's garland, her bonnet; she unpinned the broach and withdrew the shawl and unbuttoned Sarah's jacket—her finery, thought Christine. Sarah's head bowed, her hair fell over her face. She partially sat, slumped and supported by her father, while Sister Clinch and another nurse folded back Sarah's covers and pulled her nightdress up and off over her head.

"Oh, my child, my child, my dear little Sal!" Hannah said. "Don't do her any harm! Don't hurt her!"

"No harm, no harm," one of the nurses said to Hannah in Welsh. The men were dead silent, expressionless, didn't move even to shift as they watched the nurses scratch fingers through Sarah's hair, raise her thin white arms, slide their hands over her back, down her torso and legs. Little girl, child, thought Christine, as if her thoughts could comfort Sarah. Slumped, a flush had spread from Sarah's bowed head down her neck and over her slight, exposed shoulders. Her flat child's chest was gray in the shadow of her slump and she didn't swoon again, submitting to the procedure as if she deserved it. On it went, ears, buttocks. She coughed, and the coughing continued until she was forced to sit up to regain breath. The nurses stopped, and for a moment, sitting up, her hair fallen back, Sarah confronted the crowd—her astonished eyes, her flushed nakedness in her father's grip on display.

Acid rose into Christine's throat, but she could not leave, she knew she must suffer it, and it continued, the only sound Hannah's soft whimper, "My child."

When, at last, it was finished, Sarah was dressed. The nurses pulled off the curtains from the parents' bed and then the bed was removed to the kitchen and taken apart.

While this went on, Dr. Lewis, who was sinewy, white-haired, and gentle, examined Sarah cursorily, taking her pulse and temperature as Dr. Harries Davies stood by. It was said these were the doctors sympathetic to the Jacobs.

Christine learned that the other children had been sent away to wait in the loft above the byre, thanks be for this bit of decorum. When the room was pronounced ready, Dr. Lewis gave directions to the nurses in the kitchen.

"You are to watch to see if she takes food or not."

"What about giving her food?"

"If she asks for food, then supply it, but you are not to offer her food. Sometimes they moisten her lips; give her water if she asks."

Christine wondered if, through the passageway, Sarah listened. She noticed the vicar, once Sarah was dressed, adjusting his shoulders, as if he suffered stiff neck.

Visitors could be admitted to the room at the discretion of the nurses, and family members could shake Sarah's hand. The sister-nurse told Dr. Lewis and Dr. Harries Davies that she refused to take the responsibility on herself unless the medical men attended every day, and she was reassured.

"A doctor will come every day?" repeated Elizabeth. "Else I cannot—"

"Now, now," said Dr. Lewis with a glance at the vicar, "five medical men are available day and night."

An official report was written and signed by all, stating that the room and the girl's body had been thoroughly searched and that no food, "save for an old shriveled-up turnip under the parents' bedstead," was found anywhere. A certificate of Sarah's condition was formally made: "Cheerful; face flushed; eyes brilliant; pulse regular, averaging 86 per minute; temperature in the mouth, 98 deg., after two minutes' rest. She has a warm-water bottle at her feet. She seems quite well, and says she has no pain anywhere if not touched."

Everyone trooped back to Sarah to say good-bye. When her turn came, Christine said, "Are you all right, dear?" Sarah managed a lips-only smile. Hannah had left off the ornaments while redressing Sarah. Why did she deck her up on this day? Christine thought. It was as if mother and child were so at the mercy of reality that the one possible response was to ignore it and live in an alternate world, and that world was shattered.

Sarah's dark hair was damp at her temples, curling against her soft brow like a babe's. They were alone, Christine realized, and bearing down with her voice, she said, "What have you to tell me, Sarah?"

Sarah's lips parted, showing her glistening white teeth. "Talk to me; you know you can," Christine said. "It isn't too late."

"May I help you, Mrs. Thomas?"

Christine whirled about to the vicar in the doorway; Sarah withdrew, deep into her suffering body. Failed, no rescue, no liberation. Children are a captive population, Christine thought, and this one is pinned to her prison bed.

"Sarah," she said, trying again. "Listen. I will visit tomorrow—"

"Mrs. Thomas, the press is banned from the watching," said the vicar.

"Oh? When was that decided?" she asked.

He didn't answer, just stepped to her side, guarding the unresponsive child.

"*Fine*," said Christine. "To see it would sicken me," and with a last look at Sarah, she turned and left the house.

She followed reports, gossip, she sent her dispatches to Brooklyn, and when it was finished—and she heard the statements and spoke with people involved—she pieced together the daily events. It would take longer to sort the events' implications, and longer yet to determine how best to speak for Sarah.

An hour or so after the search, Sarah's flush whitened, and she awakened and calmly read to herself from her books. The room's musty odor, the skin-shrinking cold and gloom were habitual to Sarah, the sister-nurse thought.

Neighbors, as well as the brothers and sisters, bunched up in the doorway late in the evening and wished Sarah good night. The parents spoke to her as any good parents might, Elizabeth thought, and awkwardly shook her gloved hand— but the absence of bedsores on the child's perfect body made it difficult for the nurse to meet the parents' eyes.

Elizabeth and Ann Jones sat at either side of the bed until midnight, and in the morning, when they resumed duty and sent the other two nurses back to the farm to sleep, Elizabeth washed Sarah's face and combed her hair. The mother refilled the stone warm-water bottle. Sarah read to herself, and when Elizabeth asked if she would like to be read to, she said, "Oh yes!" and listened attentively to Shakespeare—*Othello*, as Sarah liked Desdemona—and psalms from the English Bible.

"Sarah," Elizabeth reminded her, "if you want anything at all, you are to ask us, and you shall have it directly."

"Had I known what nice ladies you were," Sarah replied, "I should have had you before!" At such moments, she put Elizabeth in mind of a miniature woman. Then, in a trice, she reverted to a sick child.

Off duty, Elizabeth Clinch and Ann Jones compared what they knew of the case's history, filling the gaps of a scanty briefing.

Elizabeth noted in the diary, which became the official log, that Sarah seemed well all that first complete day and had slept peacefully the night before. Also noted was the absence of any doctor on Friday.

WHEN SARAH AWOKE SATURDAY MORNING, Sister Clinch and Ann Jones removed her from her bed to a chair-bedstead. Sarah's nightdress was soaked with urine and, Elizabeth wrote, "there were three other marks, from her bowels. These stains were fresh, and all the nurses saw them."

The girl looked unwell to Elizabeth—sunken-eyed and pinched-nosed, and though she regained equanimity back in her bed, she remained subdued.

At three o'clock, a doctor arrived to examine Sarah, under the supervision of Evan Jacob, who insisted on overseeing the doctors, since "by one she was roughly used." About the stained nightdress, he claimed that shock brought it on—it had last happened after the death of a family cow. Elizabeth noted Sarah's abstraction, how she existed outside rather than within the ministrations.

Dr. Rowlands, a gruff, fast-moving man who had not been consulted before his appointment to the medical committee, spoke to a reporter after his visit and was summarily dismissed by the local committee when his report was published in the *Cambria Daily Leader*: "Mr. Rowlands found that the little girl showed signs of great prostration, as compared with her condition on Thursday; that the pulsation was above 100; and that water and excrement had passed from her during the preceding night."

To which Gohebydd responded in a letter to the editor:

> *If, as is alleged in your issue of today, that a medical gentleman visited the girl on Saturday's last and discovered a "mare's nest," would it not be more courteous and honourable towards his colleagues, before rushing into print, that that gentleman should first take means to acquaint the Committee of such "discovery"?*
>
> *The case is submitted to the decision of four experienced nurses chosen specially for that purpose from a leading London hospital. These persons know their duty. I would therefore respectfully, Mr. Editor, submit to all whom it may concern—to doctors, lawyers, preachers, poets, and correspondents—that while the case is pending, while the "jury" is sitting in judgement, that the word should go forth, "Hands off, and meddle not!"*

The nurses had seen combinations of diminished appetite and wasting from chronic disease, seen the effects of malnourishment alongside demises hastened by other organic causes. However, the case before them was different. They had read Dr. Fowler's diagnosis of hysteria but had no experience of the so-called disease at Guy's.

Later Saturday, following Dr. Rowland's visit, Sarah acted quite well again. When asked what they could get her, she'd call for a book. She slept peacefully that night, except for a short time restless and grating her teeth.

"Wasn't she flushed?" Ann Jones asked Elizabeth.

"Perhaps."

But on Sunday, Dr. Harries Davies called in the afternoon and wrote in the log, "Not so cheerful as when I last saw her, but her pulse was regular, she had no pain whatever unless touched, and a mild headache—nothing for concern."

WORST FOR THE NURSES WAS NIGHT DUTY, and on Monday Elizabeth and Ann Jones watched from midnight until eight in the morning. Sometimes Ann half-dozed, and Elizabeth let her. It was harder for Ann to stay awake, and if fully conscious, she liked to talk quietly, sentence here, sentence there, in counterpoint to the sleeping girl's breath.

"I expect she will ask for a morsel tomorrow," Ann said.

Optimistically, Elizabeth thought. Sarah seemed to her under a spell, in thrall to an invisible directive. Sweet girl, affectionate girl; a single candle burned so they could see her. She had fallen asleep at seven-thirty, the other nurses said, and slept deeply. Even in sleep she did not move her left arm, the arm said to be paralyzed.

Elizabeth ached. Cold or the damp, she couldn't say which bothered her more, and the stale urine stench pricked at her sinuses and stung the back of her tongue.

"Try the window again," she said to Ann. "I don't mind freezing if we can just get a mite of ventilation."

The hefty shoulders on Ann, Elizabeth thought, would

budge it if anyone could. But the window stuck fast. "Ice," Ann said, "or the wood is too swollen with damp." Thankfully, the day's rain had stopped; the night's coldness would have brought snow.

"The wind's eerie, thin but always there," Ann said. "It doesn't sound like wind, but you know it is."

"'Devil's breath,' I've heard it called," said Elizabeth.

Ann's head dropped onto her chest. Feeling drowsy herself, Elizabeth got up and stood by the doorway, where it wasn't so cold; a passage led to the smoldering fire in the kitchen. If they were desperate, she and Ann took turns going out and warmed their hands over the embers.

Elizabeth was from a prosperous family, and she had lived in Italy for parts of her girlhood. She recalled the Italian sun, the warm trees shedding blossoms on grass. Her father had died in Florence. Her mother grew permanently sick and her brother married. Elizabeth, enlisted to care for the widow, found herself at her mother's death too old—or uninterested, that may have been it—for a husband. All she had known in her adulthood was care for her mother, and nursing seemed a natural profession. Idiocy, volunteering herself to the whims and directives of men, not one as in marriage but passels of them, the doctors who had come and gone during her tenure at Guy's and the latest batch, who had ordered her here.

A person walked in the kitchen. Elizabeth strained to see out. The shape of the white nightdress and the hitching step told her it was Margaret stalking the room.

Elizabeth got the candle in a holder and lit it from the other near Sarah. She whispered to Ann, "Wake up. Watch her." The candle before her, Elizabeth quietly went to the kitchen and saw Margaret toss herself into a chair.

"Is anything wrong?" she asked. She believed all the children knew some English, by observing their listening faces.

Margaret didn't answer, didn't look at her.

"Go to bed," Elizabeth said.

The girl heaved an exasperated sigh and, without words, refused to bestir herself.

"Don't, then," Elizabeth said, and returned to the bedroom. But in a while she heard a door creak and suctioning wind. The brat had opened the front door! She rushed and closed it. "What are you doing?" she asked. Margaret had just opened it, didn't go out, but stood placid as an inanimate object by winter's gaping maw.

"Don't do it again," Elizabeth said.

It was two in the morning, and at three—Elizabeth looked at the clock—Margaret did it a second time, stationed herself as sentry at the maw, her gown whipping in the wind, eyes fixed straight ahead.

Elizabeth shut the door once more. "Why do you do that?" she asked, but of course she got no answer. "Shall I call your father? Go to bed."

Margaret sat on the hard settle, as if to appease her, and then she lay down and stayed there through the night.

WHEN ELIZABETH AND ANN RESUMED DUTY at four o'clock in the afternoon, Sarah looked weaker, her eyes more sunken and her cheeks flushed.

"Has a doctor come?" Elizabeth asked Sarah Palmer, who replied in the negative, adding that they had not deemed it necessary to summon medical assistance.

"Still, someone should come," said Elizabeth in annoyance.

"But kiss me!" Sarah said urgently from bed. "You haven't today."

"How are you, Sarah?" Elizabeth asked.

"The same." She opened her book and read aloud, a poem in English, a poem in Welsh, voice raspy but recognizable.

The parents came in and out with hot bricks and flannels and Sarah's replenished warm-water bottle. Margaret lurked in the doorway. The boys and the sister who wasn't quite right stayed, mostly, away. The eldest sister often came in, though Sarah ignored her. Elizabeth noticed that Sarah would speak to her family members if spoken to, but she acted more interested in the nurses.

"Did you see my geisha?" she asked Elizabeth. "Dr. Harries Davies brought her to me. There, on the mantelpiece."

Elizabeth had asked Sarah again what she could get her, and the girl asked for her geisha. It was a hard-backed photograph brilliantly painted.

"Brocade, silk, satin," Sarah said, pointing. "You see her face? It is the ivory white they esteem."

Over the whole of Monday, no doctor came, but the local committee met and received a report "that she was fresher and brighter than on any day since the watching commenced."

"From whom did they get the report?" asked Elizabeth later, and no one could say.

At eight o'clock Monday night, she and Ann grew aware of a fresh unpleasant smell, examined Sarah's bed, and found she had passed a large quantity of urine. The warm-water bottle had lost its cork and, as the bed was on an incline, the water had run down. The father brought in the chair-bedstead. When Sarah was put in it, she closed her eyes, and Jacob said she was about to go into a fit. "No, she is not," Elizabeth said, "are you, Sarah?"

Sarah opened her eyes and said, "No, Sister."

The mother helped strip the sheets and fussed over Sarah, and after the parents had gone out, Elizabeth said to Sarah, "Let us know when you want to make water."

"I cannot tell when I pass it," Sarah said.

"Why can she not tell?" Ann asked Elizabeth, back at their lodgings.

"I don't know, but I'm wondering how much dissociation is going on. While awake, she keeps her attention on books and her little objects and ideas she has. . . ."

"Her lips were very dry," Ann said.

"Losing color."

THE SISTER-NURSE LEARNED THAT at six o'clock Tuesday morning Sarah awoke and read aloud to the Queen of Heaven. At seven-thirty, a rope of the bed sacking broke and the warm-water bottle smashed to the floor. "She fainted," Sarah Attrick reported. "Not one of those fits, but a real faint, she was so startled." The father had repaired the bed and Sarah lay patiently in the chair-bedstead while the mattress dried, her paleness alerting Elizabeth to further deterioration in her condition.

Shortly after Elizabeth and Ann Jones took up duty again, the vicar and a Dr. Corsellis arrived. The vicar's take-charge attitude had slipped, Elizabeth saw. He acted warier, ill at ease at the bedside. Dr. Corsellis said that, at eighty, he did not practice medicine anymore and did not know why he had been selected for the medical committee. He felt Sarah's pulse, the vicar prayed with her, and they soon left.

At noon, Dr. Harries Davies called, cheerful and bustling. "Now then, Sarah! How are you on this fine day? Any day it doesn't snow, we send up prayers, else how would we get to our darling?"

"You'd come on a sled," Sarah said.

He took her pulse and said, "Good, good, my precious, my pretty one," and Sarah laughed.

"I am not pretty, I am a fright and you are a liar!"

"You hurt my poor feelings, girl, don't do that or I shall go into decline. How are your serving women doing for you, fair princess?" She giggled again and said he was the silliest man she ever had met. "Oh, little bird, little bird, I am not silly!"

"And I'm not a bird!"

"No? You have the shiny black hair of a crow."

"And you are plump as a spring robin!" she said.

It was unnerving hearing them joking like that, Elizabeth would say, because the girl was more than pale now; she had gone a bit ashen.

After the plump doctor left, Elizabeth checked the log and saw he had written, "Sarah Jacob is subject to the same variation in pulse and aspect as has been the case since and during the previous watching; no indication of danger."

"I thought he might move her to hospital today," Elizabeth said to Ann.

"Well, they can't force-feed her here," Ann said.

Then at two o'clock, another doctor came by, Dr. Vaughan, an elegant man, as Ann described him, with silky flaxen mustaches and hair.

He was shocked by Evan Jacob's restrictions and insisted, "I must examine her."

"You cannot."

Vaughan was allowed to take her pulse—and read it at 144.

He wrote in the log his agreement with Dr. Harries Davies—no indication of danger—and when the sister-nurse asked his opinion of Sarah's countenance, he acted rushed and said he would return tomorrow.

"Would you like me to read to you, Sarah?" Elizabeth asked.

"No, thank you." Elizabeth followed her gaze to the window, where Margaret stood wrapped body and head in a rough blanket, which framed the oval white of her face.

Beside her stood a boy with intensely blue eyes that cut the gloom. Elizabeth, suffering cold, again recalled blue Italian skies, the yellow orb of the sun. But that boy—she peered at him, thinking she saw a trickle of blood on his forehead.

Just then Mrs. Jacob entered the room, wanting to shake Sarah's hand. Mother and daughter sat holding hands, watching the window.

Elizabeth looked irresistibly back at the wrapped girl, the sentry and giver of oatcake, and the blue-eyed boy with the bloody head, who brought to her mind the curse of Cain.

She stole a glance at the mournful woman in the snowy white cap, and the woman caught her and, how could she? Elizabeth thought. Incongruously, horribly, as if sweetness could right this, Hannah smiled.

At midnight, Elizabeth and Ann, resuming duty, passed by Hannah and Margaret, who were still up and sitting at the kitchen table. In the bedroom, the other nurses looked harried, and Elizabeth marked this, since those younger two were ordinarily flat in affect, dull, unemotional types without the gumption of Ann.

"We could not get her warm!" the two said, their voices overlapping.

Sarah was sleeping now, under more layers of flannels and a heavy quilt. Near the patient, Elizabeth detected a new smell, one she couldn't identify.

"Smell her," she whispered to Ann.

"I don't know what it is," Ann said.

No usual smell of the sickroom, more like rotten fruit, Elizabeth thought. "Nothing in the bed?" she asked Nurses Attrick and Palmer.

"Nothing," they said, and it wasn't urine; Sarah had passed a small amount of water in the late afternoon, but not since.

"Go, then." They left. "Tell Mrs. Jacob and Margaret she is resting comfortably," she said to Ann. Elizabeth sat watching Sarah. Every eight or ten breaths, Sarah's mouth opened wider and she panted in quick gasps, and then she settled back to breathing regularly.

"Is she congested?" Ann asked, upon her return.

"I don't know."

"Are you sure the bed isn't wet?"

"I don't want to check and wake her," Elizabeth replied.

At six o'clock, Sarah awoke, and they confirmed the bed was dry. The parents entered for Sarah's ablutions.

"How are you, Sarah?" Evan Jacob asked.

"The same, Tad." She flinched under the face washing and hair combing.

Jacob said, "Do not change her linen, as I feel it disturbs her."

She was settled back into bed in the same gown, black jacket, shawl, and the red woolen cap that helped her stay warm.

"May I get anything for you, Sarah?" Elizabeth asked. "Anything at all?"

She shook her head.

"Books?" She didn't want books.

They departed at eight o'clock, remarking that the smell was the same. "It may be endemic of her condition," Elizabeth said.

"And what is her condition?" Ann asked. "It isn't any stench of death I know."

"She isn't dying," Elizabeth said. "There are no other signs except the pulse and the weakness. I do fear damage to her organs. Too long for a child to go without food." She hoped that the doctors would make a decision today. But one had to be careful with doctors, and what was to be made of these? The lack of organization disturbed her, and she felt one doctor, instead of five, would have been more prudent.

Returning at four o'clock, she learned Dr. Lewis had come. In the log, he had noted Sarah's pulse at 120, said they had conversed pleasantly, and was satisfied there was no immediate danger.

Elizabeth and Ann were relieved that the smell was less keen, but when Sarah requested eau de cologne to scent her handkerchief, they wondered if she smelled it herself. They applied the scent, and Sarah fell asleep at seven o'clock with her handkerchief pressed to her face.

"Should we have given it her?" Ann asked. "Is she sucking the liquid?"

They both leaned in close to Sarah, and Elizabeth whispered, "No, she isn't sucking it." And if she had been, even if the moistness hadn't evaporated and could have served to alleviate Sarah's thirst, Elizabeth wouldn't have cared. She'd have welcomed it, welcomed an end to the travesty, an utter misuse of medical attendance—they were not to *do* anything; how could she nurse and not *do* anything?

She thought of sly remedies, throwing the washing water on Sarah, forcing the wet towel into her mouth, remedies that would avoid, perhaps, a dismissal from Guy's. If she was dismissed, she had income anyway, unlike the three younger nurses.

Sarah awoke in an hour, shivering so hard that they heard her teeth clack. They sent for the parents to bring more hot flannels.

That morning, she still hadn't passed urine; by afternoon, it had been over a day, and she slept fitfully through evening, flailing about, her paralyzed left arm moving freely now as her right. Ann was sent back to the farm at midnight, but Elizabeth stayed the night with the two youngest nurses and the parents, who were up, trying to keep Sarah warm.

At eleven the next morning, Sarah read a little without much interest, and when the vicar called shortly later, he startled—saw her parched, dry lips, her ringed eyes, detected the smell, or so Elizabeth thought, for how could he have failed to? He stared at the listless girl. "Sarah . . ." She closed her eyes, and he hurried to the kitchen to speak with the parents.

Elizabeth went to the passageway and, though the voices were low, heard the vicar express his concern for Sarah and the parents say they had seen her worse before.

The mother said, "If she is weakened, it is the result of the watch and being without her younger sister."

"Call it off," said the vicar, and the father said, "Nay, sir."

"There was no reasoning with them," the vicar would later say—but on this day, when he left, he sent a message to Dr. Harries Davies, who came quickly.

Davies felt Sarah's pulse, assured Sister Clinch in front of the parents that there was no danger, and then he rode off in the sleety midday on his pony, Anastasia, to a cottage nearby, the home of Hannah's sister Nell and her husband, John Daniel.

"You've word of Sarah?" John Daniel asked at the door.

"She is in grave danger," the doctor said. "Will you come speak with the parents?"

As he had at the time of the first watch, Daniel considered the doctor too easily influenced by Jacob; Davies half-believed that the watching and not lack of food endangered Sarah. This fasting balderdash, John Daniel maintained, was the reason he had distanced himself from the Jacobs.

"I think it wise," the doctor repeated, "that a family member step in."

"I'll try, then," the uncle said, and he set off into the sloppy day. He was a steady, physically powerful man with canny hands that held his horse's reins lightly, guiding the mare with the subtlest twitch, hands that had fascinated his niece when he fitted her for a new coat once, her first that hadn't come down from her sisters—Evan had had a good year. She had asked why she could not have a purple coat instead of a black, and he'd marked her curious and agile mind—as intelligent as she was pretty. It had sickened him to see her stripped—how Nell had talked him into being there for it, he couldn't say— and what he could do for Sarah now, he didn't know, either, but if she was in danger, he had to go. He had warned his wife that it wouldn't end neatly—last spring, he had predicted eventual shame for the district from Evan's obsession.

At the house, he learned Evan was at work on the property and Hannah was asleep in the children's room after Sarah's fitful night. Mary said Sarah kept talking to herself and the Welsh nurse couldn't say in what language.

But when John Daniel entered the parlor, the sister-nurse said Sarah was better, had rallied. Goodness, how? Daniel thought, confronted by the pained face within the red woolen cap. "You do not look so well as I used to see you," he said to her.

Ann Jones surrendered her chair to him, and near to Sarah, he said, "Would you like the nurses to go away?"

"No, thank you, Uncle."

"Will you take a drop of water?" he asked. "Or a simple bite?"

At that, she closed her eyes, turning her head from him.

"I will sit by you, Sarah, if you change your mind."

The sleet clouded the window and thickened to snow. Elizabeth Clinch—unaware that Dr. Harries Davies had summoned the uncle—had been reassured by the doctor's note in the log: "Thursday: Passed rather a restless night. Pulse excessively variable. Owing to a little anxiety on the part of the sister-nurse, I thought it advisable to send for Dr. Lewis and Dr. Vaughan for consultation." She expected them presently and believed the doctors would act.

Sarah opened her eyes but would not look at her uncle. "Snow," she said. "Look, Sister."

"Yes, dear."

"It is God, purifying the world."

The doctors arrived at four o'clock. Harries Davies would say that he had felt the responsibility too much to bear by himself.

Hannah was displeased to see Dr. Vaughan, the flaxen-haired gentleman who had earlier challenged Evan. "Only Dr. Lewis may see her," she said.

"Mrs. Jacob," Lewis remonstrated, "as a member of the medical committee Dr. Vaughan is perfectly within his rights to examine Sarah."

"Mr. Jacob is not here," Hannah said, "and I cannot allow it."

"Never mind, Lewis," Vaughan said. "Go in if the girl is ill or dying; I don't want to see her." Vaughan sat by the fire, where the children huddled, the three boys, Esther, and Mary knitting furiously. John Daniel came out and said he had noticed a strong smell of eau de cologne; the sister-nurse had given Sarah the bottle at noon and Sarah hadn't returned it; when she was asked for it back, Sarah drew it out from under her nightdress. She was given the bottle again at two and surrendered it shortly thereafter.

Dr. Lewis went in to Sarah but soon came out and told Hannah that he needed Vaughan; he had difficulty reading Sarah's pulse and required a second opinion.

"You may just take her pulse," Hannah said. "I won't have her pained or upset."

Dr. Vaughan greeted Sarah and knelt by the bed, read her pulse after several attempts at 160. "How are you feeling?" he asked the girl.

"As usual," she said.

"Better keep back the scent," Dr. Lewis told the two younger nurses before he and Vaughan withdrew from the room.

The doctors conferred in the kitchen and Dr. Vaughan left. Lewis said he would speak with the father when he returned to the house. He went in again to Sarah, followed by the uncle. But when Sarah saw John Daniel, she closed her eyes once more and turned her head away, so Daniel went out.

"Well then, Sarah, you are displeased with your uncle."

"But, Dr. Lewis, I am glad to see you," Sarah said.

"Where are your books, dear?" he asked her.

"Sister-nurse put them away for me, back on the shelf."

"Why?"

"I want to think."

"And what are you thinking of?"

"School."

"You liked school."

"Very much. I imagine it in my mind, and it is almost as if I am there."

"They must miss you at school," he said.

"Four of the girls agreed to watch with the kind nurses. But they were forbidden."

"Have they been to visit?"

"Yes, they came."

The father entered, conversed with Sarah about the snow, and then went out of the room with the doctor at his behest.

Dr. Lewis stood silently for a minute with the parents in

the kitchen, his white eyebrows furrowed, arms crossed in thought against his chest.

Dr. Lewis said, "Jacob, the pulse is excessively variable and rapid, and the sister-nurse feels she threatens to sink. I must know if you wish the watching called off and if Sarah should be given food."

"I will on no account offer her anything," Jacob said. "I made a vow two years ago I wouldn't unless she asked for it, and I have seen her worse."

Given Sarah's rally, Dr. Lewis did not prod him further; he was less distressed by the pulse than was Vaughan, in the absence of other symptoms of sinking; there was no clamminess of the skin, no delirium, no disturbance of the intellect.

John Daniel stepped forward and confronted Evan. "You know your daughter better than anyone. If there is anything to be done, you must do it."

"Must I, now?" Evan said. "What would I do?"

"I simply know Dr. Davies called at my home early today, saying Sarah was in grave danger."

"Is this true?" Evan asked Hannah.

"I didn't know of it," she said.

"Why would he do that?" Evan said, his voice rising. "Leave us!" he shouted at the group by the fire, and the children scattered, flying out to the children's room and up to the loft. Evan hadn't removed his wet coat and boots, and he yanked off the coat and threw it to the floor; Hannah took it up to spread by the fire.

"He did," John Daniel said, "because she may be dying."

"He would tell me himself."

"But he didn't, he told me, and I went in and asked her to have a sip of water. Have you no mercy? Give it her!"

Evan grabbed the larger man by his coat collar. Hannah

cried, "Don't!" Evan let go and John Daniel, taken off guard, staggered back.

"We have told you she worsens if offered anything!" Hannah said.

"You could have killed her," Evan said.

"I? *I?*" the uncle said.

"Get out," said Evan, "before I kick you from the house."

Dr. Lewis, much moved by the uncle, interjected. "Dr. Davies telegraphed Dr. Vaughan and me for our attendance and opinion, fearing she was in danger. It must have been shortly after he went for John Daniel."

Evan and Hannah exchanged a look, and then Evan said to John Daniel, "I have asked you, sir, to leave my house."

Daniel stared at the Jacobs and, briefly, tears lit his eyes; he expelled a quick breath and departed.

Evan withdrew to the fire, where he sat at the table and pulled off his boots.

Lewis approached with Hannah, and still standing, he said, "I ask you once more, Evan Jacob, for clarity—is it your wish to continue the watching?"

"Aye, it is," Evan said. "Daniel knows nothing of the affair, and I am disappointed in you, Dr. Lewis, for you have shown sympathy with our cause and the trials we have faced."

"It could be that she weakened from so many doctors in attendance," Lewis replied, "as she has been upset on other occasions."

"Yes," Hannah said, "and she recovered! We have seen her very bad before."

"Then you will not call off the watch?" Dr. Lewis repeated.

"Not for the world," said Evan.

Dr. Lewis calmed the nurses, and before he departed, he wrote in the log that Sarah's livid tinge had disappeared; he noted her lack of the usual symptoms of sinking, ending by writing, "No material change has taken place in Sarah's state."

Across the district it was by now believed that Sarah had beaten the watch and would prove her authenticity. The committee released an announcement that Sarah had assuredly lived since the previous week on nothing and asked for nothing, and so said the witness nurses.

The local committee was pleased to receive confirmation that Sarah was unchanged on Thursday evening. Dr. Harries Davies, after speaking with Dr. Lewis, sent the telegram himself.

At midnight, Sister Clinch and Nurse Jones arrived, to find Sarah thrashing in bed, only secured by bolsters. She had been restless for hours, convulsively shivering but tearing away the covers, and the bed reeked of eau de cologne.

"How did she get the bottle?" Elizabeth asked Sarah Attrick.

"I couldn't keep track of it," Attrick said.

Elizabeth quickly searched Sarah, found nothing, and thought that it didn't matter. Her breath didn't smell of cologne; it was foul.

Sarah tore off the red cap; Ann put it back on. Sarah opened her mouth wide and with those quick gasps turned her head about, as if seeking air.

"Why does she do that?" Ann asked.

"I don't know," Elizabeth said. "Sarah. Sarah, are you awake?"

She curled into a fetal position and then, with a powerful thrust, kicked off the covers and lay on her back, seeking air.

"They did nothing?" Elizabeth asked Sarah Attrick, who

didn't know what she meant. "The doctors," Elizabeth said, and the young nurse shook her head.

"Wake the parents," Elizabeth instructed her, "and then you and Nurse Palmer go ahead back to the farm."

"Look at her lips," Ann said.

"I know." Sarah's lips were white, parched, cracking. Sarah bit at them, trying to soothe them. Elizabeth lay her palm against Sarah's mouth and felt the girl's tongue, dry and harsh, lick her skin. Sarah's shivering rattled the bedstead. The candlelight showed blackened skin around her eyes, her nose beak sharp, her cheekbones pushing out of her face, the cords of her neck drawn taut as bowstrings, holding the shivering child together with fearsome effort.

Shortly, the parents brought more hot flannels and the father sat by Sarah, rubbing her hands, speaking softly to her in Welsh. The mother sat at the other side of the bed, also speaking to her. The sister-nurse felt their nearness would do no harm. Mary came in with a second warm-water bottle. Margaret lurked in the doorway.

The snow had stopped at dusk, but it crusted the window, and Elizabeth thought that the crystals were the same color as Sarah's lips.

"Sarah has taken our eau de cologne bottle," Ann Jones said to Evan in Welsh. He put his hand under the covers, quickly retrieved it, and gave it back.

By one o'clock, Sarah seemed to have settled, and Elizabeth told the parents to go out to the kitchen for a while to let the girl sleep.

Ann went to the passageway and reported that all the family was up, and Elizabeth said it was for the best, but if Sarah could sleep, Ann should keep them out.

"Dr. Harries Davies came by again, they told me," Ann

said, "at quarter past eight. But she was still rallied and didn't begin like this until nine."

"Where was the bottle?" Elizabeth asked.

"Under her arm, I think," Ann said.

"I didn't look there."

"She's shaking again," Ann said, and Sarah sat straight up and shouted, "Tad! Tad!" She looked about but did not see him when he rushed in. Focused on a blank space beside him, she told it, "Come in, and close the door." When he drew near to her bed, she at last saw him. "Go out," she told him, "go away, and close the door."

In a few minutes, she shouted a second time, "Tad! Tad! Come in and close the door," but once he returned, she said, "Go out, go away, and close the door."

This happened repeatedly, with the beleaguered man in and out of the room. Mary brought more hot flannels, and Sarah called, "Mam! Mam!" When her mother came in, Sarah's face opened with recognition, then crumpled like a baby's about to wail. "Ma-ma," she said, relaxing, and didn't dismiss her mother.

But the shivering didn't stop. Jacob watched from the doorway and, distraught by the rattling bed, he finally turned and picked Margaret up in her nightdress from the kitchen and brought her to her sister.

"We would put her into the bed to keep Sarah warm," he said to the Welsh nurse.

"It's worth a try," Ann said.

"No, no, Tad," Margaret whimpered, clinging to her father, crablike, her arms and legs curled up and grabbing onto him.

"Sarah, it is your dear sister Margaret," Jacob said. "Here, shake hands," for though Sarah shivered, her eyes were open and she seemed sensible, and the girls clasped fingers.

"We'll have to search her," Ann said. Elizabeth was about

to say no, they did not, when Evan removed Margaret's dress as she struggled and put her, naked, in the bed.

She whimpered and wiggled but presently lay still beneath the covers, nestled against Sarah; the rattling stopped for half an hour and Sarah breathed regularly. But then it all started again, the shivering, the gasping for air, the delirium, Sarah muttering to herself between breaths words that no one could understand.

Jacob took Margaret out from the bed. The child's limbs were still pulled in tight to her torso, as if frozen stiff. Hannah re-dressed her, rubbed her, but Margaret's arms and legs wouldn't release, she spoke miserably to her parents, and they took her out to the fire.

"What was she saying?" Elizabeth asked Ann.

"'Don't kill me,'" Ann said.

"Oh, God," Elizabeth pulled the covers from the red-capped head and said, "Sarah, you may have anything you wish. What may I get for you, Sarah? Say it in Welsh, Ann."

"Beth ydych chi eisiau? Sarah."

The clock read five. "I'm going to talk to them," Ann said, and she went out to where Hannah held Margaret in her lap, wrapped in a blanket, by the fire and squatted down beside her. "Sarah is very bad. If she were my child, I would give her brandy and water in a spoon."

"I cannot offer her anything," Hannah said weakly.

"We took an oath we would not," Evan said.

Ann returned to Elizabeth and said, "They don't understand."

"Tell them she's dying," Elizabeth said.

Ann went; and the father came and said, *"Sarah, beth bynnag yr ydych ei eisiau, bydd gennych."*

"She cannot ask for anything," Elizabeth said, "He must

give it." But he would not, and Elizabeth ordered a doctor, and Emyr was sent to fetch him.

When Dr. Davies arrived at eight o'clock, Sarah continued to be restless but was "quieter than in the night," Elizabeth wrote in the log. "We think she is sensible."

The other nurses took up their duty, and Ann and Elizabeth sat with the family by the fire.

Davies told Jacob that Sarah was sinking. "Will you give her brandy and water?" he asked. Jacob would not, but—a glimmer of doubt in his eyes—he told Davies that if he liked, he could give it to her himself.

Davies went in again purposefully to the room, but he soon emerged, showing anguish. Boldly, Elizabeth asked, "Did you give it her?"

"No," he said softly. "She has been so long without fluid, I was afraid she might choke." He appealed to the father to call off the watch, and again Jacob said, "Not for the world." Davies dismissed the young nurses from Sarah's room and told them to wait by the fire with the rest.

At ten o'clock, the vicar appeared, summoned by Davies, and found Sarah speechless. He stood at the bedside, trying to get a response from her, but none came.

By the fire, they heard him say over and over, "Sarah. Sarah. Sarah."

Then again, his voice: "The Lord is my shepherd, I shall not want," and the words going on, thudding against the silence.

At noon, the children were brought to say good-bye to Sarah, and when at two o'clock John Daniels and Nell arrived, Evan Jacob did not send them away. Hannah rushed to her sister, weeping, and said, "The watch has told on her, Nell."

"Little shred in a red cap," Nell would later report, "that's what I thought at the sight of her, and it was enough to break your heart. The light of the winter's day was just leaving at three o'clock, when they let us go in. Everyone else was then out by the fire, for Hannah wept so hard that Evan was holding her, and the children were frightened.

"It was myself and John Daniel, and we had a bit of water I'd brought in a bag. We dampened a handkerchief and put it to Sarah's white lips. But it was too late. The sister-nurse came and checked her and said she was gone.

"Then everyone entered again; all of the light left the room except for a single candle. No one knew what to do, for it didn't seem real, until we were brought out of our shock when Margaret took up a shoe and smashed a pane in the window.

"The smash brought us back, fierce little Margaret, a clog in her hand. A gust from outside snuffed the flame, and when I looked again at Sarah, I could not see her face. Darkness covered her, covered us all."

"We offered to wash the body," Elizabeth said, "but they sent us away."

It was 17 December 1869, day eight.

SARAH

MARGARET, I WAS TRYING TO TELL YOU what I could not tell you. At the touch of your hand, I warmed, for you were truth and sustenance. If your warm flesh could have read my life, you would know.

I asked them to put away the books and I watched the scenes of my life in the window, where in the light was the key.

The four girls didn't come, but as I faded, they silently stood at the foot of my bed. If I shifted my eyes, I saw others, two tiny girls the size of mice perched on the shelf, hugging each other.

Comforts, there when I knew I wouldn't be saved. If I turned my head, I saw another Sarah, on a bed in a red cap, and as I spoke to her, she spoke to me.

There, now, there, now. The first Sarah and the mirror Sarah were white, transparent like fairies.

Mam didn't save me, but I forgave her, for I knew she loved me. You couldn't save me, nor the nurses, nor the American woman reporter, though I had dreamed her country reached out and took me into itself. Japan, when I dreamed, sent an emissary, who said, Now Sarah, don't cry. You are needed here, so say good-bye to your mother and father and come through the window, through the light, because We have the key.

I did not deserve to be saved. I was not strong enough to

walk down to the river bottom and breathe water into my lungs.

Margaret, I tried to tell you I couldn't breathe, and if I could not breathe the air, I could not be on earth, and I prayed for the angels to take me.

I was bones. I was turned inside out, a cold, sinning creature the Lord must forgive, yet in my sinning heart I wasn't resigned, because of desire for life that would not go away.

You were too young to remember the shining boy with the bloody red badge laid on the table and close to death.

Tad himself dug the stuffed muck from his mouth and nose and the boy breathed and lived and I knew my father's power.

As for the boy himself, I gave him scant thought as I grew, but I felt myself watched sometimes, walking to my lessons or back, and when I looked about, I imagined I saw his blue eyes.

People said I was beautiful, what did that mean? Mountains were beautiful, food was delicious, rainstorms were ecstasy, wind spoke, and I listened and felt and ate and saw.

One day when I had begun to add and read and the symbols were flowers, I sat by myself on the way home from school, chanting numbers, I think it was that day, and laughing because they arranged into posies, and how lovely. I basked in the satisfaction of how things could cluster and join together and mean, as flowery numbers and words didn't mean to me quite yet but I sensed they would, sensed how the whirl about us could slow down and break into patterns and open to me. Prideful I was even as a young girl, desiring knowledge, worldly order and harmony, and desiring a part in everything I heard about. I didn't know then that such pride is wrong.

I lingered that day by the river, postponing the walk through the door to people and chores that would pull me from my dreams, and the older boy saw me laugh, trailing my hand in the water with all my capacity for delight, my sinful hunger and glee.

"Emyr!" I said, for he was there.

"Why do you laugh?" he asked sternly. He seldom smiled; like a man, he just stared with his cutting eyes.

I laughed more and ruffled the moss, enjoying its sponginess on my palms.

He knelt beside me and stared more.

"What?" I said.

"I would like—"

"What would you like?"

"To touch your hair."

"And if you did?"

"I would know what it felt like."

"Then do it."

He did, and I laughed, because he picked up a hank as though it were a baby rabbit, cupping it in his hand. "Don't laugh," he said.

I learned he didn't want me to laugh.

From then on, I always walked to and from school by the river, so if he could get away, he would find me. In the house or in the fields if we came upon each other, we had this secret between us, tethering us.

One day, one of the bright, exciting days he found me, he showed me a wooden spoon carved with clusters of berries and a squirrel's eyes and whiskers—a love spoon.

"When you are a woman," he said, "I will make you the best spoon. We'll bundle and soon be married and go away and live in our own house."

Bundling, he said, was how you practiced sleeping together and how you became betrothed.

"Betrothed?" I asked. Not knowing the word made me angry.

"Pledged for marriage," he said, "like your mother and father."

Like Tad and Mam! I nearly laughed, the idea was so impossible, but I knew better than to laugh at his seriousness and didn't.

We lay back on the bank side by side and listened to the river and that was nice.

"You were dead," I said. "I saw you."

It was another secret between us, to say it, to talk about it.

"I came out of the mountain and lived. I can never die."

I held my breath.

"Your head," I said. "Your wound."

"My badge. I was born with it."

"I want to touch it," I said.

"You can."

I had thought it would come off red and wet on my fingers, but it didn't, and after he let me, he wanted to look at my legs.

I knew to let him would be wrong and I leaped up and told him, "You'll die like the rest of us and you can't see my legs."

I flounced off to school, glancing back as he rose unconcernedly, putting on his cap. It bothered me that he seemed not to care much one way or another, and clearly, he didn't love me. Thinking about it, I was relieved. I was learning new things every day, entranced by the possibilities in life, and I didn't want a love spoon, to bundle, to be Tad and Mam.

I felt free; I nearly forgot him, until I noticed him watching me like a sad cow in the open, when we were working or if I passed by him in the house. I hated it, believed that he taunted me, and if it wasn't a secret, then it was no good.

I tried to ignore him, spoke harshly to him, even laughed, but he wouldn't stop. I no longer walked to school by the river. I walked partway through the fields and met up with the other village girls in my class. By then I was just the age you are now,

Margaret, nine, and you and I had our bond, after I nearly killed you in the storm. I was chastened, loving the Lord, and I wished for this bigger and bigger boy to go away.

"Hit me, then," I said to him finally when he was doing it, watching me and hanging his head. I thought hitting me might get it out of his system.

"I could never," he said.

"Don't stare at me anymore."

"Sarah, I must." That particular day I was already angry—Margaret *fach*, how shall I number the sins of my outrages, my hot blood?—because Mary had told me to shove Bronwen's face in a bucket, and I said she'd drown. Mary said that's what you did when a cow wouldn't drink, and I had to learn. I refused, Mary did it herself, calling me Miss High and Mighty, Miss Delicate Feelings, she acted like Mam when Mam was away, and Mam was away at Aunt Nell's for a baby. I was angry over the baby, too.

Mary said to put Bronwen back in the barn, and when I did, Emyr was there, sharpening tools. He stared at me whilst he scraped the blades and wouldn't hit me, and the fool could have cut himself, he was so stupid. I said, "Oh, all right," to stop him, to regain my freedom; I didn't care if he cut himself to bits. I took the rope off the cow, tossed it to the ground, turned to Emyr, and lifted my skirts. "There, are you satisfied?" I said, and the barn went black: Tad had come in, and before I could let my skirts down, he grabbed my arm, nearly pulling my shoulder out of the socket.

"What is going on?" he said.

I was frightened enough, I couldn't see, but stubbornly I said, "Nothing. He wanted to look at my legs."

"You are asked to show your legs and you show them?" Tad said.

He flung me off; I fell into the hay; the cows in the barn

sensed trouble and moved about. One shat. The odor pungent around us, Tad took a peat spade from the wall and told Emyr to put down the sickle. Emyr set it at his feet, Tad raised the spade and bashed it on Emyr's cowering back once, twice, and Emyr fell.

"He didn't do anything!" I cried.

"Be silent," Tad said. "Stay away from her," he said to Emyr. Mary had come to the open doorway, and when Tad dragged me up and took me off, we pushed by her.

My father took me to where he had been mending the pasture fence and threw me to the grass. "Stay," he said, as if I were the dog. He must have remembered then what he had gone to the barn for, went back, and returned—he'd brought shears—and clipped a length of cord from the spool he had for the mending.

"Am I allowed to go?" I asked.

"I told you to stay, and if you don't, I will bind you to the fence until I am finished."

Never had Tad spoken to me in such a way. He loved me especially—I had felt it for as long as I could remember. In the time I've had since to think about my life, I wondered if maybe his love was why I thought so much of myself, was the force that drove his pride into me. I wish, now, he had loved me less.

He finished the fence, and then he worked on the sheaves whilst I sat on the ground. It went on like this for the rest of the day, his work, my waiting for him to release me. The next day it rained, and he would not even let me get up and help work to stay warm when I said I was cold.

He kept me from school for the four days this treatment continued, and if I protested, which I did—I was not easily mastered—he said I would not go to school again until I learned what I needed to learn from him.

Up to then, I had thought he was keeping his eye on me because I couldn't be trusted; that's what he had said. I asked, "What is the lesson?"

"That you are a vain, haughty girl."

I wept, believing he hated me, being changed this much toward me.

Sometimes, going to the fields together, he would speak of the Lord and he made me feel the Lord hated me, too.

Yet still, I protested. "I didn't mean anything by it, Tad."

"Mean what?" he asked.

I didn't know. I was uncertain of what he wanted me to say. If I'd had the words, the comprehension, perhaps I could have stopped the worse things that came.

The fourth day, I carried a rake back from the fields behind him, the others ahead of us, and I stubbornly said, "I'm going to school tomorrow. I'm punished enough."

He went mad, I think. He grabbed me, his face a fist, and said I would not say what I could do, said he was my father, who'd given me life, and if he was displeased, I should be sorrowful and that his pleasure should be what I wished with my sinful, roving will.

I felt I was terrible, knew it then, that I could do this to him, change him into another person. He said we would go back to the fields, and far out, as God watched from the sky the punishment I must have deserved, Tad made me kneel and put my hands on a part of him I didn't know and hold my hands there as he told me that if I was to be with anyone, it would be him, my father, to whom I owed my life, and I *would* be obedient, and I *would* not protest, and I *would* never say what happened between us. I must beg for providence from him, and what we did was the way of the world, his pleasure was mine, and I was a bad, sinful girl and if Emyr asked to look at my legs, I must have provoked him, and when

I couldn't say what I had done, Tad prompted me, and then he stopped. We went back to the house and that night and until Mam returned, he took me in his bed, telling the others he could not trust me anywhere, even at night, and each night he did things to me like the animals do.

None of you shall approach any blood relative of his to uncover nakedness; I am LORD.

If I wasn't lost already before it happened, I truly was then.

Margaret, the Lord is a great God, and a great King above all gods. In His hands *are* the deep places of the earth: the strength of the hills *is* His also. The sea *is* His, and He made it: and His hands formed the dry *land*.

In cold February, my sick blood entered my flesh and I was glad, because Tad seemed to forgive me, and I had my good loving father back. But the sickness hurt so, fresh wrath of the Lord, and in my suffering, I heard them say that my life rested with the Great Doctor—so. I surely would die. This was right, and I knew that He *must* not save me. I tried to be reconciled, ease myself down in the choking, the stakes driven into my spine, the fire of dying, but I was the same willful girl; I struggled for life.

In sleep, I dreamed of Emyr. I saw him rise like a black angel out of the mountain to find me. Like him, I was marked. Like him, I wouldn't die.

My pride!

Then there was my precious dear, my Margaret, sitting patiently by the bed, wetting my lips, and what would become of her, alone without me? I saw the world was a black place— Tad had taught me this—and I must remain for my sister.

To my shame, the food from my parents' hands choked me. Only from you could I feed, a little, then more; a long journey it was, and a puzzlement: My sinning body wasn't mine, my will split; there were days the painful knowledge of what I had done destroyed my resolve and you weren't enough and nothing was enough and when I could run, I would run in the night, hoping to outrace my body, to blend into night, to be one with the darkness, the wind, the rain, to wash Sarah, renew her, become a girl I lost.

In time I could read again, write, search in my books for the quietness that had abandoned me, bury myself there.

In a poem, I read about a girl who walked into the river and was free and I read of saints who lived only on God and died happily, taken to where angels dwell beyond misery and corruption.

But I could not walk into the river, and I was no saint. I *should* not be saved, and I did not deserve nourishment, sustenance.

I won't eat anything, then, I thought.

But I did eat.

I lay in bed, feeling my legs, in the night hating their power, which could not save me. I prayed and prayed, dreaming myself into Christ our Lord, into His agony, as if it were the dark, deep water.

Black world, black sun, and still my good father forgave me, nursed and protected me as if I were again his good child.

I took back the world in books, Margaret, gorged on them, fed my ambitious yearnings until for moments, then hours, I escaped the room. I turned words into keys and I grew despite everything, sin, justice, the Will of our Lord, for I was to lie peacefully in the bed He had sent me to, only I had no peace. I was a ravening plant, growing larger each day and bursting with blood, my hair coming in long and thick again, as if I were an ordinary girl, as if I ate in a kitchen by day, as I used to do, peacefully, loved my dear parents and all the authorities

I was meant to, and instead I fed my brain and went places and loved language and perceived how the special smell of the vaporous fields could rise up from sentences, as if I still lived where I had. I hadn't lost it, not really, the grassy dirt wheat smell watered by urine and rain mixed with shit purified by the sky; it was mine, and in my throat, saying the words, I lived even better and stronger than before—many days.

But still I hated myself, this selfish girl who took and took and sinned and yet lived, and I feared for my soul.

There was this pressure.

I LOVED ENGLISH, LOVED SCHOOL, and the vicar came and talked to me as I recovered. We discussed the Welsh saints, who had crossed treacherous water to bring us God's light, the merger of pagan religion with Christ. He was a different sort of vicar, who loved Wales, though he had gone to the Anglican seminary. He hadn't turned from his people, still loved the Fair Folk and valued their lessons.

I asked to be baptized and taken into the Anglican Church, to ready myself for a Christian death.

I knew what Mam said, that I was a miracle—miracle, ha! Silly woman, dumb animal; I thought this of my own mother.

I had never thought much about her before all that happened. I felt her, just as I felt the air on my skin, in my lungs, and thought nothing about it, as if the world I had then couldn't be lost. Mam.

You see, Margaret, I could not leave the bed, could never leave the bed, although the reasons kept changing. I learned to live there with the vicar's help.

He began coming regularly, bringing me books, speaking with me about their connections to history, law, nations. The Bible, for instance, isn't only about religion, and Shakespeare wrote for all people and represented all things, the actual, yes, but also the deep shifts of our minds.

The vicar knew so much that sometimes I believed he could see into me, and if he did, he must have forgiven me, this man of God.

Visions of food didn't trouble me much anymore. I fed in the night quickly, my eyes turned away, and I bore my pains in the day with near equanimity most of the time. If I didn't, it was *that* girl and I knew she would soon subside, stop making her silly racket, that ugly child.

I thought I was gaining assurance from the vicar. During his visits, he spoke more intensely than when I was just one of his pupils, I was his special pupil. I knew I was marked; was I also special?

The vicar stressed that we are all saved, in spite of what we are. If we are certain that we are God's Children, that our sins are forgiven and we are going to heaven, we *will* know assurance and joy. The Word instructs us on how to find this certainty and I should search there.

But as much as I studied, I did not feel release, the click of the key in the lock, in the light. The vicar said assurance wasn't simple belief or cold knowledge, but Christ Himself becoming real to you, a felt Christ. He said I had a special talent for feeling religion, and it was true I could transport myself in words, with words.

When the vicar's wife died, I read to him and comforted him and loved him because he had brought me assurance.

But the fact was, though I could soar, I would soon be dashed on the rocks, and the vicar said sickness tests our willingness to bow before God.

I wanted to be good for the vicar and for my father, and when people came, I tried to be good for them and for Wales.

Always, Margaret, you helped me; you would have stabbed me dead had I asked you to, as I deserved.

There were days I wanted to live, days to die.

Do you remember? The sun drying the fields, our shoes in the earth, singing and Nest, her magical listening to music, and the baby rabbits we saw once, killed by the scythe.

MARGARET, I WAS A BROKEN, BITTER GIRL. If I saw Emyr—who had gotten two strokes of the spade and walked free—I hated him with all my sinning soul.

People kept coming and I was tired. At first, I had liked it, the work the vicar said I had been called to do, and I liked the coins and gifts, dressing up, and I didn't mind the lying in service to Wales—and I don't mean lying in bed; I mean fabrication, untruths. I don't have to tell you. I began to feel I couldn't do it anymore, I couldn't pretend to the doctors and I couldn't submit—they hurt me, their hands like my father's hands and I asked, "Can I stop, Tad?" He said I couldn't, but tenderly, with only the tiniest edge of the knife in his tone I remembered. "I know," I said, and I lied, saying I wasn't fearful of death. "You will not die," he said, "for you have been very sick and always lived, and when you are proclaimed, the doctors won't hurt you anymore, dear Sarah." His hand was on my shoulder, the hand that could love me so and hurt. But never had he hurt me in the way he had before, since I lay abed, and he never would if I obeyed him, went through with the watch, as he asked me to, as the vicar and the famous Welsh patriot asked me to.

But I *was* afraid and thought constantly about what to do, I wondered if the reason that I hadn't *intended* to sin held weight before God. I could have talked it over with the vicar, but I was afraid of what he might say. I tried to talk to the

American woman reporter, hoping that if she believed me, then she would be able to save me—great America! She would take me far away from the bed and this house and land I so loved and now on many days in my sinning heart, hated.

The moment, however, slipped away, I wasn't strong enough to speak and I wasn't strong enough for Wales. I knew the rules: my sister kept from the bed, nurses awake at night, impossibility for me, but maybe, I struggled to think, Tad was right, there was a chance I might live.

Peacefulness washed through my body, the sense of an ending, and I could even be my old self, the laughing girl, the beautiful girl, the kind, good girl who loved and did not hate.

If my body protested, well, there was nothing to be done anyway anymore; if it hurt, well, hurt! Hurt, then!

Sometimes I couldn't feel it, but other times I could. It would start in my stomach, as so often over the months when I was in bed and seemingly well, it hurt, grinding pains, pressures that threatened to burst my flesh. And there was the shame for what I had done, and new shame, for my body opened to eyes, my filth. I read when I could and said my poems, hymns, prayers silently in my mind to keep shame away, and I lifted up out of myself, watching the window for light, but I was driven relentlessly back in the bed. It was so dark and cold, my head hurt too badly even to recite to myself; in the flickering candles, I saw my flickering life, my power of will gone, I had never been free and never would be; I would never ride on a train, feel the speed, travel to the country of the English poets, and assurance? I couldn't remember for the pain of my body that lived and lived and hurt.

Soon I stopped thinking of food at all, just thirst. I dreamed rivers and oceans, water that flowed over rocks; the ground of the earth was just rocks, long, smooth, rounded stones, all of them flowing with water and warm mist, rising.

I felt refreshed, I awoke and remembered the vicar crying at my bed when his wife died, and I wondered at that kind of love, one I knew I wouldn't feel, and I didn't think it existed between Mam and Tad, though I saw it sometimes for Tad in Mam's eyes. I thought I had tasted a corner of it with the shining boy, and he stood in the window beside you, sister, and I saw my loves.

Came the snow, Margaret, and I was dying; the white at the window was finally there against black. Breath, breath, I tried.

Thirst.

The girls came and stood motionless, silent, around the bed. The tiny ones hugged each other on the shelf and it was the two of us shrunken down in my dying; they were trinkets, reminders of my life.

I told the sister-nurse to put away the books, to take away words, for I didn't need them anymore.

I watched the snow.

Breath. Thirst. I wanted to tell you that I tried to live, I could not; forgive me. The snow was water and light in the dark window, or I turned my head and saw the other Sarah, that other girl, and when I was dying, I called for Tad, but when he came, it was another man, I tried to reach him, but it was not Tad, and so I called for my mother and she came, and I said to her, "Ma-ma, where are they taking me?" But she did not understand. She said I must give back my keys and go into the dark that first held me before the naming, before words, said I must give back my keys and go away.

In the window, I saw them! Angels! They broke free and flew through clouds and drifted in skeins across the sky, until the mountains were covered in white, fluffy like petals, as though in winter the mountains bloomed.

Their light filled the room, lit up the dark, secret corners.

Again, I smelled the vapor of summer fields and *heard* the rivers and *tasted* rain. And then, as Tad would touch the knob and turn down the lamp, everything faded, and I closed my eyes.

PART TWO

Do you not see the path of the wind and the rain?
Do you not see the oaks beating together?
Do you not see the sea scouring the land?
Do you not see the truth preparing itself?

—Gruffudd ab yr Ynad Coch

Whoever you are, we too lie like drifts at your feet.

—Walt Whitman

THE CORONER'S INQUEST

A GUARD ON THE LATE-AFTERNOON TRAIN from Pencader brought the news of Sarah's death to Carmarthen, but it wasn't believed. False rumors had circulated for days. It wasn't until ten o'clock on the night of the seventeenth, seven hours after she died, that an official telegram was received at the *Carmarthen Weekly* confirming the outcome. Christine had spent the week conferring with reporters, reading news on the wires, and poring through British newspapers people bought to the last copy. Brooklyn, Philip wrote, did the same, and he said to forge on with the excellent work. He expected daily missives—bother the content, because it all sold. Sarah Jacob was not the first and would not be the last fasting girl of the period, but she was the single one to die while nine members of the medical profession looked on.

Pary returned late on the seventeenth from the telegraph room to his office, where Christine sat with Lloyd, and said, "It's over."

"And?" Lloyd asked.

Pary stared at Christine. "You were right," he said, and she did not understand. "They've killed her," he said.

Lloyd released a long whistle. "Now there's hell to pay."

"I didn't actually think—" Christine put her face in her hands and pushed at her eyes.

"It would seem," Pary said, "that for all our skepticism, we

179

believed in science, believed the doctors would—protect her," and he dropped to the open chair. "Poor little girl."

He collected himself and informed them about the committee meeting the following day, at which they would hear the nurses' report.

Christine added dates and times to the dispatch she had composed for this possibility, sent it off, and went home to the inn.

The house was pitch-dark. Mrs. Owen ordinarily left candles burning for her in the front window at night. Christine felt for the door and found it locked. Everyone had deserted the offices when she had, in order to snatch a few hours of sleep in preparation for the long days ahead. Cold and tired, she rapped the knocker hard. When an abashed Mrs. Owen in nightcap and winter shawl creaked open the door, Christine said, "What happened?"

"The child's dead!" Mrs. Owen exclaimed. "I assumed you'd be working the night, with it all going on."

Well, I hadn't decided, Christine's inner voice said, to go over there and bury her myself. She pushed by Mrs. Owen and started upstairs, furious, for a second unable to comprehend the Welsh words that followed: "I didn't expect it."

Christine turned back: "None of us did. There's nothing else to be done tonight. I'll attend the committee meeting tomorrow."

"Will there be an inquest?" asked Mrs. Owen.

"Oh, surely," replied Christine. It would not be enough for a group of Welsh neighbors to blacken their faces and bang pots outside Evan Jacob's door, under cover of night—a local tradition still in practice—with the intention of impressing on him the displeasure of the community.

"How did you find out?" she asked Mrs. Owen, as an afterthought.

"Dr. Lewis got a telegram," she said. The Lewis family lived on the block.

In her room, Christine took out the bottle of gin she kept for nights like this when it was the only foolproof way to sleep. *Foolproof*, she thought, funny word. What Pary meant when he said they'd had faith in science was that they'd had faith in themselves, in the educated class, to correct the peasants and those who slathered it on in the name of the Lord, that myth who had gone incognito, who didn't dare show His face in this smashed-up world.

We botched it, she thought, sipping her fairy milk in bed. How she had accepted the vicar's response to her concern about Sarah's poem was, in light of what finally happened, unconscionable. Just because Sarah had written the poem two years ago didn't mean that the *message*, the sign she had given Christine to interpret, was defunct. Sarah had spoken, and she hadn't heard.

"Your face is—very alive," she remembered saying to Sarah. Stop it, she told herself, or you'll never get through tomorrow. Why could she not have been wrong? Why could she not have found that people were so much better, so much more careful than she had feared?

The gin eased her. The questions and self-recriminations stopped—for now. She curled beneath the blankets and felt that unreality one always felt at the very beginning of a death, death from the perspective of the living, the "beginning" meaning that of course it would go on and on, and what you first felt was the unreality of any walls, the insubstantiality of the solid world, because of a solid creature passed into spirit: black like smoke from the candle, definite, visible, then drifting fainter, gray into white, and merging at length with air into incomprehensible invisibility.

In the morning, she would awaken to learn that every

London paper was full of, and every London hoarding and waste wall was placarded with, the news. It was up in the same words of the telegram sent to the *Weekly*: "The Welsh Fasting Girl Is Dead."

THE GENERAL COMMITTEE MEETING was held at two o'clock on Saturday afternoon. Talk among the reporters on the train was about how silent the committee had been throughout the watch, how unforthcoming with any news. They kept saying the girl was the same, that there was no change in her condition straight through Thursday night, the night before she died. *Why?* Had the doctors withheld reports? The nurses? She must have been failing for days. What kind of a man was the coroner? Christine asked. George Rees was half Irish, pugnacious and apt to go after the doctors as well as the parents. But do you think the doctors may be charged? Why not? They're guilty, too, aren't they? Put a blush on it like that, and you could charge the entire committee. No one could imagine the nurses would be charged, but anything was possible. The majority opinion was that the Home Office would become involved, although it was too early to predict in what way or when. It was too much to expect, someone from *The Welshman* said, that the case could be locally contained: There was the involvement of London's Guy's Hospital, the widespread reporting, and the trend away from the local in criminal law. Carmarthen Jail was about to undergo modernization, in alignment with the new single-cell jails of England, along the American model.

With talk of the jail, Christine's attention shifted to thoughts of how hard Hannah and Margaret must be taking the loss. Of Evan Jacob, she had a fantastical flash of him whipped in the street.

The meeting was held at the Eagle Inn. The room was again lined with benches, its tables—except for one, at which the committee was seated—pushed to the walls. The head nurse's chair had been placed at the table's end, facing out, as if acceding to the legal direction the case was now bound toward.

Jones. Black slash eyebrows frowning, complexion pale. Marles looked wearier, if that was possible, than when Christine had seen him last. The dapper solicitor Thomas Davies was unchanged. "Gohebydd hasn't come," she whispered to Pary.

"For the doctors, nor has Vaughan or Rowlands," Pary replied. The other doctors sat in the first row of benches with the three younger nurses, facing the committee and the sister-nurse, Elizabeth Clinch. She was gray-haired and unadorned: a utilitarian bonnet, a solid black coat and dress.

"Who is that?" Christine asked Pary and Lloyd, referring to a husky man she recognized from the day of the search.

"The child's uncle," Pary said. John Daniel sat in the middle benches among the reporters. There were nearly fifty from the press, as the room wouldn't hold more and today's meeting was closed to the public—and had been kept from the public, who might have amassed outside in force. Gwilym Marles called roll and announced, "Dr. Vaughan declined to attend, having resigned his office as a member of the medical committee on Thursday night."

This was news. Marles continued: "Dr. Rowlands also declined because he had nothing to do with the case after Saturday, eleventh December, when he saw the girl and was dismissed for his statement to the press. Dr. Rowlands noted that the father refused to leave the room during the medical examination."

So, Jacob interfered, Christine thought. Not a surprise, though his interference could tell on him in any number of ways, most of them damning.

The white-haired Dr. Lewis moved that the Reverend E. Jones, B.D., vicar of the parish, be voted to the chair, and Thomas Davies seconded.

Jones stood at the table and plainly said, "When we last met here on a former occasion, we rejoiced at the prospect of having the alleged fasting of Sarah Jacob thoroughly investigated." He paused. "We now meet as much sadder, but not wiser, men. I hope for enlightenment from the nurses' report."

The sister-nurse opened the puffy brown soft-covered book, adjusted her spectacles, and delivered the contents in a staid, officious voice—how else could she have read it? Christine surmised concealed emotion, a caring for Sarah. And perhaps disdain for the entire proceedings? Christine felt connected to the nurse as she recited the grim tale: the records of pulse and temperature, Sarah's spirits, her color, her sleep, the output of bladder and bowels, the reading, the conversations, the belated visit of the first doctor and the doctors' intermittent visits thereafter, the goings in and out of the family, the additions made to the diary by the doctors, their reports sounding increasingly terse and, Christine adjudged, more obfuscating, less and less in tune with what anyone clearly could tell was a steady decline in Sarah from the third day—clearly could tell, that is, if you were there day by day, moment by moment, as none of the doctors had been.

There was much yet to be learned, but already before them was evidence that Sarah had eaten before the watch, and that Evan Jacob had interfered and been eerily nonplussed until near the end—and that from the perspective of the doctors, there had been stormy confusion: false rallies, a perplexing mixture of symptoms. Christine felt mounting horror as the record progressed and the doctors kept telling the local committee, "No change." In the eye of the storm was Sarah, wanting nothing, refusing food and water—as if a part of her desired death?

And yet, what might happen to one's volition and life force under Sarah's circumstances? What were the biological changes, wondered Christine, the physical sensations she'd undergone? Sarah could not tell, the nurse reported, when she was about to make water.

"We could not get her warm." Mention of a cap, coverlets. The doctors afraid—so the nurse seemed to suggest—and the vicar asking Jacob to call it off and the parents' bloody pact and the statement that "they had seen her worse before." Margaret stripped and put into the bed—Christine closed her eyes at this. The father's phrase "Not for the world." The delirium at the end was the hardest to listen to, the thrashing, and the thirst.

"I pronounced her at three in the afternoon," concluded Nurse Clinch. "Ann Jones and I offered to wash the body, but Dr. Davies reiterated that we'd been dismissed."

The vicar was the first to speak after the recitation. "You say she was insensible at the time of death?"

"Yes, and had been for an hour or more."

"And you say she was frequently asked if she was in any pain?"

"Frequently. She always said no, just the one complaint of headache. When I changed her nightdress, she thanked me and said I did not cause her pain."

Marles asked, pro forma, whether with surety Sarah had not been fed for the entire term of the watch and it was confirmed; he asked for corroboration that she had been offered anything she wanted and was told yes, many times each day.

"Only the uncle explicitly offered?"

John Daniel rose and said he had asked Sarah to take a drink, and the sister-nurse said that nothing had passed Sarah's lips except for what was offered by her uncle and aunt when she was unconscious and near death.

Thomas Davies asked Dr. Lewis if it was true that on Thursday he had conveyed to the father that Sarah was sinking.

"I said the nurses had told me she threatened to sink," said Lewis.

"You did not agree?" asked Thomas Davies.

"I was uncertain, as I saw the pulse as the one possibly alarming symptom. The nurses were more familiar with how she had changed."

"Dr. Harries Davies," the vicar said, "We received a report from you on Thursday night that there was no material change in Sarah Jacob's condition."

It was just short of an accusation.

Dr. Davies stood at his seat. "She had rallied, sir, when I saw her. And I had never seen starvation in a patient who was otherwise free of active disease."

There was a long silence. Davies seemed to await permission to sit. No matter the sincerity and obvious pain revealed by the young doctor, his report had been misleading, had been, even in view of the rally, egregiously rose-colored. So thought Christine.

"Then your summation would be starvation as cause of death," said the vicar, "even though the onset of delirium was late and the usual wasting didn't apply?"

"'Usual wasting'?" said Marles.

"The nurses have said she was—plump," said the vicar.

"Without the results of an autopsy—" Davies began.

"Will there be an autopsy?" asked Marles.

"It is being arranged," Davies said.

"John Daniel!" said Marles.

Again, Daniel stood. "Dr. Davies told the parents the child

was fine on the day he went to fetch you. Then why did he fetch you?"

"He told me she was in grave danger."

"Early on Thursday, sir," Marles said to Davies, "you said 'grave danger' and that night you reported to us 'no change' in her condition?"

"The rally—" said Davies.

"Rally or no! You said she was 'grave,' and you told us 'no change'?" Marles turned to Evan Jones and said, "We were not kept informed."

"As the nurse reported," the vicar put in, "I saw her myself on Thursday and I asked Jacob to call off the watching. He would not."

"Madam," said Marles to Nurse Clinch, "you stated to the father on the girl's last night that she was dying, and he would offer her nothing?"

"I told Nurse Jones to tell him in Welsh."

Nurse Jones stood. "I told him. Then he went to Sarah and said she could have anything she wanted, but he would not offer it."

"And he never would call off the watching?" said Marles to Dr. Harries Davies, who was still on his feet.

"He would not."

"Sit," Marles said to Harries Davies, and Marles turned away in his chair in disgust.

"Are there any further questions?" asked the vicar.

Thomas Davies moved that the committee adjourn until after the postmortem and this was seconded and carried unanimously.

"I should like," Marles said, "before we adjourn, to read the letter of resignation sent to the committee on Thursday by Dr. Vaughan."

Vaughan resigned because he was not allowed to examine

the patient. Taking her pulse was all he could do and that, given Sarah's hysterical condition, was not a reliable measure. Vaughan respectfully reminded the committee of his earlier letter of 6 December, when he advised a single doctor to better assess subtle changes—the test, he wrote on the sixth, could well result in the girl's death.

"MARLES AND JONES TRUSS UP HARRIES DAVIES as the sacrificial lamb," Lloyd said on the train, "and in big splashy colors illustrate to the press that they were uninformed. Read: They had no reason to appeal to a magistrate to remove her to hospital. Davies knew she was dying, but not them—and then!" He chuckled and cracked his knuckles.

"Could you desist?" asked Pary.

"Sorry, old chap. Then Marles reads the letter from Vaughan, throwing culpability back on the committee! What's his intention? They were informed that she could die! They were advised to select one doctor and they stuck to five."

"But advice probably came from several doctors," said Pary, "and the doctors disagreed. Davies was the man most involved in the case straight through—the committee knew him better."

"They all want to distance themselves," said Lloyd. "Fritter and scurry like rats from a ship." Christine hadn't seen that. She had seen upset, remorse—but Lloyd was right: Despite any regret, they would save their own skins; they were highly educated survivors, people who thought a lot of themselves. Where they were blind was in their belief in empiricism, the age's faith in evidence and experiment, as if these could not be as flawed as intuition and reason, and as if there weren't things necessarily barred from experimentation.

"The only ones in the clear," said Lloyd, "are the nurses.

They had their marching orders. Four lowly nurses, up against doctors and preachers and lawyers."

"Oh, to hell," said Christine. "They let her die, just like the rest."

"Why did I not see it!" Pary exclaimed. "The vicar reminded Marles that he had asked the father to call off the watch on Thursday. Why did the vicar himself not tell the committee that night how bad she seemed?"

Vested interest, Christine thought, same as the interests of Lewis and Davies that clouded their diagnostic vision.

"You didn't see it," Lloyd said, "because Marles turned attention off Jones and onto Jacob's refusal to do anything." Vaughan's letter had shown the doctors disadvantaged by Evan Jacob's directives. Marles established Jacob as the guiltiest party.

At the *Weekly*—lately the *Daily*—the correspondents scattered to sift through their notes and write up reports, and the rain that had threatened since afternoon, when the temperature climbed, poured down, melting the carpet of snow.

CHRISTINE AWOKE IN THE NIGHT and the rain had stopped, but it started again in the morning. She dressed, donning clogs, her cropped flannel skirt, and an oilcloth coat. She expected a great deal of company at the vicar's Sunday service and saw many people she knew on the train, and at the church, people drawn there perhaps by talk at the smithy's, at the butcher's, the public houses, the parlors where the newspapers were read; drawn perhaps by memories of Sarah, for neighbors who had helped bring in the potato crop and the hay on the Jacob farm, who had formed their own opinions, people who may have braved repugnance or deep disappointment to call on the Jacobs yesterday, while others hadn't yet decided whether to shun the Jacobs or to embrace their pain, their morally suspect but understandable capitulation to the will of the powerful, their going along at the instigation of flamboyant words, their neglect to grasp that they were pawns in the Big Men's Game. But yet, she thought, observing the horses and vehicles lining the road, and the wet folk inside filling pews and crowded against the stone walls, there would be those who were aware that they themselves had blindly lashed out, propagated a wish or a simple opposition sprung from their powerlessness, from a shamed history, and were in emotional league with the vicar: They had embraced Evan Jacob's decision to let his child die.

What would the vicar say for himself? What would he say for them? Or was today just one more act of the carnival show, the type of excitement they had attached to since Sarah put away her bowl.

Christine saw the boy guides, the old man who had first driven her to this church. She recognized dairymen and a group of correspondents—no one from the *Weekly*—and there were a remarkable number of women, more than she had seen anywhere except at market, women of different ages and stations, and some had brought children. She doubted that many were regular congregants at St. Michael's. Of the farming women, she had to suppose that they were Nonconformists who did not, as a rule, worship here but had come on Sunday to the Church of England in witness, in the trench of profound sorrow.

The organ began, and Christine worried that assigning blame out of the mishmash of the eight days would be impossible and that nothing at last would be construed as actionable or worth anyone's while. But no, the English would not let the Welsh get away with a well-advertised and witnessed murder of a child, for all their part in it.

The vicar rose to the pulpit in his clerical garb after the first

hymn was sung. His Scripture reading and prayer acknowledged the Christmas season. The people sang again and listened quietly to the vicar's bland sermon about the birth of a
holy babe. He then announced a birth in the village and the
death of Sarah Jacob, "a member of this congregation." Christine heard a woman nearby say in Welsh, "Now." But at legal
risk, Christine knew, there wasn't much he could say.

It was humid and cold, wet clothes breathing rain against
stone, everyone waiting as the vicar's pale hands set aside his
Bible and took up another smaller volume and opened it to a
page marked by a ribbon and read in Welsh, in his *hwyl*, in his
hiareth, from the *Hebrew* prayer book.

> Verily, we confess,
>   we have sinned
> We have trespassed
> We have dealt treacherously
> We have stolen
> We have spoken slander
> We have committed iniquity
>   and have done wickedly
> We have acted presumptuously
> We have committed violence
> We have framed falsehood
> We have counseled evil
> We have uttered lies
> We have scorned
> We have rebelled
> We have blasphemed
> We have revolted
> We have acted perversely
> We have transgressed.

He shut the book to a long silence as people absorbed his confession and negation of confession through the couching of his regret in printed words and the assignment of blame to the community rather than to himself. How could he? Christine thought, with his responsibility and power? Or was this the best he could do under the circumstances? Did he show humility, including himself with them? Before she thought further, he left so suddenly, nobody knew it was over. People whispered, craned necks at the altar, and Christine slipped out and set off around the church to the only exit, in back, he could have taken without processing down the aisle. She didn't think what she might say if she caught him—but no. Already he was briskly walking across the fields behind the graveyard, his open coat swinging, getting smaller across the rain-driven winter fields, away from their eyes, to his womanless house. He soon disappeared, and only then did the bewildered congregants emerge from the church.

On Monday, the rain bore down again and the lane to the Jacob farm grew impassable. Sarah's body was wrapped in a blanket and tarp, roped to a constable, and galloped over the fields on horseback.

The autopsy was conducted in an upper room of the Eagle Inn. When the rain ceased and the temperature dropped and the authorities learned the lane had frozen, they returned the body by wagon early on Tuesday morning. The coroner's jury was required to view the body in situ. Thirteen parish men completed their viewing in the parlor bedroom where Sarah had died. The traditional Night of Tears, and the burial, would not occur until after the inquest. "It was a blessing the cold came," said John Cross, who, with Neville Watkins, had performed Monday's postmortem examination and who testified on the Tuesday at "The Inquest on the body of Sarah Jacob, the 21st day of December 1869, commencing at noon at the house of Ann Charles, New Inn, in the parish of Llanfihangel-ar-Arth, in the county of Carmarthen, before George Rees, Gentleman, Coroner of the said county."

The public room of this landowner's house was high-ceilinged, gloomy, and adequate to the emergency accommodation of the jury, the witnesses, and the inevitable press. On Monday, George Rees had already compromised his high-principled view of the gravity of the situation with the public-house postmortem procedure, for lack of nearby facilities. But with the cleared weather, he chose his neighbor's house to better serve the formal approach he deemed right and proper. Enough had already been slapdash. If they did not do this right then, by God, everyone in this damn country deserved what they got.

The *Carmarthen Weekly*'s publisher, George Rees's good friend, gave a sketch of the man to reporters that Tuesday, who passed word along.

The outspoken Rees blustered into the house on the dot of the scheduled time, and Christine was impressed by the figure he cut, dark and forceful, though he wasn't amused when the medical examiners were considerably tardy. "Will they in the end come?" he asked. "Have they been given the correct location? Will someone explain why nothing is managed as I ask it to be?" The order of witnesses was then rearranged.

"The jury has seen the body," he said, "and I called their attention to its state particularly to enable them to appreciate the medical evidence. Our purpose is to ascertain how Sarah Jacob died. We are not here to criminate anyone, but if anything crops up that indicates a breach of criminal law, it will be for us to advise that those so criminated take their trial on the charge."

He sat in an ornate straight-backed chair beside a matching table, on which he drummed his thick fingers, which were adorned by two heavy gold rings. Every so often his rings hit the table with startling loud cracks. Others were seated in plainer chairs at tables or in rows of hastily arranged groupings—and he could have been a gamekeeper on a country estate, confronting a poacher gang brought before him. That is, until the proceedings got underway. The medical talk, the detailed exposure of a body in extremis, the ghastly *matter* of their purpose, thought Christine, scraped off the room's civilized sheen.

The sister-nurse repeated the facts, and a series of questions were posed, which offered up no more insight.

By then, the two tardy necroscopists had dashed in, very red from the cold. Their evidence was taken, John Cross going first.

He stood at the other side of the coroner's table; a steely, thin, blond man, he was sworn and seated. He said to George Rees, "I am a surgeon in practice at Newcastle-Emlyn. Yesterday, in conjunction with Mr. Watkins, I examined the body of Sarah Jacob, said to be twelve and a half years old. It measured fifty-four inches, was plump and well formed, and showed indications of puberty. The brain was perfectly healthy. The incision made from the top of the chest to the lower body displayed a fine layer of fat. The lungs, heart, and great vessels were healthy, and contained little blood. On examining the alimentary canal, I observed there was not the slightest obstruction from the mouth to the termination of the gut. The stomach contained three teaspoons of dark gelatinous fluid, having a slight acid reaction with litmus paper. The small intestines were empty, but the colon and rectum contained about half a pound of excrement, in a hard state, which I handed to P. Sergeant Scurry. The liver was healthy, the gallbladder distended with bile; kidneys and spleen perfectly sound, urinary bladder empty. The body was free from disease, judging from the healthy appearance of the organs. Judging from the appearance of the excrement, I should say that it might have been there a fortnight. I attribute the death to want of water and food; I also believe the child labored under hysteria, showing itself in fits, and in her case by refusing to take food before the public."

He sat, and Neville Watkins, a short, tentative person who was thrice instructed by George Rees to "Speak up!" was sworn in and said, "I am a surgeon in practice at Newcastle-Emlyn. I joined the last witness in the postmortem examination of the deceased. I agree with his testimony in every respect. I add that on examining the feet, I found that the nails had been carefully trimmed within a week or ten days. Under the nail of the right foot's great toe, I observed a dark mark, as if pinched by the scissors—but it was a large bruise and fresh, and I am unsure of its cause. On looking at the girl's shoulders and armpits, I found the right shoulder much more prominent than the other, the left armpit being very hollow, sufficiently so to contain a half-pint bottle."

Reginald Pary, seated beside Christine, wrote on his pad, "BOTTLE, BRUISE." In parentheses, he wrote, "COLON."

Dr. Harries Davies was sworn and asked to corroborate the key points in the sister-nurse's testimony. He concluded that as late as Thursday evening, at the time of Sarah's last rally, her temperature was normal. Temperature was a sure sign, according to diagnostic theory, that a patient was not close to death. In hindsight, however, Davies thought she died from want of nourishment. He stressed that he never conversed with the child about taking food, because of the parents' strict orders.

At that, Mr. Rees called an adjournment until two o'clock,

when Evan Jacob appeared voluntarily, without his wife, and reopened the proceedings.

Christine couldn't help feeling pity for him as he took the witness spot at the coroner's table, his pale eyes focused beyond the horizon of heads. Darkly chapped about the face, his hair lank and oily, he cleared his throat and said, "I was not made aware by the doctors that my daughter was in danger of dying of starvation. I believed her incapable of taking food, though I cannot say how she survived so long without. If anyone had clearly told me that she was dying for want of food and drink, I would not have refused her access to any."

His claim, and his misconceived, outrageously detailed answers to the coroner's questions about Sarah's excretory history—after what the sister-nurse and the pathologists had said—sounded baldly mendacious, and discomfort at hearing it was barely concealed by many in the crowd. "She had no motion from the bowels," Jacob said, "for the first three weeks of her fasting, but then she had daily motions for a week—very large stools once every day, quite hard; and for the same weeks she passed the usual quantity of water, as much as a girl of her age could be expected to pass. Her very last stool, in November 1867, was large, and she had no stool again until the time of her death.

"From the end of December 1867 until the watching, she didn't pass water, and if she did, it was from shock. I am sure of what I say, because I myself made her bed from 1867 to the day the nurses came. Nobody else could make it so well and so smooth." At last, Jacob signed his deposition and sat beside his solicitor while John Daniel and Gwilym Marles deposed and the three junior nurses were questioned, driving Jacob's statements further out of the realm of credence.

The winter gloom of the high-ceilinged room descended as the day passed; Christine could barely see to write on her note-taking pad. Lloyd had ceased writing and threw back his head to observe the dark uppermost reaches. Pary scratched away. Dark figures brought lamps, and as they were lit, the smart coroner connected the cologne bottle with the hollow beneath Sarah's left arm. "The sister-nurse testified," he said to Ann Jones, "that when you told Evan Jacob the cologne bottle was missing, he reached into the bedclothes and took out the bottle from under Sarah's arm."

"Yes," said Ann Jones, "where the sister-nurse had forgotten to search—the armpit."

"He did it quickly?"

"Yes."

"Automatically? Did it seem as though he knew where it was liable to be?"

"Yes, sir, I would say so."

Christine had already presumed that the bruise on Sarah's toe was evidence that she had tried to prize the cork from the water bottle in her thirst. Poor creature! Desperately thirsty, and ironically how she had laughed when the bed broke and the water ran down—and Christine remembered that, according to the nurses' testimony, the bottle had been uncorked that previous time water flooded the bed.

And the parents had said, "We wet her lips once every fortnight." And they had said on another occasion, "We wet her lips several times a day." Which was it?

Sarah had probably taken the cologne bottle for its liquid or mistaken it in the beginnings of her delirium for the bottle of sustenance, milk or the like, she may have concealed in bed beneath her left arm.

And if Jacob hadn't given it to her, he had known it was there.

George Rees finished with Ann Jones and began his summation.

"I cannot understand how rational persons could believe the story of the girl's fasting. The father deceived the doctors, however, and I think they are not to blame. We have two branches of inquiry before us: first, the cause of death, and, second, who is responsible. The cause—there can be no question—was starvation, and the responsibility was on the father. In law, the father was responsible not merely to provide but also to induce the child to take food. The mother was not responsible, unless it could be proved she was given food for the child by her husband and withheld the food from the child. The criminal negligence is on the father only, but it is a question of degree." His rings sparkled in the lamplight. "I cannot understand how the father could tell such a story on oath today and endeavor to impose on the jury such hideous nonsense.

"From the start, I say, which was it easier to believe, that the natural laws were reversed, or that the father was stating falsehoods? The latter," he said drily. "To these falsehoods, life has been sacrificed. It is for us a question of murder or manslaughter—which?"

In just fifteen minutes, the jury was back.

The foreman said, "Died from starvation, caused by the father's negligence to induce the child to take food."

The murder/manslaughter distinction was up to the coroner.

"He offered her anything she wanted," Rees said, "but failed to induce her, and therefore the negligence constitutes manslaughter."

The coroner made out the warrant for Evan Jacob's committal for trial, and as expected, Jacob was granted bail.

All anyone knew of the present activities at the homestead consisted of conjecture and rumor. Since Friday, the family had closed themselves off to the larger world that

Jacob had, earlier, stridently invited in. Christine wanted to pay her respects for the sake of Hannah and Margaret, but it would have felt unseemly under the circumstances. In truth, she was relieved to be spared seeing Sarah's body. Its endless detailing was already exhaustive, as in her life, and the irony of its exposure, its use, when the person herself—the *soul* had cried out to be seen, understood, loved, and had not been in any way that did her a whit of good—*that,* Christine thought, was a crime that could not be assigned or even named in any satisfactory form.

CHRISTINE TRACKED THE MAJOR PRESSES as they weighed in on the case. Harold Turner, superintendent of Guy's Hospital, who had granted permission to send the nurses to Wales, took the onus on himself, writing in a letter to *The Times* of London that no one else at Guy's had known of the plan. He emphasized, however, that he had counted on the local doctors to do their duty. Had the girl been in Guy's, no parent would have prevented measures to preserve her life.

The Lancet spoke out under the headline STARVED TO DEATH! They wrote that the only medical aspect of interest ought to have been the cure of the child.

> *That someone had been fraudulently and surreptitiously supplying this miserable girl with food, there can be no shadow of a doubt, and the medical attendants should not have allowed themselves to have been in the least degree influenced, as two of them appear to have been, by those who were obviously interested in the maintenance of the fraud. The practical lesson is clear—the medical profession should have nothing to do, directly or indirectly, with the investigation of any of the absurd stories*

> *arising, from time to time, out of ignorance, deceit, or*
> *superstition. The sacrifice of this child ought to be enough*
> *to make any future attempts at similar impostures penal.*

By no one was the verdict of the coroner's jury considered sufficiently conclusive. Blame was attributed to the committee, the doctors, the parents, and Guy's Hospital. The public, and science itself, it was written, ought to be put in the dock. Christine saw that for many, Sarah Jacob had begun a new life as martyr.

THE MAGISTERIAL HEARING

Summonses are issued in Wales

Special dispatch to The Sun, *23 February 1870*

By Christine Thomas

Evan Jacob of Lletherneuadd, in the parish of Llanfihangel-ar-Arth, in the county of Carmarthen, farmer, and Hannah Jacob, his wife, were yesterday cited to appear before the Magistrates at Llandysul on Monday, 28 February 1870, on a charge "that you did on the 17th day of December last, at Lletherneuadd, in the parish of Llanfihangel-ar-Arth, in the county of Carmarthen aforesaid, feloniously kill and slay one Sarah Jacob, of Lletherneuadd aforesaid, against the peace of Our Lady the Queen, Her Crown and Dignity and contrary to the statute in that case made and provided."

Most in the vicinity expected a renewal of judicial proceedings under a government prosecution. As reported last month by this correspondent, the coroner's inquest is to inquire and ascertain all the particulars, but no person is sent to trial on such an inquiry. Whenever the case is so serious that death has been caused and a coroner's inquest has been held, the next probable step is a hearing before the magistrates, where a person or persons are charged with the crime and have opportunity of a defense, so that the evidence may be fully investigated prior to placement to trial.

At first it was under the consideration of the law officers of the Crown that the whole of the committee should be summoned, but it was later and recently decided that proceedings should be taken only against the medical gentlemen who superintended the watching, as well as against the parents of the deceased child. The doctors were therefore also served yesterday, additionally, to appear.

❧

Carmarthen, Wales
5 March 1870

Dearest James,

Vinnie Smyth has written to me that a case such as Sarah's is a correspondent's refining fire. And indeed, I feel closer to you, dear, than before Sarah's death—is it wrong? Women must, as the best minds have told us, go into the world and be a full part of it, roll its marred soils against our own fingertips, stain them, confront the most baffling crimes.

The hearing is presently adjourned until the fourteenth because of the opening of the Spring Assizes. If the hearing drags on and concludes that Jacob and others will be sent to trial, they will have to wait for the Summer Assizes. Evan Jacob's solicitor applied to the court for an earlier trial, but his appeal was rebuffed in favor of the hearing's completion, and Jacob's bail will then be enlarged accordingly. Jacob has already sold portions of his land, and if the hearing finds him guilty, he will have to sell more. I should have thought help would come from a few of the prosperous parties involved, but it seems Jacob is left to fend for himself. The turnabout of Hannah's summons is another surprise. I cannot imagine how she will weather this latest development alongside the loss of her child.

As the hearing approached, I felt I had to make contact with Hannah, and yet the delicacy of the situation forbade it. At last, I took the lock of Sarah's hair that Hannah gave me to a jeweler and purchased a portraiture case on a chain for Hannah to wear around her neck. A side sealed in Sarah's black curl and on the other I had inscribed *S.J.* and the dates of her birth and death. I hoped it would comfort Hannah. No matter the outcome of any hearing or trial, as a mother myself, she haunts me.

There remained the problem of how to present my remembrance to her. I settled on the vicar to take it, having heard that he has called on the family each week since Sarah's death and would know how to give it to Hannah discreetly. I didn't want Jacob to claim and sell it. I went to St. Michael's but found the church locked. I located Sarah's grave by the names of Evan Jacob's dead parents: the still-unmarked mound stiffened by cold. It took my breath. I sat on the bench under the yew tree and waited for the vicar. In the distance, the uppermost slopes of the hills were covered in mist, as you said they would be. Were they still even there? I couldn't remember their shapes before the shearing of winter. I couldn't fathom how I had backed down to the vicar on the day of the search, or believed the watch safe, dismissing my own intimations.

When the cold encased me and Jones didn't come, I left. I sent a messenger with the necklace and a note to the vicar's home. He wrote back and promised to take it. I did not understand how the vicar continued relations with Jacob. He had seen Sarah die. He had publicly blamed Evan Jacob. And the doctors! When they appeared on the first day at the hearing, it was without legal representation. They were so convinced of their innocence, or so unconvinced of any will to hold them accountable, that they believed they'd been summoned merely to testify as they had before. Were the wordings of their summonses different from those sent to the Jacobs? I asked fellow reporters, and the received wisdom was that they were not. We hold firm assumptions about ourselves, and others, and though a fact may be placed squirming and bleating straight in front of us, do we see it?

How *may* we see? Truly see?

Always,
Christine

THE MAGISTERIAL HEARING WAS CONDUCTED over a stable and a brew house, belonging to the Wilkes Head Inn, not far from where Christine had visited Harries Davies and his birds. The three of Her Majesty's justices of the peace for the county sat beneath the pitched roof of the loft, which was drafty and stank of rotted straw and hops.

Alun Lloyd's stomach kept him at home, and Christine traveled to and from the hearing with Pary and sat with him in the fumy loft. Nights, they compared notes, once at his house near the newspaper office. He had the dark lower floor of a ramshackle town home. His rooms were tacked, like his office, with charts, maps, and clippings—but these walls, layered and peeling, were unhealthy skins, a sad palimpsest of the news.

His kitchen table was cluttered with books and magazines, just a free square on the surface for his cup and plate.

"I've lured you here with gin," he joked. As if I were young, she thought, catching the tiny bat squeak of sexuality, easy to ignore.

"Reginald, this is an awful place. Why don't you move?"

He wasn't offended. "It suits," he said. "I grew up in a

rambling house in a big family, but I'm rather happier here. Do as I please. Study."

Upstairs, his neighbors spilled marbles onto the floor—or that was the sound. "What's that?" she asked, startled to her feet.

"Day and night," he said, unconcerned, "they're tromping about."

"There's your insomnia," she said, but he only shrugged.

Throughout the hearing, the Jacobs sat tucked away by the fire, Hannah wrapped in a long black shawl. Christine asked herself for the hundredth time if she should suspect Hannah, and of what? Had she been afraid of her husband? I have been afraid, Christine acknowledged, without men's rights.

On the first day, Mr. Coleridge, for the prosecution—the only one wigged and robed, which rendered the loft environment sadder, shabbier—faced the bench and gave a brief history of the case, asserting that parents were not allowed to suffer their children to starve themselves, but were obliged to use every means of providing food. He drew attention to the cavity found beneath Sarah's left arm, suggesting that a bottle was kept there for Sarah to feed on under the covers. He detailed the rules of the watching and read the agreement signed by the father.

Mr. Fitzwilliams remarked, "That is just a granting of license to watch."

Fitzwilliams, the chief magistrate, commented frequently, while the other two, nestled in lap robes, hung on his words. The chief's unprepossessing troll-like appearance would come to belie his unyielding intention—so Christine would see.

Mr. Coleridge paused, then continued: "As I am instructed, the mother was involved during the entire period in looking after the child. The father would often be absent, as was his duty, to work for the family. The mother would both by law and custom be expected to attend more to her child, and we have therefore brought an action against the mother.

"When money was given, we find the father said, 'Do not give it to me; put it on the child's bosom.' And no doubt plenty of money was given. Then we find that all sorts of gifts were also given the child. Looking at the whole matter—the child's fantastic dress for the purpose of exhibition, the money, the gifts, and the secret bottle of nutriment under her arm—it strikes me as a sort of dramatic performance! For gain and to defraud the public, and the performance brought about death.

"As to the doctors: In law, any people conspiring together for an unlawful purpose from which conspiracy death happens are guilty of manslaughter.

"I submit that the doctors having acted on the committee, although the committee are not before you—I repeat that the doctors having accepted the invitation of an illegally constituted society—for had it not been for the watching, the child would not have died—they undertook to perform an illegal act.

"The doctors undertook charge of the watching; they were to see that the child was not to go on in this deceit. But what did the doctors do?

"They went on occasion to see the child; they received the nurses' reports. When symptoms of exhaustion set in, they should have insisted upon the girl's being fed, but instead they said, 'She may last a little bit yet; there is still heat about her mouth.'

"Dr. Davies, very much frightened, went to the brother-in-law of Evan Jacob on Thursday and asked him to go and get the father to give food, instead of the doctor giving food himself. It might have been given by the stomach pump, or by injection into the nostrils, and if the parents refused to cooperate, he could have brought in the aid of the law.

"But nothing of the kind was done. The brother-in-law went, but the father refused to give the child food, the mother refused, and the child wouldn't even take water.

"If, as I am told, two of the doctors tended to believe in the fasting and the others did not, it seems to me the unbelievers were most guilty. They had perfect knowledge of the outcome."

The medical men applied for an adjournment in order to employ counsel and the hearing adjourned until the third day of March, at 11 in the morning. Mr. Marles was called to witness and, at the request of Mr. Clifton—the young, nervy solicitor to the doctors—read a letter concerning the rules set forth for the test, "that it must be distinctly explained that the object of the watching was not the withholding of food, but ascertaining whether food was given." Mr. Coleridge interjected: "I said that in my opening address."

Mr. Clifton said, "It bore repetition."

Coleridge: "We say there was gross negligence in carrying out the test."

Fitzwilliams: "We have read in the depositions that parental control of the child continued during the watching."

Coleridge: "But the child died, and the medical men should have prevented it! A committee was formed. They appointed a subcommittee of doctors, who took the responsibility by committing to act."

Fitzwilliams: "The doctors were to see if there were dangerous symptoms, and they said they did not see any."

Coleridge: "They did see! Dr. Davies sent for the brother-in-law on that account."

Fitzwilliams: "I think Dr. Davies would not admit that he saw such symptoms. Therefore, all that Mr. Coleridge might contend for him was crass ignorance."

Coleridge: "I would rather say gross neglect."

Fitzwilliams: "No, if you look at it as gross neglect, it then tells against the nurses. They were continually with the child."

Evan Jones sat for a long examination and cross-examination, tracing the rise of the case that led to the watching and minimizing his own part. Gohebydd emphatically spoke to the Jacobs' desire for the watch. On the fourth day of the hearing, Dr. Fowler was sworn in. All he had observed, the stately, thoroughly confident Dr. Fowler put forward.

He was cross-examined by Clifton, who asked, "How long, in your experience, may persons live without food?"

"As to persons in a normal state of health, my opinion formed by my reading only," said Fowler, "is that they may live lacking food from seven to ten days without serious symptoms, or death, arising. If water is taken, a person may last much longer."

Mr. Bishop, solicitor to the Jacobs—kind-faced, polite, and ill-prepared—inquired about the possibly different survival rates of a person who suffered from catalepsy, the disease Harries Davies had cited in his early attendance on Sarah. Christine had read that hysteria, catalepsy, and epilepsy were allied conditions on a continuum of nervous disorders, each bearing a relation to mind and body, and she expected the eminent man to clarify their relationships.

"I know nothing of catalepsy," Fowler said. "But I shall say that hysteria can mimic any disease. These patients have the propensity to deceive and malinger. Hysterical patients are prone to sham living food-free. Children who don't take food in the presence of their parents are called 'night feeders.' My opinion was that she was a night feeder."

Mr. Coleridge rose to reexamine and asked, "If you had

been attending her, how long would you have let her go without food?"

Mr. Fitzwilliams cut in: "That is a long question; it assumes a fallacy against the doctors. They were not in the position of medical men attending her."

Coleridge: "We are assuming that the medical men misconducted themselves in their dealings with the girl."

Fitzwilliams: "You have no right to assume misconduct, Mr. Coleridge, since there is no evidence of it whatsoever."

Coleridge: "We say the medical men did not interfere and administer food when they ought to have done."

Fitzwilliams: "But the doctors were strictly to look on and to be consulted by the nurses. Take it at the worst, you cannot put it otherwise than that the doctors erred in judgment." Pary scrawled exclamation marks on his notebook, which he showed to Christine.

She scrawled back, "WHY DO THE OTHER TWO SYCOPHANTS GO ALONG WITH WHATEVER HE SAYS?" Their job, evidently, was silence.

Coleridge: "The doctors were there as medical practitioners, to pronounce upon the girl's condition. We say they combined together and are responsible for the consequences whatever they may be. That is a principle of law. There is a case in the books that if a man be not a doctor and undertakes to give medicine and attend to a case, and death ensues from his negligence, the crime is manslaughter."

Clifton: "But it is a very different thing altogether, where a man is not a doctor."

Coleridge: "But if he be a doctor, you seem to infer that he may kill the entire parish and escape!"

Fitzwilliams: "But in that case, he would be an *unskilled* doctor. That is your misfortune, if you submit to an unskilled doctor, and you must suffer the consequences. Every man is not as this man," and he gestured to Fowler.

Mr. Coleridge persisted that he had a right to put the question to which Mr. Fitzwilliams had taken objection.

Fitzwilliams said, "I cannot allow it to be put."

Mr. Coleridge claimed gross neglect; Mr. Fitzwilliams said he could only claim gross neglect on the part of the nurses in not consulting the doctors.

Clifton: "Then bring action against the nurses for manslaughter."

ATTENDING TO THE TESTIMONY of Elizabeth Clinch once more across the next days, Christine distinctly heard how Clinch was the first to identify the progressive decline in Sarah, rightly estimating the daily changes and the danger. Nevertheless, in reply to the court, the nurse said, "I did not appeal to the father to give her food; that was not my duty. My instructions were only to see if she took food. When the doctors arrived on the Tuesday, I did not ask their advice. On that afternoon, there was nothing to indicate danger to a person seeing the child for the first time. She was not looking so well as at the start. But for a person said to be suffering from disease and lying in bed so long, she looked pretty well. The only unusual thing—and not until Wednesday—was a nasty smell."

Then the sister-nurse flatly contradicted part of the testimony she had given at the committee meeting: "On the last morning, I made no suggestion, either myself or through Nurse Jones, to the father or mother as to the child's treatment."

Was it a united front on the part of the medical people? Or, thought Christine, had the sister-nurse determined this the best course to protect her own neck?

John Daniel testified: "Evan raged that my offer of food could have killed Sarah. 'Offer again,' he said, 'and I will kick you from the house.'"

Mr. Bishop objected.

Mr. Coleridge said, "This is such strong evidence against the father that it is essential."

"The case is already so strong against the father," Fitzwilliams replied, "I do not think it could be made stronger."

Dr. Cross and Dr. Watkins reiterated results of the postmortem examination, and Dr. Fowler was brought up again to interpret those details and others pertaining to Sarah's condition in the official log.

This time, Fitzwilliams did not restrict Mr. Coleridge's questions. By then, he must have considered the hearing's outcome a fait accompli.

"Assuming a child kept from food," Coleridge said, "showing signs of 'restlessness' and 'restless sleep' as described by Nurse Clinch and Nurse Jones thirty hours after the watch commenced—to what, as a medical man, would you attribute these symptoms?"

"Signs of early exhaustion," said Fowler.

"If on the next day—after continuous absence of food—what would 'eyes rather sunk' and 'nose rather pinched' indicate to you?"

"Important symptoms of exhaustion."

"What, in your opinion, as a scientific man, should have been done?"

"In any case with these symptoms," said Fowler, "added to the antecedent circumstances of this particular case, and with the knowledge of total absence of food—I would give food."

"Supposing," Coleridge said, "the child expressed loathing for and refused to take food, what would you have done?"

"Having previously obtained the parents' consent, I

would have forcibly given food. In the event of the parents' refusing to allow food, I should have declined all further responsibility and retired from the case.

"But, let us say," Fowler persisted, "hearing of symptoms on the *fourth* day as 'face flushed,' 'eyes unnaturally bright,' 'not so cheerful,' 'pulse averaging 112,' I should say those symptoms indicated increasing exhaustion. Assuming the fasting to have continued for *five* days, and the symptoms being 'not looking so well,' 'appearing weaker,' those symptoms would indicate still-increasing exhaustion. If on the *sixth* day the symptoms were 'a fainting fit from excitement, much flushed, lips dry,' I should consider such symptoms signs of even further increasing exhaustion.

"Suppression of urine is a serious symptom," he sternly said, "and should have been investigated. And on the eighth night, 'very difficult to keep in bed, only ten minutes' sleep at a time,'—I should say the patient was hourly getting worse. If on Wednesday came a 'peculiar smell,' it would be one of the symptoms, recorded in authorities, of death by starvation. There were cases observed during the Irish famine, though these were cases of chronic starvation, as opposed to acute starvation. Acute starvation would account for the fat layer found in the girl's autopsy. In chronic cases, I would expect but little fat."

"You have successfully cleared up a mystery," Mr. Coleridge said. "But if you consider the girl's rallies, her cheerfulness and so forth, would that have changed your opinion at any point?"

"No, by Wednesday the bad so preponderated over the good, I would easily consider the case a serious one affecting life." He pronounced, "Any doctor should have seen it."

"You earlier said," Mr. Coleridge concluded, "you believed that Sarah Jacob deceived her own parents."

"I do not believe it now," commented Fowler. "I have heard quite enough to refute such a belief."

The notorious and mysterious Dr. Pearson Hughes, rumored present in the court, was then called, since Jacob's assault charge against him was said to show that the father never surrendered control of Sarah to doctors.

Belligerent, brash, in a Scottish brogue he barked, "I put my hand down her back, I did, but gently, gently! I did not employ unusual force! I was feeling about for bedsores, and there were none. I told the mother that it was a pity to keep such a pretty little girl in bed, and that she ought to be up at once!"

Mr. Bishop, for the Jacobs, rose and said, "Were you kept from examining her?"

"Not completely. But they invited me to come and they said go away. What is this but shameful deceit? Then I'm charged with assault! Is a medical examination assault?"

"You implied," said Mr. Bishop, "that the girl could get up and out of bed had she a mind to."

"There was nothing wrong with her legs."

"What was your diagnosis?"

"Hysteria, by miles."

Titters in the court.

"Sirs," Mr. Bishop said, addressing the magistrates. "This doctor did not attend Sarah. The only doctor who looked after her across any span of time was Dr. Harries Davies, and Davies—and the vicar, too—has spoken of the girl's dire sickness two years ago, which may have left residual damage to the nerves."

"Do you claim she was diseased?" Fitzwilliams asked.

"It would have bearing upon her death and the parents' alleged guilt."

"But the necroscopists have testified that the body was healthy," Fitzwilliams said.

"Perfectly healthy!" barked Hughes.

"Be quiet, sir," Fitzwilliams said. "At the commencement of the watch, she was healthy, from all indications, and death was caused by lack of food."

"Or by the excitement of—"

"No, Mr. Bishop, do you claim to be a doctor?"

Cowed, Mr. Bishop sat. Pearson Hughes, reluctantly, gave up his spot in the box.

Thomas Davies spoke to the agreement signed by the father, saying that it was invalid except as leave and license from the parents. "No one instructed the doctors that they should apply to a magistrate to compel the father to supply food. Nothing was said beyond withdrawing the watch."

The court had received the depositions taken at the inquest. Now Henry Giles, reporter of *The Welshman*, submitted his shorthand notes from the committee meeting and testified to their correctness—although to what use, Christine would see, the notes ever were put was anyone's guess.

Fitzwilliams announced the conclusion of evidence. The parents were not to be called, nor the five Welsh doctors. Coleridge—his wig askew—rose again to sum up. When he maintained that Jacob *intended* to give his authority over by signing the agreement and *only later* interfered, the chief magistrate had heard enough.

Fitzwilliams: "I think we must heed what was stated by the father—in the nurse's report—that upon the last day of that poor girl's life, Mr. Jacob gave his permission—*gave his permission*, the report said—to Dr. Davies to give the child food, and Davies did not."

The bookend magistrates nodded, and Coleridge sat.

On the morrow, Fitzwilliams announced, "We have

considered the evidence very carefully, and by majority of the bench we think that no case can be made against the doctors. Our opinion rests upon that of Mr. Baron Alderson, who says there must be some personal act committed. I do not think that any personal act has been committed in this case. The doctors were retained, if I may use the phrase, to advise the nurses if their advice was called for. The doctors came up for that purpose and the nurses never asked for it. We cannot assume that the doctors undertook any other duty than that which they actually did undertake. That relates to the four doctors. As to the fifth, Dr. Davies, he went to the father on the morning of the death, and the father gave him permission to give the girl food. It is possible if he had done so, the child might have lived—it is possible it was already too late. But in any case, Dr. Davies—who acted foolishly—still had done nothing to bring himself under the operation of the criminal law.

"We then come to the wife, and because the law is doubtful in regard to her position, we agree that she should be sent to trial with her husband, where the court will decide.

"As to the father, there are circumstances which might be given in evidence upon the trial—such as the father's belief in his child's fast, the influences under which the girl labored, the differences of opinion amongst the doctors; I say that all these might be placed before the jury in his defense and might bring about mitigation."

The chairman formally announced that Evan and Hannah Jacob would be committed for trial at the Summer Assizes, and he set bail.

Hannah wept, shuddered convulsively, cloaked in her shroudlike shawl. Throughout, the hearing had been conducted in English, and translation had not been provided. But yet she knew, saw by the turned heads and expressions and probably knew from the beginning, from the wordless attitude of the troll, what the situation would be. When Evan attempted to comfort her, she wrenched him off.

There would be a trial, a victory of a kind. But what of the points of law, as Christine understood, no one had sufficiently addressed? There was "no personal act" by the doctors, and the legal problem of fixing criminal liability for omission rather than action was real. But nor had the parents committed an action, since they were not charged with a hoax, but with manslaughter. Throughout the eight days that killed Sarah, they had, like the doctors and nurses, done nothing at all. Coleridge hadn't made legally clear how far the father's responsibility for force-feeding would really extend. He didn't designate primary or accessory responsibility on the part of the doctors in relation to the parents' crime. Instead, he allowed Fitzwilliams to box him into a corner. Fowler's convincing performance made it easy to feel that the head magistrate's single intention was to get off the medical men, the five of his own class. The vicar, who started the ghoulish circus with his published letter, slithered away like an eel. Two peasants would go to the dock, and a pack of people who ought to have known much better had aided and abetted their crime and would slither off just like the vicar.

Reginald Pary audibly gasped when the bail was set. It would go hard on them, he said. Long before the Summer Assizes, they would be ruined.

That night, Christine wrote to Douglas and Gwen that she must stay in Carmarthen well into the summer. She must bear witness, stay for a rightness she couldn't at this low moment perceive. Might they understand?

Her letter crossed Douglas's latest. He wrote that he had decided to journey to Wales. He had long meant to visit the country, and his mother's descriptions of the events had quite moved him. He could get away in late spring and would try to convince Gwen to come.

There is good yet in the world, Christine thought, in her American children and still, yes, in Wales, despite the chief magistrate—she had learned to believe in the Welsh, across the long months she'd abided with them. But life this long winter felt thin. Trust, that elusive component of anything valuable in human affairs, frayed like the weak winter light.

THE FAMILY

WE STOOD IN THE DOORWAY AS THEY TOOK OUT the bundle of her. We stood by the house as they lashed her to the man's back on the horse. We watched him ride her away until they were a black dot far off over the fields.

They brought her back, and Mam said we must wait in the loft whilst new men came and looked at her.

That is when it started, Mary watching me and saying, "If there is anything I can do for you, Margaret," and "What have you to tell me?"

They laid her out, and Mam made me kiss the hard flesh—gray-white—and I saw her eyes flattened beneath the lids.

I didn't sleep. Mary said, "You are not to worry; I will take care of you."

Mam made me wash, dunked me in the cooling water after the boys and scrubbed me down.

I was glad they took the thing to the graveyard and laid dirt upon it, because it wasn't her. At home, Tad sat us down and we put our hands on the Bible and vowed to pull together and never to speak of what we knew. He gave Mary and Esther her combs and me the spinning top. Baby David had her bell—he lost it the next day, throwing it at the wall, and it fell between cracks—and the other brothers had the monkey book and Mam had the shawls and the bonnets, but soon Tad took the gifts back to sell at market. Under my blanket I had the geisha and the portrait of a girl that did not look like Sarah. I tore the portrait and Mam found the tatters and cried. But always she cried, lay sick in her bed or else cried. At table when Tad read from the Bible—for we must take strength now—Mam cried and set Esther off, so the two of them wailing angered him. Esther would not sit at table, but stayed on the floor, sucking her bloody fingers and drawing a circle with her scrawny body and crying if Mam did, and Tad said, "I will send that one to the workhouse."

Mary said, "Try it." I looked at Mary, and Mam looked at her. She was a new Mary we didn't know. But Mam was quieter then to keep Esther out of the workhouse and would go to the dairy to cry.

Work and cry, work and cry. "Look," she said one day to me in the dairy—I didn't cry. She took a package from behind a vat and showed me a gold chain. On it was a tiny gold box, and inside a piece of Sarah's hair.

"Then see," she said, "S.J., and the numbers are for her birthday, in May, and the day she died."

I thought of the hair in the cupboard bed and nothing left but this bit behind glass. Mam must have seen my thoughts on my face. "Someday," she said, "it will be yours. But not now." She stuck the chain inside her dress and probably hid it another place later, so I wouldn't steal it from her. And I wouldn't have done that, I would have broken the gold box in two and left her the side with the letters and numbers.

NOBODY WENT ANYWHERE EXCEPT TAD AND EMYR, no chapel, no school, only everyone working and pulling together. I washed clothes and cooked food. I learned to milk, churn, and knit. I had to replace good-for-nothing Esther. Mary taught me my work, but I still didn't like her. Sarah and I didn't like her. I kept my eyes from the fallow fields and said to myself, work, and it's another day gone. Work, and the green will come, and the air will turn warm again. Tad sold the chickens and pigs and smashed up their shelters for firewood, and strangers led Nansi, Malt, and Eilund off in snow. We children followed them across the moor and onto the lane, where the cows vanished in whiteness and we were too cold to track them. Then Tad sold the goats.

I heard Mary and my brothers talking at night. David slept in my arms—I had claimed him, needing someone: Dilly, the dog, and David, the baby, were mine. Nobody knew what would happen if Tad and Mam went to jail, and the boys thought we might all go. Before that, they'd run, the boys said, they were old enough to go to the steelworks or the mines, and Emyr knew how to get there. Mary laughed and said, "You boys didn't kill her now, did you?"

"The doctors killed her," said Samuel, and asked were they going to jail?

"Doctors don't go to jail; jail is for the likes of us," Mary said.

"Then shall we not go?" Saunders asked.

One night as we lay in our shelves in the children's room, Mary told us that she had found out: The family doesn't go to prison with the parents, and Tad and Mam only were to be tried—in summer. That we hadn't been summoned to the hearing meant we were safe.

Belle, Clovis, Bronwen, and Rhian were taken, and we had just four cows left. I milked with Mary outside in the yard, and pulling Ruth's long, warm teats, the steam when the squirts hit the bucket rising and warming my face, I asked Mary one day, "Will they calve in spring?"

"You've decided to talk to me, eh?" she said. "Yes, they

will calve, and then he'll sell the whole lot, mothers and babies, and that will be that."

"Why?"

"He owes it."

I didn't know whether to believe her. She was a grown person, and those you couldn't necessarily believe. I got up from the stool, and she said, "You are well, then, Margaret?"

Well? How could I be well?

She said it again, so I kicked her.

"Heathen!" she shouted. She grabbed my arm and threatened, "Do I have to take a shovel to your head?"

"Let me go," I said.

She did, but her face descended to me and held me there—I smelt her rank sweat—she sweat even in cold—and she had black pinprick spots on her nose and a taint to her breath that took me back to when Tad put me into the bed with Sarah and I couldn't breathe for the smell—sometimes for no reason the walls seeped the smell and I was there again with Sarah's coldness, her labored breathing, her clinging to me, and the blankets piled on us, trapping and smothering. "Your dear, dear sister is gone," Mary said. "And Tad and Mam could well be gone soon. You may be better off if they go, but in the meantime, is a child barely up on his feet and a dog enough companionship for you?"

They are enough, I thought. We brought the cows inside, and she pinned me again: "Who killed her?" she asked. "How did she die? Do you know?"

Of course, I wasn't out of my mind like Esther. They kept me from her and so she died. "They" were Mam and Tad and the doctors and nurses and the vicar and the Welsh patriots. All of them, but I didn't say anything. Did Mary think I had no ears, that I heard nothing?

"Miss High and Mighty, just like your sister. Butter

wouldn't melt. Your father killed Sarah, miss. Just as sure as he put her in the bed."

What she said kept me from leaving the barn. Tad didn't put her in the bed; she was sick and then she wanted to stay abed. But Mary had tied up a knot in my mind because Tad had stuffed me in the bed with Sarah against my will and I thought I would catch the dying from her, and my arms and legs wouldn't work, wouldn't thaw, and often still they got stuck with cramp and I feared that any day my own death would erupt from my bones that held it. "There," she said. "I've got your attention, haven't I? He did it," she said, "and you need me to look out for you whether you like it or not. He heeds me." Of this she was proud, and I had seen it, though I didn't know why he would listen to her. "Just work," she said as she set to mucking. "The more you can do, the better off you will be. You can go into service with me perhaps," and I couldn't keep the awfulness of that possibility from my expression, thinking of being with her forever and smelling her breath and always being reminded. "Or you can race the devil!" she said. I thought I could go to the mines with the boys. We would all have to go somewhere when they put Tad and Mam in Carmarthen Prison.

ONE NIGHT, MARY CAUGHT ME SETTING CREAM in a saucer on the ground outside the parlor window. Tad and Mam were asleep, and though I was quiet, as ever, Mary had heard. "Look at you! Have we food to waste?" But she herself picked up the saucer and tipped the cream into the dirt. "There, she can lap it up in hell, where she lives."

"Please don't tell Tad," I said.

"I won't. Come inside."

But I wouldn't, I was so afraid, for it seemed to me that

Mary knew everything I had done for Sarah, and if Mary knew, maybe Tad also did, and Mam, and even if I hadn't been summoned to the hearing, they could still come and get me if they found out and put me away. I would be killed, or else I would go to prison—and the shame of prison, Mam said, was as good as death. I sat on the damp ground and took hold of my head and pushed hard, trying to push out the thoughts, I was stupid to offer the cream, she couldn't eat anymore; she had no mouth or eyes or fingers or legs. She wasn't anywhere, I offered cream out of habit, there was no person to feed, and I pushed harder at my dumb head and Mary touched me. I stopped.

"It is cold," she said kindly, and I followed her inside this time. Anything was better than being with me, with my thoughts.

"I am sorry I said she was in hell," Mary whispered, when we were in bed. "She isn't. It wasn't her fault, Margaret."

Esther keened low in her sleep. Mary nudged her, and Esther stopped. I pulled sleeping David closer. Mary asked me if I would just promise to come to her if Tad did anything I didn't like, and I agreed. And she said Tad would heed me, as he did her, for the reason that he knew I'd fed Sarah and pretended not to. If I spoke, I could doom him, did I understand?

He knew? How? He knew and still he had let the nurses come? He killed her? He wanted to kill me?

GRONWY, MEGAN, RUTH, AND SALOMÉ were full of calf. Their sides bulged, and the weather went milder, and I saw a little hoof kick from inside Gronwy.

"Put your hand on it," Mary said, seeing me looking at the skin.

"I can't."

"Then let me feel it," and she held her hand on the skin that covered the calf's foot and said, "This one shall live."

It saddened me to think of the cows and their calves being taken, especially since the buds were coming on trees and my dark thoughts had lightened.

I avoided Tad much as I could. I worked and was obedient, but I did not meet his eyes or seek him out. He cornered me by the fire on a night after the others had gone to sleep and I was up knitting. If I'd known him awake, I'd have gone to bed. He emerged in the kitchen. I stood.

"Stay."

I sat.

"Who do you think you are, girl?"

I knit.

"Answer me."

"I am Margaret and I will be ten in July."

He took a paper from out of the Bible and said, "You cannot read, can you?"

"You know I cannot."

"I will read it to you, then." He sat too close, and I barely breathed. He read by the firelight: "'Poor murdered girl. I was sure the doctors would finish her off when they got her into their hands. . . . The sudden plunging of her into the adverse influences of a posse of doctors and nurses, the majority filled with suspicion of her and hostility to her . . . was . . . like being plunged and kept down in an atmosphere of carbonic acid gas. . . .'" He folded the paper. "It is a letter," he said, "from the solicitor—the man who helps with the false charges against us. Did you understand it? Did it not say what I have told you?"

I understood well enough. Even if the doctors had killed her, he had asked them to come. I willed myself to look at him and say, "Carbonic acid?"

"Poison," he said.

Poison, she wasn't poisoned.

"What do you hear from people?" he asked.

"I don't talk to anyone."

"You talk to your sister Mary."

"I don't. She talks to me."

"You have vowed never to speak of our business."

"I have kept my vow."

"I do not feel from you the love a daughter should bear her father." I heard the bed curtains and then I could fill my lungs, and Mam came into the kitchen.

"Leave her alone," she said. "She is a good loyal girl."

"Go to sleep," he said to Mam.

"I don't sleep anymore," she said. "Or I sleep with my eyes open, as well I should."

"This girl," he said, jerking his head at me, "is cut in your stamp. You should be womanly once more and soften your heart!"

"I shall not soften my heart," she replied, "and live in the hardness that is yours!"

He lurched up and lunged at her, and before she could step back he struck her to the floor. I leaped away; he stood over her, saying, "More? You will know hardness you cannot conceive," and he toed her back, pushing her face into the clay.

Mary came in, followed by Esther clinging to Mary's nightdress. "No, no!" Esther said, "No, no!"

Tad took his foot off Mam, but she didn't get up. He looked down at her, "Do you believe I do not miss my Sarah?"

"No, no!" Esther cried, "No, no!" Tad turned to her, grabbed her by the arm, and led her to the front door.

"Where are you taking her?" Mary said.

"To the barn, where she'll sleep the night."

"Let him," Mam said. "She may be quieter there."

Mary helped Mam get up, and Mam sat at the table, whilst Mary did a thing I would never forget: She sat in Tad's chair by the fire.

"I should not have questioned him," Mam said. "I should not disobey him, Mary. I was wrong. I must not. Else what will become of us?"

He returned and saw Mary in his chair. He said nothing and went back to bed. Mam and Mary stayed up, but I went to David and held him. The big boys pretended to sleep. I could hear Esther wail in the byre through the wall; I felt the cramp stiffen my limbs.

TAD LEFT ME ALONE UNTIL CALVING. He said I should be there for it, since I was almost a fully grown girl. The barn was emptier daily. He had sold the new plow and most of the tools. The fields near the house lay unseeded, since we couldn't pay the rent, new tenants sowed the outer fields, and Mary told me the house would go after the trial. "He's given up," she said; "he may as well have already been tried and convicted." He roused himself when the vicar came by and they spoke of the future. Between them, it was as if nothing had happened. If it came to prison, the boys would go to one of the schoolmasters, who wanted to encourage their studiousness. If the worst came about, the vicar said, there were ways to begin again, smaller farms where we could all be together. "You are a fine man, Evan Jacob," the vicar said, "and young enough to rebuild your life." This was all I overheard. I supposed I would go into service with Mary, and that didn't seem bad anymore. I worried over Esther and Dilly and David. Mad Esther was quieter. A doctor came and bandaged her bloody hands, but she sucked on the dirty bandages and tore them off, and we put them back on; we cut strips from old linens and boiled and hung them from the line, and if she was too violent at herself, we tied her hands to her sides, and at night we stroked her and hummed to her until she slept.

Except for Esther and David, we were all in the barn when Gronwy birthed the little kicker. In the beginning, it was horrible, how she groaned and pushed out the calf in a slimy sack. Only then the calf struggled, tore itself free, tried to stand, fell, and Gronwy licked off the awfulness and you could see the black fur of the little man, a little bull. On the fourth try it stood! I heard myself laugh; then I clapped, and Mary laughed and clapped too and then Mam, and even Tad and Emyr smiled.

It wasn't long, however, before Ruth began her labor, and it was endless and painful, and Tad and Emyr soon said the calf was dead, but Ruth had to push it out anyway and we waited for it to come. It dropped, and I saw its slit eyes through the caul; its body had barely any hair and was purple, splashed with Ruth's blood in the hay.

A sound must have oozed from me, because Tad turned and noticed me. "Bury it," he said.

"I can," Emyr said.

"No," Tad said, "Margaret will do it."

I stared at the dead calf and didn't move. Ruth lay and heaved—she wasn't tending to it, and it just lay there.

"Take it," Tad said. "I must save the cow."

Mary and Mam had gone to the house for more water from the fire. Emyr helped me wrap the dead calf in burlap and put it in the small wagon. I buried it near where the chicken house had been, and the ground was soft. There were two more live births afterward from our other cows, but I didn't see them. I told Tad I wouldn't, and he didn't make me.

MAM SOFTENED HER HEART AND DIDN'T CRY ANYMORE. That is, not until Tad planned to take her best dishes to market. "They are the only pretty things I ever had," she told me. "They were my mother's. Do you remember your grandmother?" I did not. Mam kept these plates propped on the upper shelves of the dresser, and when I was small, I climbed up to the ledge and saw my reflection in their copper shine. Sarah had told me I would. After that, Sarah and I dusted them often, studied our faces, talking to them as if ours were the most remarkable faces in Wales.

Mam put the plates in a heavy bag, with each one carefully wrapped, and we set out—Tad gave us permission—for Uncle John and Aunt Nell Daniel's. It was a fine clear day and Mam smiled at the sky, as if almost happy. "Hopeful," she said. "It is the first day I have felt hopeful since they took my Sal." I thought she'd start in with her crying again, but she didn't. "It is hard for Tad, Margaret," she said. It was hard for us all. I didn't say anything. "But hard or no, my girl, I know what is right and what is wrong."

"He hit you," I said. "He put your face in the dirt."

She was quiet a minute. "He never did it before," she said. "And I don't care about myself; all my thoughts are for my children. And my plates! Oh-h!" She pressed the bag to her breast, and it brought back the weeping.

She sat on a ridge of rock halfway up the moor to cry to her plates. It was nothing to me; I was too glad to be away from the house and to breathe good air, not warm air but thinking of being so, air brewing summer. The mist on the mountains was thinning and soon we'd see their tops. Everything would change come the warm weather, as everything changed when my sister died. Whilst she lived, I was a child, and now I was not.

Mam dried her tears with her shawl and we continued our journey along the river. I felt it running in my heart! I stared at its sparkle, drinking it into myself. At last, we went up the short rise to where the two-story blue-painted house perched above the river. The sky was pale today, but when it blued, the house hovered against it, merged with its color. A small house, it flooded once, and we helped bail and sweep the lower rooms. I hated to think of my aunt and uncle and cousins floating away in their beds if it happened again. But after the flood, they slept upstairs, and the shop was moved to beside the kitchen down below.

"Daughter," Mam said as we neared. "I will ask money for the plates to satisfy Tad. And if God wills it, I will someday buy the plates back."

I had figured as much.

"But, daughter," she continued, "I will leave you there with them if they agree."

"Why?" I asked. This was a completely unexpected development and I wasn't challenging her, I was just surprised.

"Margaret *fach*, do as your mother says," Mam instructed. Geof, Cam, and Hank huffed up from their play at the riverbank. "Where's Dilly?" asked Geof.

"We didn't bring her, dear," Mam said. "We've come to see your mam and tad." Geof snapped his fingers in annoyance and my cousins hurried back to their games.

Aunt Nell came out to the steps, calling, "Hannah! Margaret, come in!" She had thickened across the midsection. I knew she carried a baby she would push out from her body to live or to die.

In the wee kitchen, Aunt Nell packaged clothes my uncle made. Shelves ran up the walls, rolls of paper and twine, boxes, and dry goods for sale—baskets, ribbons and thread, a black velvet backing laden with scissors, hanging rugs and lops of yarn, natural and dyed, and the paper flowers Aunt Nell made herself—we had some of these flowers left back home. I detected my uncle in the other room, behind a false person covered by clothes. The river's light slanted onto the floor, and you could see slices of silvery water from the windows.

"Soon we'll have spring!" said Aunt Nell.

"There's been little rain," Mam commented darkly.

"And there was little snow," Aunt Nell agreed. "Sit," she said, and she got us tea and slices of barley bread with butter. We quickly ate. At our house, we did not have enough. The threshed grain was low, and the yarn finished. Mary said we would scrape wool from rocks, the sheep's leavings. Tad and Mam had thinned, as they ate less than the rest of us, and Aunt Nell hadn't brought food in several weeks.

"I've been feeling a mite poorly," she said, "but I am better now."

"It carries high," Mam said. "A girl this time, Nell." My mother's mouth trembled, and I wished for her to control herself. She busied herself with the bag. "I've brought the plates," she said, putting them on the table. "They go with your others."

"Yes," Nell said.

"I thought if we kept them in the family."

Aunt Nell called, "John!" He came, with a tape around his neck, and I noticed, as I always did when we were here, how he filled the room. He had tried to save Sarah. He had dents and dings on his hands from his work.

"Good day, Hannah, good day, Margaret."

"John," said Aunt Nell, "why don't we pay Hannah for the use of the plates that match the others?"

He didn't run at the offer. "Does Evan know you brought them?" he asked. "For I cannot give you as much as he might get at market."

"It is better so," Mam said. "It will be easier for us to buy them back later."

"You put me in a position, Nell," he said.

"Sit with us, John," my aunt told him.

He sat beside me, and I wondered if every day I might sit beside him at table.

"Well then, what news?" Aunt Nell asked Mam. "It is nice to see you about! You ought to go back to chapel, Hannah."

"There is more sympathy for you abroad than you know," Uncle John said.

"I never will," Mam said, and she rubbed her hands, which pained her.

"And whose decision is that?" said John, and Aunt Nell touched him.

"I would see her there," Mam said. "I see her everywhere! I wanted it. I prayed, heathenlike, for Sarah to appear in my sleep, to live as a ghost anywhere that she could, just so I would have her and she wouldn't be gone! But it is terrible," and tears dripped onto her rubbing hands. "Take them," she said, pushing the plates toward John. "They are the only pretty things I ever had, them and my Sal. To think I birthed such a beautiful daughter—me. And then she died. And the shame, Nell, the shame," and then came a fresh surge of weeping. I watched the light on the floor. Aunt Nell and Uncle John regarded Mam with a patience and kindness I didn't feel. At length, Mam snuffled and pulled herself up.

"John," Mam said, "Nell. Isn't Margaret big and strong? She has turned a fine worker and a good loyal girl."

"We are pleased you comfort your mother, Margaret," Aunt Nell said. Not out of choice, I thought—mean girl.

"I didn't just bring the plates," Mam started. "Only the plates. I brought the girl in hope you would take her—house her. Before the trial, I must find—"

"Why, it hasn't come to that yet," said Aunt Nell. "You must have faith and courage, Hannah."

Mam shook her head. "Better she stays here."

"If the worst happens," said John, "we will do what we can. But I have five to feed and six by the harvest and we are not wealthy people, Hannah, as you well know."

"She'll work," Mam put in weakly.

"It would displease Evan," said Nell. "Even if we had the gold of England, surely you see it wouldn't be smart."

John got us a handful of coins for the plates, and Mam put them into her dress. Nell packed us a basket of food, and we set off home.

At home, Esther had unwrapped her bandages and they trailed in long dirty and blood-flecked streamers around her where she sat on the floor and circled and hummed. Dilly lay on the floor beside her, as she often did, her eyes rolled up at Esther, whimpering in tune with the humming. David had wrapped Esther's leavings around his own hands and he showed us them as we came in. Tad sat by the fire, reading his paper.

"Mary!" Mam shouted, and Mary came down from the loft, where she was working, and she and Mam took Esther to the children's room to attend to her. I unwrapped the dirty bandages from David's hands and put his jacket back on, as he was shivering in his shirt. I picked him up and took him to the fire to warm, standing as far from Tad as I could and pressing my face into David's soft curls. David was thirty months and I was teaching him to speak. I had taught him "Margaret" and "Sarah," and I regretted it. At the worst times he had said, "Sarah." At table when Tad read the Bible, David would brightly smile and say, "Sarah."

He did it now. He looked straight at Tad and said, "Sarah."
I corrected him: "Margaret."

"Teach him his father's name," Tad said.

"Say 'Tad,'" I said to David.

"Sarah," said David.

It was time for the late-day milking, and I carried David with me to the barn. Dilly rushed after us, and Dilly and David chased Gronwy's black boy calf and Megan's brown girl to the yard as I brought out the cows. Our remaining cows were barred from the pasture. Megan and Gronwy strained toward the field, and I reined them in.

Mary came, and we milked.

"You have returned," she said. "Anyway, Tad would have brought you back."

I would have missed David and Dilly.

NOT MANY DAYS LATER, MARY AND MAM had just gone out for water, with David and Dilly along and Esther bound to her bed—and this late afternoon, Tad walked in from market as I tended the kitchen, my face to the fire.

Without turning to him, I continued my tasks. He didn't sit, didn't come close; he watched me work.

"Your leg," he said. "Does it pain you?"

I didn't answer.

"Does it pain you?"

"No."

"I had no money when you were injured for its proper repair."

I stirred the broth thickened with potato skins.

"Do you accuse me?" he asked.

"No." I could see his bony countenance and dirty hair with the eyes of my back, and I felt his energy push at me.

"I have been meaning to talk to you about Sarah, but always you flee."

I rested the spoon by the tongs on the fire plate.

"You very well do!" he said.

I turned to him. "I don't flee."

Satisfied at keeping me there, he sat at the table.

Where is Emyr? I thought. Then I remembered he worked away from us now on some days.

"Bring me food," said Tad.

When I set the bowl down, he saw my hand shake.

"You have forgotten the spoon," he said. I brought it.

But it wasn't food he wanted. He let it sit and said, "What does Mary pack your head with?"

"Nothing."

"What does your mam say to you?"

"Nothing."

"Always nothing!" He scraped up from the bench and said, "Sit. You will sit down and listen." I sat, and his strength shooting across the table frightened me and handily struck—as the stroke of an ax may release a hidden spring—at the innermost part of my body, which harbored to bursting the water I'd held back, and out it poured. He didn't force me to look at him; he allowed me to sit, crying, and listen. "You fed her; I didn't. I learned of it. But when I learned, there were plans already made and they couldn't be altered. It was explained to you and the rest as the watching was planned. Wasn't it?"

I nodded.

"But you said nothing. If she was fed and did not die, would she not die if she was not fed?"

I nodded.

"Then I didn't kill her, now, did I? Did I?"

"No."

"Who killed her?

"The—"

"Who?"

"The doctors?"

"The doctors. Well now, it was either the doctors or it was you—what are you trying to say?"

"Not me."

"And why not you? You could have told, and then they wouldn't have done it."

"I—"

"What is it?"

"Tried."

"How did you try?"

"I don't know."

"You don't know. Listen. I will not have a person who abhors me in my house."

"I—"

"What is it?"

"I do not—"

"Hate me?" he said.

"I do not hate you."

I had said the right thing at last. He regarded me differently, as a person who needn't be killed. "I am a merciful father, Margaret, and I will not tell them what you did. Thank me."

"Thank you."

"But I am tired of women and wee girls thinking I am to be mastered. Do you understand?"

"I understand."

"I am going to lie down for a nap. You are to say nothing to Mary or to your mother or anyone else of our discussion."

"No, Tad."

"To whom do you owe duty?"

"To you."

"Who gave you your life?"

"You."

"Who every day returns it to you?"

"You do, Tad."

I smelled Sarah's breath and felt her hands—the house reeked of her breath and the smothering blankets came down. "Look at me," he said. "If I go away, daughter, if the dogs, the captains of life in this bloody land, take what is left to me, I'll get it back. And you back. Why do I say this?"

"I don't know."

"Why, to convince you!" He sounded pleased with himself. "I think now, Margaret, that you will carry conviction."

I didn't move until I heard his steps recede and the click-hiss of the bed curtains. I ran outside and didn't stop running until I was up the steep path and to the clearing where she would pray by the wild oaks in the lee. I fell onto my fours and stayed as the water kept coming out of me and out of me until the flood weakened and didn't come anymore. I sat up, recalling as if it was again how he shook my sister, when Mam went to deliver David. I recalled Sarah's empty bed until Mam came back. I gripped the rough bark of an oak, fingered the knots and whorls, I gripped it—whilst smelling my sister's dying breath and clutched by her clawlike hands—and by this method, at last I returned to myself. I wasn't going mad anymore; I wasn't swallowed by what had escaped from me, what he had pulled from me.

I said to myself the story I repeated most since she died, about the lady of the lake. I had thought of the story at the river and imagined that Sarah lived in the river as the lady lived in the lake. So much desired was she that a man coaxed her from the lake along with her fairy cattle. But she warned him that if he hurt her three times, she would go back. Though he didn't intend it, he hurt her once and then again, and after the third time, she went with her cattle and the rest of the stock she had accumulated whilst she lived on land. The oxen plowing the field escaped their yokes, and even the dead animals came back to life and followed her to the water. A little calf hung from a bloody hook climbed down and flexed his muscles, a sizzling goat wiggled off from the spit and trotted after the rest. The lady was never forgotten. The children she had with the man were great healers and carried her lessons to people for all their days.

I would have to return to the house. Mary and Mam would be there. All I had to do was not say anything. When I looked up at the sky, it was clear and pierced with a faint light of stars, blocked for months by weather. I believed them a sign, because I felt her as she used to be—alive. I stayed watching starlight come, brighten—the stars were her breath and their glow her breathing—until I was too cold and could not any longer.

CHRISTINE'S REPRIEVE

Carmarthen, Wales
29 May 1870

Dearest James,

They will be here in two days! I settled upon a domicile for the three of us, of which I think you would approve. I was tempted to lease a Regency house on fashionable Quay Street, but except for their colorful washes they are similar to our row houses in Brooklyn. At last, I found a thatched cottage not far from the Parade, where there is the expansive view of the river and the valley. There are two nicely appointed bedrooms in the cottage's loft for Douglas and Gwen, and I have a bed and a desk in the main room by the kitchen. Mrs. Owen and Mrs. Morgan labored mightily with me on preparations. The cottage was already modernized before I let it, but I am anxious to render it spotless for our month in June.

The children stayed with Vinnie in London, and then Vinnie traveled north with them along the Welsh Marches. They are coming south via the western coast and must be stopping at Dyfed about now. Vinnie will stay at the widows' inn here, although she has vowed to intrude on us incessantly. She said it was what I deserved for refusing to join them on the trip north.

I'd work to do, the human-interest stories for Philip while his readers hang fire for the trial—and I just did a piece for the

Weekly on the Carmarthen Literary Institution at the Assembly Rooms at Guildhall, where the assizes will convene in July.

"Really, Christine," Vinnie wrote, "you haven't seen Douglas and Gwen for a year, and soon you'll return to the States and may never come back. Don't you want to see the north once more?"

Vinnie is still enthralled by North Wales, considers it more spectacular even than her beloved Sussex Downs. "The children have you to show them James's place," I said, "and we will have June." I was concerned about news leading up to the trial as much as about my various little assignments, but finally I saw it was more than that—it was you. I didn't want to pass through the spa towns and seaside resorts for new tourists brought by the trains. I wanted only the coaching inns on the road to the north. I didn't want to see Gwynned with my old eyes, apart from you. All of it, the Irish Sea off the coast, Ireland pressing out of mists on fine days, the ancient abandoned Town of Giants, the slate quarries where you were proud of remembering slates named according to size, Duchess, Viscountess, Broad Ladies, Narrow Ladies . . . and were astonished by how strong your father had to have been in his prime to lift them, and the northern rooms where we slept, rife with the atmosphere of turf and bracken, water and wind, the pungency of everything tufted, ferny, and mossed, peaty, the bed linens fragrant of mushrooms, and outside the spurt of springs and the squelch of morasses, the waterfalls pouring through rocks, our sighting of Snowdon, how I fell to my knees in ecstatic shock and you helped me up and said you cherished me for my capacities and I wanted to know what capacities you referred to, of feelings, of brain, of love prowess—laughing—and you said for all three, but mostly for my sturdy feet and stomach and I said that you weren't romantic and you took me back to that day's particular inn and ravished me nicely before starting, once more, to the mountain—all of it, my darling, lives in me. I want it safe and not nudged aside by a fresh trip without you. I would argue that this is healthy of me, that preserving instincts are needed in this rushing life. You are, you know, with me. And now the children want to see Wales—to have it, belatedly, with you. I wouldn't be honest if I didn't acknowledge poor Sarah's part in healing our family. Would she not have died, for our healing could have come in another way that didn't include this weight, this new loss, this regret that lives in me now as much as anything else.

In Gwen's recent letters, I hear more enthusiasm than I have in years—and she, like Douglas, has read my dispatches and is anxious, she claims, to discuss the case with me. Shall I attribute this broader interest in the world to the change Douglas intimated from Brooklyn? I should wait and see and not get my hopes up. But why else would she have agreed to the trip?

Gwen is quite taken with the *tylwyth teg* and has put aside novels for myths—only in Wales, they don't seem myths, but nearly firm as the land and people they grew from, or as flimsy, the slippage the magic of enchantment, I'd venture to guess.

The trial will take place in Carmarthen after all. It would have been fairer in London, with a chance that a disinterested jury could be found. But given the newspaper coverage and prejudice against the Welsh, possibly I am wrong. *The Law Times* is concerned that the intermingled issues of law and science are too complex to be left in the provinces and that experts are required for "this great scientific contest." The reporters at the *Weekly* say the English are cognizant of the fact that Welsh juries seldom convict, preferring still to take criminal matters into their own hands, particularly when it comes to crimes with a distinctly moral component. So much depends on the will of the Crown, on the message they propose to send with their approach in court.

The family continues to live in the house, the acreage shrunk down to nothing. They have the yard and a dog. The cows are gone, and what's left of the milk and cheese go to feeding the family. Jacob resigned his posts at the chapel and as overseer of the poor. He was seen until recently at market, terse in his dealings and otherwise speaking to no one. A plain wooden cross now marks Sarah's grave, and people leave flowers there. After the heavy rains last year, there is drought. It is Sarah, some say. God in His heaven is displeased. People think they have seen Sarah, heard her—a shiny black splash of hair sighted through blossoming trees, her distinctive voice riding the wind. Others curse her, saying she should have died sooner, before the publicity. The pride of the Welsh is to behave as if never crippled by the big rich neighbor to their side, and in July the neighbor will arrive, exhume the starved corpse, and crow.

What I say is this: Evan Jacob wanted to be important. He developed an obsession. He could not stop. The forces of modernity entered his blood and were fed by disputes and lay in the bed with his daughter. *But how did it unfold?* Motive. Personally, I can't wait for the trial, if it will reveal what we don't already know.

I must return to my floor washing. I've got back my health. The tromping through fields and rain has toughened me up, and a tincture provided by the local chemist has helped to restore my equilibrium. I plan to be a long-lived, hardy old woman fighting the forces of evil. From heaven, you'll see me beside the young knights.

Meanwhile, I lay my hands softly on your closed eyes, comforting them. I look to our children. I hold you close in my heart.

Always,
Christine

◌

ON THE MORNING OF THE CHILDREN'S AND VINNIE'S arrival, Christine's entourage at the station included two carriages, the Welsh widows, Pary and Lloyd, and the chemist and his wife, Christine's new fond acquaintances. Mr. Brigstock was a modern chemist, but he also did sheep and cattle dips, gaining the confidence of doctors and farmers alike. A splendid lunch awaited the travelers at the cottage. They needed guests, Christine had decided, to anoint this reunion.

"Do we look a batch of country bumpkins?" Christine asked Mrs. Owen.

"We are country bumpkins," Mrs. Morgan rejoined.

"The Americans!" Pary and Lloyd shouted at the rumble of the train.

Mr. Brigstock and his wife, dignified gray-headed people very like in appearance, spoke up as one: "The Americans!"

"Should we have hired a band?" the chemist asked.

"We'll sing!" Lloyd said. "Welsh songs!"

"Best we don't," Mrs. Owen said, "as we may frighten them back to Brooklyn."

And it was uncanny that the first thing Gwen said when she stepped down from the train was, "Mother, you look Welsh." It was her garb, Christine realized, the short skirt and clogs, the plain cotton bonnet—her American clothes long ruined.

Gwen: luminous, womanly, Christine thought as the day progressed and she watched her daughter with rabid eyes—the young woman, emerged from the chrysalis of petulance into life, chatting amiably to the Welsh at table on the grass, sunburned, her brown hair streaked gold, and she was delighted by the cottage. "How does it keep out the wet?" she asked, observing the thatch. "Do you see," said Christine, "how the stalks lie along the roof's plane? Long wheat straws they are. Placed like that, they shed the water. Slides straight down."

Douglas was tan, and he had grown a full beard. He charmed with his interest in what they had seen of the north and his questions about what to see in Carmarthen. "She wouldn't come home," Douglas announced to the party when after lunch they lingered in sun and shade, "Refused! And we had to come here." He proposed a toast and gave it in Welsh, impressing the Cymru. Vinnie Smyth, always competitive in a genial manner, chimed in with a more accomplished phrase flavored by a northern accent.

Vinnie had hurt her foot walking the shore in Dyfed, and though she didn't complain and limped only a little, Christine saw, abruptly, her age—the thinner white hair, the lessening flesh at her shoulders. Alun Lloyd was back at the office after his illness, but though it wasn't hot, he mopped sweat from his yellowish face.

All the more reason *to have this day*, and when Lloyd went off with Pary, and the Brigstocks and the widows said they would see Vinnie to the inn, Christine walked with the children along the Parade in the long summer light—down to the riverside, where the hobblers still worked, and coracle men climbed out of boats, strapped the curved boats to their backs, and walked off with their haul, looking like upstanding turtles. She walked with Douglas and Gwen along Dan-y-Bank, a lane under the bank inhabited by the Irish, and ascended the steps to Castle Hill, passing near the newer tent settlement, near the people Christine had been drawn to the night she discovered gin with Pary.

Viewing the castle, that threatening pile on the rocky eminence overlooking the river, Douglas and Gwen spoke of garrison towns they had visited and remarked on the sheer number of castles everywhere in the country, towering over towns or lurking, half-hidden, six hundred across Wales. Christine hadn't before heard the number.

"The jail's there," Christine said at the northern section.

"Where the Jacobs will go if they are convicted?" asked Gwen.

"They would be kept here just briefly," said Christine. "They'd go to Swansea." A chill prickled her scalp. To speak of it made it more real. They traversed Market Square and went by the Guildhall, an imposing stone building adorned by columns and distinctive classically arched windows. How would it be, Christine thought, for the Jacobs to go through its portal, to pass by the oil paintings of noblemen staunch against smoky battle—or seated at desks, feather pens sharp as swords?

They walked back on King Street as the gaslights came on and cast an amber glow within the narrow medieval layout of adjoining lanes and crisscrossing alleys.

"Will they be found guilty?" Gwen asked.

"It's hard to say," Christine said. "No one thinks the Crown would have taken it on without the will to convict. If the trial is here, the grand jury has to submit a true bill. I'd be surprised if they didn't. But actual trials are heard by a petty jury composed of farmers, and the farmers are more unpredictable." She sketched out the Jacobs' fate over the months since Sarah's death. "One daughter," she said, "has gone quite mad." This she had learned only that morning. Crofters at work in fields that had belonged to the Jacobs heard screams issuing from the homestead. They went to the door, and when Evan Jacob refused to speak to them, Evan Jones was called on and vouched for Esther's condition.

"How dreadful," Gwen said.

"They keep her at home?" asked Douglas.

"The rural Welsh hate institutions. It would mean the most extreme defeat if they couldn't maintain her themselves."

"But what if . . . ?" said Gwen. "What will happen to her?"

Christine shook her head. "I don't know."

"I found much of what the prosecutor said at the hearing sound," said Douglas. "His naming the committee an illegally constituted society made sense to me. I felt the whole committee ought to be tried."

"But you see," Christine said, "no one imagined she'd die. They thought she would outwit the watchers or confess deception. They didn't expect Sarah would allow herself to be starved to death and her parents would just—look on."

"Are you defending the doctors?" Gwen said. "Their job, then, was what?"

"They had signs," Douglas said, "that she was dying. The pulse was enough."

"Was it?" said Christine. "Isn't it easy to be wise in retrospect?"

"In this situation and from a disinterested party, Mother, I would say no. On the day before she died, Lewis and Vaughan got different readings, but they weren't far apart. Vaughan claimed the pulse isn't a good indicator in persons of a hysterical nature, but Sarah had the same nature as at the start of the watch, when her pulse was half what it became. As for the rally, people do rally before they die. It isn't unseen. A bedridden woman I treated got up and fed her horses one final time and then crawled back in bed and died ten minutes later. Any doctor has seen this."

"The problem was Jacob," said Christine. "Maybe they could have convicted the doctors had Jacob not interfered."

"The father is guilty," said Gwen, "that much is clear."

"The cologne bottle was damning," said Douglas.

"That Jacob knew it was under her arm!" said Gwen.

"Mother, do you think lasting the watch was discussed between the girl and her parents?"

"Nothing may have been overtly said. But Sarah knew what was expected of her." Christine explained how the vicar had walked in during her last contact with Sarah, how he had guarded the girl—as it happened, into death.

"There!" said Douglas. "They should have charged the entire committee!"

"She was trying to talk to you, Mother!" said Gwen.

"I'm not sure," Christine said. "But I should have challenged him, should—" She stopped, for it was too much to explain.

"It isn't your fault," Douglas said.

"No," Gwen agreed.

They went into the cottage and sat drinking mulberry wine by the fire, since no one could yet think about dinner.

"Fowler's diagnosis was vague," Douglas said. "The current attitude is that everything can be learned from the physical examination, but it can't. Fowler elided what he didn't know under the blanket diagnosis of hysteria. When in doubt, say hysteria."

"I've gathered," said Gwen, "that that's what hysteria is. But what was wrong with Sarah, then?"

"I couldn't say," he replied. "I am in agreement with Reverend Jones in one respect. He was right to call medicine the most uncertain and immature science." The science, thought Christine, that hadn't been able to save his sick wife.

"Because it is," Douglas said. "It is muddled and new, only just regulated. Tremendous discoveries are on the brink, but they aren't here yet. I doubt that a courtroom of medical experts, even in London, could blow the fog off the lingering questions in the case; they'd disagree, and cancel each other out."

"Can you answer this?" Christine asked. "Did Sarah have

volition before her death? I mean, did she have functioning, rational volition throughout the watching?"

"She couldn't have had," Douglas said. "It would have been compromised by the third or fourth day."

"It is why the suicide theory doesn't hold," said Christine. "She must have thought she could last, but by the time she perceived she couldn't, she only half-knew what she did anymore."

They pondered that, drinking wine.

"It was a lovely party, Mother," Gwen said. "Is Mr. Pary your beau?"

Christine blushed, told herself they couldn't see it in firelight, and laughed. "Gwen, why would you think that? Beau? *Beau?* I think not."

Gwen shrugged. "I wouldn't put anything past you." But she said this with a twinkle, without any judgment.

How did Gwen know? It had happened, and it was mad that it happened twice, and Christine hated his cluttered house, and they were old. It had been the gin, combined with her sense of physical rejuvenation. Inappropriate, but then, it was pleasurable, and she was the instigator. Oh dear.

She grinned and said, "Food?"

But Gwen shot up from her chair, replenished her glass, and swilled down the wine. "I'm leaving my husband," she said. "But I hate how I'll hurt him! Don't gloat, Mother, please." Christine went and put her arms around her daughter. When Gwen drew back, her cheeks were wet, and she said she was tired and left for bed.

"She must have just decided," said Douglas. "I think she's been mulling it over since we've been abroad."

Restraining her joy, Christine said, "It won't be easy."

"Is it true?" Douglas asked. "You and Reginald?"

"No! For God's sake!"

"I wouldn't blame you," he said, reassuring her.

She asked, "Have you given up smoking?"

"No, all your dreams aren't coming true in one day."

She expressed her gratitude that they were here, and he said coming was brilliant of him, that he had seen parts of Father he wouldn't have, otherwise.

"Douglas—you said I came to Wales to find him. I did, or that was a very large reason. Strange as it sounds, there were qualities in him that puzzled me always. His audacity and determination, his emotionalism—these, I've learned, are keen in the Welsh. I didn't want him to report the war. I see now, he had to. What he had lived as a child couldn't have been resolved otherwise."

"I've felt that," said Douglas.

"I've heard that the words to explain Wales exist only in Welsh."

"You've heard the words?"

"Not yet." No one, so far, had said them adroitly enough for her to hear.

THE NEXT DAY, THEY DESCENDED BY THE PARADE to the railway station at Kidwelly Fach and traveled to Llandysul, where Christine showed off the medieval church by the river and the region's fattest and oldest yew in the graveyard. The yews were associated with the land of the dead, and some, Christine said, were a thousand years old. Churches were often built beside rivers. They needed a water source, to be sure, but as well, in medieval times there remained an adherence to water gods, in Celtic beliefs that located the numinous spread throughout nature—trees, dirt, water, sky charged with spirit and quickened by faith. When Douglas and Gwen continued on with their sightseeing, to the place where the chained Merlin, historical soul of Carmarthen Town, sang in his cave, Christine returned to the cottage to meet Vinnie Smyth for tea.

"How is your foot?" she asked.

"Strapping, almost," Vinnie said. She removed her boot and rested her foot on the damask stool. Vinnie, born in 1804, was fifteen years older than Christine and James. The three of them had spent a good deal of time together on that first trip abroad. Vinnie had later visited Brooklyn, and correspondence by letter, except for a few years during the war, had always bound them.

"How did you get away from the paper?" Christine asked.

"I haven't taken anything off since—" She couldn't recall. "And I should work less."

"Really?"

"It's so. And you, my dear, you're well? You look strapping!"

"You promised news from London."

"The talk about Sarah is quieter," Vinnie said. "We have so *much* crime in London. Sarah was set apart while she lived, but now the Jacobs seem common criminals."

"What of the Crown?" Christine asked. "What are their intentions?"

"They have run down their authority as protector of children. The poor law system has failed; the baby farmers leave infants for dead in the streets—yes, I have seen it, once a tiny face in the gutter beside a dead dog. No, she wasn't alive. She may have died in the night, because when I saw that little oval of white staring up from a bed of wet leaves—her little eyes were open—it was early morning, and as I drew near she was grayer than white and dead as can be. It was probably weeks I nightly patrolled the gutters in my stretch of London, but I didn't see or save anyone else." She stared ahead for a moment and then said, "There is the economic depression, the pauperism in and out of the workhouses. We've a bigger mess on our hands than what we did to the kids in factories."

"So the Jacobs will be a test case," said Christine.

"I'd say so, alongside the insane obsession with the Welsh, an attitude that fascinates me. You look at the Irish, such stormy, obdurate people. The Welsh are evasive, God knows, but they are conciliatory, if given a chance."

"Isn't it simpler, though?" said Christine. "Sarah amassed a following, and they can't let the forces of unreason and superstition gain the power her myth had, not today."

"And certainly not in Wild Wales when they're in the process of taming her. Yet again."

"Too many factions latched onto her here," said Christine. "The Welsh have plenty to blame themselves for. Gohebydd and Marles and Evan Jones—they used her."

"Are you still taking it on?" Vinnie asked.

Christine got up and went to the small front window, a square of blue sky. She turned back: "I'm not out at night patrolling the streets."

Vinnie smiled. "Let me serve as an example."

"It's just—" Christine sat. "I knew her. I loved her." Vinnie's brow lifted and Christine herself hadn't expected the overstated "loved," unless, she realized, it was not overstated. "Sarah was an individual to me," she said. "Increasingly, as I knew her, she was utterly real, and herself, and if every side of this case has its champions—some for the doctors, the Welsh, the law that's arisen, our dying God—I keep thinking that Sarah, the girl, so brave under everything all of them did to her. . . . I think she only had me."

"Had you? Has you?" Vinnie said.

"I profited by her," Christine said.

"Well then, when it is over you can write letters to the editors. Perhaps you can find another fasting girl to save. But I do think their days are numbered. I do feel this death has served a sort of purpose in putting the battle to rest."

"A purpose . . ."

"You disagree."

Christine didn't answer, and Vinnie said, "Gwyneth's strapping! Isn't she! And Douglas. I've enjoyed them immensely, Christine."

"And they you."

"When Gwen learned that the cromlechs were old as the pyramids, she began drawing them. It is inspiring for young people to see things endure, even if it is just a pile of rocks."

"She's leaving Blunt."

"You don't say! Jolly good news, she's got her confidence back. I wish you had yours."

"But I do."

"I apologize."

"No need. You're right. Vinnie, how is it that we don't *get* anywhere? How awful it is to think I'll die knowing so little."

"We get somewhere. Trust me, you would not have preferred living two hundred years ago. And to realize how much you don't know, and will never know, is a mark of wisdom, by my lights."

"Move to America, please. Live next door and remind me. I will feel stable, I will feel accepting, I will feel peace, and then everything turns, I'm confused; I'm sixteen at fifty-one!"

"It's being alive," Vinnie said. "I am most sorry to tell you."

"I hoped for mastery."

"You've a bit of it, don't you?"

"I have no idea."

Christine had never had a mother or a sister, and Vinnie was the closest she'd come to both. She hated to think of living beyond her, of living beyond all the elders, with nothing between her and the grave.

"The children honor James by their visit," Vinnie said. "And they honor you. Will you go back with them?"

"I have to see the trial through."

"Of course. And then?"

"Why, yes. I'll go back."

GWEN AWOKE IN THE NIGHT AND CAME DOWNSTAIRS, finding Christine at her desk.

"What are you writing?" asked Gwen.

"Oh, notes. I'm always at it, even when I'm not," and she took off her spectacles and watched Gwen in her dressing gown sit at the table. "Nightmare?"

"No, I've been thinking about what to do. I read the John Stuart Mill in London, *The Subjection of Women*. Vinnie has seen him speak."

"Read Mary Wollstonecraft," Christine said. "Most of what he wrote she said eighty years ago."

"I've decided to go to college," said Gwen.

Christine took a bracing inhalation and said, "I shall not react with too much enthusiasm. I shall pretend, Gwen, it's all one to me." She swooped to the table. "It's wonderful! Nothing could make me happier. Nothing could make *you* happier, darling. You've a very good mind and you love to read, and the excitement in colleges now for women! It will be such an adventure!" She stopped herself and said, "Well, good."

"I wrote to Mr. Blunt yesterday," Gwen said. "My letter should arrive before we do. So it's done."

"That was smart," said Christine, "and brave, dear."

"Brave. Selfish. It's one. But I have only one life and I don't love him. I thought I did. But, Mother"—her voice had gotten low and distressed—"I could not have been pregnant, ever.

And don't say anything about it, please, because I know—what I did, lying about it, and that I must leave him."

Christine obeyed and was silent.

"Still, it's terrible, to hurt him as I will," Gwen said.

"Despite our best efforts and intentions," Christine said, "we hurt people."

They both looked up sharply at a shriek from outside.

"What is it?" Gwen asked.

"A fox," said Christine. "It's riven the silence. I can still feel it, can you? Flowing over your skin." The vixen. Blood on her mouth, scampering into the scrub with her kill.

"Father's dead," said Gwen, and Christine reached across the table and lightly took up the fingers of one of Gwen's hands with her own.

"Yes, he's dead," said Christine.

"They'll never find him."

"I think—finding his body doesn't matter anymore."

One day, Gwen, Douglas, and Vinnie decided they wanted to see the vicar's church, the public house, and St. Michael's graveyard.

Sarah's grave was a tourist destination, and limp bouquets rotted among the new offerings—golden poppies, wild thyme, clematis, and the first summer roses on thorny stems.

They didn't enter the church, but they refreshed themselves at the Eagle Inn. When they emerged, Vinnie Smyth said, "I say!"

"Jones," Christine said.

"The famous vicar," Vinnie muttered under her breath. He walked straight toward them, having come from down the road. Then he passed by them, as if they weren't there.

"Reverend Jones," Christine said.

He turned back and squinted at her. She had both hoped and dreaded to see him. Her feelings about him were outsized, as if dastardly acts he'd committed might lift from his brain and become fully discernible cartoons around him, might become people capable of attack—he seemed to vibrate today with something of the like. His jacket was covered in dust and his hair, too, was dusty. He'd walked long and far, or had cleaned out an attic.

Mrs. Owen had recently seen him at market, the four-year-old daughter tripping along many paces behind.

He grimaced, and then, reaching a decision, he turned away again and continued on.

"Not very sociable," Douglas said.

"What's wrong with him?" Gwen asked.

"The vicar is drunk," Vinnie said.

Christine looked over Vinnie's shoulder at Jones's diminishing form down the road, intrigued to see if he'd stumble. "Really?" she said to Vinnie. "Was he?"

"I could smell it from three feet away," she replied. "But if he's High Church, I suppose it's all right."

"How gothic," Douglas said.

"How Poe," Gwen said. "I love Poe."

Christine wasn't shocked by his behavior, but rather pleased. Her senses had dilated, fluttered and flapped in a state of high stimulation.

≫

Carmarthen, Wales
2 July 1870

Dearest James,

They've gone. I felt bereft. Worst were the last words Gwen said to me, "You will come back, won't you? To Brooklyn?"

I felt I am someone and no one. I exist, and I don't. I render thoughts into solid words on a page, but I live in a kind of twilight. Not young and not yet very old. Not here and not there. Am I *afraid* to go back?

I am afraid to leave bearing my failure—my hand in digging Sarah's unquiet grave. In the blankness of my family gone, I felt shrinking faith in the resolution I'd once hoped the trial would bring. I slept poorly these last three nights since they departed.

Then today came a turn. I'd gotten up, disgusted with bed, and dressed. I perceived light, heard the twitter of first morning birds. I walked out to the Parade, where another dry day would dawn, and watched Wales appear. Through pearly gray I heard the sheep faintly bleating before I could see them. They were being driven out into the valley. White dots skittered and pulsed light, as if the motion spun brightness. Grass greened; the sky blued. I intimated the river's shape, and, upon it, the fluffy mist drew away like an eiderdown from the sleeping water. The tinworks glittered on the far shore and the riverbanks populated, embroidered detail, chimney smoke whirled, and the river gleamed. I heard lowing cows, the tones like distant sonorous organs.

Gwen had told me that if a Welshman longs hard enough to witness the land of the *tylwyth teg*, invisible to mortals, he may be invited to place his foot on top of a fairy's and from the touch another world opens in a chasm before him, teeming and real.

A cart trundled down the Parade and day arrived. I headed back to the cottage, and when I drew close, I saw that someone had gone through the gate and stood at the door.

I picked up my pace and called out, "I'm here!" The man turned; it was the boy Emyr.

"Good morning!" I said. "You're out early today."

"Good morning." But for the red stain at his hair, I thought him handsome. "The mistress sent it," and he tried to hand me a small parcel.

I brimmed with the confidence of the new day, singing within me. "Come in!" I opened the door and went into the front room. "Have tea with me," I said. "Emyr, isn't it?"

"I've work," he replied, and he stayed on the stoop.

"I cannot accept the parcel," I said, putting more age and authority into my voice, "unless you take tea to repay your trouble."

I lit the fire under the kettle, and he reluctantly entered and crossed to the table at which I gestured him to sit. When I brought tea and poured, he put the parcel on the table and pushed it in my direction. "Not yet," I said, and pushed it back. I couldn't take the chance that he'd bolt. "And what is your work today?"

He had been astonished at being forced to come in, but now he relaxed. "I'm at the stables by the Eagle Inn. Then I go down to the Jacobs'."

"I admire you for your loyalty." I served bread and butter and saw he was hungry. "I was fond of Sarah, as you know," I said.

"I saw you," he said.

"Often, didn't you? Now I'm staying on through the trial and probably longer. I care, you see, about Sarah's dying, and about Margaret and Mary and the rest."

He looked at a book on the table. "*Tylwyth Teg*. Illustrated and in Welsh."

He could read. "Would you like it? I have it in English; you take the Welsh."

"No," he said. "I have a book," and he sat up straighter.

"This book?"

"A book."

"Another book. Ah."

He finished his repast and eyed the parcel; I ignored it. "I came to care deeply for Sarah," I told him. It could have been the wrong thing to say, but at my emphatic words, our eyes met—and held. "Sarah lived for her books," he said.

"That she did. More bread?"

"No, madam, I—"

"I wanted to help her," I said with all my passion.

He brought out an object from his pocket, and, keeping it a distance away so that I couldn't touch it, he showed me a love spoon. Flowers and leaves wound its stem and painted petals curved into an *S* and a *J*.

"You made it for Sarah. It's beautiful."

He put it back in his pocket. His gaze lit once more on the parcel.

"I'll take it," I said, "but in a minute. Something's not right, Emyr. Wait. Please don't be frightened. I want to know what happened to Sarah, and I will know. I have no confidence in the trial, of any true justice." Did he comprehend? "If you know anything, tell me. You don't even have to until after the trial—if you are worried. You'd be safe."

He clumsily stood, and I saw that I had, in the end, frightened him.

I opened the parcel I'd barely considered until then, and it was the necklace I'd given to Hannah.

"Mistress wants you to keep it for her," Emyr said.

"Why then, she trusts me, doesn't she? And look, do you see what it is?" He was turned to the door. I dangled the necklace. "I had it made for Mrs. Jacob, in memory of Sarah. One side is a lock of her hair and on the other side—see?"

He wouldn't look, but he listened.

I didn't recognize that what I did was reckless, that it could potentially endanger him and the others. I was desperate and proceeded along the sole path available to me: this boy. "Good-bye," I said, and opened the door, and he fled.

Out of the twilight, out of the black empty hours. He was the access I had waited for, and I believed that in time all would come clear.

It is night again now as I write, and I still believe.

His spoon was a declaration.

As ever,
Christine

THE TRIAL

Opening of the Summer Assizes and the Madness of a Daughter

Special Dispatch to The Sun, *12 July 1870*

By Christine Thomas

The Courts of Assizes are periodic courts held around England and Wales, where the most serious criminal cases are committed to it in quarter sessions. The holding of the Assizes is a significant event in the life of towns where these sessions convene.

On this hot morning in Carmarthen, Wales, crowds thronged the street and the Guildhall Square as the presiding judge, arrayed in red robes, the black-robed barristers and solicitors, the high sheriff, chaplain, and the twenty-two magistrates comprising the grand jury marched to the Guildhall to be met by the clerks, court reporters, and the twelve members of the petty jury, local workingmen who hear the cases deemed fit to stand trial. Inside the opulent rooms of the court, sunlight poured across the crowded lower floor and, even at ten in the morning, overheated the packed ladies' gallery above.

The grand jury having been sworn, and the proclamation against vice, profaneness, and immorality having been read, His Lordship, the Honorable Sir James

*Hannen, knight, delivered the charge to the grand jury.
The grand jury was then excused to consider the case of
Evan and Hannah Jacob. The petty jury was next sworn
in, and shortly the grand jury returned a true bill, committing the Jacob case to trial.*

*The indictment will be read and translated into
Welsh for the defendants on the morrow, when the parents of the dead Sarah Jacob are scheduled to appear.*

*It had been rumored that Esther Jacob, elder sister
of the deceased girl, has declined in her mental health
since shortly after Sarah was buried. Upon confirmation
from officials at the Joint Counties Lunatic Asylum, it
was reported that today Esther, sixteen years of age, was
conveyed by her father and an unidentified assistant to
the stately hospital, built in 1865, where she will reside
for the foreseeable future.*

≈

A HUSH FELL OVER THE COURT WHEN THE DEFENDANTS were
brought in. Jacob, rail thin, morose, was put into the dock—
the wooden stall reaching his waist while he stood, the glass
his chest. Christine imagined his pale eyes locked with His
Lordship's, as Sir James watched from his platform as Jacob
settled. Hannah moved to the dock as in a trance. Swathed
in mourning black, she wore a flower-trimmed bonnet in an
eerie echo of the lost girl.

Christine sat toward the rear of the lower floor with the
other, male correspondents, but was constantly drawn to
the sight of the women in the gallery above. The petty jury
was seated to the right of His Lordship. The prosecution and
defense teams had tables in front of the Jacobs. The Reverend Jones, the nurses, the five doctors, Gohebydd and Marles,
the pathologists, John Daniel, Dr. Fowler, and Dr. Pearson

Hughes were seated behind the defendants, ready if called as witnesses.

When the indictment was read, Evan Jacob rose to say, "We are not guilty."

Mr. Hardinge Gifford, in black robes, white lace at his throat, and an unusually lengthy white barrister's wig hanging down at either side of his aged face like long ears, then stood and opened the case for the prosecution. "May it please Your Lordship and gentleman of the jury—I am instructed by the Crown to conduct the prosecution against the two prisoners at the bar, who are indicted for the manslaughter of Sarah Jacob.

"Gentlemen, this you may take as common knowledge, that on seventeenth December 1869, Sarah Jacob, then between twelve and thirteen years of age, died at her father's house. It is alleged on the part of the prosecution that her death was caused by manslaughter, by the culpable acts of the prisoners. The allegation is that they engaged in a scheme of imposture upon the public. As time went on, they found that they must either avow themselves imposters, or else persevere in the scheme. They did persevere until seventeenth December, when the child died."

Light bounced off the brass chandeliers, washed the white walls and pillars, richened the wood, and the court was still as a church.

Christine glanced at Reginald's pad and read "HOW MANY OF THE JURY SPEAK ENGLISH?" She scanned the twelve, thinking they seemed to follow. But who could tell? Mrs. Owen had said that, if necessary, the men would explain to one another and compensate.

"Now, gentlemen," said the distinguished Mr. Gifford, "the principal question for you to consider is whether, when the child was wasting away, the parents abstained from giving her food." Standing quietly and speaking with utmost respect to the farmers, Mr. Gifford continued: "Shortly related, about the year 1867, Sarah Jacob was afflicted by fits of hysterics. Gentlemen, I use a popular phrase, because in the depositions are scientific words that mean the same thing"—"DO THEY?" Christine wrote—"but which you would not understand. This girl being in that condition, it is likely that what happened afterward was suggested by something that was really true. The scheme, the trick, the imposture was derived from the *real truth* that the girl was able to exist on comparatively little food.

"Then from its being a remarkable thing, there came a gradual agreement to make it a miracle. And so instead of saying that the child lived on scanty food, the parents told their neighbors and friends that she lived on no food at all.

"It has been well established that the mother and father took money for the child's display—though it seems they got it into their heads that they were absolved from theft if the money was placed on the girl's breast and not directly given to either of them.

"Gentlemen, it may strike you as wondrous that a child of this age participated in the deception. But apart from the girl's complaint of hysteria, which wise people say induces a propensity to conceal, you will find that modes were adopted to render extremely agreeable to this child the lying abed to which she was subjected. The child, who was intelligent and precocious and certainly vain, was led to believe she was special. Her hair and person were decorated in styles far beyond her condition in life. I understand she was a pretty child and looked very well in her adornments. She was made much of. You have, on the one hand, financial motive, and, on the second, you have an exhibition profitable to the child's vanity. This little girl was compelled, by acts of the defendants, to keep up the impression that she was a miracle person who did not eat: a supposition that the slightest knowledge of physical function would show to be folly.

"Unfortunately for the child and the parents, too, some people, in this nineteenth century, began to believe in the miracle, and it acquired wider influence. An appeal was made to the newspapers, and medical men were invited to visit.

"People took various parts; some were simple enough to believe the pretended miracle, while others adhered to the skeptical view of the medical men. Doctors debated the case in the press, and eventually a sort of watching was conducted; but it was inept. In time, a rigorous watch was arranged— and an officer at Guy's Hospital, London, consented that four nurses be sent to the family's house to observe the child day and night.

"Gentlemen, one can hardly speak with forbearance about a child allowed to die in the presence of experienced persons without a single one of them attempting to force the child to take food. That is not the question, however, before you. The question is whether the prisoners at the bar are responsible, and you will find overwhelming evidence that both the one and the other were parties to Sarah Jacob's demise."

"NO MERCY FOR HANNAH," Christine wrote, "THEY WANT HER, TOO."

"You will find that from the year 1867 until the ninth December 1869, the child was thriving, instead of becoming emaciated. But from the hour the watching began, she wasted away. In the autopsy report you will hear evidence that she ate prior to food being kept from her during the watching, and if you arrive at the conclusion that she died because she was starved, who is responsible?

"In the nurses' reports, you will have minute—indeed, appallingly minute—descriptions of the symptoms that this unfortunate child displayed. I say 'appallingly minute' because it seems to be something beyond one's experience, and beyond one's reading, that you should have symptoms of a person dying from starvation described with minuteness until death occurs.

"Now, though you may regret that others are not on trial, this does not relieve the prisoners from responsibility. The mother and father assisted in the watching. No one knew better than they did that the child had been, by their act, carrying on an imposture for months; I might say for years. And they knew that during the experiment in front of the nurses the child could not get food. The parents—both the one and the other—assisted in an experiment that, no one knew so well as themselves, was most unsafe."

He spoke of Sarah's allegedly paralyzed arm and how it waved about as she neared death; he spoke of Evan Jacob's interferences; he described the small room where Sarah slept near her parents; he asked the jurors to pay careful attention to the hollow found beneath Sarah's arm and the waste in her colon; he suggested that the parents hoped against hope that their daughter would outlast the watch and establish their reputation forever; and he concluded, "But about the third or fourth day, dangerous symptoms began to set in. The uncle of the child went to the father and appealed to him to give the child food. The father refused, determined that the experiment should be continued at all costs, at the cost of his child.

"The result is that the child is dead. This child was starved to death. I am sure you will entertain no doubt about it."

The jurymen sat there, their expressions impassive; His Lordship looked down from his eminence; and the lower floor popped with coughs and adjustments. No one in the gallery stirred, and throughout the trial the quality of the women's attention never wavered: In their patient absorption, their attention was rapt as prayer.

When the court was adjourned at noon until one-thirty, few women left, reluctant, perhaps, to lose coveted seats.

Christine went outside to the crowded square. Catching sight of Mrs. Owen, she excused herself from the other correspondents and rushed to catch up with her friend. The noon sun beat down and the aroma of bodies and horses hitched at the posts and in alleys was a wall she pushed through. Men, women, and children awaited word. People hawked newspapers and refreshments and locks of Sarah's hair. Signs advertised that the pink-ribbon locks had been tied by the mother's own hands.

"I must get back to the inn," Mrs. Owen said, turning to Christine.

"What was the mood upstairs?" asked Christine.

"Intent. I felt no excitement, as you would have if they had come for the spectacle, and few of them ordinarily attend the court. I think they are there for Hannah and Sarah."

For the remainder of the trial, Christine sat upstairs beside Hannah's heavily pregnant sister Nell, who hadn't been summoned to witness as John Daniel had. At days' end, Christine returned to the newspaper office and filed her reports, and at night, back at the cottage she'd meant to give up and hadn't, Reginald was with her; yet when they discussed the events of the day, she avoided the subject of why she had chosen to sit with the women. "It calms me," she told him at last; "I am accustomed to their perspective." Upstairs, she felt more human somehow. She didn't try to engage Nell in talk, but Nell and many of the rest knew who she was and accepted her, saving her spot if she was late and loaning her fans on occasions she left hers at home. During delays, the women talked softly among themselves about the drought, the health of children, the cost of necessities, the chapels to which they belonged—talked of those things that were the underpinnings of the lofty surface, the skin that was the court; discussed the fleshy interior tissue that supported the stiff, brittle bones of men's courts and fired its muscle. How could you separate women from men? And yet here they were. Their attention became even more acute when the nurses spoke, as if they were running the words through themselves. Strong in their long, deep knowledge and patience, though a few had embraced the miracle while Sarah lived, the women watched. They inhabited Sarah's outrageous story as if it were familiar.

THE PROSECUTION CALLED THE SAME WITNESSES questioned at the magisterial hearing, and while the trappings of the trial were respectful and grave, apart from the skill and preparedness of the legal men, little was different. Cross-examinations by the defense were effective, challenging issues dismissed at the hearing. But the finer legal aspects some had expected brought up in this court were left aside. There was no debate about crimes of omission; and the law of coverture—dealing with wives—that could have exonerated Hannah was dismissed so fast that, as Reginald posited, the defense must have decided that insisting upon it would hurt the interpretations of Hannah's actions they chose to highlight. The case would not become a leading case in the law because the aim, Reginald said, was to win. Neither side wanted to confuse the jury, not because the jurymen were illiterate farmers, but because keeping their arguments direct and clear was what barristers and solicitors did in criminal court. Disputed facts that required analysis were, more or less, glossed by emotive appeal. The law, Reginald said, was an arm of the present, the will of immediate needs. The fissures that had determined Sarah's fate were let lie. Religion? How the narratives Sarah interiorized from the vicar, the Bible, the chapel, the teeth of the revival played into her fate—this was buried with her.

A WELL-PREPARED MR. BISHOP OPENED FOR THE DEFENSE. While the prosecutor depended on gravitas, Bishop took a humbler tact.

"Gentlemen, I am here on behalf of a ruined man, for Evan Jacob's worldly prospects are abolished. To meet bail, his land and livestock are gone. . . . He is accused of starving his little girl, Sarah." Bishop adjusted his wig, as if it rested uncomfortably on his self-effacing Welsh head. "Let us examine the facts.

"All the doctors agreed on Sarah's hysteria, that it caused her desire to conceal that she ever took food. It has been established that the whole neighborhood believed that she actually abstained from food. Even persons much higher in life than the Jacobs entertained faith in the possibility that Sarah was a being free of human laws.

"I do not ask you to decide whether such an occurrence is possible. But every doctor here in court said that hysteric persons exist—may exist—on small quantities of nutriment insufficient to sustain a healthy person. With that fact, my learned colleague opened his case.

"But we must inquire more stringently whether the prisoners knew that the girl was surreptitiously getting food. As the jury knows, the father was a farmer occupying some hundred acres of land, a man who from his position in life was necessarily out about his farm during the major portion of the day. And although I am only defending the father, Mr. Michael will have no objection to my saying that what applied to the father's absence from home would also often account for the mother's absence.

"Women in this country, in the position of life of the

prisoners, are obliged to contribute their energies in the field as well as at the hearth. In this instance, since there was just one manservant employed, the mother would often be, necessarily, absent from the house. Sarah, therefore, had ample opportunity of secretly obtaining the food she required. You know the arrangement of farmhouses, and the Jacobs' dairy was attached to the house. Cheese and buttermilk stood in the dairy. Oats simmered all day on the fire.

"My learned friend says that the girl died for lack of food during the watching. But *I* say there is no proof that the parents knew the girl fed up to that time; they were convinced that the watching could bring her no harm.

"The father was said to be angry when the uncle offered her water and food, but this was because he believed that by the offer, his child would be injured and thrown into fits! It was suggested that the father had, by means of keeping his child in bed, been getting money from the public; but the girl fasted long before any money was given.

"It was suggested that the girl concealed a bottle under her arm and by that means fed; but there was no need of concealing a bottle if the parents were parties to the fraud! The house was shut up early in the evening and the girl could forage for food whilst the hardworking parents slept their hard sleep.

"Gentlemen, where is the evidence of the prisoners' guilt? No one has disproved that Evan Jacob believed his daughter's long fasting."

The jurymen straightened as Mr. Bishop spoke, and the tiny shifts and throat clearings in the gallery quieted when Mr. Michael next took the floor.

Tending to flash and gifted with a resonant bass voice, Mr. Michael dramatically waited a moment after he stood and turned to the jury. "Did the mother feloniously slay Sarah

Jacob?" His voice seemed to open a cool channel through the stifling heat; upstairs the soft whirring of fans continued.

"Hannah Jacob's daughter Sarah, for two and a half years, was subject to a disease. Please bear in mind that it is a true disease. When it is described as simulative, this does not mean that it is any less a disease, but that it mimics other diseases. You have it from the medical witnesses that it is protean, that it changes character—varies so much that it is impossible to tell, day by day, what form it may assume.

"Two and a half years ago, Sarah Jacob had the symptom of spitting blood, which you all know alarms parents, and she had some form of obscure disease that confined her to bed. One of her doctors at the time said it was inflammation of the brain; another said, 'I can do nothing for her. I ought to have been called in earlier.'

"Gentlemen, Sarah Jacob had a disease that was extremely difficult to cure, a disease that, evidently, may deceive even doctors and require special medical skill in order to discover, not whether the girl was ill or no, for there is no dispute about that, but whether the symptoms pertained to the hysteria, or whether her paralysis, blood spitting, and fits, epilepsy or whatever it was, derived from some other disease, superadded to the hysteria."

He allowed his recitation to settle in.

"I ask you to consider the parents' position: The highest men in their district, the clergyman, the esteemed Mr. Marles, the wordsmith Gohebydd and the other committee members, including a band of doctors, induced, 'in the interest of science,' this poor man and wife to consent that the child be tested.

"I ask you, if this man and woman were attempting to deceive the public, what more fatal issue could they have thrust upon them than nurses from Guy's? And what could the authorities of Guy's have been about? If the girl's fasting was so assuredly impossible, why conduct a watching at all? If it was so positive that she would die—it is the clergyman who ought to be in the dock; it is the committee and the doctors who *induced* these poor ignorant people to the loss of their child, their goods, their reputation—to their own fall.

"Before you can find the female prisoner guilty, you must be satisfied that there was no other way of perpetrating the fraud but by her consent and interference.

"I ask you, where is the manservant, that he is not called? I ask you, where in the court are Sarah Jacob's brothers and sisters?

"You cannot find the prisoners guilty on the violent presumption of my learned friend until he has excluded all possible sources of the fraud, as he calls it, except the persons charged on the indictment. I say he has not done so. The manservant or the brothers and sisters may have supplied her with food. She may have kept nutriment in the abnormal hollow beneath her arm. According to the evidence of one of the learned pundits, who wanted to assure us that the girl got out of bed one hour in twenty-four to avoid bedsores, that time might well have been spent obtaining food.

"Gentlemen, I urge upon you that there is no conclusive evidence, nor a particle of evidence, to show that the prisoners had anything to do with the fraud, if fraud there were. I urge upon you that the innocent parents joined in the watching—and with great shock to them, death supervened."

He paused to bring his case home, and then he launched brusquely back into his speech. "Now, gentlemen, is it at all proven to your satisfaction that her death was caused by starvation? According to the statements of the dissectors, the postmortem didn't find any evidence of disease, and they jumped to the conclusion that death occurred from starvation. Well, I must direct your attention to this one point. This was a nervous disease; this disease especially affected motion; one foot remained stiff and unnatural; there was coldness on one side; these symptoms were written about and discussed by Dr. Fowler in court. And was she paralyzed on that left side, or not? The four nurses who watched by the bedside never for a week saw a movement of the arm or leg and only saw these at last when death encroached. One nurse saw a convulsive motion of the girl's arm whilst she slept, and another nurse saw a motion of the leg.

"Consider. The gentlemen who conducted the postmortem looked at the brain, stomach, heart, and chest. But the spinal cord, which affects motion, and the great nerve, described to you by the doctors as the great sympathetic nerve that supplies the stomach and whose morbidity would prevent taking food, they did not examine.

"None of the traces of progressive starvation were prominent in this girl during the entire week of the watching, until the very last. I claim the evidence of the four nurses. Where were the symptoms? The warnings? How was Sarah Jacob the exception to the ordinary rule? People cannot abstain from food, and have pangs of hunger and thirst, without manifesting dreadful symptoms!

"Is it right, in a case acknowledged 'in the interest of science,' to be surrounded with so much difficulty? A case in which it is said we are sitting in order to free the ignorant Welsh mind from the trammels of superstition and darkness? Was it not the duty of my learned friend to put into the box every scientific gentleman, and the best he could find, to show the vulgar and ignorant and benighted and superstitious Welsh mind that there was no truth in this case? To show by their expertise that the girl really died of starvation, and died at the instance of a loving father and mother?

"When the doctor from Cardiff, Pearson Hughes, came to the house and was at first refused permission to examine the child, as soon as the mother knew that he really was a medical gentleman, what did she say? Although hysterical persons dislike the slightest touch, and although, as a medical witness told you, a mere puff of air will produce pain and terror—what does the mother say to her daughter? 'Allow the doctor to examine you, because he will cure you.' And again, when the child drew back from another doctor, Fowler. 'Be good and let him examine you.' Consider the kindness and affection of the mother, who selflessly subjects her daughter to that which she knows will pain her, in the hope of relief from a terrible and long-standing disease!

"And are you to presume—according to the perverse ingenuity of my learned friend for the prosecution—evil intent from the directions that food not be offered? How evil is *his* supposition that this mother, for a few shillings, trafficked in the blood of her child?

"I ask which is more likely, that the mother turned back the unstoppable tide of motherly love? Or instead the more natural suggestion that the mother, throughout the entire illness and up to its fatal result, attempted to save her child from any pang and pain she could?"

The lower floor erupted into applause. The ladies' gallery waited, and then shyly joined in. His Lordship called for order; the clapping resolved; Mr. Michael held the floor half a minute, blotted his brow, and sat.

Two interpretations, two conflicting narratives of what might have happened; the defense rested their case.

Mr. Gifford rose to refute. He, too, brought out a handkerchief and dabbed his face. "I compliment the defense on their vigor," he said, unfazed. "Even while I must respond to Mr. Michael that it is not the duty of the counsel for the Crown to endeavor to procure a verdict unwarranted by the evidence.

"If the parents' story is true—that they believed in the fast—the child, for two years, must have evaded the vigilance of the parents and the elder sisters, presently sixteen and eighteen years old. If the jury is guided by reason, what is *most* probable? That the parents aided and abetted in pursuit of this scheme so profitable to them? Or that the child was able to evade vigilance in a crowded household for two years, the functions of nature suspended, the parents seeing to her bed and person, and they sleeping in the same room with her? As to the claim that 'nerves' caused her death—all the evidence supports starvation.

"I have no interest in bringing you to a wrong conclusion. It is not the duty of the counsel for the Crown to call witnesses unless the counsel for the Crown deems them necessary—witnesses whose testimony, far from being calculated to enlighten, might, on the contrary, be calculated to deceive. The reason why the Crown did not call the manservant and brothers and sisters is apparent; the reason why Mr. Michael and Mr. Bishop did not call them for the defense is a whit more obscure.

"Did the parents encourage inquiry into the truth about their daughter's condition? Why, the father refused to allow Dr. Vaughan to touch her! Of what did the so-called fits consist? Merely closing the eyes, and that is what they called a 'fit.' At least two of the doctors advised the father to withdraw the watching, and he replied, 'Not for the world.' Why? It has been said that others forced the experiment upon the parents, and yet the father, despite the advice of the medical men, persisted in maintaining the watch.

"The parents were fully acquainted with all that was going

on, and from first to last they participated. I cannot tell where Mr. Michael gets the idea that the trial was intended to dissipate the darkness of Welsh ignorance and superstition. I have used no such phrases. There is no more darkness in Wales than in England. But this alleged darkness is immaterial.

"What is material? To show that if persons engage in any such dangerous practices as these, the protection of the law will surround the weak against the strong; and if those who should be the natural protectors of children engage with others in dangerous experiments, no matter if it is with people of authority and reputation—clergymen, newsmen, doctors—they will be punished. And if the local administration of the criminal law should be faulty, then they shall be taught that there is a central authority that will not balk at a criminal prosecution but will bring the offenders before a jury, independent of, and uninfluenced by, local authority, and possessed of firmness sufficient to enable them to give a verdict, according to what is true and right in the case."

After a brief recess in the afternoon of 18 July, the court reconvened, and His Lordship summed up to the jury, cautioning them that the case really involved the consideration of but a few facts. The red-robed lord remarked that one of the dissectors used a strong expression: "He said that her body presented the appearance of a freshly slaughtered animal."

Beside Christine, Nell lowered her head.

"There was no trace of disease," said His Lordship. "It was suggested that the dissectors ought to have examined the spine. All I have to say about that is this. Counsel for the defense presumes a greater amount of knowledge, or ignorance, than belongs to me. In the evidence, the girl's only disease was hysteria. The seat of hysteria is in the mind and doesn't cause death. Of what, then, did she die?

"The object of the watching was to see if the girl could live without food. Put it in other terms, to see whether if she had no food she would die. They kept watching her and saw that she had no food, and she did die."

Nell slumped from her shoulders. "Do you need to go out?" whispered Christine.

She shook her head no.

It went on—the evidence of the excreta, His Lordship's pronouncement that the watching was perfectly natural, forthright, conducted as it was by concerned, educated parties. "The unavoidable death," he said, "was just the sort of experimental proof by which we arrive at such certainty that humankind can possess on any subject whatever."

"Do you need to go out?" Christine asked again.

She nodded yes.

Christine helped Nell from the gallery and down the stairs to the shady corridor through to the foyer, and outside to the dazzling square.

"Will you sit?" Christine asked, spotting a bench vacated at their approach. Everywhere, sprawled on the grass, draped from open shop windows, eating and drinking and selling wares, currying horses, they waited—at least a hundred. Up the brick rise at the end of the square, the castle prison awaited, a short journey from the Guildhall, which faced the square and would soon, they hoped, open its doors with news.

Dully, Nell sat, the color high in her cheeks.

"Shall I take you home?" Christine asked.

"I couldn't," she said. "I'll wait. It's better out here."

But as the wait extended, Nell sweat so profusely and sighed so often that Christine got up and said, "Stay here; I'll get you a drink."

She crossed through the crowded square to where she saw a vendor, but reaching the man, shoulders knocked into her, and the crowd jostled and leaped. "Stand back! Stand back!"

The javelin men from the court were pushing people away from the Guildhall columns and carving a path through the square. Shoved-off people cluttered the margins and blocked Christine's view of Nell. She glanced up at a beam of altering light and gray clouds just above the farthest rooftop in her line of vision—and thought that, finally, it would rain. Then from between the front columns emerged Evan and Hannah Jacob, their arms bound behind them. Evan looked about; Hannah, thought Christine, was choking, but it all happened quickly. Single sounds blended, the pitch altogether had dropped, and the muting continued as Evan and Hannah came into the square.

The Guildhall expelled the court. The people who had waited outside fell in behind the advancing prisoners, first in groups of three and four and then five or six, fanning out into rows. Men and boys doffed their hats and children held parents' hands. Some from the court fell in behind the first rows. The crowd went up the rise, the lines of folk proceeding and snaking back all the way to the courthouse steps as people kept joining.

Christine saw Reginald on the steps with Lloyd and the other correspondents. John Daniel had found Nell.

The gallery women were coming out now; they completed the retinue. Christine walked with them, and one of the women confided that Evan had gotten a year of hard labor and Hannah six months.

It wasn't far to the castle. They were too much in the rear to see well when the prisoners vanished inside. But as the Jacobs arrived at the top of the ascent, Christine saw Evan turn and look at the sky. Only a moment it was, and the castle had him.

As those at the front of the crowd began to disperse, the gallery women pushed forward. "Her hat!" a boy cried. He held it aloft. Hannah's flower-trimmed bonnet had fallen from her. Christine saw it smashed, waved excitedly by the boy. He tossed the hat into the air and children scrambled to catch it and fought over it on the ground.

"Give it," a woman said, pushing off the roughhousing children. She secured the hat and delivered the coveted object safely to one of the javelin men, who took it into the castle.

The light changed. The dark clouds had dissipated, exposing enamel blue and dashing the possibility of rain. Christine and the gallery women pressed closer.

She pictured the stables at the Eagle Inn, where the red-marked boy worked. She would call on him in the morning, only to learn he was gone. She wouldn't know for some time that in Hannah's womb Evan Jacob's eighth child already quickened.

Only women and children remained at the castle, standing respectfully near the gate. A girl looked up at the highest reaches, and Christine followed her gaze, imagining she could see Hannah brushing the dust off the flowers, reshaping her hat.

SWANSEA

CHRISTINE FOUND IT SLIGHTLY ALARMING that Reginald, self-proclaimed lifelong insomniac, achieved narcotized nirvana when he slept in her bed. His soft snores accompanied her pen's scratch. Lying spread eagle on top of the quilt in his nightshirt, he might have been flung into a poppy field and settled there, full of bliss. His kinky black head was turned to the side and he seemed to be smiling.

At seven o'clock in the morning, four days after the trial, the cottage was cool. The Jacobs were gone from Carmarthen, transported by train to Swansea Prison. In an earlier era, they'd have traveled south via the river. Christine wondered how it had been for them to ride the train, to arrive in a foreign place where no one would know them. She assumed they'd have no visitors. The ironworks and other major industries had transformed Swansea; transient workers populated its prison, alongside sailors and prostitutes from its rough seaport. Carmarthen Prison was beginning its renovation, while Swansea had completed its alteration to the silent, single-cell system. Quiet labor. Aloneness. Dung heap in the prison yard.

She had been shocked to find Emyr gone. "Went south," the man at the stables had told her. "To the mines, surely," he said, "like so many of the young." The south was stippled with mines and she'd never find him. Even if she did, what would he say? Was there anything to say? That he had left on the morning after the trial must have meant something. He didn't want to talk to her, since Evan Jacob would return in a year? Or maybe Emyr wasn't afraid of Jacob; maybe he didn't blame Jacob. Jacob had once saved the boy from certain death, and Emyr's loyalty to him could have remained paramount, bigger than his childish love for Sarah. Maybe concern for the other Jacob children, if he spoke, caused him to flee. She had heard that the elder brothers had already moved in with the schoolmaster. She hoped Mary and Margaret would go, along with David, to stay with John and Nell Daniel.

When Reginald slept on, she dressed and went outside and sat with her back against the cottage wall. She could see a wedge of the Parade, the tinworks beyond, grassy slopes under the hard blue summer sky. Each day she was consciously drinking her last of Wales, imbibing what this old civilization, for all its worries, had taught her. She had come to know Carmarthenshire, perhaps, better than Brooklyn. As she had expected, Reginald asked her to stay. But if she tarried, it was from remorse over what she hadn't done to save Sarah, what she unreasonably still believed she should rectify, somehow.

Everyone else was satisfied that it was over. Vinnie had been correct about the case's being tried as an example. But the message surpassed the welfare of children; it warned against conspiracy and chastened the local magistrates for how they had let off the doctors. The prosecutor's closing remarks also warned against extra-legal dealings with crime; the Crown proclaimed those days finished, as so many old Welsh ways were through.

A year for Evan and six months for Hannah wasn't much. All that to-do for not much—why, more had been blurred into nonexistence than had been revealed. The Crown took a stand, Reginald said, because of the death and Sarah's fame. The sentence was a nod to the unusualness of the case. Of late, harsher sentences had been imposed, but for more overtly violent crimes. The parents of a boy they kept locked in a henhouse until he died of exposure were sentenced to twenty years.

The sun brightened, warming her face—well, well, she missed her sleeping paramour. She couldn't deny that her feelings for him had deepened, and with a burst of enthusiasm she rose to go back inside—and lifted a rock near the front door. A whiteness edging it had caught her eye.

The white was a piece of paper, folded once and hidden beneath the rock the size of an unleavened bread loaf—well enough that she could have entirely missed it and almost had. You dear, she inwardly said to the vanished Emyr.

But then she read it: "Evan Jacob interfered with Sarah, and she lost her faith."

She read it again, mistrusting her Welsh.

She looked back out at the Parade and went to wake Reginald.

She sat carefully down beside him and rubbed his back. "Good morning."

"Have I done it again?" he mumbled.

"You have. Wake up. Quickly," she added.

"It's come to that, has it?"

He sat up, and she gave him the paper, asking, "What does it say?"

He repeated, in English, what she had thought it said.

"Am I misinterpreting a sexual connotation?" she asked. "Can it mean, improper relations?"

"Who wrote this? Where did you get this?"

She told him the story from the beginning: how Emyr had whittled spoons at the fireside with the family when she was with them; how Hannah had told her about Evan saving the boy; how she had counted on Emyr knowing what she could not see of the family life and how, when he brought her the necklace from Hannah for safekeeping, she had inveigled him inside and he showed off the spoon he made for Sarah; how she had discovered him gone, probably south, where he couldn't be found.

"I wouldn't think he could write," Reginald said.

"He read aloud to me the name of a book when he was here."

Reginald's alert eyes held the surprise she often saw in him when it came to her actions. "How would the boy know?" he said.

"Proximity, extra awareness because of his feelings for Sarah."

"Anyone could have written the message," Reginald said. "You're a well-known newspaperwoman. Some might wish to extend the viability of Sarah's powers, or, at any rate, the cause it brought forth."

"But who else could know this? If it's true—and I couldn't publish unsigned speculation."

"The writer might think otherwise."

"Reginald. Did the jury convict them because they feared reprisal from the English if they did not?"

"What reprisal? Strong words were said, but they were words. The jury convicted because it was right."

You could not shake his faith in a system that had, overall, served him well. He had never needed to grab at tenuous clues, to watch closely what the powerful did in order to evade possible danger. Although he had his Welsh pride, he wasn't a farmer, and he wasn't a woman.

"Let me ask you this," she said. "Why wasn't Emyr called into the court by the defense? Why weren't the brothers and sisters called?"

"It's obvious," Reginald said. "What credence would have

attached to witnesses economically dependent upon the defendants?"

"But they may be the only ones who really know what happened!"

"We know enough about what happened."

"We do?"

"Wrongful death, and it was prosecuted. I, for one, am glad about that. A Welsh farming girl's life was valued by the Crown."

She got up and went to the stove and put on the kettle. None of this was Reginald's fault. Courts dealt with the shell of life and set their precedents. Shells, one could hope, were protective. "Tea and toast?" she asked.

"Why are you angry?" he said.

"I'm not. Anyway, not at you."

She laid the table and he came with the paper and read it again. "Even if this is true and comes from a person who could know it true, it's immaterial now."

"Really?" she said, turning to him.

"It couldn't be brought before a court of law, of course," he said.

"Of course."

"And if it could, it is small compared to the matter of—"

"Small?"

"Christine. These things happen, probably often, and more than we would care to know."

"Can you hear yourself?" she asked.

"She's gone," he said. "You cannot do anything else for Sarah Jacob."

At this, she emboldened; her mind cleared, she took back the note and informed him, "I'm going to London to speak with the sister-nurse."

"Why?"

"Hunch." She left off making breakfast and started to pack. "I'll stay at Vinnie's. Will you telegraph, care of her through *The Times*, if there's any news?"

ON THE TRAIN, SHE STUDIED THE PAPER. "Interfered." Did it simply signify Jacob's orchestration of imposture against Sarah's will? No, Emyr wouldn't have said it like that. And "lost her faith" was heartbreaking in how it suggested lack of protection and unpunished sin and destroyed comfort for a sick, religious girl. Her thoughts tumbled over one another. Reginald was a very good man. She would love him, in her way, always. But her passion, now, was elsewhere. James, she thought, you and Father protected me too well. What did she know of the vagaries and varieties of life? When Douglas and Rupert were small, they loved lifting up rocks, the larger the better, to examine the mucky, buggy swirl underneath. Gwen loved the dollhouse James had built for her precisely because who didn't want to take off the wall of a house? Holding the paper, she studied her hands, thinking how strange they were, her skin creased by time. When you were young, you tried, through your own body and its concrete environs, to understand who you were in the world. As you got older, you came to accept it all, yourself, four-walled houses, sun-warmed rocks half-dug into earth, without thinking of what you couldn't see or know. How else to get on?

If Jacob had done this and if, as Reginald said, it was a thing that often happened, the world was new, and she would have to question everything she had ever thought.

Did it make the starving worse? Did it nullify the starving? It did not nullify. It intensified. It made the starving infinitely worse.

She was going to Swansea, having decided that London

could wait. As the train neared the industrial city, smoke watered her eyes—the town she remembered, clustered below the hills by the sea, had been visited by a plague. The green sulfurous glow of the smelters lay in a haze across the sky. The ships tightly packed against the quays could have been castaways, thrown at the shore, thirsty and gaunt. Nothing lived by the shore. The trees were stunted or gone, the grass blistered off. The flickering furnaces were the glare of success, but the rivers were black, and along the banks, even in summer, there were no flowers.

She went straight to the prison. Already she had investigated what it was like for dispatches she wrote throughout the trial. The prison currently housed around two hundred inmates, and of these, fifty or sixty were women kept in a separate ward; Hannah and Evan would not meet during their terms. Hard board beds had replaced the more comfortable hammocks once used, and in the small single cells, each with one high barred window, prisoners were meant to reflect on their misdeeds. Transportations and executions weren't working against rising crime, and the new prisons had been expressly designed to deter, in an effort to keep the masses under control. Food was poor and intentionally monotonous. Work was tedious and taxing. Hannah would grind soaked laundry through mangles for ten hours a day, unless she picked oakum—took apart tarry rope fibers for reuse on ships. Evan would walk the treadwheel, a huge drum that prisoners rotated by climbing everlasting stairs, each step three feet in height, work designed to leave the men gasping. At Swansea, the treadwheel pumped water, but in other prisons the treadwheel turned without purpose except to grind men. Prisoners daily climbed the equivalent of nine thousand feet, which, if straight up, would have brought them in three days to the top of Mount Everest.

The massive stone building took up a block on Oyster-mouth Road. In the reception cave—a dank niche—Christine pretended to be Hannah's sister and was told to wait. She fingered the necklace in her pocket, asking herself, once more, why Hannah had sent it to her for safekeeping. Surely there was a reason for Emyr's note, the note she had no intention of sharing with Hannah.

The key-clanking guardsman returned and said, "Come back tomorrow at four o'clock."

She wondered about the souls she encountered as she asked in the vicinity for an inn, the foreigners—she heard German, Russian, and Nordic words—and those like Emyr, the Welsh who'd worked the land and found themselves here, trying to live. At the inn she located nearby, the white lace curtains were black at the hems, and so sad they seemed that she almost walked on, but what else would she find?

Inside, she spent the rest of the day writing and then staring up at the cracked ceiling. Why go out? What was there to see? Count the hours, sleep, perchance to dream—of another world, a better place.

THE GUARDSMAN USHERED HER INTO A CAVERN and told her to wait at a long table. Something dripped behind the walls, and the rocky expanse she faced glistened with moisture. Far away—bells, then the sound of a train. The heavy door swung with a spine-tingling creak and Hannah was brought in and seated across from Christine. Hannah didn't let on that Christine wasn't Nell, but she looked wretched—dirty, thin, humped, her hair going gray, spewed from the meager flannel cap. One of her cheeks was swollen.

They were alone.

"Hello, Hannah."

Hannah stared as one would at an ethereal manifestation. "Why are you here?" she said at last.

"Out of care for you. I received the necklace you sent back to me from Emyr and—" Hannah's features contracted; her long nose dipped to her mouth. "What is it?" Christine asked.

"I—did not send it. I gave it to my daughter Mary to keep for me." Fearfully, she continued, "I would have given it to you, but I thought you were returning to Brooklyn."

"It's yours! You can do anything with it you like," said Christine.

"You shouldn't have come, madam. I am ashamed before you." She brought up one outsized red hand and touched her cheek.

"Do you have a toothache?"

Hannah rapidly nodded.

"I will see it is tended. Are the children housed? Shall I visit them for you? I am going back to Brooklyn, but I'd like to help first."

Slowly, Hannah brought down her hand and it fell, as if weighted, into her lap. "Do you believe in me?" she asked.

"Believe what?"

"That I tried to do right by my daughter."

"It is why I am here."

Hannah trembled, and tears welled in her eyes, but she blinked them back and said, "I cannot—ever again live with Evan Jacob. I think—he wanted Sarah to die!"

"Why?"

"I don't know! My daughter Mary says that she does!" The tears spilled, and Christine said, "Hannah, please don't cry. Talk to me. Tell me what I can do."

"I will die here if I must," Hannah said. "I will die in the workhouse. If I am alone, I will die thanking the Lord. Evan promised me she would live through the watching. Then it would be over, you see? He promised Sarah could last fourteen days. He swore! I thought it, too, for she had been very bad in the past and must have eaten so little!"

"You knew?" Christine said. "You knew she ate?"

Hannah had found the secret soft shoes on the day she and Evan emptied the cupboard bed for the watching. Hannah, in consternation, asked Sarah how her shoes came to be fresh with mud. Margaret liked using her shoes, Sarah told her. Evan counseled Hannah to leave it alone and not to upset Sarah. He assured her they would prevail, and he instructed Hannah to fashion the hair they found into souvenirs for friends and to sell, enjoining Margaret, too, in the task when she entered the room and screamed the hair hers.

"Nothing is yours in this house except by my leave, girl," he said.

There were times he talked wickedly to the children, Hannah said, as he hadn't done before Sarah got sick. Hannah and Margaret set to the task of tying the locks with ribbons. Since Evan had grown accustomed to plentiful money, he often sought means to have more. Hannah didn't know what he did with the money. All she cared about by then was getting the watching over with, having their tribulations—and Sarah's—finished and done. But the shoes had worried her. The shoes, like so much else in her life, sent a message she couldn't read. Always she was ashamed for what she couldn't read, couldn't see, and if she saw, what of it? What, madam?

Nothing, she was. Oh, she had never thought much of herself. Nell was the smart one, the pretty one. But handsome Evan Jacob, who had risen from rags, set to courting her. Already when he was very young, people saw size in his future, and he, for inexplicable reasons, chose Hannah. They pulled well together. She knew how to work. She had the strength of five women in her youth. She learned that he had his weaknesses. He even spoke to her of them in the nights of their betrothal, their bundling, spoke of hauntings—desires and guilt that surged when fate tightened around him. He learned to work, pray, and think—he had taught himself to read—to control, to reroute temptation. She thought his struggle made him all the finer.

It was difficult in the beginning, learning his ways and accommodating his plans for their future. He was never an affectionate man, not to her, but she felt his pleasure in her as a helpmate. Together they achieved much on the land and in the community, and at moments she saw a new pride in him and felt a sort of pride in herself. Sorrows came, as they do. But every one of their children lived, the farm expanded, and if Evan had an especial dislike of Mary, for mysterious reasons, and if Esther wasn't right, Hannah couldn't expect perfection. Eventually, he stopped paying any attention to Mary and Esther, and it happened when Sarah began to become who she was.

Sarah was beautiful and bright, like her father—more beautiful even, more searching and brave. Sarah had, furthermore, what Evan never would, a capacity for contentment. You could see him watch her closely, and Hannah thought Sarah inspired him to surpass what he had already done in his life. Sons? It was as if he had no sons, after Sarah took his heart. Impish Margaret he liked periodically, but always he turned to the girl who, for him, was the shining answer. Hannah saw tenderness in him, studying Sarah, and she, Hannah, the mother of Sarah, felt reflected warmth.

Then everything changed. The change didn't come with Sarah's sickness, she had realized later; it began at the time baby David was born. She returned to the house to an Evan in turmoil, an Evan who treated her coldly from then on, whatever she did.

Throughout Sarah's sickness, the land came second; the animals waited for water and feed. He seemed to be proving a thing to himself in his care for her, a debt repaid, a crumbled hope mended; he could not let her die. It wasn't the same as his caring for Sarah before her sickness. It looked to Hannah desperate, compensatory—though she did not use these words. He was paying for sins and earning salve for wounds; this was what it was like, how it seemed to Hannah.

Sarah was blessed with the physical strength of both her parents, and she recovered. Hannah thought their trouble was over. The exceptional girl didn't feed yet flourished. She was a miracle, Evan said. Yes! The grace of Sarah's survival elevated their daughter to a plane far above. Evan had heard of holy fasters, and he told Hannah about them—she had vaguely heard of them herself, but what she knew about anything was so much less than he knew. She accepted the miracle, and for a time it drew Evan closer once more. But his friendship with the vicar and his rule over the miracle bringing them all Evan had ever wanted—money, respect, and dealings with people who could impact reality—changed him again. He became two men, the first man torn and suspicious and the second bloated with pride. And, too, Sarah was doubled. Her little girl suffered. Miracle or no, the child was sick, and not just sick in her body, but torn, as Evan was, in her soul. Mothers know this, said Hannah; they see, even if such a one as she neglected to see far enough.

Now, when all she had was time to brood on her wrongs, she remembered sounds in the night, when Evan would say it was nothing and tell her to go back to sleep. She remembered how harshly he spoke to Sarah before the watching, as if she no longer mattered to him, not in comparison to the grand gentlemen to whom he swore she could last!

Did Sarah eat? Her daughter Mary was shrewd, and in

these modern days young farming women could learn a lot if they were out and about. After the hearing, Mary learned in the villages from other girls what had been said at the inquest about the bottle beneath Sarah's arm, and about other proofs. Did Sarah eat? As the watching neared, Hannah suspected she did eat a little—that Margaret fed her—but if it was the single way Sarah could eat and it kept her alive, why, then, was it wrong? She'd think it wrong, but she'd banish the thought, for she loved her daughter. Evan wouldn't listen to her, and when the celebrities came to the house and required their vows that Sarah could last fourteen days, she vowed at Evan's insistence, and from his assurances, she believed: Fourteen days and it would be over. Now, it would never be over. Heaven was shut to her. She was humbled now, lower than low. Now all of her life with Evan Jacob flared up in back of her eyes, clouded by Sarah's death. Clouded by what Mary said to her, clouded by what she suspected after the worst had happened. That he was cruel. That he cared about none of them—that when he was stripped of his pride and ambition after Sarah died, they were all nothing to him.

She was a bad woman. She deserved to suffer, but her children did not. She feared for Margaret. He went after the girl, accusing her as the animals sold and the land slipped away. Mary feared for her, too. Esther was slipping, and Mary was rising against her father, threatening him, and he listened, he obeyed Mary, and Hannah didn't know why.

Mary did not say; she was looking ahead, gathering strength from the ruins of what Evan Jacob had wanted and lost.

"Why would Evan want Sarah to die?" Christine asked. "It behooved him, as you say, that she should last out the watching."

"I don't know," said Hannah. "It was a feeling I had. Before he knew he would be charged with a crime, he acted relieved.

He grieved his good name, but not for his girl. He grieved his ambitions, but not his girl."

"Will Mary talk to me?" Christine asked.

"I think so."

"Will Margaret?"

"Give her the necklace," said Hannah. "Tell her I sent it and asked you to see her. She has gone to John Daniel and Nell."

"I will see what I can learn," said Christine, "and do." She wouldn't encourage unreasonable hope, although she suspected that Hannah had no definite expectations. The lady reporter came, and Hannah reached for a way ahead.

Leaving, Christine wished Hannah courage. Sarah, said Hannah, came to her in dreams, blazing the prison walls with heavenly light.

It took three visits for Hannah's confession, and prison rules dictated that they were days apart. After the third, Christine went to London, having written ahead to Elizabeth Clinch and to Vinnie. No letter awaited Christine from the sister-nurse, but from Carmarthen, Reginald wrote that Esther Jacob had died of sepsis.

Christine pictured the girl's bloody, bitten fingers, her mad open wounds. Another blow. The bigger the wound, Christine thought of the Jacobs' lingering troubles, the more it festered, spreading infection and pain down deep into the system.

Christine walked throughout London, drawn to the elegant galleries, bridges, riverside promenades, and to the grim East End, where hunger announced itself at every corner, and she understood how dreadful it would have been for the local child savers to hear of a Welsh girl who intentionally starved and a family who aided her in the ruse. She found herself missing the country, took solace in parks. She wrote everywhere, trying to find the right words for what she had seen and heard, imagining links between the pieces. She sent the sister-nurse another letter and several days later sought out her residence on Weston Road, not far from Guy's Hospital.

It was a rather fine house for an underpaid nurse, terracotta and brick, black shutters matching the wrought-iron grillwork. She waited hours across the street in a tea shop for life from the house to announce itself.

An elderly couple started down the front steps, trailed by a white poodle that scampered as if it were weightless. They descended, clutching their brass-handled canes and the woven pink leash on the skittering sprite.

"Excuse me," Christine said. "I am looking for an old friend, Elizabeth Clinch, and I have this address."

They said Clinch leased the garden flat below, but she hadn't been well and didn't need to be bothered.

"But a friend, dear?" the woman said.

The three of them stood on the sidewalk, the poodle playing a spinning top around Christine's feet. She glanced down and saw the dog lasso her tightly by wrapping her ankles up in its leash. She pulled one way, the dog pulled the other, and Christine fell.

Good, she thought a second before striking brick. Next thing she knew, the woman's face peered from above, framed by the sky. On his knees beside her, the man unwound the leash, and Christine was able to sit up, bleeding from the head.

"Do we fetch someone?" the woman said. "Naughty Clementine, bad girl."

The woman pulled the dog back.

"Are you hurt badly?" the man asked. He handed Christine a monogrammed handkerchief, which she pressed to her forehead and then removed, finding it soaked with blood.

People passed, Christine heard boat whistles on the river and the bang of a gate, and black skirts joined the elderly couple.

Clinch knelt and said to Christine, "Here, show me."

The nurse sopped up the blood with the handkerchief Christine handed her, and with her cool fingers probed the wound's edge.

"Are you dizzy?" she asked. "Headache?"

"Ache."

"It could be from the cut. I'll see to her," she told the couple, and Clinch helped Christine up as the couple caned away, the poodle prancing behind.

Clinch guided Christine into the flat through a shadowy passage opening onto a spacious parlor that, while still dark, was richly appointed. The nurse came in and out, setting a bowl of water, ointment, and bandages onto the marble-topped table by Christine's chair. "How is your vision?" Clinch asked. Christine studied a painting of cypresses waving against sunny skies and said, "Normal." Her reading spectacles were in the reticule by her feet, as was the missive from Emyr.

"Did you hurt yourself intentionally?"

"Why, no," Christine said.

The nurse bathed the cut, dressed it, brought tea, sat across from Christine on a satin loveseat, and said, "The press have hounded me since I returned, and I don't appreciate how you refuse to take no for an answer."

Christine sipped her tea.

"The cut's superficial," the nurse said. "I had both your letters. Show me the note." Christine took it out and handed it over. "Did you forge it?"

"No, I didn't."

"There is no signature." Christine regarded her silently. "What do you want from me?" Clinch asked. The nurse appeared worn, though less so than Hannah; her hair, more silver than gray, was attractively arranged around her face.

"As I wrote, I plan to return to Wales and see what I can do for the mother. I will seek counsel from contacts I have in the community, who will know best how we should proceed. It is my hope that the eldest daughter, Mary, may clarify matters that have given Hannah cause for concern. But for myself, I want to better understand the disease of hysteria, what drives these women and girls into bed."

"Theories are plentiful and abound."

"I want your theory." She wanted a nurse's perspective, a woman's.

"I attended no one at Guy's with the disease," said Clinch. "I heard a series of lectures last year by an eminent man at St. Bartholomew's Hospital who claimed that these girls, before they grow ill, exhibit unusual force and decision of character—that they have plenty of nerve. It would seem the wan, spiritless girls might be more prone to the illness, but then, think of it: Doesn't it make sense that girls of greater vitality would be more affected by society's limitations? Doesn't it make sense that energetic, bright girls, deprived of active spheres, might be driven into themselves? Where does energy go if it cannot be used?" She had become almost instantly animate, but then she pulled back, saying, "I really know little about it."

"Your observations are sound. I can see girls of about my daughter's age of eighteen fitting the portrait you draw. Even Sarah would loosely fit. I often felt that the trauma of Sarah's first, severe illness might have been enough to drive her to dissimulation and fasting. Except I kept coming back to the parents on guard beside her bed, and the father making the bed, loath to let anyone handle her other than himself."

"The lecturer said the parents are controlling," said Nurse Clinch.

"Hoverers?" said Christine.

"It is supposed to be typical."

"So—when I got the note and put it together with what I wrote to you of my various interviews with Sarah . . . I was dismayed." She had written down for the nurse Sarah's cogent words: "I sin very much. I may not live long. I am afraid. Not good enough. I did a very bad thing, but I didn't mean to." Yet she knew the words could be read with meanings more innocent than those she suspected.

"What is the aim of our speculations?" the nurse asked.

"It is whether Evan Jacob should be returned to the community."

"What else can be done? If he interfered with her, it isn't even a crime."

"Not to the law, but it would be a crime to the community. He could be shunned, maneuvered to seek his living away from his wife and children in another district."

"They'd shun him?"

"If they thought it just, they'd cut off whatever he needed to reestablish himself. I have lived in Carmarthenshire for a year and I know the people."

She had also written to the nurse about Esther Jacob, that in her estimation two daughters were gone as a result of Jacob's obsession—that the dismantlement of the family and the farm had broken Esther's mind. She hadn't expected Clinch to speak with her, no matter how hard she tried to see her. Perhaps Clinch was as changed by Sarah as she was herself, out of her own sense of culpability.

"Has illness kept you from work?" Christine asked.

"I have resigned from Guy's."

"Have you given up nursing?"

"I never cared for it," the nurse said.

"What will you do?"

"I'm going to Italy."

"Alone?"

Clinch didn't like the question. "Madam, I was most discomfited by the girl, and by what followed after her death, the questions unanswered, the uses they put her to." She paused. "There was something about her physical symptoms and how she would shift her attention away to bear them, as if her body were speaking of that for which she had no words.

"Even before she died, I thought the father had at her. How much that was the origin of everything else, I cannot say. But I felt . . . a recognition, because when I was young, it happened to me."

THE SUMMER'S DROUGHT WAS THE WORST in living memory, Christine read in *The Times*. Dry leaves rustled above her, brushing the skylight of her room at the top of Vinnie's house. Soon daylight would fade, and Vinnie would return, calling up to her from the vestibule.

Since leaving America, Christine had thrilled to the freedom of traveling about, riding boats and trains alone, released into an anonymity she had lacked as a young woman and girl; burst out of roles, expectations, and habitual thoughts. If she had her life to do over again, who would she be? With complete choice, would she drown in the ocean of possibilities? Or would she enlarge, stretch until she could see beyond her own patch of familiar life, feel what daily ritual numbed her to, predict, out of the formidable breadth of her freedom, how events might fall?

It wasn't as if she had no knowledge of incest and child sexual molestation. Incest seemed, though, so aberrant, so unusual, that it was easy to accept the tropes made for it in literature: People twinned, seeking closeness; in literature, it wasn't about betrayal. No literature she had read described brutal sexual acts doled out by parents, the very people children depended upon—an immensity crushing, twisting, and excising your meanings. That might be the worst of it, being unable to articulate what had been done.

She took up the newspaper again, but the words lay inert, didn't convert into meaning but cut meaning off, because all she could think about were the counterworlds outside the paper—interior, hidden worlds. Catacombs, warrens, tunnels for the stalked, the trapped, the maimed, the blind, and the dead. We lived there. We lived at the mercy of the owners, the day walkers, the travelers, the movers and shakers. Darwin, she saw, hadn't startled her in the least: The ascendancy of the mighty? When had it been otherwise? You could pray all you liked in the church, and you might very well get in the next life what you didn't get here, but if a man ran the place, you'd better hope that when you entered the pearly gates, you were free of your feminine gender.

She ought, actually, Christine realized, to be outraged by the likelihood that Evan Jacob knew all along that Sarah ate, that he had coerced her to starve, to undergo the watching, and to die as he watched with those pale reptilian eyes. She *was* outraged, as much as by whatever other obscene acts he had committed. But she had considered the outrage of his intentionality in the case for some time. She had grown, in a sense, accustomed to its horror. Not to the other, the boundary crossing, what they called the "nameless outrage," the "cruel immorality." If James had touched Gwen in that way—her perfect innocent child—she would have murdered him, if she were physically capable, with her bare hands. So much, she thought, for the gentler sex. But what had given Evan Jacob license to do as he pleased with the eight human beings under his roof? Men's laws, laws so imbalanced that they could even, if momentarily, cast her good husband into suspicion's shadow, laws that put everyone into hair shirts, men and women alike.

Where was Vinnie? Come back. Release me. Teach me how to live with this. Tell me, friend, what I should do. Two girls, one Welsh and one English, one relatively poor and the other probably wealthy—the suggestion being that it cut across country and class.

"Tallyho!" Vinnie called. "Back from the wars!" Then came a series of thumps as she put down her bags, released her hair to a frothy whiteness that fell to her shoulders, removed her working clothes and her stays, donned her at-home dress, and heated the water for her tired feet. Christine went down, took charge of the tin water basin, and set it by Vinnie's chair in the kitchen. Tonight, Vinnie had brought home a roast chicken, a quarter wheel of cheddar, and beer. They ate in the kitchen, the city sounds humming in the open window. Vinnie liked to be quiet until she had eaten and soaked out her soreness.

"What news?" she asked, settling back in the candle-light she preferred to lamps. *This room, this time,* Christine thought—they were among the most precious rooms and times of her life. To what she had already told Vinnie, Christine added what had happened that day with the nurse.

"Are you saying these girls in their beds were all raped by their fathers?"

Christine started. "I cannot think it is that pervasive."

"Don't be so quick to dismiss it! There are, after all, brothers and uncles and cousins; I should think variations would count."

"How can you joke?"

"Oh, darling." The white walls had grayed, and the green velvet chair by the window was lumpy and mended; James had sat in it once. Vinnie poured more beer. "There may very well be a connection between the sexual aberration and the girls getting sick, and, too, a distaste for food. How can I feed if charge of my own body is torn away? How can I feed that which I loathe? Stouthearted girls of the past, raped by soldiers, took up the sword of the brigands and drove it through their own guts. Most of us are milder types. We languish. We kill ourselves slowly. We finish the job after our own fashion and in our own time. Do you know what took me to economics? The Irish famine—that was a story. The scientists studied the problem of the blight and concluded that the Irish just didn't know how to cook the rotten potatoes; the scientists taught them a method of removing the rot and grating the rest into a cloth that they were to wash repeatedly, until what was left was a mush they must dry and bake into bread. Well, the method killed off the very young and the very old. Meanwhile, there were those who said, 'Why don't we just feed them?' America sent ships of cheap corn, which sat on the docks in Cork and Dublin while the politicians argued over whether imports would undercut the English grain markets. The markets—that was the key. Will *we* be all right if we feed them? Or will we starve, too?

"In the end, nothing helped. While scientists studied and politicians declaimed, others attributed the rotten potatoes to divine plan; they sanctified the lack of any solution and we were let off the hook. Who were we to interfere?

"A million starved. To help, to change, threatens. There are no guarantees that we won't be worse off when we've done the right thing.

"We cling. We accuse. We, most of us, know what we should do, but can we do it? To act, that is the step we cannot quite take. We moan: It is so complicated! Who can we trust? Who can we believe? The one tiny next step: to act. And we don't. What if, what if drives out our wit, and the unfortunates are consigned to misery, over and over.

"The Woman Question, however, is being unraveled. Cases of child molestation are being fought in the courts. They're infrequently won, and the age of consent, which is twelve, isn't doing us any favors. Naturally, upper-class girls are better believed. And some of those at the forefront of the battle, some of the do-gooders, are barmy fools. They don't want girls 'spoiled,' not because it is wrong but because they're afraid the 'spoiled' will go out into the pure sea of life and corrupt everyone else.

"I worry about how your Carmarthen friends may react to your news, if the daughter Mary corroborates what the note claimed and the mother suspects—she suspects. She may well have known. But how much can a woman in Hannah's position acknowledge? What could she do if she knew the worst of her husband? Divorce is impossible for her. Let's say he was locked up for twenty years. She wouldn't be a widow and could not get a job. If she could, she is already getting too old to go into domestic service. She could take in washing, or eke out subsistence as an agricultural worker, but for how long? She could do needlework if she has the skill, but young eyes give way from the hours it takes to survive by the thread.

"You could take them all with you to America. Don't look alarmed. You could. I wouldn't rule it out, given your feelings, but so many of the same problems would continue there. And if she were younger, stronger, there would still remain the question of who Hannah would be apart from Carmarthenshire, outside of Wales.

"Your friends may not welcome this news. They have already suffered the indignity of the case, and now this? They haven't forgotten the Blue Books—and neither, unfortunately, have the English. The dirty, immoral Welsh, their bundling before getting married, their language, they starved the girl, and now this?

"And, Christine, the Welsh may trust you well enough not to publish the news, but are you completely satisfied that you will not? Someday? What do you owe to the community and the family, and what do you owe to this knowledge—the pattern you may have stumbled upon through your inquiries?

"We're years from confronting and understanding any of this, I think. Here you are, holding it. Here you are, worried about the other little girl, Margaret? It goes beyond the mother. But what can be done? If Jacob was capable of these crimes against Sarah, will he accept losing his family? What would remain for him? How unhinged may he become in prison? Drive him out of Carmarthenshire? Possibly.

"Go to your friends and see. They may be able to frighten and humiliate Evan Jacob enough, as you say. But, what then?"

They sat a while longer in the candlelight, discussing rough justice. In England, it was called "rough music"; in Scotland, "riding the stag"; in France, *charivari*; in Wales, *Ceffyl pren,* or "wooden horse." Christine had discovered it written about as "remaining barbarism" and "characteristic of a rude state of society."

Twenty-five years ago, during the Welsh uprisings, it had often been used, against people as high as the mayor of Cardigan. But the practice was extant yet, and who could she find to strap Evan Jacob to the wooden horse and ride him through fields, over hills, across the river, and up to the castle: mock trial, burning in effigy, black-faced marauders teaching him that he wasn't above the will of the neighborhood, the social law—wake him, get him down in the dirt, strap him, and let him think he would die.

When Vinnie had gone to bed, Christine lay in the dark under the skylight, the dry leaves brushing the glass, seeing torches, riders, hearing him scream. For Christine, in and out of sleep all night, the morning came like hallucination.

She dressed, packed up, kissed her dear Vinnie, and walked the mile to Paddington Station for the train.

MARY AND MARGARET

Carmarthen, Wales
31 August 1870

Dearest James,

It was late when I arrived back from London. The warm night was a bowl of soft calm I felt I could lie down in and float on like water. The sky was a moonlit lilac; pink clouds were outlined in gray. The gate to my yard, the rock I checked as if it hid more notes, the squeak of the door's hinge, all said hello.

From upstairs, taps and a bang took me by the throat.

Moonlight spilled into the parlor. I moved to the fireplace and grabbed the poker. Raccoons, I reckoned; they had gotten in before. No. Footsteps. The poker preceding, I ascended the stairs. I approached the closed door and hit it. A step answered; I reached for the knob, turned, but when I pushed, the door stayed shut, secured by a chair from inside, keeping me out. Turn around and go away, I thought, but I spoke up. "Who's in there? Declare yourself!"

"Mary Jacob!" The chair scraped, and the door swung in to an apparition: The girl I most wanted to see had materialized, but in her displacement and my startled state, I shuddered, as if my peace had been stolen by jackals.

"I knew you would come!" the girl cried.

"What are you doing here?"

She wore my dressing gown, her dark hair tossed upon

it, and her visage was vulpine, entirely different from what I remembered. But it was the context. The moonlight. The whole displaced world I'd entered since I found the note. I knew that with her size and strength she could easily kill me.

"Mr. Pary from the newspaper put me here."

"Put you here?"

Poor girl, a certain thuggish quality stamped her, and probably garnered reactions like mine to her often. Yet despite my sympathy, I needed to get away from her and to sleep. When I encountered her freshly, then we would see.

"All right. Go back to bed," I said.

"I need to talk to you," she replied hotly.

"Yes. Tomorrow."

I headed downstairs, relieved she didn't follow, and before I sank straight into sleep, a part of me wanted to take it all back, my offer to help, to know—I wanted away from the awfulness I had encountered since meeting the Jacobs.

And Pary had done it: *Put her here?*

Come morning, I felt again I was alone, and I was right. The room upstairs was vacant, the bed neatly made, my dressing gown hung on the hook at the back of the door. Newly disoriented, I quickly washed and dressed and set off to the newspaper office to confront Reginald.

Neither he nor Lloyd was in their office, and I found him on the second-floor landing, where he was about to march down.

"Pary."

"Christine!" he exclaimed, delighted to see me.

"You put Mary Jacob in my house?"

"I telegraphed. It must have crossed. How are you? Lovely to see you!"

"I near died of fright, and how *could* you without consulting me? Now this morning, she's gone. Where did she go?"

"We got her a job at the tinworks!"

So pleased with himself he was, despite my disgruntle-ment, that I deduced he must have a tale. Mary had gone off, it seemed, to her new employment.

"Thank goodness you're here," he said. "You don't know what I've been through over the last days." What *he* had been through? "I've tried to do what you would have wanted," he said.

"Well, I've had a time, too."

"Let's go out," he said, and we left the building.

"Where's Lloyd?" I asked.

"Another story. Unwell. But his wife has a little cottage—a near ruin, but it could be fixed—that we might get for Han-nah Jacob when she's released. Shall we go over and see them?"

"There isn't a rush on it, Reginald."

"True, true." He must have felt bad for his first response to Emyr's note. "Tell me about London," he said.

"No, first tell me about Mary Jacob."

"It was Alun and I got her the job, but she said she already had a place to live. Though it turned out she didn't. She pre-ferred to sleep outside near the hospital where Esther was, so in the morning she could change—bandages? Esther had at her hands and—"

"I know."

"The matron let Mary in to care for her sister. Then Mary would go to her work. Then the matron decided that Esther got agitated from Mary's ministrations, and Mary was barred. A couple days later, Esther died. That's when I wrote."

"Yes. Got it."

"Mary is the daughter of Evan Jacob, I'll tell you that. She talked her way into the hospital and attacked the matron."

"Physically?"

"Yes, attacked. Had her down on the floor for a pummeling,

and the attendants put Mary in a cell and called the sheriff. I got wind at the office and went over there—"

"Thank you."

"You're welcome. And I talked them out of taking her to the castle, and out of the Magistrate's Court."

"Oh my."

"But I couldn't just leave her in a mad cell, could I? They had iron rings on the wall and she threatened to dash out her brains."

Once more, I shuddered.

"They tied her up," he said, "while I got her aunt Nell. She came and talked Mary down. It's a decent hospital. Nell didn't think they did anything wrong. It was just very unfortunate— and very sad. Mary had to go somewhere, since she was barred from the hospital grounds, and Nell and John Daniel had no more room. They took in the two youngest—and the dog."

"I know."

"You do? Well. That's why we took her to your house. Since you weren't there."

"You did right," I said. We'd descended the road and crossed the footbridge and stood in the dry pasture. I'd been unaware of the grazing sheep, and when one wandered over and nestled my hand with its woolly head, I thought I might cry.

We were in plain sight of the Parade and the riverfront, after the talk we had caused from our cohabitation, and now Mary Jacob stayed in my house and— To hell with it, I thought. I told him briefly about Swansea and what Hannah Jacob had said. I only alluded to my interview with the nurse and didn't mention Vinnie's comments. That could wait until I spoke with Mary and, possibly, Margaret. Then I would sit down with him and the widows and the Brigstocks and Alun—if he was able—and get their advice.

"What is wrong with Alun?" I asked.

"Belly," he said.

"Bad?"

Without answering me, he asked, "How did you hurt yourself?"

"Tripped."

He touched the small bandage. "Sorry. Be careful, why don't you."

It would be hours before Mary would finish at the tinworks, and I told Reginald that, yes, we ought to go to the Lloyds' and see about the cottage.

We walked back over the footbridge and to the east side of town, where Alun and Braith Lloyd lived with their children in a pretty house in a yard of tumultuous flowers—a real English garden in Wales. But the stalks were limp, the petals singed from the drought, and it was a miracle anything grew. The children, four boys, hauled buckets of water from the well, Braith said, since seeing the flowers made their father glad. Braith and three of the boys had flaming red hair. The fourth boy, the eldest, looked like Alun, slender, with dusty brown hair. Braith told us that the eldest, Lyn, stayed most of the day with Alun and read to him.

In a front bedroom, Alun sat up in an overstuffed chair, but he was wasted and sallow and I was shocked by his rapid decline. The room was papered with bluebells and the bedspread embroidered with roses. I don't know what I'd expected at Alun Lloyd's house, but it wasn't this. The brown-haired boy sat on the bed and Braith brought in chairs.

"Lynie, go out," Alun said. "We've business Mam and I mean to discuss with our friends."

"I'm old enough to stay," said Lyn.

"No, you're not, Lynie, go on." He left.

"How are you, Alun?"

"Done for, Christine," he said.

"Oh, now," said Braith, "I won't have you speak darkly."

Alun laughed. "Dark, light. If speaking could rescue me, Braith, I'd learn the words. You have come about the cottage for Hannah Jacob?"

"We thought we could take up a collection to pay," Reginald said.

"It's tumbledown," Braith said. "It's hardly habitable."

"We could get people to put it right," Reginald said.

"The daughter Mary could help," I said, "and live in it herself when it's ready enough before Hannah comes home."

"Such friends Hannah has!" Alun said. "And she not two months behind bars."

"She's pregnant," said Braith.

"How do you know?" Alun asked her.

"Everyone knows," she said.

Alun, Reginald, and I glanced at one another, for *we* hadn't known. The information complicated matters.

"I've seen her in Swansea," I said to Alun.

"Before or after the other daughter died?" he asked.

"Before," I said.

"The vicar went down to tell the parents about Esther personally," Alun said. "But he hasn't returned, and it's been what, Pary?"

"A week."

"What other news of the vicar?" I asked.

"He isn't himself," Alun said, "and he hasn't been since Sarah died. He had better brace up, or he'll lose the parish."

We fell quiet. To cushion the silence, I said to Lloyd's wife, "Braith is a beautiful name."

"It means freckled!" Alun said. Braith was freckled indeed. The couple laughed together, but laughing caused Alun to wince.

"We'll go," I said. "We'll come again soon."

"I would like Hannah to have the cottage," Braith said.

"Thank you," I told her.

We said good-bye to Lyn, who was seated on the front steps. The other three boys, more radiant than all the flowers, came into the yard from the street, carrying packages. Reginald and I walked on to the chemist's, near the Guildhall. The Brigstocks lived above the shop and they had a storeroom where Mary Jacob could stay until the cottage was ready.

But I shan't write of that now; I need to get on to Mary. I will just say that, hearing of how she attacked the matron, I planned to act gingerly with her and welcomed the storeroom.

I picked up my letters at the newspaper office and left Reginald there. Philip had telegraphed, "WHAT NEWS?" Whatever I had begun writing in Swansea and London, it wasn't for newspapers. And I wasn't for newspapers. I quickly composed my resignation to Philip—with gratitude—and sent it off.

It darkened before Mary Jacob came up the Parade, swinging a lantern. The air was thick with humid heat and the clotted clouds signaled rain. It would rain soon and overnight, but not much. It had already been hours since I'd laid the table, and I had already eaten.

She came in; I told her to sup and that then we would talk. When she eyed the food as if she didn't know how to handle it, I cut her cheese and passed her the loaf. She tore off the bread piece by piece and devoured the loaf, pushing aside the cup of cider I poured for her. Without asking, I brought her tea, which she drank. I got up and tidied the kitchen, unnerved by her silence and her black eyes pinned to me as if I might run away.

"It is hard work there, isn't it?" I asked.

She didn't answer; she'd always worked hard.

"Well," I said, "I have been to see your mother in Swansea. I mean to help, and to listen." After the urgency she had expressed to talk the previous night, her silence was baffling. She must have been tired; I already knew she was half mad with grief. "We seem to have panicked each other last night," I said. She wiped her mouth with the back of her arm. "More tea?" I asked idiotically.

"You write for the newspapers," she said.

"I do." Did. "You sent Emyr to me with the necklace I gave your mother. Would you like to say why? Where is Emyr?"

"Gone."

"He left me a note," I said.

"No, he didn't; I did. He just wrote down what I told him." She lifted her chin proudly. "I've not been to school."

"That is unfortunate."

She shrugged. "I don't like the factory, being indoors all day. It's loud."

"I'm sure."

"I like to work outside."

"Perhaps I can help you with that. Perhaps—"

Abruptly, she stood and roamed the room, moved in a nervous rush to a spot and then observed baubles—a shepherdess figurine, a silk pillowslip, a gilt bowl—with comingled wariness and awe. She may have latched onto the objects to collect herself, to get away from me. I thought she didn't trust me and, actually, I couldn't see why she would trust anyone. Then we both started at a faint ticking: rain. She rushed outside. I, too, couldn't stop myself from seeing it and raised a window, not the one near the door, because I sensed I should give her privacy to be in the rain, to feel its novelty and refreshment. Water. Life. The scent of it was like no other, releasing from earth the best smells, the magic. I put my hand out the window and the rain anointed me.

It stopped. She came in and sat at the table, licking rain from her mouth. "What did my mam say?" she asked.

I stayed where I was and told her, describing exactly what I'd seen at the prison and what Hannah had said.

"Do you think she will survive?" Mary asked.

"I do, for the child in her."

Mary didn't respond to this information; she just stared. I went over to the table and sat down, my fear of her having melted away.

"If I say," Mary began, "if I tell you things, you mustn't tell Mam; you mustn't upset her too much, as—" She broke off.

"You may advise me on that," I said, struck by the extraordinary mix in her of tender feeling and rage.

"I didn't like Sarah," she said. "I didn't! Never." Hard. "But Evan Jacob took her life and took my Esther and he must pay. I believe—he loved Sarah, as Mam said. But his kind of love— you can see where it got us."

Jacob had tampered with Mary first, nine years ago. He repented when Hannah interceded, and I can only imagine what that may have cost her. The oddity of it was that Mary was certain her father despised her—and I'm sure he did, because every day her presence reminded him of what he had done, of his weakness, as Hannah had euphemistically phrased it. Mary's goal, her own obsession, had been to protect Esther. Mary had felt Sarah was safe, since Evan loved her and would not wish her harm. The erotic seemed to be no part of it from Mary's perspective, and maybe in such cases it seldom is. If I could peer into Evan Jacob, drill into his body and brain as he lifts a foot onto each everlasting stair, feel his strained muscles, sit in his cell, confronting the walls, remember with him how he stood by Sarah while she was dying and touched his firstborn so that she would never on this earth be right—even then, would I grasp his essence, realize his impetus, find words?

The household lived in silent knowledge of what Sarah

and Margaret did in the night. The other children enacted the vow the parents had made when Sarah was first ill and near death: She shouldn't be offered food, shouldn't be harried. The visitors, the miracle, all that came later arose out of the silence, the circling by the others of the dance between Sarah and her father.

The dance, the avoidance, the penance—Mary just wanted peace. She lived to go off with Esther someday, although it barely seemed plausible. But she dreamed of it, milking the cows, churning the hard winter butter that wouldn't come, washing and mending and cooking and planting as the seasons came and went and the drama in the bedroom got stranger.

She had thought it an outsized, tangled love. She had thought it Tad and Sarah's web her mother was caught in. Margaret was just a little girl; you couldn't blame her. And she, Mary, was chastened by how she had blamed Sarah, who wasn't much older than Margaret, for her fate, even believing that headstrong Sarah deserved what she got when Tad roped her to his bed for those nights Mam was away. Roped her to his bed for punishment, Tad said. For whatever Sarah had done to provoke the scene Mary had come upon in the barn.

Everyone thought Sarah's celebrity would, someday, just stop. How could it continue? And yet it did. Mary learned, as the boys did—as Esther did before it went too far—to subsist with it, to wait for the eventual day when the interest people had in them—them, farmers!—would finally cease.

It was lonely, as if they had no mother and father but show performers enslaved to an act the children were led to perceive as the one path that would keep Sarah alive. Sarah must have thought it her survival, too—that if she stayed in the bed, she was safe, that if she ate in the dark, where he couldn't see, she had an escape.

But the truth came to Mary; its contours bled through in

how Tad grew to hate Sarah as he saw that he would be found out, that there was nothing he could do to fend off discovery.

"They'd take his money, his reputation!" Mary said. "That was what he loved by then. He walked about that last year as if he wore a noose and they'd put him up on a chair and the vicar would kick it out!

"Sometimes I would feel happy about it. I'd prayed he would be arrested. But as the grand people came and planned with my parents the watching, and Sarah got frightened and different and I saw it would really happen—then I knew.

"Sarah kept her soft shoes in the cupboard bed, to go out at night, and Mam found them. Yes. Oh, I'd seen tracks on the kitchen floor, mornings. I had seen food taken, and I had to suppose that Mam saw it, too.

"But maybe she didn't. I can't know. But I wanted my mam to know enough so that we could be safe after it all came to light when Sarah died and they charged him. I feared for Margaret. He went after her, and he was out of his mind.

"We started to talk, me and the boys, about what we had seen."

Mary reinterpreted the events during Hannah's confinement with David: the attack in the barn, the four days Evan hauled Sarah from place to place as he worked, how, one night, he took her back out to the fields and then kept her in his room until Hannah returned.

"I had to be sure," Mary said, "and so I bribed Emyr. He wanted to go to the mines and needed money. I'd stolen a coin at a time from the box Tad kept under his bed all the while he ran his show. I had to buy yarn and extra food for the children. But I had enough left."

The meetings between Sarah and Emyr by the river; Emyr's watching Sarah; how she had shown him her legs in the barn and Evan's anger—that was enough for Mary to put together what was going on, especially after what had happened to her when Hannah was gone to deliver Margaret, and what happened to her beyond that time, until Hannah stepped in.

Evan must have sworn he'd never do it again. He may have come undone when again he sinned. It all made sense to Mary then.

In retrospect, Sarah's behavior in bed didn't seem inexplicable, willful, for it was an outgrowth; it wasn't how she was originally, active, haughty, inquisitive. Even Mary could see that Sarah's religious strivings, her fretfulness and pain, were not part of her character, but a response.

And him! Watching her. Guarding her.

What Mary could not understand were the others, the fine men; they were the ones, along with her father, she would curse forever.

Maybe Jacob was glad, I considered, for Sarah's transformation into a sick, utterly dependent miracle girl who wouldn't tempt him, until the solution became its own problem. The father and daughter, both caught.

"Is there enough proof?" Mary asked.

"I believe you completely," I said.

"We'll punish him, then?"

I couldn't tell what she meant.

"Get him tried for murder."

"He has already been tried. What we can do is protect innocent parties and see that you and your mother—"

"He killed my sisters! I'll testify then, all right? I will, even if Mam must know everything."

"Mary. It is too late." I didn't say it would be too hard to prove, or that the Welsh wouldn't want the exposure, even if legally it could be done.

"He was convicted of manslaughter," she said. "I know

the difference between that and murder. The one is minor and the other is not."

She got up, and I thought she might throw down the table. I stood, so she could not hulk above me.

We stood, I in the grief of my age, she in her rage at a reality that defied reason. I had to be the bearer of what the law was and was not. Of what was deemed significant and valid and what was not. I couldn't, for all my years, explain to her why what was just and right was out of the question.

"Legally," I said, "it's over."

Mary's pupils dilated—I'd put out the light—and I nearly swooned into their fathoms.

"Over," she said. "Then what good are you?"

She took her lantern and left, slamming the door.

It helps to write to you of it, James. It is comforting. I decided to write while I waited for her to come back. Light now is bluing the windows.

I'll go to bed, since she hasn't returned.

As ever,
Christine

◦❧◦

TIED UP BUNCHES OF DRYING HERBS FESTOONED the chemist's storeroom. The riot of them pointed down from the low ceiling, so if you woke in the night and lit a candle, you'd confront an earthy, prickly heaven, rest beneath herbal clouds in a healing sky. A cot spread with a colorful quilt had been placed in the corner, and a table cleared.

Two days after Mary left in the night, Mr. Brigstock, the chemist, turned the sign to CLOSED and went upstairs to the living quarters for the meeting Christine had called.

Present along with the Brigstocks were Mrs. Owen and

Mrs. Morgan, Reginald, Braith Lloyd, to represent her husband, Alun, and Nell and John Daniel.

Nell had her baby in tow, an early-born infant, a weeks-old girl. The parlor was crowded and hot, and Christine nervously drank down a tumbler of water before she spoke. Mary hadn't returned to the house, though Reginald said she had reported both days to her work.

Christine struggled with how she was about to let Mary down again—knowing Mary might never have spoken had she been aware that the information would not meet her goal. Christine felt fresh grief, facing her friends, about to say what she had learned from Hannah and Mary, and although she had rehearsed to herself the part about Elizabeth Clinch and the conclusions the nurse had led her to, she was unsure of its relevance to any steps they would take now. Still, it felt right to deliver everything. The stakes involved precluded catering to the delicacy of the subject, and her skin flushed with shyness, most of all before Nell and John Daniel. A relative or a neighbor would have been a more appropriate bearer of such hurtful news. But Pary had thought it best that the Daniels hear it straightaway, along with the others, as their opinions and wants would be most important. He had reassured Christine that she would present the news frankly but with compassion.

Christine was seated beside the tea table. Mrs. Owen and Mrs. Morgan, carefully dressed for the occasion, regarded her from the divan, where they sat alongside Pary in their familiar stern-kind manner she loved; the calm of the neat gray Brigstocks encouraged her from their straight chairs by the window; Nell, body lush from birthing, her spirits protected by new life, sat queenly in the stuffed chair, John Daniel's sheltering frame perched at her side on a stool. And Braith's flaming hair! It cheered Christine, even as it reminded of her absent friend. This was the real Wales, she thought, these people, and she told them what she had learned in the best words she had.

The baby slept while she talked, but as she neared the end of what she had to say, it wailed, and Nell rocked and quieted the infant.

"I have brought this in confidence to you," Christine said. "Forgive me if any of you feel I have overstepped bounds. I merely give you what I have heard, and you will decide how best to proceed."

At first, Nell appeared confused. John Daniel got to his feet, as though to confront the phantom Evan, and then he leaned down to his wife and whispered to her before sitting again. The others, too, evinced shock, and gazed into space and not at one another. Then they adjusted, seeming to psychically rejoin their friends and neighbors.

John Daniel said, "Well, what do you think yourself, Mrs. Thomas? On the issue of Margaret."

Never, thought Christine, had trust meant so much. "How she is feeling of late," she replied, "should be considered foremost. Hannah asked that I speak with her, but do we need further corroboration?"

"Margaret speaks very seldom since the trial," John Daniel said.

"Might it help Margaret to unburden herself?" Mrs. Morgan asked.

Christine looked at John Daniel, who thoughtfully frowned.

"Hannah's pregnancy complicates matters," said Christine.

"Will Mary be riled again, do you think?" Pary asked. "By our interposition?"

"She could have been here today," said Mrs. Brigstock. "We'd hoped she would come."

"Where is she, then?" asked John Daniel. Pary said she

went each day to her work, and he thought she slept nearby. "I'll find her," John Daniel said. "She may be made to understand that short of a new trial, other actions could bring results."

"We should make a list," said Mrs. Owen, "of what should be told to whom. Only—Mary said we should keep back from Hannah? I don't see why."

"Whatever the reason," said Nell, "it is Mary's request, and Mrs. Thomas agreed. We must be directed by Mary on that."

"She will tame down," Pary said, though Christine wasn't convinced.

"You are sure there is a baby?" asked Mrs. Brigstock.

"Yes," said Braith. "Hannah confided it to the vicar and the vicar told me."

"The gall of that man!" John Daniel said. "Why must he continue to be involved?"

"We needn't involve him," said Mr. Brigstock.

"We won't!" John Daniel declared. "The man talks! The man publishes vile letters! How he persisted in his infernal meddling even after Sarah died, I—"

"John," Nell said. "I think we all agree. What to do about Hannah is the most troubling course. What to do about Evan . . ."

Further questions were posed to Christine, for clarity and detail. At length, Nell and John asked that Christine come to their house and give the necklace from Hannah to Margaret. If Margaret wanted to speak, why then, she'd speak. Any additional information would help to guide them. They would reassure Margaret as best they could. Christine reminded herself that she would be gone when the day came for significant action. She would talk to Margaret and see Mary housed, and then she could go.

❧

THERE IS A CORUSCATING AWAKENING IN THE BRAIN when the innocent are harmed, a crackling snap of the nerves and a leap of the limbs that, nonetheless, are immobile, stuck like trunks rooted to the ground for all the reach of the tree, if the innocent harmed cannot be saved. Innocence dies fast and hard in life, and thus it is holy when it exists. Christine would always think about Sarah. She would hold the importance of comprehending, in her own aliveness, how Sarah was harmed for as long as she drew breath—stay in hard thought of Sarah, every so often, as she lived her life.

When she came in sight of the blue house by the river, she saw at once the white-blond shock of hair. Taller and stronger, but with the same sawed-off fringe, Margaret raked the ground, clearing the trees' summer droppings. She didn't stop until Nell came out on the steps and waved. Nell went and spoke with the girl, who looked up as Christine neared.

"I've just told Margaret," Nell said, "that her uncle John will mind the baby whilst we have our visit." Nell leaned toward Christine: "She finds it amusing. The tad and the baby!" Margaret did not at the moment appear amused.

"Will you sit down, please, Mrs. Thomas?" said Nell. "I'll bring us tea!" Nell was affecting that extra false cheer one sometimes couldn't help around children.

Margaret didn't approach the table beneath the rowan, and so, nor did Christine.

"It's a wonderful rake you have," Christine said.

"It is my uncle's and he lets me use it," said Margaret. "A proper rake must be as light as possible, to avoid weariness during harvest. The handle must be smooth, to slip through the hands with ease. The teeth must not be set at too sharp an angle, or the rake will not gather the hay efficiently. But if the angle between the teeth and the head is not sharp enough, then the tines will stick in the ground and break off. This is a good rake," she said in conclusion.

Nell, who hadn't yet gone in, said, "That is the most I have heard you say in a time, Margaret! And eloquently put." She smiled at Christine and went into the house.

"Do you fare well here?" asked Christine.

Margaret hesitated, then nodded.

"Dilly and David are here, too, I've heard."

"They are down at the river with my cousins."

"It's lovely here," Christine said. A breeze riffled the grass and the metallic river scent washed the air clean. She sat at the table, and then Margaret did also, keeping the rake, laid crosswise on her lap. She held the handle, wistful, Christine thought, to go back to work's solace. Nell returned bearing a tray of tea and biscuits. She poured and said, "Well, Margaret. Mrs. Thomas has been to see your mam in Swansea."

Margaret's head tilted quizzically. "It is the prison, dear, where your mam is being kept."

"She misses you and is very concerned about you," Christine said. She drew the necklace from her pocket. "She sent you this."

Margaret took it.

"You've seen it before?" Christine asked.

The girl nodded, making no move to open it.

"Put it on!" Nell said. "It belongs to you now."

Without expression, Margaret did.

"There," said Nell. "To have a memento of Sarah close to your heart is a blessing. What other word from Hannah for Margaret, Mrs. Thomas?" Nell asked.

"Your mam talked to me," Christine said, "of events surrounding the watching." Margaret tensed.

Christine looked at Nell, who continued, "Mam has

reason to believe there is more we should understand about what occurred, and about what occurred more recently, over the spring and summer before your parents were tried.

"And then your sister, Mary, confided in Mrs. Thomas how she worried for you throughout the last weeks you lived in the house."

Wild to get away, Margaret gripped the rake and said, "I don't know anything."

"All right, dear," said Nell.

Nell told Margaret to go, so uncomfortable did Margaret seem. Even freed, she had lost the taste for raking, left the rake propped at the table and dashed away to the river, to be, Nell said, with Dilly and the boys.

"I like when she wants to be with the other children," Nell said. "Often, she doesn't. You see how she is very afraid."

"We shouldn't bring her more fear," said Christine.

"We will keep Margaret with us," said Nell.

"You've told her?"

"Oh, yes. It was what Hannah wanted, and Margaret is a fine child and exceedingly fond of my husband. Mrs. Thomas? There is no malice in my sister. She has had—a difficult life."

There was something of Sarah in Nell—the slightly winged black eyebrows. Of Hannah, only the thick lashes spoke their relation.

Two sisters, so differently treated by life and fate.

The fineness of Nell and John—the loyalty and help they continued to provide in itself spoke well of Hannah. With the little they themselves had, the Daniels buried Esther and took in the progeny of a man they must despise.

In the end, Margaret told her story to John Daniel. Christine didn't know how he had reassured her enough. She hoped he had told Margaret that her father knew all along that Sarah ate. She hoped he had told her that what happened wasn't her fault and that, every day, Margaret had helped Sarah live.

Valiant Margaret—her dancing limp, her giving of oatcakes, her jumps for the Lord, her rake—was braver even than Christine had known.

SHORTLY AFTER JOHN DANIEL SPOKE WITH MARGARET, Nell reported to Christine all that Margaret had said. She granted Christine permission for the story to—someday—be widely told.

Mary never returned to Christine's. Nor was she interested in the chemist's storeroom. She slept outside until Daniel found her and showed her Braith's cottage. Mary chose to sleep there, under the gaping hole in the roof on a pallet she bought with her pay from the tinworks.

Well before winter, before Hannah's homecoming, neighbors would help put the cottage to rights.

❧

Carmarthen, Wales
15 September 1870

Dearest James,

I leave for New York in two weeks. Reginald Pary is to go with me and we will marry.

I know you would want it.

As ever,
Christine

❧

IT HAD COME ABOUT LIKE THIS: She announced the date of her departure, and Reginald dropped to a knee.

"Reginald," she said, "I'm fifty. One."

"You look all right to me."

"High praise." She couldn't bear an ocean between herself and her children, grown as they were. She wanted to be near her grandchildren if they came. She needed to live in the house she had shared with James.

Reginald's parents were gone, and to leave Wales had become possible for him.

It was decided as simply as that.

As they prepared for the journey, one day Christine asked, "How do you think John Daniel will proceed with Evan?"

"I would think go to Swansea and speak with Evan. Perhaps he'll wait until Hannah is released."

"He'll speak to Evan alone?"

"Well, surely he will confide in others in the district, apprising them of the plan for Evan, and of its necessity."

"That's it?" she said. "He'll just speak to him?"

"My goodness, what else did you think he would do?"

As the Welsh had trusted her, she had to trust them. And she began by allowing her Welsh paramour to keep to his own discretion.

EVAN JONES

"JONES," CHRISTINE WROTE AT THE TOP OF A FRESH PAGE in her newest notebook. She pondered the name of that ever-elusive figure.

"Suffers. Drinks. May lose the parish."

It wasn't as bad as all that, the word abroad was that his suffering was appreciated, since its public nature proclaimed his regret. He had been spotted by others traipsing tipsily about, and the workingmen with whom he drank at the Eagle Inn said he had come down from his high horse.

Nell had visited Christine the previous day, and after Nell left, Christine had walked miles, absorbing the information from Margaret. Then she sat down and wrote and thought throughout most of the night.

Now Christine prepared to call on Jones, who had summoned her once more, as his letter had lured her across the ocean. They were, if she was honest with herself, accomplices as much as adversaries.

It was nearly October, three days before she left for New York. If the vicar hadn't invited her, she'd have sought him out anyway, confronted him one last time. But a formal note had arrived requesting her company on Friday at four o'clock at the parsonage, and it wasn't luck, serendipity—anything of the sort. Suffering or no, he was still crafty, still invested in the Jacobs, and because he had been turned away by the

Daniels at their riverside home, and had heard, Christine presumed, of her friendliness with them—and of Reginald's involvement with Mary Jacob—he hoped for as much out of her as she hoped for from him.

She wanted to hear what Hannah had said and had not said to him at the prison. Why Hannah had confided in him, prior to the sentencing, about her baby was unclear. But Christine doubted that she had said anything more. Whatever she said to the vicar could prove a conduit to her estranged husband.

Christine wanted to know how much of what Evan Jacob and Evan Jones did had been planned. She wanted to grasp how Jones could testify against Jacob, after telling him, finally, to call off the watching, and witnessing Sarah's death when Jacob wouldn't, and yet remain loyal to him, as Margaret had reported: "You are a fine man, Evan Jacob, and young enough to start again. There are other farms where the family can be together," the vicar had said.

Not likely. Not anymore.

His infernal meddling, John Daniel had said. What was his investment at this point? Guilt? It was impossible that he knew what she did about the most intimate matter, and she wouldn't tell him. The Daniels emphatically wanted him uninvolved. She would honor their wish and leave the two Evans to each other.

THE EARTH WAS SERE, THE HARVEST PALTRY. The rain stayed up in the thick, pregnant sky. She would leave with a distant memory of mist and rain.

A house and sixty-four acres accompanied the vicar's post. Common knowledge was he had two farmworkers, a dairymaid, and a single domestic servant. The traditional cottage was protectively set against a hill's fold, the windows small to keep out the usual wet. The lime-washed front was its soft complexion, the windows its eyes. To look across the valley at the cottages placed with skill and care was to see Wales, the Welsh and the land coexisting in harmony.

He answered the door himself and led her to a sitting room at the back of the house that served as his study.

"Now then," he said, getting right down to business. "My house maid's away, but I can make tea if you like."

"It isn't necessary."

"I've a decent claret." It stood close at hand, in a crystal decanter on his desk.

"Do you have any gin?" she asked.

He did, in a cabinet under the window.

Glasses in hand, he sat at his desk and she on the settee.

"Ask me what you like," he said.

"And in return?"

"I will ask my own questions."

"I reserve the right not to answer."

"I wouldn't force anything out of you."

"You'll try," she said.

"You haven't changed."

"You have."

Acceding, he drained his glass.

"Have another," she said.

"Not now."

She sipped hers and set it aside.

"You have ingratiated yourself very prettily, Mrs. Thomas," he said. "It is what you sought. But do you believe that in a year you have learned all you need to know?"

"About—"

"Us. Wales. Sarah Jacob."

"I should stay longer."

"Stay if you like," he said. "You still won't understand."

"And why do you care?"

He made a snuffling sound, indicative of a cold, anxiety—grief? Indicative of the edge he walked between control and collapse.

"I don't write for *The Sun* anymore," she told him, "but I suppose you already know that."

"You may yet again," he said.

"Certainly, and what harm may I possibly do to you, more than you've already done to yourself?"

"You *don't* understand."

"This is my translation of that," she rejoined. "If I understood, I wouldn't blame you. Everything you have done would blush with roseate rightness."

His lips quivered. "Great trials coinciding with great opportunities, Mrs. Thomas, demand nerve. Quick action. Sacrifice. Your President Lincoln did what he had to, at incalculable cost."

"How sure of yourself you still are," she said. "And how do you know that just because I am American I approve of our bloody war?"

"How could you not?"

"Easily, or at least not wholeheartedly. Some of us think the results could have come to pass by other means."

"Because you're naïve," he said.

She laughed. "You seem to be thoroughly conversant with America, yet I do not understand Wales. And do I mean to understand? You rate understanding too highly. It is an excuse for relativity and justification. There are things that must be weighed by themselves."

"So you think."

"So I know."

"Ask," he said.

"All right. Tell me about Hannah, how she took the news."

"Bravely."

"And Evan?"

"Evan Jacob is an extraordinary person," he said. "Do you know that?"

"If I don't, I surmise you will teach me."

"Why did you go to see Hannah yourself?" he asked.

"She was led by Jacob."

"And what have you said to her?"

"Good grief! Are the Jacobs yours to guide as you like?"

"I took my lead, madam, from Evan and Sarah."

"From a child? Did she dictate your letter?"

"I will tell you this: Child or no, she comprehended everything."

If so, Christine thought, how sad.

"When did you decide to do it?" she asked. "To publicly claim you had no doubt? Oh, you modified your words later, said just that there was strong evidence in favor of the miracle. But in your original letter you wrote you had no doubt whatsoever."

"Faith," he said, "is to believe there is divine truth in all things, and to have this persuasion stronger than what we see with our eyes; such an assent is the peculiar work of God's spirit.

"Doubters have always asked for miracles," he continued. "We live in an age riddled with doubt and questioning." He replenished his glass. "Sarah was there. I supplied what was necessary."

"But the watching was desperate and bound to fail, and you knew it."

"I didn't. Gohebydd and Marles interrogated the parents stringently. Jacob insisted she'd last."

"But he had his own intentions! When she was dying, you told him to call off the watch and he wouldn't."

"He still believed, and Sarah was ready to die. Remember," he said with chilling calm, "that she had been sick for a long time."

"A person of sixty may or may not be ready to die, not a child of twelve."

"A Welsh child."

"Oh, don't." She stood, repelled by the sight of him. She studied his books: theology, philosophy, Welsh history; he must have felt that modern times were about to render his entire life obsolete.

She turned back. "If you are so sure of yourself, why do you grieve?"

Why did he drink?

A heart-shaped glass dish of potpourri on the window ledge exuded a spicy, dusty fragrance. His wife must have put it there.

"For years," he said, "I read the latest periodicals. Science, progress, I welcomed both. We thought—even Darwin did—that science would prove instead of refute the creationist claims of the Bible. It would validate man's special place in the world. And where are we left? Where are we going? The trains brought only crooked values and devilish enticements. What is to become of life on the land, of community, of continuity? When I met Evan Jacob, it was in autumn. He stood in his field of ripening corn, and he said to me, 'It makes you want to take it in your arms, and to be with the scythe. The corn bows with the scythe,' he said, 'as it swings, and it falls curved. The corn falls curved. . . .' All of that love, destined to be swept away. . . . My father was a farmer. We didn't have much and I never thought I would be off to the seminary at sixteen. But during the bitterest times, when I was growing up, we had more than most. My father took me along to those with less, people who lived like Evan Jacob once did and to whom we dispensed our charity. The Poor Laws, you see, meant they had less than before. They would go to the workhouse if they were abjectly impoverished, but most Welsh would rather die. And did. The families lived in single rooms where the windows were holes in the wall, bunged up with bundles of rags at night. There were no chairs or tables, no beds but loose straw and filthy rags, peat packed in the corners and a kettle set straight onto the fire."

"I know this," she said, sitting again. "My husband's family had little more."

"Yes," he said, "many emigrated if they could. But many remained. What is it for? Such a life, if there is no world beyond? How can people live? How do we persist if miracles are vanquished?"

"They aren't," she said quietly. He poured a third glass for himself, and his hands trembled.

"We have a power in us," he said, "we don't understand."

"I agree." She added, "I'm sorry for how you have suffered." One pale hand brushed her words away.

"You have no one to talk to since your wife died," she said.

He had stopped looking at her and stared at the glass dish.

"You're ousted, Reverend Jones," Christine said, "as the keeper of one particular miracle. It's over, and there is nothing left for you there."

"No one," he said, "has moved me as Sarah did since my wife died."

"Stay away from Evan Jacob."

"Why?" He looked back at her.

"You may find out soon enough."

"He is in agony, you know," said Jones.

"I hope so."

"We have tried to fight great crimes," he said.

"And committed crimes as great."

"Yes. . . . I thought, what is one little girl?"

"Everything," she said.

"I've paid," he said. "I have been shamed and ridiculed."

"Welcome it. Learn."

"My mother has taken my child."

"I'm sorry," Christine said.

"I was a distracted father."

They stood.

"I wish you Godspeed, Mrs. Thomas."

NEITHER HAD GOTTEN MUCH OUT OF THE OTHER, and yet the meeting surpassed what she had expected. She felt now she could go. The carriage she'd had wait sprayed billowing dust as it set off back to the train station. She couldn't see the Jacob homestead from here. She wouldn't again see St. Michael's, the Eagle Inn, the graveyard she had meant to visit once more— she said to herself, enough.

She imagined the sisters laid side by side, Esther's grave a fresh mound. Fly away, little birds, she thought.

She could see Sarah's plain cross. Fly away, pretty crow.

She could still see the vicar's pale hands and his short glossy beard, its strands of gray, his gaze on the glass dish.

ONCE THERE WAS A HANDSOME BRIGHT BOY who suffered. At night, he dreamed. By day, he cursed his blocked dreams.

He learned that for hundreds of years others like him had suffered. He found out why and felt the relief, the directness of a tangible answer—

And a goal: one foot in front of the other, and the exaltation of finding a road! Strength flowed from it. Others had started with little else and they had succeeded.

Whole villages met on the hilltops to worship together and discuss the steps necessary for what should be theirs. Newspapers came, factories, foreigners, and yet life on the land didn't change in its difficulty. Hard, grinding days mixed with the assurance of heavenly rest: The sermons and tracts, the Sunday school stories and biblical tales ran, like light, below everyday life.

On the curved earth stirred change. He worked and established a family, a farm. He would pause in his toil and observe the sky, watch the wind ruffle the crops. He protected the sheaves and exploited the sun and drew sustenance from his wife and children and felt himself a Lord, a man like any other.

An angel was born to his woman, as proof.

With Sarah, he felt that his sins were forgiven, his memories eased, his fears soothed—a beautiful girl.

He strengthened; he rose in stature and felt he could bear his hardships and was patient for the heavenly life his daughter's existence announced.

Blessed years, immanence, the numinous earth and sky one.

Wales shone in its future glory, bathed in restitution.

He walked his land as God walks, and almost believed it entirely his.

They lived amid great change like giants, sang on the hilltops and bore up together, beings charged with purpose, a marked generation.

At night, he knelt before sleep, thanking God. He worked, his eyes lifted to heaven, and it was enough.

And then—the fall came, the blackness rushed forth, the world flooded in, and the equilibrium he had briefly enjoyed was banished forever.

After he failed the test, others trailed closely upon it like devils, disguised. Sarah sickened, and he was nearly relieved of his heaviest burden, but the devil kept the girl with him, sliding between life and death.

The devil of sickness, devil of rain and desire, devil of past actions, weakness, the girl in the bed living on, and what to do?

One day it would be one thing and the next another.

To save her, to wish her dead, to love and hate and be always reminded, and through it he worked, a beast of burden, a devil himself, the black child he'd been alive in the man. The labor no longer settled him, but was his penance unending.

Weighted and chained to her slight fevered form, the days came and went, and at last she flourished—her hair growing back, her skin regaining color: a sign.

By God's grace she lived, by the bread of God. They stopped feeding her and she lived. He stopped castigating himself and she lived. Devilish, infernal soul in the shape of a child—such ardor she had! Such assurance.

Two beings in her, mighty devil, hurt child, and what was he in it? What was his place?

Caretaker, Joseph, he was a little Lord. Great as the revival, an intoxicant nearer than the Promised Land were the new opportunities, in life, for a man of his capacities.

He settled into the new way and riches accumulated, the temporal riches of power, among men.

His angel resurrected, a saint in the house unnerved him at first, the knot seemingly untied, the unsought forgiveness, the suspect solution, a voice from beneath the mud floor mocking and mourning.

But by what other means could he continue?

Destined. Chosen. They lived the miracle as if it were real. They lived as if it would last. He worked the land as ever, welcomed the pilgrims, and counted the coins he kept under the bed.

Mary pilfered from the box, but what could he say? She, mobile devil, observed him out of her omniscient eyes.

Mary was a black shadow.

Sarah was white.

People read about the saint in the papers and came on the train.

They performed their act.

He slept, and woke to the girl in the bed.

Sometimes as he cared for her, she dislodged the old tenderness, a type of love he had experienced before she betrayed him.

It was as if, then, nothing had happened.

Rebirth. His fate linked to the fate of the nation.

Importance and size were flavors he tasted.

Now she must live, now she must ensure his redemption, and if she did not? Why then, she must die. He could not know God's purpose for Sarah.

Fourteen days she could last, he swore it, and though he knew all along that she ate, he believed against reason, caged by desperation, in her ability to survive.

"Come, girl," he said to her.

"Come, wife." They were his, after all, and could not live apart from him.

Devilish doctors, the vicar he had always pretended to respect yet reviled, celebrities and newspaper reporters, how were they less sinful than he?

And Mary, black shadow, knowing, watching, threatening. They should all go down to the devil and leave him in peace!

For what is the peace of a father with all his burdens? In a burdened land, where in an instant they could take everything from him and did.

She died.

At last, the girl died, ascending to heaven, dissolving in dust to hell.

He walked in the wilderness alone.

He walked the everlasting stairs, his strong body caretaker of his black soul.

He envisioned the land, the ruffling corn; he lay in his cell with his eyes to the latticed glass near the ceiling and swallowed the sky: sheeting rain that flattened the grass, grayness that showed before wet, blue of the sun and gentle white streaming clouds that sang the fields into their growing.

Her name was Sarah.

Sarah meant purity, happiness, and princess of the multitudes.

Sarah was gone.

But his strength wasn't exhausted, nor were the notions his fatherhood and his fame had injected into his brain.

He would live again.

By his wit and brawn and unfailing maleness, he would survive.

IN JANUARY 1871, HANNAH JACOB BROUGHT her baby, birthed in prison, to the cottage and lived with Mary until Evan was released in July. Mary was forced to leave the district soon after her mother chose to start anew with her husband.

Nell wrote to Christine that to think Hannah could bear up alone would have been asking too much of an already weakened woman.

Nell hoped that Evan had changed, was softened and grateful for his freedom. In any event, Margaret remained at the Daniels'—and Evan and Hannah continued on with the boys and the new baby girl, also named Hannah.

After a year as an agricultural laborer, Evan took out a lease on a modest plot of land, and in two he had built a house and lived as a farmer once more.

Evan was always included by the community in the system of mutual help—in Welsh, *cymortha*. John Daniel had waited for a cue from Hannah to act. No one but those at the chemist shop meeting would ever know what Evan had done.

Mary Jacob lay in wait for her father at the side of the path that led from the cottage to the well and ran at him from out of her hiding place, wielding a freshly sharpened pitchfork. But Evan's reflexes were swift, and with the steel-like sinews from his prison labor he intercepted the thrust by grabbing the handle and throwing Mary to the ground.

He held the tines an inch away from her breast. The witness, a weaver who also used the well, said father and daughter were very like in their rage, as if each saw in the other the fieriest pit of hell.

POSTSCRIPT

Brooklyn, New York, U.S.A.
23 May 1875

Dearest James,

My best heart, I could not have foreseen the bilocation that would be my life. You, Reginald, America, Wales. Our children are well and bring me much joy. The bunting across the street has come down, the people who flew it like eternal banners long moved away. New neighbors painted the house an incongruous sea green.

I have finished my book.

Therein lay my recent vexation.

So much has changed in five years. In 1871, Dr. Robert Fowler published his tome on the Sarah Jacob case. It contained nothing notably new. His many extractions from the trial transcripts, his exhaustive medical discussion of fasting in a variety of situations—we still know so little about the biological changes during abstinence—were interesting to doctors, I'm sure, or to the curious who had followed the trial at a distance. But the book most impressed on me how not a single doctor asked Sarah, "Why do you not eat?" The etiology and not the proof was, for me, always the question. Now Fowler's book has been rendered passé, except as an artifact of a perplexing period and event.

It is one of the ironies of the case that while Sarah lay sick and finally dying, research was being conducted at important hospitals on women and girls who fast. Fowler diagnosed the distaste for food as arising from the hysterical willfulness of deceptive, always feminine persons. Then in 1873 W. W. Gull of London and Ernest-Charles Lasègue of Paris published nearly simultaneous findings on a new, independent disease: anorexia nervosa. Gull differed with the French doctor's name of "hysterical anorexia" because of its derivation from the Greek *hysteros*, meaning "uterus." Gull preferred "nervosa," implicating the central nervous system instead of the uterus and allowing that the condition could exist in males. Distinct from lack of appetite caused by organic disease, anorexia nervosa, according to Gull, is attached to no unusual amount of hysteria but can hardly be called insanity, either. It appears to stem from multiple sources. From what I have read, Elizabeth Clinch was correct in identifying Sarah's trouble with food as bodily speech, a physical communication of a disturbance for which she had no words.

Watches on these girls today are rare, as consideration of them has shifted almost entirely into the secular realm. Thankfully, the days when fasting girls lived out symbolic denials of science and provided points of connection to past religious tradition as a miracle-working process—those days are gone.

Few cultures, over time, were more rooted than that of the rural Welsh. Ideas about the disciplining of society, which were increasingly driven by progress, were applied to an area in which stasis and continuity were still, in the 1860s, prominent forces.

Welsh celebrities of the era presided over a span of revolutionary social change. Religious ministers could be harsh and uncompromising and often led controversial lives. Conventional, respectable vicars failed to contribute to the liberal political breakthroughs that made the 1860s the years that ended the tyranny of the landed classes. The actions of Evan Jones and his committee can be viewed in this context. Socially, workers are better paid and are shown more respect. Taxation adjusted. The schools are better, and all children attend. Many more ordinary people can read. Yet the progress that benefited the Welsh dashed the stability and continuity that had been their strength, and sacrifice across many lives was its price.

The phenomenon of the Welsh Fasting Girl was explicable. Her death was not. The adults involved in the watch dithered, trying both to do the right thing and to evade responsibility when the outcome was clear. The Welsh doctors were medical men, and yet Welsh. They were at once scientists and mortal, fallible creatures. They were being taught, at a faster rate than had ever occurred, the fact of our animal natures and the split between body and soul. The law and the penal system struggled to support advancements and keep the peace. Corrections to well-intentioned yet fraught and outmoded middle-Victorian institutions were a necessity.

I have heard the Evan Joneses of the era called "antimodernists." I often thought of Jones as a modern-day druid, those ancient priests of Celtic Wales.

But I resist pasting impressive labels on persons who so egregiously erred, as I did. I soften, some, in consideration of life's confusion in the thick of it, and in acknowledging our interdependence—how much we count on the will and spirit of the group to move us beyond past limitations.

Here in America, ten years from war's end, the land is scarred and the freed encounter new bonds: The quality of their freedom is only potentially better.

Life's high stakes are vastly out of kilter if you consider the ephemeral nature of substance, and are of necessity shouldered by sinning men and women, regardless of whether doctors or priests are the gods.

How do we approach the buried lives of women and girls?

When a crime cannot be proved, does it vanish?

Where has Mary Jacob gone?

I have waited for word of her these five years and it hasn't come. I think she works deep in the airless mines, walks the London streets, has found a position in a grand house or as a dairy worker on a northern farm. I think she stole onto a ship and came to America, where I might suddenly see her seated out on the stoop next door. I fear she is dead or incarcerated for assault or murder.

In 1872, a ninth Jacob child, Rachel, was born to Evan and Hannah. Early this year, the vicar remarried and accepted a prestigious position as the rector of Newport. Margaret remains with the Daniels, and all along I've had word of her progress, her devotion to John Daniel's trade and, recently, to her schoolwork—this last, Nell wrote, was a grudging concession, but one that Sarah wanted for Margaret. I have tried to digest and articulate what Nell passed on to me from Margaret—as I have tried to speak for Sarah—to inhabit their story and feed comprehension. But every day I thought and wrote and paced my eight-foot-square attic room, I worried for Margaret.

Evan Jacob resides at New Inn. He has most likely encountered the Daniels at the markets and fairs. I wonder if Hannah calls on the Daniels, if she is allowed to.

Reginald believes that John Daniel privately told Evan Jacob what he knew and promised to speak throughout the district if any of the children were harmed.

He must be right. If I worry, John and Nell would worry also, and act.

My worry extended, recently, to the possible consequences of my book's publication. Nell wanted the story told, but when?

I wrote asking for her directive, and her answer was the advice I'd given myself. I shouldn't jeopardize Hannah's and Margaret's precarious safety.

Wait. The four letters evoked an image of Jacob on his thirty acres, as much land as he had in the beginning at Lletherneaudd. That he should thrive! Father more children. Be thought well of.

It went hard with me.

I returned to work desultorily for Philip Beckwith, researching innocuous subjects. Reginald is the reporter in our house. "Write another book," he said. But it wasn't writing the book I cared about; it was the cause.

I couldn't contradict Nell's course. To honor her wisdom was my holy writ. And so I decided to give the manuscript to Gwen. Someday she will choose what to do, probably after I'm gone. "By then my book may be as passé as Fowler's," I told her. Accepted knowledge is already altered, and who, in ten or twenty years, will care about the trials of a little fasting girl? "Bury it under the floorboards, then," I said. "Maybe someone will dig it up in a hundred and fifty years."

Will they be enlightened? Will they be kind? Will they have moved far beyond the crimes of my story?

If so, let it lie.

Gradually, I arrived at acceptance. What regret remained was alleviated when, yesterday, I received another missive from Nell. I opened it and my residual unease dissolved. Nell wrote only three lines, about the weather, and enclosed a scrap written by Margaret, and they were the words, her words, I needed.

She formed the date and her address in a bold hand on a piece of foolscap. I pictured her at a desk, scowling, anxious to return to the river and the trade she had chosen, as seamstress. I imagined her hands, the dents and dings from scissors and needle, clutching the unfamiliar pen.

She wrote a salutation and my name, and
"I am well."
Yr wyf yn dda.
I am well.

As ever,
Christine

AUTHOR'S NOTE

THOUGH THIS BOOK IS A WORK OF FICTION, it is based on real events and is grounded in the history and culture of rural Victorian Wales. Sarah Jacob is still well remembered in Wales today. She is the subject of plays, books, and legal articles, and in Carmarthen she remains a local celebrity. Theories regarding her life and death abound. But the essential facts are exactingly documented across numerous sources.

I first read about Sarah Jacob in *Fasting Girls: The History of Anorexia Nervosa*, by Joan Jacobs Brumberg. The medical and historical details of this landmark study were the ballast of my understanding of Sarah's plight. The author's recounting of how the parents put Sarah's little sister into the dying Sarah's bed, in an attempt to keep her warm, led to my focus on Margaret in the novel. Others have also mentioned Margaret as the person who probably supplied Sarah with food. Sian Busby's *A Wonderful Little Girl* was the first account I read of the whole story, and I am grateful for how it acquainted me with the general outlines of the Sarah Jacob case. *Wreath on the Crown*, by John Cule, was another account I read early on that proved useful.

I traveled to South Wales in 2011 and was greatly assisted by Richard Ireland, who showed me around Sarah's village. I saw the family grave, the public house where the autopsy was performed, and the church once presided over by the Reverend Evan Jones. As a legal historian, Mr. Ireland was especially helpful in explaining the complexities of the parents' trial and sentencing. His article "Sanctity, Superstition and the Death of Sarah Jacob" guided my approach, as did his books *Land of White Gloves?* and *A Want of Order and Good Discipline: Rules, Discretion and the Victorian Prison.* Mr. Ireland kindly put up with me again in Wales in 2014, when he patiently answered my questions as I began to penetrate the many aspects of the story I was attempting to comprehend.

The text I am most indebted to is *A Complete History of the Welsh Fasting Girl,* by Dr. Robert Fowler, who did indeed examine Sarah when she was alive and testified at the parents' trial. The excerpts Fowler included from the trial transcripts were the loam out of which I fashioned my trial chapters and the tragic eight days of the watching. I tried to remain as accurate as possible to the testimony of the nurses and of the doctors who performed the autopsy, and to the characters of the various players in the legal proceedings as I perceived them from what they said. The character of Dr. Fowler in the novel was shaped out of his testimony and what he wrote to *The Times* (London) in his original letter about Sarah that led to the watching.

The letter by the Reverend Evan Jones that catapulted Sarah's local notoriety to worldwide fame is included verbatim as it appeared in the press. The vicar's dead wife and his relationship with Sarah and her father are true to what I learned throughout my investigation, from news reports to transcripts of the local committee meetings where Sarah's watching was organized and later discussed after her death. Likewise, the political figures are based on real activists of the day and their involvement with Sarah and her family.

Christine Thomas is my invention, out of my early sense that I needed a guide to open up the story to readers unfamiliar with Wales, and to provide my contemporaries with the context necessary to grasp the cultural and political forces that determined Sarah's fate. I invented other, small characters as well, and built up characters who seemed vital but remained shadowy in my sources. The doctors involved in the watching adhere to how they are presented by Fowler, though the character of Dr. Harries Davies is expanded, imagined from his reported actions and what he wrote about the case. The sister-nurse and Sarah's aunt and uncle also play expanded roles in my novel, as do Sarah's sisters and the Jacobs' hired boy, whom I call Emyr. As in the novel, Evan Jacob saved Emyr as a child from certain death. The Welsh reporter characters are inventions, intended, along with Christine, to convey the active participation of the press.

Of necessity, there came a time when I had to frame a thesis about what occurred at the very center of the story: How did Sarah stay alive for so long while seeming to eat nothing? And *why* did she do it? There is no hard evidence of incest. Yet it is well documented that a high percentage of women and girls suffering from eating disorders were sexually abused, and Evan Jacob's behavior supports this speculation. Louise A. Jackson's *Child Sexual Abuse in Victorian England* allowed me to see this possibility in a Victorian context. A recent social history, *The Girl Who Lived on Air*, by Stephen Wade, set out compelling conjectures about the Jacob family dynamics that added to my dramatization.

Wales itself, its landscape and history, is an important character in the novel, and visiting there contributed more than I can say. Wales is a beautiful, passionate, and fascinatingly complicated place I would never have known without researching this book. *The Matter of Wales: Epic Views of a Small Country*, by Jan Morris, a Welsh Republican and one of our finest living writers in English, prepared me to appreciate her beloved country. Other books that showed me Wales were *Life and Tradition in Rural Wales*, by J. Geraint Jenkins; *This Small Corner: A History of Pencader and District*, by Steve Dubé; *Carmarthen: A History and Celebration*, by Wendy Hughes; and *A Welsh Way of Life*, by Iwan Meical Jones.

ACKNOWLEDGMENTS

I WISH TO THANK Richard Ireland of the Welsh Legal History Society for his hospitality and valuable information. Thanks to Michelle Latiolais and Daniel Stewart for their keen readings. My agent, Joy Harris, also offered valuable insights; my thanks to her and to her assistant, Adam Reed. Thanks to my mother, Louise Varley, for her support of my writing. And thanks to the Department of English and Sponsored Programs at Kent State University for their support during the composition of this work.

Special thanks to Erika Goldman, publisher and editorial director of Bellevue Literary Press, for her vision and commitment. I am honored to know and work with her and the rest of the terrific BLP team.

More than anyone, my husband, Joel Wapnick, enabled my Sarah Jacob story to come into being. For his belief and support every step of the way, this book is for him.

CREDITS

Page 77

A happy place I was in today,
Under cloaks of lovely green hazels . . .
And the eloquent slim nightingale,
From the corner of the grove near by,
Wandering poetess of the valley, rang to the multitude
The Sanctus bell, clear to its trill,
And raised the Host
As far as the sky . . .

> —Dafydd ap Gwilym, translated by Jan Morris

Jan Morris translations reprinted by permission of Oxford University Press, Oxford Publishing Limited, Oxford, UK. Excerpted from *The Matter of Wales: Epic Views of a Small Country* by Jan Morris, published by Oxford University Press. © 1984 Jan Morris

Page 95

old pond . . .
a frog leaps in
water's sound

> —Basho, translated by William J. Higginson

Reprinted by permission of Kodansha USA, Inc. Excerpted from *The Haiku Handbook: How to Write, Teach, and Appreciate Haiku* by William J. Higginson and Penny Harter by Kodansha USA, Inc. © 1985, 2013 William J. Higginson and Penny Harter

Page 95

> On hill, in valley, in islands of the sea
>> Every way one goes,
> From Holy Christ there is no escape.
>> —Anonymous, translated by Jan Morris

See note on page 349 regarding Oxford University Press permissions for translations by Jan Morris.

Pages 121–122

On the Death of a Little Girl

A little girl went home today
She rests where she belongs,
And now she plays upon her harp
The sweet and heavenly song.
And though she was so precious
To her parents dear
Christ He sent to fetch that girl
A pearl whom he'd have near.

She leaves behind a world of grief
And all it's tempting gain
She leaves behind her troubles
And all this world of sin.

And now she stands beside the throne
With Jesus and the holy throng
And in her hands she holds a harp
And plays the Heavenly song.
>> —Sarah Jacob, translated by Geoffrey Ballinger

Printed by permission of Dr. Geoffrey Ballinger

Page 177

Do you not see the path of the wind and the rain?
Do you not see the oaks beating together?
Do you not see the sea scouring the land?
Do you not see the truth preparing itself?
   —Gruffudd ab yr Ynad Coch, translated by Jan Morris

*See note on page 349 regarding Oxford University Press
permissions for translations by Jan Morris.*

BELLEVUE LITERARY PRESS is devoted to publishing
literary fiction and nonfiction at the intersection of
the arts and sciences because we believe that science and the
humanities are natural companions for understanding the human
experience. With each book we publish, our goal is to foster
a rich, interdisciplinary dialogue that will forge new tools for
thinking and engaging with the world.

To support our press and its mission, and for our full catalogue of
published titles, please visit us at blpress.org.

BELLEVUE LITERARY PRESS
New York